TO TURN THE TIDE

TO TURN THE TIDE

S.M. STIRLING

To Turn the Tide

A Baen Books Original

Baen Publishing Enterprises
P.O. Box 1403
Riverdale, NY 10471
www.baen.com

ISBN: 978-1-6680-7263-9

Cover art by Sam R. Kennedy

First printing, August 2024
First trade paperback printing, May 2025

Distributed by Simon & Schuster
1230 Avenue of the Americas
New York, NY 10020

Library of Congress Control Number: 2024012526

Printed in the United States of America

10 9 8 7 6 5 4 3 2 1

To Janet Cathryn Stirling, 1950–2021, dearest of all.

Thanks to—

Judy Tarr and Harry Turtledove, for the loan of Nicole Gunther-Perrin, Attorney-at-Law of Los Angeles, aka Mistress Umma, tavernkeeper of Carnuntum. She's the protagonist in their *Household Gods*, which I heartily recommend, and makes a brief appearance in Chapter Twenty, below. Second century Pannonia can get crowded with American tourists.

To Esther Friesner, good friend and talented author, for checking something out for me.

To Kier Salmon, longtime close friend and valued advisor, to whom I have always listened carefully. And for things like managing the beta-reader stuff. I owe her greatly for everything I've written since 1998.

To Markus Baur, for help with the German language and as a first reader, and for being my native guide to Pannonia Superior, which provided valuable help with *To Turn the Tide*.

To Dr. Donald Ringe, author of many insightful volumes on linguistic history, for a single piece of advice on Proto-Germanic chronology. All mistakes are mine!

To my first readers: Pete Sartucci, Markus Baur, Steve Brady, Ara Sedaka, Mike Ralls, Terri Pray, Diane Porter, Margaret Carter, Mike Ralls, Kier Salmon, Romaine Spence, Jade Cheung, Sandy Michaud, and Emily Sedaka.

To Patricia Finney (aka P.F. Chisholm), for friendship and her own wonderful books, starting with *A Shadow of Gulls* (which she wrote when she was in her teens, at which point I was still doing Edgar Rice Burroughs pastiche fanfic) and going on from there. One of the best historical novelists of our generation!

And to Joe's Diner (http://joesdining.com/) and its splendid proprietor, Roland Richter, for his help with German stuff, and the servers for running relays with my Diet Coke.

Also Tribe's Coffee House (https://www.tribescoffeehouse.net/) here in Santa Fe.

To both institutions and their staff for putting up with my interminable presence and my habit of making faces and muttering dialogue as I write.

Also, they don't have attention-demanding cats walking on the keyboard. A cat sleeps more than fourteen hours a day, yet somehow manages to interrupt you continuously—feline magic.

When you go by the Via Aurelia,
As thousands have traveled before,
Remember the Luck of the Soldier
Who never saw Rome any more!
Oh, dear was the lover that kissed him
And dear was the mother that bore,
But then they found his shield in the heather
And he never saw Rome any more!

When you go by the Via Aurelia
That runs from the City to Gaul,
Remember the Luck of the Soldier
Who rose to be master of all!
He carried the sword and the buckler,
He mounted his guard on the Wall,
Then the Legions hailed him as Cæsar,
And he rose to be master of all!

It's twenty-five marches to Narbo,
It's forty-five more up the Rhone,
And the end may be death in the heather
Or life on an Emperor's throne...

Rudyard Kipling, "Rimini"

⋙ CHAPTER ONE ⋘

Vienna, Austria
June 25th, 2032 CE

None of the five Americans spoke much as the university van took them from *Flughafen Wien-Schwechat*—Vienna International Airport, just southeast of the city—to the Institute of Science and Technology campus on the western outskirts of Klosterneuburg. Which was upstream of Vienna on the same south-running stretch of the Danube as the Austrian capital.

"All motorway now go out, go out only of Vienna, too much auto. Must to go through city," the driver warned them.

Even the chaotic traffic, the lurches and tight swearing—in Ukrainian—from the driver and once the bang-crash-tinkle of a collision right next to them didn't spark any interest, despite being normally an unthinkable anomaly in this order-conscious country.

When the world was going to Hell...

All Hell breaks loose. In the eleven hours it takes to fly from Boston to Vienna, Arthur Vandenburg thought grimly. *And maybe not just metaphorically, if things keep getting worse. Worse faster and faster.*

He was the only one of them who saw much of the city's Baroque splendors as they passed through, and then climbed over low forested hills, the famous Vienna Woods, and descended via back roads through glades and fields.

Arthur Vandenberg, graduate of West Point, formerly and very briefly captain in the US Army (1st Battalion, 75th Rangers) and newly minted Doctor of Philosophy in Ancient History from Harvard, had put his phone away with a monumental effort of will after his wife's last message—*we're praying for you*—and his reply.

He was doing his best to be in the moment.

There's nothing I can do about the world *right now. Or even Mary and the kids. Exclude the irrelevant, get on with what's on your plate.*

It was a practiced mental trick he'd acquired in situations where the ability to focus totally was *literally* a life-or-death matter.

The team of four graduate students he'd put together for this—of oddly varied specialties, as requested—were still glued to their phones or tablets, earbuds in tight and eyes locked to the screens as their fingers flipped between apps, as if a new one would yield better news. They were all years younger than his early thirties, and though he didn't know them very well yet, he thought they'd all had rather sheltered lives as far as physical danger was concerned.

It was a mild, bright day with a few lacy clouds in a pale blue sky... June in southern central Europe... but he could smell the all-too-familiar acidic rankness of fear in their sweat as they took in the babble that was the news feeds right now. It wasn't just mutual hysteria building on itself, either, though there was plenty of that. The airport, and international air travel in general by report, had locked down tight *right* after their wheels touched down on the runway. Every flight in Europe, and apparently the world, was being diverted to the nearest strip... and wouldn't *that* cause some lovely chaos.

The scariest thing was that they hadn't interned the passengers. Or done anything else with them, except tell them to get lost—or *manage their own affairs.*

A flight of F-35s had gone by fairly low right after that, and they'd watched from the parking lot as they screamed past. Probably headed for a base in Slovakia and to hell with violating technically neutral Austria's airspace. Things had gone downhill from there. Official silence echoed loudly about the renewed naval clashes in the western Pacific, and ugly, ugly rumors abounded.

And I am so glad Mary took the kids to visit her folks before I left, he thought tightly. *Boston isn't where I'd want to leave them right now. I just wish her family lived in the Falklands or Fiji, instead of Amarillo!*

That was a remote, medium-sized city in the Texas panhandle, the closest real town to their nearby birthplaces. But it also had a nuclear-weapons assembly plant and another that made tilt-rotors for the military.

When they arrived the campus of the Institute proved to be mostly a modernist anomaly embedded just west of Klosterneu-burg's panoply of the ages on the Danube's bank. It had opened in 2009, after all, though the trees and gardens were pretty. A nervous-looking academic with a white goatee and a lab coat over a suit was there to meet them, and the van drove off immediately to take their luggage to the Guest House.

If the driver doesn't just take off for the Alps the way every third person in Vienna apparently has, Vandenberg thought sardonically.

Doctor rerum naturalium Hans Fuchs didn't look in the least foxy. More like a terrified rabbit, in late middle age and skinny, with his tie loose and runnels of sweat trickling down his face and his eyes darting around or freezing on nothingness. His clothes looked as if he'd slept in them last night, and there was the slightest whiff of stale underwear.

"Dr. Vandenberg? Would you and your associates please come this way to Lab Eight? I am afraid there is no time to waste," he said—in accented but fluent English, which everyone at a place like this spoke these days. "All will—"

He pronounced it *vill*, and Vandenberg's lips quirked as he involuntarily remembered watching Colonel Klink in ancient *Hogan's Heroes* episodes... ancient even then, on VHS... with his grandparents on their ranch in the Caprock country of the Texas Panhandle as a child, back in the early years of the century.

"—be explained. Follow me."

Arthur Vandenberg's eyebrows climbed as the man turned and hurried away; the Americans glanced at each other and followed at a brisk walk. This was all about as far from normal Austrian-German academic etiquette as it was possible to get and not suspect the man was on drugs or had just had a psychotic break.

They went into a large, anonymous building with white stone cladding on the outside and institutional-bland decor on the interior, almost painfully new. People pushed past them, apparently headed out; many of the offices were empty and littered with the paper detritus of rapid departure. One half-open door showed a man slumped unconscious over his desk with his face in a puddle of vomit and a bulbous flask-shaped bottle labelled *marillenschnaps* lying nearby, empty.

By contrast the big open lab they came to had people in plenty, with purposeful movement under the harsh light of overhead floods. Many focused on readout screens, and equipment ranged from standard laptops on tables to hulking and mysterious *some-things* amid snaking cables roughly taped to the concrete floor with metal protective runners over them. Other lines vanished into the steel vaulting above, crossing in front of the big row of windows just below the roof.

Whatever the machines were, they were eating a lot of power and not just by plugging into the wall socket—the slight ozone smell was fully familiar from deployments where field genera-tors were the only electricity you got. The improvised look of parts of the ensemble was familiar too, however alien and high tech the details; the unmistakable look of things put together on the *whatever works, get it done in zip time, to hell with the paperwork* principle.

It was an air you expected in a field encampment in an active zone, but distinctly odd in an Austrian research lab.

In the middle of the great room was a clear circle of space yards across, with stacked boxes and bales and bundles inside the taped perimeter, all resting on a big circle of gridwork. The Austrian led them over to it, and Vandenberg's eyebrows did another rise as they got closer. It was the sort of gear you'd expect at an unusually period-conscious historical reenactment LARP meeting—

Don't say period Nazi *around here. Deeply untactful. You're a prof now; gotta learn tact.*

—which was an occasional guilty pleasure of his he had to hide to keep respect among the notably snooty Harvard faculty. It was bad enough in their eyes that he and his family attended a Baptist church.

The irony there being I haven't been sincere *about it for years. But ten thousand times better the faculty look down their noses in the common room than my causing Mary hurt.*

The crates were wood fastened with crude nails, the parcels wrapped in tanned leather or coarse canvas with hemp or leather binding ropes...

And an honest-to-God *gladius* on top of one of the wooden boxes, with sheath and red-dyed leather *balteus*, the Roman military belt. In a second-century style with over-the-shoulder baldric to hold the sword and openwork silvered-bronze plaques on the part around the waist. He walked over to check, trailing grad students like ducklings.

Drawn a few inches, it revealed that it was even a specifically Pompeiian type of short sword with the sides of the twenty-inch blade parallel before the point. That was the final form that had come in with the Principate, and continued through to the third-century collapse.

Before he could organize a question, Fuchs handed him something he recognized just as easily: a *dolabra*, the Roman soldier's classic entrenching tool. One side was an axe-head, the other a narrow mattock, and this one was mounted on a three-foot shaft of wood he recognized as from an ash tree.

It was a fine reconstruction; the surface of the metal part even had a pebbled finish, and the marks and filed-out nicks of hard use. Then he looked more closely; the material was wrought iron, not steel.

And his eye recognized the slightly porous texture that came from iron made in a bloomery. A Catalan forge or the like, producing a glowing ball that was hand-hammered over and over to get the slag out, the small-batch, labor-intensive method the Classical world had used to make iron. That was authenticity taken to absurd lengths. Who went to *that* much trouble with a reconstruction? And the shaft had a worn look he knew from a rural childhood. It was a hard-used tool kept strictly for function, where you didn't waste time on pretty.

The quick surface coating of rust was also far too authentic, and when he raised it to his nose and sniffed, he smelled rancid vegetable oil of some sort, layers rubbed in over years and left.

"No, *Herr Doktor*, it is not a duplicate," Fuchs said as he saw Vandenberg's face change. "It is real. This you see around us is not apparatus for dating historical artifacts dug up by you historians and archaeologists—I implied that because you would not have believed what it really is, not without seeing it for yourself."

He'd *said* they'd developed a method for giving an immediate, nonintrusive and really reliable absolute calendar date for any artifact, which would have been an archaeological Holy Grail and very, very important for historians too.

"My apologies for the necessary deception."

Vandenberg felt a surge of anger replacing bafflement; he'd been lied away from his family, and it had been done *now* of all times!

The Austrian waved around them. "This... it is an apparatus for temporal displacement. A radical breakthrough. The first small-scale experimental confirmation a year ago... you are holding it... very rapid progress since."

Time travel? Vandenberg thought, his fury growing as he dropped the *dolabra* on a bundle. *Where's the big lever and the upright circle of fake CGI mercury rippling?*

He very nearly turned around and walked out then. What stopped him before the weight came off his foot was a quick glance around the chamber; there were several score million euros or more on display, possibly *much* more. And the Institute in general and Fuchs in particular had excellent reputations: he'd checked when Fuchs contacted him months ago, talking with people he knew in the science departments back at Harvard.

Whatever this was, it wasn't a total crank playing make-believe in his mother's basement. Serious R&D money was involved; so was the Institute's reputation.

And I can't get home anyway, not right now. Air travel's locked down.

Just then his opinion of the Austrian physicist became moot, because his graduate student Filipa Chang screamed.

It was an ear-piercing shriek, and she was clutching her phone in both hands and sobbing and looking as if she was about to puke, too:

"Seoul! Seoul was bombed, nuclear!"

Her parents had been born there, and he knew she had family ties that she kept up.

The other graduate students—Mark Findlemann, Paula Atkins, Jeremey McCladden—brought up the phones or tablets they'd let fall to their sides while the senior academics spoke. They began babbling in chorus, and he had to focus totally to pick out the separate threads:

"—there's a flash from over Seattle—city communications cut out all of a sudden—"

"Tokyo's gone—"

"Russian troops crossing the Lithuanian border from Kaliningrad—"

"Tactical nuke at—"

"London! London's been bombed, multiple hits!"

"New York—shit, my family's there! Shit, shit—"

"Hundreds of launches incoming to North America. From China, and what's left of Russia too!"

"We're launching back—subs—"

Somewhere in the background a siren began to wail.

Professor Fuchs reacted instantly, as if he'd been thinking of just this; he turned and ran for one of the computer stations and started hammering two-fingered on the keyboard. One brief set of entries, and he was up and running back toward the Americans.

There was a bright flash through the high windows. Then a sudden high-pitched whine from the electronics all around them, earsplittingly loud, and after a split second beneath it came a bass rumble.

Arthur Vandenberg had never heard those sounds before, not in person. There hadn't been any above-ground nuclear tests in his lifetime, though his father's grandfather had been in a slit trench a mile and a half from one in 1957 in Nevada. He'd heard the recordings in classes at West Point, though, and recognized it instantly. The hairs tried to stand up along his spine.

This wasn't a scratchy analogue-to-digital recording. He could feel the shudder beneath his feet. A high-yield fusion bomb had detonated within—at most—ten miles from where he stood. Several hundred kilotons at least, a city-smasher.

Flicker.

Everything seemed to freeze for an instant, and the light dimmed.

Then it was back to normal and Fuchs was dashing for them, face twisted in panic as pieces of equipment began to short out spectacularly in the background amid showers of sparks and:

Flicker.

And Fuchs was launching himself through the air in a dive like someone going for first base, headfirst with arms outstretched. Other people all through the big lab were starting to run toward them, or just sat there screaming. And the screams went up and down the scale, from normal shrill to dull sonorous tones that stretched out like molasses in January.

Flicker. Flicker.

Fuchs stopped in midair; then lurched forward; then he hung again impossibly suspended.

Light swelled through the broad, high windows. Everything turned a washed-out faded color.

Flicker. Flicker. Flicker. Flicker.

Faster and faster, strobing, and now Fuchs's leap was in jerky slow motion and there was a vast bass rumbling like the sound of a world breaking. The big windows began to bulge inward, fractures in the tough glass spreading as Vandenberg watched.

He knew with some remote part of him that he was about to die, and the faces of his son and daughter and Mary were there. He hadn't really believed in Heaven for some time, but now he *wished* he still did.

Flicker. Flicker. Flicker. Flicker. Flicker. Flicker. Flicker. Flicker.

His own mind telling his body to hit the dirt, close his eyes, put his arms across his face, but the response of body to thought was absurdly slow, as if he was encased in amber honey. Heat beat against his face. A taste grew in his mouth, acrid and metallic and burnt all at once.

FlickerFlickerFlickerFlickerFlickerFlickerFlickerFlicker...flick-flickflick...

Blackness.

⋟ CHAPTER TWO ⋞

Provincia Pannonia Superior, Imperium Romanum
Consulate of Marcus Gavius Orfitus and Lucius Arrius Pudens
Fourth year of the joint auctoritas of Imperator Caesar
Marcus Aurelius Antoninus Augustus and Imperator Caesar
  Lucius Aurelius Verus Augustus
Ante diem VII Kalendas Iulias CMXVIII Ab Urbe Condita
(June 25th, 165 CE)

The merchant Josephus ben Matthias—it was Lucius Maecius Josephus on the *libellus* that attested his Roman citizenship—rode northwestward from Vindobona on a fair summer day, along the Roman highway that ran not far from the west bank of the Danube. Which river hereabouts was the border of the Empire as well, or at least the boundary of direct control. His young nephew Simonides rode at his right hand and his Sarmatian freedwoman Sarukê came behind, managing the remounts and the packhorse whose panniers contained very little right now except a goodly sum in coin.

They passed through the well-cultivated land that surrounded the city: truck gardens, rich grainfields shining golden, orchards and vineyards on slopes, woodlots higher up. Scattered farmsteads stood among the fields, and hamlets huddled together. Rarer but imposing were red-roofed villas stuccoed in cream-white or brighter colors, each with its dependencies and the distinctive luxurious glitter of windows made with panes of glass in wooden frameworks. Rows of workers in the fields were taking the very first of the winter wheat with flashing sickles, looking up now and then to gaze at the road.

At travelers on foot or in the saddle, groups of belated migrant harvest workers trudging with their bundles and tools on poles over their shoulders soldier-wise, and long trains of two-wheeled carts and bigger wagons inbound toward the city with fodder and fruit and vegetables and firewood and charcoal. Or at donkeys nearly invisible under bundles of this and that.

Plus the odd herd of docile sheep or obstreperous pigs or smaller groups of cattle headed likewise, and once a coffle of twenty German slaves yoked neck to neck and supervised by several armed, mounted guards with clubs and whips. Some of the human merchandise were young men with healing wounds— warriors captured in some intertribal skirmish across the river, and sold to Roman traders. They'd probably be kept going to markets further away, for safety's sake.

The numbers on the road dropped off as the day progressed, and there were only scattered groups after they stopped for a noon meal of bread, oil, onions, smoked mutton sausage and fruit. Now and then cavalry patrols from the *auxilia* went by, giving them sidelong looks, sometimes swinging across the road and asking questions, then riding on at his cheerful greeting and mention of his name and residence.

"More patrols than usual," he said. "The Lord of Hosts grant it's just the commanders being nervous."

"Amen," his nephew said.

Sarukê snorted; she knew better.

For that matter, so do I, Josephus thought, pressing his lips together.

Out on the blue river itself, barges and sailboats passed, and rafts of timber and little fishing smacks. Twice a light patrol galley, swift as a serpent among the tubby cargo vessels, its fifteen oars a side beating the water into froth and a gilded bear or boar's head and painted glaring eyes above the bronze ram. The water smelled cool and fresh when the wind came from the northeast, leavening the earthy-dusty scents of farmland, the green growing tang of woodlots and pastures and the barnyard odor of livestock and their own horses' sweat.

Birdsong was loud, louder now that the sound of human voices was rarer. The hooves of the horses clattered on the concrete-set paving stones of the road, or thudded on softer dirt when they could ride beside it to spare the beasts.

Josephus was in his thirtieth year, and Simonides only just adult at seventeen, but otherwise they had a strong family resemblance: both of medium height, olive skinned, wiry slim in a well-muscled way with big dark-hazel eyes and black hair and long faces with bold noses. Josephus wore his dense curly beard short cropped, in the Greek-philosopher style that Marcus Aurelius had made popular, and his nephew's was so tufty-patchy to date that he shaved in the older fashion to avoid humiliation.

They both wore openwork *cothurnus* boots, tight knee-length leather riding breeks—called *femoralia* because they covered the *femur*, the thigh—and short-sleeved tunics. Those were of tough linen bloused up through their belts to knee length too, but of good dyed cloth with embroidery at the hems, and they had broad-brimmed leather traveler's hats on their heads. On a warm summer's day like this the practical hooded cloaks woven from grease-in wool were rolled up and strapped behind them; unlike the lands further south, it could rain here at any season, which made the cloaks a wise precaution.

"Usually nobody minds much if you dodge *some* of the import taxes on amber and furs, provided you—" the merchant said.

With a gesture that involved fingers stroking palm and meant *grease the right hands.*

He spoke in Greek, which was the language they usually used in his family; Josephus had been born in Syrian Antioch, and so had the boy's father, who was his half brother and elder by fifteen years, by his father's first wife. Simonides spoke Latin as well, of course, and Aramaic; Josephus had those and a few others, including Persian and the local varieties of Gallic and German.

"But lately the Marcomanni"—he inclined his head toward the river; that was the German tribal confederation that occupied most of the other bank here—"have been kicking up their heels. Raids, and not just by a few hotheads. Prince Ballomar swears he's a loyal Roman ally, but he's the one behind it, and his father's too old and doddering to stop him. So the new legate of the Tenth—"

Which was the legion long stationed at Vindobona, though seriously understrength right now. The previous commander had been sent to help wage the war the emperors were currently fighting with the Parthians in the east. He'd taken large *vexilliationes*, detachments, from all the Danubian legions with him and a goodly chunk of their auxiliary archers and cavalry too, and nearly all their catapults and siege gear.

That was one major reason Prince Ballomar was getting playful, insofar as a German warlord needed reasons to cut throats and burn and steal.

"—he's getting tight-arsed about enforcing the duties and regulations on cross-border trade. Still, it's worth a *little* risk. It increases the margin of profit on the goods by, oh, two parts in ten or a bit less. Which is the difference between *not worth bothering* and *nice tasty morsel*."

Simonides frowned, memorizing the information. Like his uncle he was a younger son—youngest son, and third youngest of six living children, in fact—and would have just enough of a patrimony to get him started. He was staying with Josephus as an apprentice, more or less.

Though of course all the extended family's heads of household helped each other at need, contributed local connections, partnered on ventures, and corresponded and exchanged valuable news from Massilia in Gaul all the way to Seleucia over the border in Parthia. They all collaborated on charitable works too, and on supporting rabbinical students from the family or bright youngsters from poorer ones.

Josephus was moderately proud of how he'd turned a small inheritance into a fair degree of affluence, though trading on the frontier had its risks.

No risk, no profit, he thought, slapping the hilt of his sword, a plain practical cavalryman's weapon like the bow cased at his knee with its built-in quiver. *And hereabouts . . . sometimes it's not just money you risk.*

Hence this trip to dicker with a minor landowner who sidelined in smuggling because his Norican-Gallic family had old blood links over the border. With absolutely nobody along he didn't fully trust to keep their mouth shut. Fortunately, amber was very high value in relation to bulk. One packhorse could anonymously carry far more than was practical to buy, hidden among nondescript bundles. Ostensibly he was buying beeswax, which was perfect for concealment and quite plausible, since it was moderately high value itself.

Sarukê *dhugatêr* Arsaliôn—the middle word was "daughter of" in her tongue and the last her father's name—looked carefully and methodically both ways down the deserted stretch of high-way and said:

"Leave road here, lord?" in rough but fluent Greek; she spoke equally bad Latin too. "For villa of Lord Marcus? I go first?"

Josephus checked the road in his turn; they were alone and she was reliable, but you couldn't be too careful. Nobody was in sight, and there weren't any of the border watchtowers overlooking this stretch either.

"Do it," he said. "Nephew, take the extra horses' leading rein, she'll need both hands."

Sarukê was probably about two or three years younger than the merchant, and a full four inches above his middling five foot five height. Sarmatians were a tall folk; she also had the pale skin, almost colorless gray eyes and reddish-blond hair common among those nomads of the Pontic steppe, and was beaky faced and built like a leopard.

Fighting women were not unknown among them too, though not exactly common. Josephus suspected the old Greeks had gotten their legends of Amazons from that source. She'd been captured when a raiding warband was smashed on the northern border of Dacia, the trans-Danubian province further east that Emperor Trajan had conquered a lifetime ago, and sold to the arenas further south as a slave gladiatrix.

The merchant had bought and manumitted her after he saw her win a bout in the arena, thus almost certainly saving her from an early, nasty death.

Right now she was dressed in her native garb, or as close as you could get here. Leather jacket and baggy woolen trousers that were tucked into soft strapped boots; a knee-length coat of riveted mail went over it, and a dagger and a ring-hilted longsword were belted to her waist, along with a steppe recurve bow in its quiver-case. The round shield slung over her back was painted with a triskele pattern of gryphon heads.

When armed as now, with the domed helmet on and its horsehair plume nodding over her head, and the hinged cheek-pieces that tied off below her chin covering much of her face, she was usually taken for a man among Romans. Ex-gladiators were commonly hired for bodyguard work, though Josephus' friends had twitted him about a female one, with rough jokes about dual jobs and sly digs about excessive thrift on her purchase price. But he'd found it very useful indeed to have a competent bodyguard who did *not* look like a fighter when she was in woman's garb.

Not to ordinary Roman eyes, at least. That had given several robbers and one unscrupulous business rival a very nasty...very *pointed*...surprise.

And she's more loyal than a man in her position would be, he thought. *She can't go home again.*

She also had an uncanny memory for terrain; they'd only been this way once before, and that in wintertime, but she never hesitated as they crossed the roadside meadow and went into the wood beyond on a deer trail leading northwest. Big trees towered over them as they rode through low densely forested hills, beeches and ash, oak and hornbeam, elm and more casting an umbrous gloom. Brush was thick where sunlight broke through, and they could hear the odd rustle from boar and deer and aurochs and other wild beasts. A *half*-wild sounder of the landowner's pigs feeding on the rich mast of beechnuts and acorns squealed and gave them suspicious, gimlet-eyed, tusk-clashing looks as they passed, though the swineherd wasn't in sight.

Occasionally they passed a stump and chips and the drag marks of an ox team where a tree had been harvested, or a circle of saplings springing up from the roots of such. The hills began to fade as they descended to the north, and open patches showing the marks of grazing herd beasts grew more frequent.

Then he reined in and said:

"Hold!"

There was an odd feeling in the air, like the tension before a thunderstorm, prickling the hair on the back of his neck. The birds had grown silent.

And then a flick of brilliant white light came from beyond the edge of the trees, followed by a sharp, piercing whining noise not quite like anything he'd ever heard before. Almost like two pieces of metal scraping but far louder, loud enough to hurt the ears.

Another flick of light, and another. More, and each closer to the next until he closed his eyes and threw up a hand against the intolerable brightness. Then it was gone, and the noise ended with a *crack* sound and a thudding like heavy weights dropping on the ground but from no great height. The horses snorted and reared and rolled their eyes, and he slugged his back into obedience with a hard tug on the reins.

Sarukê was looking frankly terrified, eyes wide and staring beneath the rim of her helm, teeth bared in a snarl; men and beasts didn't frighten her much, but this smacked of the Otherworld. Simonides was pale but biting his lip and visibly mastering himself.

"The Lord God of Hosts is with us!" Josephus said to the boy sharply. "Call upon Him, and fear nothing."

He was frightened himself. But he was also curious; and there really *was* no profit without risk. New things were opportunities, and you had to be able to seize them. Letting terror cloud your wits didn't help.

And I'm not going to look *fearful before my nephew.*

The merchant slid down from the horned cavalry-style saddle and tethered his horse to a nearby sapling; the normal, mundane actions helped him take back self-control. The other two did likewise, and Sarukê had the remounts and packhorse calm in moments. Josephus drew his sword, his nephew a long curved *sica* dagger, and the Sarmatian had an arrow on the string of her powerful four-foot horse-archer's bow. They went forward to the northern edge of the woods, down on their bellies for the last few yards, through hazel thicket and ladybell with the odd blue flower lingering, yellow Venus-foot and others.

The stretch of meadow ahead was normally just more rough grazing on a low, gentle slope; the Danube was out of sight from here even when the leaves were off the surrounding trees. The great river did a sharp turn to run east-west a few miles north... upstream...of here, and they were in the elbow of the curve.

No birds sang, and no butterflies danced or bees buzzed about the flowers. Now it held—

You'd need a big *oxcart to take all that,* his merchant's mind calculated automatically as he blinked at the sight. *No, two of them. Or a four-wheel wagon.*

Ten yards away in the knee-length flower-starred grass was a collection of wooden boxes, fastened together with the luxury of iron nails and tumbled higgledy-piggledy, some cracked a bit. One teetered and fell over with a thump as he watched. A few chests and trunks, and a number of sacks. Many large bundles, rope wrapped with outer coverings of coarse burlap or waxed leather. A few things leaned against them; a pair of spears, a couple of ordinary flat oval shields of the type many people carried in rough country, and a Roman legionary sword and belt.

And sprawling unconscious on the ground, just to one side, five odd-looking *people*...and part of another man a little *further* aside, an older man with a white tuft of beard on his chin, his legs sliced off neatly at the upper thigh and his mouth gaping in death. There was no sign of the missing limbs, but the blood was still flowing.

Which made no sense at all.

Wounds like that killed quickly, and the red tide ebbed and slowed to a diminishing trickle even as he watched. But where had been the screams and clash of iron and beating of blade on shield? And some of the bundles were smoking faintly, as if they'd been exposed to very high heat, like cloth held too close to a crucible of molten copper but not quite long enough to burst into flame.

He rose and walked forward into the clearing, sword still ready; the air was unnaturally hot, and there was a curious smell like lightning, but both were fading quickly. The others followed, and Sarukê did a swift expert circuit of the clearing, bow ready.

When she called there was disbelief in her voice:

"Nobody else! No new man track or horse track or ox sign or wheel sign, either, lord! None!"

"Take a look at the baggage," Josephus said to his nephew, sheathing his sword.

And added to himself: "Strange, very strange. Solomon in his wisdom might be able to figure out how they got this much heavy gear here without leaving tracks. There must be a full"—he stirred a few of the bundles with his toe to confirm his impression from the way they looked—"two or three thousand *libra* of it. Thirty or forty talents."

Sarukê was *good* at hunting and fieldcraft, and if she said there wasn't any sign, there wasn't.

"But *I* can't figure it out. Unless they dropped from the sky like that Greek Icarus in the story!"

Young Simonides hastened to obey, his natural curiosity overcoming the ebbing fear. Sarukê remained tightly ready for a fight as she kept their surroundings under a ceaselessly moving eye.

Josephus examined the people, the living ones—several of them had trickles of blood coming from nose and eyes and ears, but they were definitely not badly wounded, breathing steadily if slowly, their pulses regular when he put his fingers to throats.

There were five. One *very* tall man, fully six feet, of about Josephus' age or a bit less, but clean-shaven in the older Greek or Roman way. He had light hair sun streaked with white-blond and cropped close, and out-of-doors tanned and weathered skin; the merchant raised one eyelid with his thumb, and the eye beneath was blue. The features were oval, handsome in a bluntly regular square-chinned way, and he'd have called them Gaulish or German at first glance. Though plenty of folk of both stocks had lived under Rome for centuries now, mingling their blood with all the others.

His clothes had a vaguely Germanic shape too, rather close-cut ankle-length trousers with a buckled belt through sewn-on loops to hold them up, socks of a distinctly odd make, closed leather shoes of intricate construction, a blue jacket with a white shirt beneath it that was fastened up the front with an odd arrangement of pearly disks shoved through slots in the cloth. But no single detail of cut or construction was familiar, and the cloth was of a fantastically fine weave and unfamiliar materials. The shirt might have been cotton, an eastern fabric as expensive as silk, but it wasn't—not quite. It felt too *smooth*, somehow.

Scars on his face and hands, Josephus thought. *Not quite like any I've seen before either... but a warrior if I've ever seen* that. *Strong built, out much in all weathers, but not a laborer's muscle. And a* rich *warrior, by his garb. A chief or lord, perhaps?*

The other four were younger, not much older than his nephew... though he couldn't be certain, because they were all quite *big* too. Not giants, no size you wouldn't see occasionally on a farm or city street, but conspicuous when you saw the five of them together.

Like a crowd of Sarmatians for height.

Two were women, but they were as tall as he was or nearly; two were men, and taller. All four wore tight blue trousers with copper studs, tight as his own leather riding breeks but ankle length rather than to the knee, and closed shoes even stranger than the older man's, of hard-but-flexible materials he couldn't identify at all.

Leather boiled and waxed would come closest, but not very *close.*

And tunics, small tight ones of a stretchy fabric; one bleached snow-white, one black, one brown and in one case white with a distorted dog's head drawn on the cloth somehow, and all tucked them into the blue trousers.

One of the men was skinny, with a big nose and light olive skin, a shaggy-frizzy dark-brown beard and similar hair already retreating a little; he might have been a cousin of Josephus, save that he was as tall as the strange warrior. The other man had the same Gallic or German looks as the first, and like him was clean-shaven, quite tall but not towering, broad shouldered and strong but with little callus on his hands.

Like a rich Greek who spends much time at sport.

The women were truly, deeply strange, even apart from their mannish garb. One was a black Nubian or Aethiop, ebony skinned and good-looking in a rather plump fashion. The other had pale umber-brown skin just a little darker than his own, a small nose, high cheekbones, long raven-dark hair and black eyes that had a fold at the corners, making them look tilted.

I saw a man who had those slant-eyed looks in Parthia, and he was flat of face like her, he thought, recalling a journey with his father half his lifetime ago. *Though it didn't look nearly so pretty on him! They said* he *came from far to the eastward.*

This group was as mixed as you might see in a great city, Antioch or even Rome, never mind this provincial backwater. All of the strangers also had the look of those who'd never wanted for food, and except for the older warrior didn't look as if they'd had to labor as hard as most did, either. And—he checked, on a vagrant impulse—they *all* had unusually fine teeth, white and straight and none missing.

Which meant they were all rich or raised that way, and unusually *lucky* too. Unlike hunger and toil, trouble with your teeth was one of those things you couldn't buy your way out of. If anything the rich had more of it, for some reason.

"Uncle! Uncle!"

Simonides' voice was urgent, but this time his excitement held a note of pleasure. Even of awe.

Josephus saw that he'd opened the chests—they had locks, strange and small and finely made, but the keys were still in them. The one he hung over eagerly was big enough to need two men to carry it, and had hide loops for that riveted to its sides; the construction was boiled and oiled leather over a stout wooden interior, and it was strapped with iron.

Another one, even larger but otherwise like it stood open beside it, and it was packed with *books*—in codex form, not scrolls, bound along one side, and in fancy ways with unknown lettering on the backs rather than on the cut edges of the pages.

That almost distracted him, his hands itching to examine the odd volumes, but the soft leather sacks had a magical pull.

An interior partition divided the trunk into a larger and smaller compartment. The younger man had opened the topmost sack on the larger side, and poured coins into his hand. Josephus snatched one up, bit it and held it up to catch the light.

It was a silver denarius of Antoninus Pius, the emperor before the current *princeps* and his co-ruler Verus. *Good* silver, definitely, not clipped or some cheap counterfeit—an ability to judge money accurately at a glance was a necessity in his line of work.

Eight and a half parts in ten silver, then.

He put the coins back in the sack and tossed it up and down a little, calculating the solid weight of it in his hand.

"Four hundred fifty to five hundred, I'd say," he murmured.

Simonides whistled softly, and well he might. *Three* hundred denarii was a full year's pay for a legionary soldier, *before* stoppages for food and gear; about what a skilled freeman like a smith or furniture maker would get in the same time here in Pannonia. Except that the soldier's pay was more regular and ended with a bonus of twelve year's wages or a grant of land for a farm. For the substantial but lucky minority who lived out a full twenty-five-year hitch. More than half didn't.

He counted quickly. There were twenty of the sacks and a swift check showed they all held around the same amount. That would be nine to ten *thousand* denarii. Forty thousand sestertii or a little less. A full talent of silver, and hence nearly half of his own body's weight.

The lowest rank of centurion, commanding eighty men, got three thousand seven hundred and fifty denarii a year. The *primus pilus*, the First Spear who was senior in the double-strength First Cohort and was first under the legionary legate and his tribunes, got fifteen thousand.

That nine or ten thousand was an equestrian's yearly income and not one for a *poor eques* either.

So it wasn't exactly a huge fortune, but it was more than Josephus could have raised immediately in cash. He'd need a week to do that, and possibly he'd have to sell some assets, or borrow. Most of his money was tied up in goods and property, or committed to ongoing dealings that had to be fulfilled to protect his reputation...and your reputation was the most crucial asset of all for a man of business.

His eyes skipped to the other side of the trunk, and his hand trembled slightly as he picked up one of the near-identical sacks there in the smaller compartment at the back. It was much, much heavier, confirming his guess. When he opened it golden *aurii* poured out into his other hand, likewise bearing Antoninus Pius' elderly face. He bit one incredulously, and the soft gold deformed under his teeth, only a little hardened by the silver content of one part in a hundred. Then he counted the coin in another two of the sacks, not willing to guess.

The merchant grunted as if someone had punched him in the stomach. There was a full talent of *gold* here too; worth more than three hundred thousand sestertii, most of the way to the property qualification for inclusion in the Equestrian Order.

Together, more than Deineira's weight in gold and silver! he thought, seeing his wife's clever narrow face.

He felt sweat break out on his brow and trickle down his flanks, and licked dry lips, tasting again the sharp metallic flavors.

That talent of gold *was* a fortune, even to a prosperous young merchant like him. You could buy a great deal with a talent of gold. Urban properties with rents enough to keep you at a modest gentleman's level, for example. With that sort of capital to draw on, Josephus knew for a fact that he could be in the Equestrian Order himself in a few years. Rich enough to be a noble or even in the Senate by the time he was old, except of course for the Senate being out of the question for a Jew unwilling to take part in pagan rites.

The other two were looking at him. Sarukê was fingering her dagger and raising her brows, a piratical—or border-reiver—expression in her eyes and a she-wolf smile beneath it. It was so, so tempting...

Sweat trickled down and stung his eyes.

Oh, what I could do with this! Security for my children and the grandchildren to come...no more passing up opportunities because I can't afford to risk the cash...

"No," he said, putting the sack of money back and closing the lid of the chest firmly, blowing out a long breath. "We are not bandits. *I* am not a bandit."

Then he had a sudden thought, opened it again, examined the coins from several pouches once more and replaced them before closing it for a second time...and turning the keys on both and putting them in his belt pouch, just to remove temptation.

"The coins all look *new*," he said, half to himself. "Every one! As if fresh from the mint...but none are this year's issue, they *have* to be at least four years old, that's when the old Emperor died. And it's not counterfeit, they're full weight and the right fineness of gold and silver, or I'm Prince Ballomar's second wife and eight months pregnant! But none of the ordinary wear you'd expect, not even a little tarnished. Odd."

One more strangeness among many.

There was a sound from behind him and Sarukê tensed, looking over his shoulder and half raising her bow. When he turned, the tall warrior was blinking his eyes and turning his head back and forth. He rose stiffly, wiped away a trickle of blood that had run from his nose, put a hand to his head as if it ached, and then stretched, twisting his torso and arms like an athlete warming up, his eyes flicking over the three.

Then he took a step sideways and—deliberately slowly—picked up the *balteus* with its sheathed *gladius* and *pugio* dagger and belted them on. Then his gaze shifted back to Sarukê with a frown that smoothed away when he'd studied her for a second.

Ah. He saw she's a woman. A perceptive man, keen of wit, not one to go by the first glance.

Josephus smiled—his delight at this fascinating mystery was quite genuine, and he firmly put the sensual pleasure of holding that bag of gold *aurei* out of his mind—and raised both hands with palms open in sign of peaceful intent.

"*Loquerisne Latine?*" he said, asking if the stranger spoke Latin.

That was the commonest tongue right around here, with Gallic and German second and third. He repeated it when the man frowned, speaking more slowly. A nod, and then the stranger said:

"*Latine loquor.*"

This time *Josephus* had to ask for a repetition himself; the tall man had the strangest, strongest accent he'd ever heard... and he'd heard full many of the ways the Empire's official tongue could be mangled and mutilated. It took a few minutes for them to be able to actually speak, even of very simple things...including a request for the *date*.

Not just the day of the month, but the *year*. And who the emperor was!

Another oddity to add to the mountain-high pile!

When they *could* speak a little, Josephus' puzzlement grew, because the man's Latin not only sounded strange; once you got past that odd accent and unfamiliar choice of which syllables to stress it was *scholar's* Latin. Old-fashioned and sonorous, the sort you might hear in a formal declamation or read in a proclamation. He spoke all the word endings written with *-um* and *-us* the way they were spelled, for instance, rather than the colloquial *u'* or *o'*.

"Where is the town of Vindobona from here?" the man asked eventually.

He was already shedding a bit of the weird intonation, consciously shaping his pronunciation toward the merchant's.

Which was another argument for keen wits.

"It...is...in...that...direction," Josephus replied, pointing southeast and speaking slowly and clearly. "Half...a...day's... travel...on...foot."

About the same time he'd taken coming out on horseback, but he'd been deliberately dawdling, part of the misdirection to cover his—

Ummm, my arrangement, *so to say.*

—about the amber.

The man hissed in annoyance, obviously thinking hard behind a creditable imitation of calm. The others began to stir too, and he glanced at them with a frown. Josephus' smile grew broader. He wasn't a bandit, but he thought he could profit from these newcomers nonetheless.

Mutual profit, the best and most lasting kind, if he could win their confidence. They were obviously utter strangers here, somehow, as if they'd dropped from the sky in truth, and he had connections and local information they'd need very badly.

And maybe he could learn *from* them too. Knowledge was a treasure nothing could steal away save death.

"You...will...need...a...cart. *Biiiig*"—he spread his arms wide—"cart. Wagon. And house? Place to stay?"

On an impulse he pulled out the keys to the chests and handed them to the man, whose brows rose. Josephus pointed to the chest with the bags of coin.

"And...you...will...need...*argentarius*..."

He deliberately pronounced it in the old style.

"A...banker. For...the...money."

⇒ CHAPTER THREE ⇐

Municipium Vindobonum,
Province of Pannonia Superior
June 26th, 165 CE

Arthur Vandenberg looked around the table at the other four Americans as they finished their dinners.

The only Americans in the whole world, he thought, with a thread of eeriness.

Most of the time now I can just... accept it. Then I see or hear or smell... or taste... something and it hits me all over again. Got to get my mental feet under me! Adjust or die, soldier.

The merchant Josephus had put them up here—it was a house he owned, normally rented out but empty yesterday save for basic furniture. And he'd sent his nephew on posthaste ahead to get things ready, including bedding, sets of Roman clothes, groceries and a cook, plus a couple of maids-of-all-work. They'd arrived late yesterday, later than this, eaten a scratch meal, fallen exhausted and still hurting a bit into early sleep, and then spent the next day doing essentials.

Or occasionally sitting stunned and shaking, like a steer in a slaughterhouse.

Settling in had taken some time... starting with learning how to tie on a *subligaculum*, the Roman loincloth. So had even a quick once-over of the baggage Professor Fuchs's crew had put together. Fortunately including plenty of money, equivalent to several million dollars, for which Josephus had helpfully recommended a banker.

And even more helpfully provided two armed bodyguards to escort the pair of porters carrying the chest of cash between them hanging from a pole. One guard had been the Amazonian type he'd had with him when they met, and the other a scar-faced Germanii who was hulking even by American standards, and from somewhere far west of here. The banker had been delighted too and fallen over himself to give them good terms, so the money was already at work making more. Hereabouts evidently a sack of gold was a sack of gold and to hell with formalities, documents and tax collectors.

Most of the rest of the gear would be very useful, including the several hundred books, and the medical supplies. The remainder had ranged from the outright weird but possibly valuable, like the mechanical calculators and slide rules, to a solar-charging kit. Which would keep phones and tablets and the four field-grade ruggedized laptops and their six external drives in the crates working longer. Fortunately there was a good translator AI on the laptops, so the fact that most of their content was in German didn't matter, and it amounted to well over a petabyte of stored data.

And there were even *seeds* of dozens of varieties, including things like maize and tomatoes and sacks of seed potatoes, more than twelve hundred years before Columbus sailed the ocean blue to their western home.

Home...a home that was not there even in the future. Not anymore.

There were formal reclining couches around somewhere in the house for dining lying down, but apparently only the gentry, the aristocracy and social climbers used them all the time. Now they were sitting on elaborate stools, around a rectangular table, which was...apparently...what upper-middle-class working folk like Josephus did except on special occasions.

The food for this meal had been recognizable. Warm-fresh brown bread in round loaves that was like a rustic whole-wheat variety from an organic bakery, tasty but very slightly gritty; chicken soup with vegetables and beans; a salad dressed with oil, and after they asked for it with vinegar too; grilled river fish with herbed cheese sauce; and lamb fried with onions and vegetables. But everything tasted strong, and a little strange, and the spices were *quite* strange.

And they offered to get us garum *when I mentioned it.*

Garum was a sauce made from, basically, the fermented—which was to say selectively *decayed*—guts of ocean fish, anything from herring to tuna. It was a by-product of the salted fish industry and the Roman equivalent of Heinz ketchup.

But they looked relieved when I declined, so I think it's expensive here on the Danube. We're a long way by oxcart from a seacoast.

Fortunately all of them had eaten at enough Greek and Italian restaurants that dipping the torn-off pieces of the loaves in dishes of the excellent olive oil—fruity and green tasting with a pungent peppery undertone—wasn't strange at all.

Around here, butter is what barbarian scum smear on their braided hair.

It was densely quiet at about nine in the evening, with only the long twilight of a European summer just after sunset and the oil lamps hanging in chains from the ceiling—one of them shaped like a winged penis—holding back the dark. He glanced at his wrist to check the time, then remembered with an inner stumble that he'd stashed his watch; the little moving numerals would be far too much like magic to the locals. None of the others wore one, relying on their phones, but it was a habit he'd kept from his time in the service.

You could forget how far north most of Europe was, because thanks to the Gulf Stream, climate didn't match the latitude the same way it did back in America. Vienna/Vindobona was on the same line as the south shore of Lake Superior, but they grew wine grapes and apricots here. The long summer days and short nights reminded you.

The occasional racket of wheels or hooves on paving stones from the outside only emphasized the stillness to twenty-first-century urbanite ears; that and the far-off, lonely sound of the *tubae* and *cornua* from the fort, trumpets signaling the changing of the night guards. Most people here went to bed with the sun. And there was the smell, reminiscent of some Middle Eastern towns he'd served in but worse than most, seasoned with barnyard from the horses, mules and oxen that provided motive power here. They had sewers and running water, but sanitation was...sketchy.

The house was built around a rectangular courtyard planted with herbs and flowers, which had a fountain...which was also the source of the household water supplies, brought in by a pipe from an underground aqueduct originally built to serve the fortress around which the civilian town had grown. The layout for the dwelling was Mediterranean, but wooden walls could be put up to close off the rooms from the outside in the Central European winter; the house walls were brick covered in plaster and whitewashed below, with a half-timbered second story above with brick nogging in between the baulks of wood, and red tile on the roof. It all looked several generations old, too.

The big fort by the riverside was the headquarters of *Legio X Gemina* and had been for more than fifty years; around five thousand legionary troops at full strength, the same number of auxiliaries, and their servants and hangers-on, the equivalent of a full division in American terms. The countryside round about held many who'd mustered out from the legion or auxiliaries, on land granted or bought with retirement bonuses. And their children and grandchildren and the great-grandchildren-plus of settlers from the other legions based here further back to around the beginning of the century.

About thirty thousand civilians made their homes in the town that had grown up around it, too—including the unofficial common-law families of soldiers, who couldn't legally marry until retirement at the end of a twenty-five-year enlistment. As well as sutlers and shopkeepers, merchants and artisans and their staffs and families—

And at least one banker that I know of!

—and whores and laborers and slaves. Supplying the soldiers with something to spend their regular cash pay on was lucrative; there would be trade across the border too, and up and down the Danube itself.

"Right," Arthur—or *Artorius* as the locals rendered it, spelled that way but pronounced *Artorio'*—said.

He took a deep breath. *Arthur died when Vienna was wiped out. Artorius is here. And Artorius says—*

"Does anyone still doubt we're here . . . here in the second-century CE? In the province of Pannonia Superior, in the Roman Empire?"

"Not unless we're sharing a really good immersive full-body-suit VR while tripping on magic mushrooms," Mark Findlemann said with a wry grin.

While brushing crumbs out of his shaggy beard. They'd all been famished; just existing here without a hundred unnoticed but now sorely missed machines burned calories, and they'd walked most of nine or ten miles yesterday with the aftereffects of the... transition... still making like bad hangovers. The headaches were gone, but the hunger had hit full force.

McCladden and Chang were into running and hiking and in McCladden's case also cycling, which had helped: it had been much harder on Atkins and Findlemann, who regarded walking more than a couple of blocks as something you read about. Those two had spent a lot of the last part of the trip on top of the gear in the big mule-drawn wagon Josephus had arranged.

Mark Findlemann was one of the smartest people Vandenberg had ever met. He was also an archetypical nerd, with a memory like a steel trap for historical trivia and vague about most other things, barely touching down now and then in the real world. And he had the *emotional* intelligence and social skills of a wilted turnip, occasionally stopping to look around and wonder why he was lonely.

Arthur nodded encouragingly, and Mark went on:

"I tried out a little Hebrew on our host, and he recognized it—he picked up that I was a Jew fast, too—but he doesn't know much more of it than I do, just some prayers and such. By rote. Though he speaks about six languages, and tried them out on me, I think trying to place our weird-ass English. I recognized Koine Greek and Aramaic and one I think is Middle Persian which is evidently what Parthians speak. Or at least the merchants he met there did. The one he said was German didn't *sound* much like our variety of German at all. More... buzzy and liquid, almost like something Slavic, except slower and with a lot of z sounds in the endings. But I caught a few words, which surprised me: father, mother, sleep, stand, water, white, black, some of the numbers."

"It would be end-stage *Proto*-Germanic now," Vandenberg said and nodded, unsurprised. "Technically. Starting to evolve into separate languages, but right now a dialect chain from here to Sweden."

"Like the common Latin people talk here," Filipa said thoughtfully. "A bit different from the Classical language, but not even Proto-Romance yet, not by a mile."

The sort of multilingualism Findlemann had described for

Josephus would be very useful for a trader here. Which reminded him:

"Exactly. We're all going to have to work hard at getting our spoken Latin comprehensible as fast as we can. The vocabulary and syntax we learned from the books is fine—a bit bookish, in fact, but that doesn't hurt, it's a status marker. It's the *sounds* we need to get right. Mark, Jeremey, you've got some Koine Greek too, don't you?"

They nodded, and Filipa put her hand up. "Mine's more classical," she said. "Did a course on lyric-age stuff and got interested."

"You should all work on that as well; I certainly will. It'll be useful and Roman aristos are mostly bilingual in Greek and Latin, that's a status marker as well."

Findlemann went on at an encouraging sound:

"I don't think Josephus is strict about *kashrut*... keeping kosher. Maybe just not when he's away from home, like? There's no pork in this food... but some of the other stuff would be *tref* if I remember correctly. He's from Antioch... the one in Syria... and a lot of the Jews there were heavily Hellenized, from what I've read. Well, he was *born* in Antioch, but his wife and kids live in Sirmium which is a ways south of here and a lot bigger than this little burg, four or five times bigger. But the dietary rules were different this far back too, not as elaborated. So... we're here, all right."

The others nodded. Bursts of incredulity had grown fewer, and then died away to silence when they'd walked in through the gates among wildly varied crowds. Past jeweled and painted ladies in litters born by husky bearers, past an *eques* with the narrow purple stripes on the tunic beneath his toga, surrounded by clients and hangers-on, past Suebic warriors from across the river with their long, often fair and always very smelly, hair up in knots on the right side of their heads and long swords at their hips, looking around with naked greed and wolfish smiles... and more and more.

And been crowded themselves to the side of the road along with Josephus and their wagon at a harsh shout of:

"*Make way!*"

... as a century of legionnaires went by.

The centurion at its head with a transverse red crest on his helmet and vine-wood swagger stick in hand, a chestful of medallions on the harness over his mail shirt, sword at left hip and dagger at right—the reverse of the common soldiers. With the *signifer* beside him, a bear's tanned head on his helmet and its brown fur down his back, carrying the long pole standard with its wreathed open hand at the top and unit-decoration medallions below, all polished to a gleam.

The long, heavy pilum javelins were held high on their right shoulders with their hands at the butt, and swayed in unison behind them as the hobnails stamped down on stone, with the iron hoops and bands of the plate *loricae segmentata* clinking and rattling as they moved in a smell of leather and sweat and oiled iron and brass.

The bull of their legion was on their curved rectangular shields along with crossed thunderbolts and eagle wings, and their eyes stared out beneath the beetling reinforced brow-ridge band of their bowl-shaped helmets, beneath the cross straps welded on the top. The broad flared neck guards and hinged cheekpieces made their half-hidden faces slablike and metallic, like a column of humanoid warrior ants. The *optio* had come along behind, a long staff topped by a brass ball in *his* hand.

And every one of them looked hard enough to chew rocks and shit gravel, as the saying goes.

Now he caught each student's eye around the table as they remembered ... possibly he'd have to stop thinking about them as students ... as the servants brought in some sort of honey-sweetened sponge-cake-like thing studded with dried apricots and nuts for dessert. Along with a pottery bowl of fresh fruit; this was well into the start of the picking season and it included peaches, cherries and apricots, but not grapes or apples yet. And more of the wine, a quite decent red, with a pitcher of water for mixing with it. The wine cups were well blown and mostly colorless glass, slightly tinted with green in the thicker spots.

Fortunately the supplies Fuchs had put together included large crates of long-lasting broad-spectrum antibiotics and the newer antivirals. They'd still have to adapt eventually, or their intestines would. Well-watered wine was a lot safer here than straight water, even water from a mountain brook, much less any from around people. Beer would be just as safe, but here and now it tasted like it had already been through the horse at least once and nobody in this century had even heard of hops. They had forks, besides the local spoons and knives; there had been a set of camping utensils in the baggage. Josephus had been intrigued at the clever way they packed together, and stainless steel had been a revelation.

And they were almost *infinitely* safe from eavesdroppers, since nobody would be speaking English for—

Well, we're fourteen hundred years pre-Shakespeare. Maybe nothing like English ever will *be spoken here. We'd be the first* and *the last English speakers!*

"All right, first thing: we don't have to worry about changing the future and wiping out our families and country," Vandenberg said.

"We don't?" Filipa Chang blurted. "You mean we'll start a new timeline that branches off from ours? How could we tell?"

"Without even Dr. Strange to blame for screwing the multiverse," McCladden said whimsically.

Paula Atkins shook her head. "The Prof means we...they... everybody...wiped ourselves out the day we...left," she said bleakly, stabbing the fork into her piece of cake.

She was evidently one of those people who automatically ate more when they were upset, without even really realizing they were doing it. She went on:

"*They* wiped *themselves* out. He's right. Everybody's dead, our homes are dead. The *world* is dead. *God damn them all!*"

Her voice broke on the last words, and she refilled her wine cup from the pitcher without watering it local style, drank, and refilled it again.

"I'm sorry," Arthur said, his voice gentle. "I had a wife and children."

He stopped for an instant, closing his eyes and concentrating on the gone-ness of it all and making the muscles of his neck and gut unclench. You had to function, even when...say...your best friend had his legs blown off in front of you and your own blood was running out on the thirsty ground too.

Which was something he'd done.

You just suck it. The mission comes first. And we have a mission. We need *a mission, come to that.*

"You all had families. We all had people we loved, friends... places and things we loved too. But that was full-scale thermonuclear war. *Thousands* of launches. Mostly aimed at cities. None of you are stupid."

They were all very intelligent and very well educated, in fact. Probably the average IQ around this table was somewhere north of 135, and they'd all started reading serious nonfiction for fun about the time puberty hit if not earlier. When you were under extreme stress, that mattered less than most people would have thought. Sometimes smarts and education simply made people better at rationalizing what they wanted to believe or do anyway. He went on:

"You know what *global thermonuclear war* means. And Vienna was hit *as* we...left...if left's the right word. Fusion bomb, that whine when the EMP hit the electronics and the rumble after it are unmistakable. I was looking up when it happened. There was this jerky slow motion, that must have been Fuchs's...well hell, it is...was...a time machine."

Findlemann frowned. "Well, of course it was the time machine. I remember that. As if things froze for a fraction of a second, then started again, then froze...cycling faster and faster. Fascinating!"

He doesn't mind calling it a time machine. It was a time machine, of course. But then, he's irrationally rational. One of his endearingly irritating features.

The thought was heartening somehow. He went on:

"So I could see the flash and the blast wave hitting the building, see the windows starting to blow in with the overpressure, I could *see* the cracks propagating, stop-motion in real life... and I could feel the beginnings of the heat flash. Some of the baggage was smoking when we woke up. Thank God, the Vienna Woods...the hills they're on, really...would have blocked the initial gamma radiation from a low-level airburst."

And if we'd gotten a serious dose, we'd be very sick or dead by about now, but no need to mention that. Cancer we can worry about long term.

They looked at him uncertainly, and he drove the point home:

"That was *Vienna*—a medium-sized city in a European neutral country of no particular strategic or military importance."

Paula blinked wet eyes, but drawing out deductions was a ground-in habit for all of them.

"So if they bombed Vienna...where *wouldn't* they bomb?" she said. "La Paz, Bolivia? Maybe."

"Whoever *they* were," Vandenberg said.

They'd never know for sure who'd started slinging the big one, though he was morally certain it was the Bad Guys. He went on:

"So the lab we were in would have been fire and rubble and dead bodies, everything burning, seconds later. Maybe two seconds, maybe one or less. We *just* made it."

"We can't go back, either, that's what it means too," Jeremey McCladden said, in his flat Upper Midwestern accent; he was from Wisconsin, a small-town boy from the southwestern part of the state originally.

"From what Fuchs said about that *dolabra*, his machine worked both ways," Filipa pointed out.

"Yeah, but the machinery is wreckage under rubble and all the scientists are dead and if anybody is alive, they're not going to be doing any physics research. They'll be fighting over cans of dog food and dying by inches of radiation poisoning," Jeremey said.

That was tactful, McCladden, now-Artorius thought as everyone winced and Paula cried harder and then they glared at him.

McCladden went on, after waving a gesture of apology:

"Dr. Fuchs is dead too—we buried him ourselves, remember? And even if he'd gotten here alive, and we were physicists ourselves instead of historians, we don't have the tools to build the tools to *begin* to build the tools for something like that, and a whole lot of regressions beyond that. We're here for life...however long that lasts. We don't have to worry about *the* future, just *our* future."

And McCladden has a keen eye for the main chance, which takes over when he thinks about things. Remember that.

Silence fell for a moment, broken only by Paula's final stifled sobs.

She was engaged. To that law student, the one with the sideburns, I forget his name. I think Filipa had a girlfriend; I know Jeremey did.

"But there *is* something we can do," Arthur said, organizing his thoughts.

My feelings are just shit right now, so I'll stick with thoughts. Except that this feels like the right thing.

"Besides just look out for ourselves," he added.

"What?" Filipa said. "Do what?"

"We can save civilization here, here and now," he said, leaning forward, tapping his knuckles on the table to emphasize the *here* part. "And by doing that, save the future. Humanity's future, because it won't have much of a future after twelve or fifteen thousand nuclear strikes. Neither will anything else except rats and roaches. It's up to us."

Mark giggled involuntarily. "Well, we could get *capes* easy enough, I suppose. Tights would be harder. The Fantastic Five from the Future!"

He struck a pose in his chair as if he was about to fly away with a woosh:

"I can be *Iudaeo-puer qui iter in tempore!*"

That meant: *The Time-Travelling Jewboy.*

Arthur-Artorius suppressed irritation; Findlemann *did* have the social skills of a turnip, and in some ways it made him more alien than the things with tentacles in science-fiction flicks. But he wasn't a bad sort at heart.

And I need him. We all need each other.

"Look, you're all familiar with this period. Marcus Aurelius is the last of the Five Good Emperors. This is the peak of the Roman world. After this it's all downhill; chaos, civil war, the Praetorians auctioning the crown—"

"193 CE, Pertinax," Filipa said automatically, as if this were a quiz in high school.

Then her face changed: "Twenty-seven years from now, almost exactly. I mean...we could live to *see* it."

Vandenberg nodded. "And barbarian invasions, Gothic pirates raiding from the Black Sea to Crete and Cyprus by this time next century...Diocletian and Constantine cobble some repairs, pull things together again, but a century after *them* the Vandals sack Rome and the Dark Ages are under way. Cities nine-tenths abandoned, barter replaces money, trade shrinks to a few percentage points of what it is now, populations crash back to Iron Age levels and only the Church preserves literacy. The Emperor Charlemagne, seven hundred years from now...he tries to learn to read and write as an adult and never manages it and the only thing that surprises people is that he tried at all."

They all nodded; the term *Dark Age* had become fashionable again, somewhat and unevenly, in academic circles. Over the last decade, as field research made it inescapably obvious just how far and fast most of the ex-Imperial territories had gone downhill in the phase shift after the breakup. Like mass migrations, new evidence had forced once unpopular concepts back into the scholarly mainstream.

"Literacy's fairly common here right now," McCladden said, with a determined smile. "Judging by all the graffiti. Bad as a New York subway in an old movie. *'Lucius, privileged soldier of the Tenth Legion, was here. All the women will tell you he's a stallion!'*"

The joke fell a little flat, though they *had* seen that written on an alley wall.

"Is it *worth* saving this civilization?" Paula said, wiping at her eyes with a napkin and pulling out a handkerchief to blow her nose; it was a repurposed napkin, in fact. "Presuming we could. They have *slaves* here."

They'd all known that in the abstract; meeting the reality had been both shockingly mundane and deeply repulsive.

"And that stuff outside the gates..."

Crucifixion was also a lot less abstract once you'd seen it... and smelled it. He thought they were all rather grateful they'd passed the grounds outside the gate after it was too dark to see the details, and while they were still in shock from the transition.

Arthur nodded. "Right. It's an alien world here, and no mistake. The thing is, most of that shit is just *everywhere* and *everyone* this far back. The tribes across the river keep slaves too—and sell their neighbors to the Romans. It'll be more than a thousand years before slavery becomes extinct in any large area on this planet—western Europe in the high Middle Ages, Japan a bit later."

"Shogun Toyotomi Hideyoshi abolished slavery in Japan in 1590," Filipa said; she seemed to be falling back on dates.

Then with a touch of the wasp: "Not that that stopped them kidnapping *comfort women* in the Greater East-Asian Co-Prosperity Sphere."

"And public executions went right on into Victorian times... later than that, in a lot of places," Vandenberg noted. "Christians stopped crucifying, but they broke people on the wheel and burned them alive and it was something people took the kiddies to and packed picnic lunches for."

Filipa spoke again: "When the Aztecs dedicated their Seventh Temple to Huitzilopochtli... Hummingbird of the Left, their war god... in 1487, a few years before Columbus sailed, they sacrificed *five thousand* people on the top in only three days on the four altars. In continuous shifts, more than one every minute, cut out their hearts and threw the bodies down the sides of the pyramid. The lake the city sat in turned brown and stank from the blood. And they *ate* parts of the bodies."

Vandenberg nodded again and went on:

"If we can save the Empire, start it modernizing, we can short-circuit...all that stuff...by a millennium. Not right away, but by a good long time. And the Antonine Plague is coming, Galen's Plague, probably smallpox. That'll kill every fourth or third person in the Empire, maybe ten, fifteen million, and who knows how many more outside it? We might be able to stop that—or at least make it a lot better. No nuclear war, either. Imagine one united planet, at peace or as close as human beings can get. *Pax Romana*...but *pax*."

Findlemann looked around the table. "OK, granting your point, Prof...but...but there are only five of us here," he said. "Two of them women—no offense, Filipa, Paula, but that's a lot bigger disadvantage here. We're scholars, not...not world-saving adventurers!"

"Well, neither was Martin Padway," McCladden said. "He was an archaeologist—a historian like us, only one with dirt under his fingernails."

A little to Vandenberg's surprise, all of them seemed to catch the reference to the classic time-travel story—de Camp's *Lest Darkness Fall*—and chuckled.

Most historians daydreamed about time travel, at least when they were young.

Mark went on, shaking his head: "We're foreigners here too, not even Roman citizens! Even staying alive would be an accomplishment. Hell, the locals can barely understand our Latin, and I've been studying *that* since before my first zits."

Jeremey McCladden spoke thoughtfully:

"You know, there's one thing we could do that *would* definitely have an impact pretty quick. And that's planting those seeds I checked over; at least, the ones that'll grow in this climate. If we did that *right now*, we could get more seed, even from the field corn, I think. I could handle that, Prof. And remember what corn and potatoes and the other crops did in the Old World, after the Columbian Exchange?"

They all glanced at each other. That wasn't their area of specialization, but their general undergraduate courses had covered it.

It had revolutionized agriculture—and that meant populations—over half the planet.

"Your folks were farmers?" he asked the younger man; he remembered hearing his father mentioned as a businessman, though that was sort of generic. "Mine were ranchers."

He smiled thinly. "Not in a *Yellowstone* or *6666* sort of way. More a small, sideline way."

"No, not farmers, but my dad ran a feed-and-seed business, I helped him with things through high school, and we had a *really* big kitchen garden, as in a couple of acres or so and some fruit trees and chickens and whatnot," McCladden said. "Mom grew up on a little dairy farm, and we kids helped her with the garden and picking and putting things up—we had a *real* old-fashioned cellar full of pickles and jam and veggies and such. Organic all the way!"

Artorius gave an involuntary sigh of relief. It wasn't like having an expert, but it was...

Close enough for government work. We only get one try with that stuff. Was that why Fuchs wanted someone whose speciality was Roman *agriculture?*

"Give me the land and some labor that'll do what it's told, and I could get a lot started. No time to spare at all, though, it would need to be right away to beat first frost."

Jeremey glanced upward, obviously calculating, before he went on:

"We've got two bushels of seed corn. Eighty thousand seeds per bushel, you need say twenty thousand to plant an acre...at low density, which we should because it'll be dry...but the summer days are really long here, so more sunlight...Say seventy to a hundred days from planting to maturity for the sunflowers, a hundred days for the potatoes; sugar beets grow quick too, but they're biennials, you have to leave them in the ground overwinter to get seed. Hundred and twenty to a hundred and thirty days for field corn, which is *juuuuusst* doable, which is why I'd save a quarter of the seed for next spring just in case. And I'd save all of some of the other things—they take longer but the seed should stay viable if we're careful about storing it; it's very well packed to last. And there's the canola, that's fall-planted like winter wheat...even easier for the veggies...Then increase by geometric progression."

"Numbers?"

"Say we plant six acres of corn, being real pessimistic but

not totally *depressed* we get around a hundred, hundred twenty bushels total, that's enough for planting *hundreds* of acres the next year, and so it goes. Only next year, using optimum planting time, we'd get...oh, maybe eighty bushels the acre. Enough seed for *thousands* of acres in the third year."

"Will the seed breed true?" Artorius said.

Paula, Mark and Filipa were looking at them as if they'd suddenly burst into Swahili; but then, *they* came from New York City and San Francisco, respectively, and their families had all been urbanites from many generations of the same.

"Yeah, it's breed-true varieties, aimed at the organic-sustainable type of buyer, Fuchs must have picked them for that. That's judging from my phone's translation of the labels...they were in Magyar, of all things. And I *think* it's all very good stuff. But I'd need land and hands, *muy pronto*."

"Josephus could probably help with that," Arthur commented, pleased. "Good idea! I'll talk to him tomorrow since that's time constrained."

"Thanks, Arthur...no, thanks, *Prof*!"

Not Arthur, he thought. *I'm* Artorius *now. Arthur's...dead. Died with his family in World War Three.*

"The good Doctor Fuchs packed us a *lot* of goodies," *Artorius* went on. "He must have been reading the international tea leaves for some time and getting ready to bug out. Or possibly he took a look at the *future*, we'll never know."

They all looked around at the alien room with its—rather crude, down-market—mural of dancing fauns and maidens, and its floor mosaic of fish and fruits and graphically, gruesomely dead game birds. This was *escape* with a capital *E*, like teleporting to another planet.

Vandenberg felt a slight chill at the sort of mind that could make a plan like that. And why late Antonine Rome? Why not go back to 2000 CE, or before 1914, and work from there? He'd never know.

Fuchs must have been very smart. And very weird. Even weirder than Findlemann, which is saying something.

"Fuchs got us in because he needed Roman experts along, and he wanted ones from outside his own academic circles so he could keep the secret—keep it long enough to use it while he ran for the hills...for the hills of here, the ones not covered in radioactive fallout."

"Or while he jumped in a hole and pulled it in after him," Findlemann said, and everyone nodded at the image.

"Well, we're here; we've got enough cash to make us moderately rich, now safely in a bank and shortly in several banks in different parts of the province..."

They looked at him. "Josephus' advice and I think it's very good. They do interbank credit transfers here by letter, which is mildly surprising and some of the banks are organized as *societās*...companies, pretty much...even here in the sticks. And we've got the rest of the baggage; and I think Josephus could be very, very useful, even more than he has already. A stroke of luck meeting him like that...and notice what he *didn't* do."

"He's been very kind," Filipa said with a frown, and waved a hand at the meal and the house. "What more could he have done?"

"He could have cut our throats and taken the money before we woke up," Arthur-Artorius said dryly. "And it's a *lot* of money, especially if you include those bags of synthetic gemstones"— Josephus' eyes had bulged and his jaw had dropped and his hands had shaken when he saw *those*—"and nobody would have known or cared about our bodies. Except the wild pigs and the rest of the birds and beasts. And the worms. *They'd* have cared. In a culinary sense."

The others looked at each other. Two of them swallowed visibly. Artorius remembered an old saying, one so old that the Stoics here and now were fond of it:

Anything that can happen to anyone *can happen to* you.

Similar thoughts were probably going through their heads right now.

He went on aloud: "That shows he's honest at a fundamental level. And I think on short acquaintance he's also extremely smart and very knowledgeable about this century...about the sort of thing that *doesn't* get into the books and that we *don't* know... which means, ignorance that could kill us."

The others were looking at him intently, nodding unconsciously. They needed a task, a vision, something to give this catastrophe meaning beyond a bolt-hole.

"And while I am a scholar, that's not all that I was. I've got some ideas. It'll mean hard work, and risks, but the payoff—"

❖   ❖   ❖

Hours later, Arthur-Artorius sat on the edge of his bed; he'd managed to convince the personal servant Josephus had supplied that he *didn't* want him sleeping on a pallet at the foot of it, though that probably meant he'd be dossing in the corridor just outside. They just didn't have much sense of privacy here, or didn't consider servants in that context, or both. The air had an odd stale scent from the wicks of the snuffed-out oil lamp on the bedside table. Which piece of furniture had spindly curved legs, a style familiar from countless revivals.

Wearily he dropped his head into his hands.

Our world went down in fire, and we can't stop that . . . except by making it never have existed at all. *Our loves will never have been born . . . Mary, Vincent, little baby Maddy . . . my folks . . . hell, my* grandparents *will lose their whole long lives, will never have been . . .*

⇒ CHAPTER FOUR ⇐

Southeast of Vindobona,
Pannonia Superior
July 15th, 165 CE

O*uch,* Artorius thought, shifting in the saddle.
    The *Villa Lunae* was two and a half long days in journey time from Vindobona by mule wagon on a good road in good weather, and a half day north of the little town of Scarbantia.
    Or around an hour from Vienna in a car, if you weren't push-ing it, Artorius thought dryly, feeling the ache from thighs and buttocks and back—he hadn't spent day after day in the saddle for a very long time. *Everything takes longer here, and costs more... and how! I have a* fundamental *problem with this.*
    That distance put the estate in what another history would eventually have called the Burgenland, easternmost Austria and right next to the western frontier of Hungary. But the fur-clad ancestors of the Magyars were currently in Siberia, and this was well south of the Danube. Roman territory ran east of here all the way to the site of Budapest-that-wasn't, nowadays Acquincum, capital of Pannonia Inferior.
    "So you don't actually *own* this estate, my friend?" Artorius said; the word he used could also mean *comrade.*
    The merchant had stayed behind to finish up some business, and then caught up with them late last night. He *was* used to spending a lot of time on horseback.
    "No, *magister* Artorio'—you might say I own the owner, or rent him, in a manner of speaking," Josephus replied with a smile,

riding easily next to the American beside the first wagon. "Your Latin is much improved, by the way. Very quickly, for so little time. It is a relief that we can now talk normally, and very useful."

"Thank you," Artorius said.

Understanding the spoken form was coming more quickly than speaking it well for all of them, but total immersion was a wonderful incentive. He'd even caught himself starting to think in it, for a phrase or two, occasionally.

"I am not learning the language, though. I know Latin as it is *written*. We all have that knowledge. I am just learning the *sound* of it. How, then, and in what manner is the owner of this land under an obligation to you?"

And I'm starting to be conscious of talking like a book written by someone with a serious linguistic pickle right up their ass.

He looked around. The wagon train had turned east about an hour ago, after stopping for a roadside lunch not far from a busy quarry, and come onto the estate a quarter hour later. The *latifundium* was a big irregular rectangle with somewhat jagged outlines, the product of long generations of partible inheritance spiced with purchases, sales and reversions. The long-term trend here was to bigger properties, but that was *very* long-term.

It included about twelve hundred acres of forest on the hills to the northwest, and thousands more of cropland and pasture, vineyards and orchards and rough grazing between there and the lake. According to Josephus about half of that part was rented out to free tenants for cash or on shares, and the rest directly managed from the villa headquarters. Apparently that was a standard arrangement on big properties and had the added advantage that those tenants with smaller holdings usually took temporary paid work on the estate fields in peak busy seasons like this, supplementing the migrant harvest gangs big landowners had to hire.

Both of which spared the owner feeding extra slaves who'd be underemployed most of the year. It would be economic suicide to carry enough hands for the harvest year-round.

The road inside the property wasn't a paved Roman highway like the one that ran south from the river, or as arrow straight, but it was well-tended dirt topped with gravel and well ditched.

Probably passable even in wet weather, except in a really bad storm, Artorius thought, giving it a glance.

The countryside around was very slightly rolling and mostly open, except for the range of low wooded hills about a mile to the northwest. Trees planted on the roadside broke the hot summer sun with dappled shade for long stretches, leaves flickering with a steady wind from the west, and more edged some of the fields. For the last mile or so many of them had held big, ungainly shaggy-looking nests, apparently built by the migratory storks who loved the large lake just east of here.

Around them on both sides right now was a mix of pasture studded with livestock, mainly sheep, and golden grainfields. More were expanses of pale knee-high irregular stubble, likewise being grazed; the harvest was in full swing now and well over half done.

Livestock's better looking than I'd expected. Bigger breeds, and they look fairly well fed.

Whole families from children in their early teens to elders well into middle age were cutting tallish waving wheat that came nearly to an adult breastbone—

None of our short stiff-stemmed hybrids!

—with sickles, while youngsters brought water. Teams of reapers mostly composed of young men were at work too. All pausing now and then to stand and stretch and sharpen the iron curves of the sickles with whetstones, a scraping, ringing sound that carried clearly even over the clatter and creaks of hooves and wheels. And through an endless murmurous rustling sound, the stalks rubbing on each other.

There was a peculiar smell to the harvest, familiar from West Texas when he was a child. Dry and dusty and mealy like new-ground flour, but here mixed with the sharp scent of cut weeds, and the yellow waves were starred with red poppies in spots. Behind the reapers came binders—more of them women—gathering the grain until it was a bundle they could just reach around, then tying it into sheaves with a twist of straw. Still others tossed those onto two-wheeled oxcarts to be hauled in for stacking and then threshing.

Odd to see a countryside so full of people, he thought; he was used to a wide emptiness.

That prompted a memory, one that he understood better now, down in the gut. He murmured aloud, from Homer's description of Hephaistos working a harvest scene onto the Shield of Achilles:

"He placed it on the estate of a great man
Where the hired men
With sharp sickles in their hands
Were cutting the crop;
Of the handfuls of cut stalks
Some fell to the ground
Along the lines of reaping, one after another,
While the sheavers were binding
The other handfuls with ties..."

The merchant chuckled, catching the reference despite what the American's accent did to the poet's Greek, which was as archaic here as Chaucerian English in the Americans' home century, and said:

"Some things never change, eh?"

Artorius nodded. Here and now, the Bronze Age scene was still as current as it had been in the blind poet's day most of a thousand years before this summer, for thousands before that, and would be for nearly two thousand years more.

He kept his *We'll see about that!* silent.

Josephus went on after a pause to organize his thoughts:

"How is the owner of this land obligated to me? Sextus... Sextus Hirrius Trogus... owns this *latifundium* and some others further south, urban properties rented out in Sirmium, and a large brickworks there; he inherited this land we're on from a great-uncle who died without living children just after Sextus' own father, so it's an outlier. He's of an old equestrian family and a landowner in a substantial way, his *domus*"—which meant *main home*, more or less, or *family headquarters*, in this context—"is in Sirmium, where mine is... and he owes me money and at first couldn't pay the full interest, so it compounded according to the form of the contract," Josephus said.

Artorius winced slightly. That was a bad position to be in, and he knew that from his own countryside childhood and remembering his grandfather cussing out the bank. It could be like trying to run up an ever-steeper slope of greasy tinplate while you carried a calf on your shoulders. Even owning a *lot* of land didn't mean you had a lot of cash on hand, especially since you worked and spent all year but only got *paid* when you harvested crops or sold stock. And of course you sold when everyone else did, which meant prices were low, and you sold in the first place to people who could hold off reselling until prices rose again.

Josephus went on: "I acquired the loan from a previous holder, heavily discounted, as part of a complex deal, and it had already changed hands more than once, losing value every time...it was a big risk, my biggest so far, I had to borrow myself to cover it, from kinfolk at that. I refinanced it in a *new* contract with Sextus, and gave him a grace period on the compounding of interest. He's paying the full interest again now, and in a while he'll start repaying the principal. In the meantime he owes me favors for that, since otherwise he'd have had to sell land from his patrimony to keep the debt from grinding him under. I'm calling in one now, giving your client"—by which he meant Jeremey McCladden and his sacks and crates of seeds—"and now you and the others the run of the place. His widowed youngest sister and her daughter—the daughter is nine—and his mother live in the villa here, but I've assured him you and yours will not trouble them. He himself usually only visits here around wine harvest."

He cocked an eye at Artorius to make sure he understood that *his* word of honor had been given. Vandenberg replied:

"There's plenty of room from the sound of things, so I'll make sure we don't get in each other's way."

"Good. He doesn't get on with the sister. He fell out badly with her husband before the man died, he was a wastrel, and she took her husband's side. Which is only seemly; he was the father of her child, after all. But family is family, blood is blood. Sextus took her in and turned the *pars urbana* of the villa here over to her together with an allowance when the brother-in-law died and left them nothing but debts, debts Sextus had to pay in large part."

Artorius made an enquiring sound.

"He stood surety for some. And it would be a disgrace if she and his niece were thrown onto the street!"

"A stain upon his honor?"

"Yes, it would undermine his reputation badly. And I think he persuaded his mother to join her here...for propriety's sake, you understand, a widowed woman still of childbearing age needs a chaperone...because his mother nags him and this way she has to do it by letter rather than in person and morning, noon and night. This property is the furthest he owns from where he lives! And I asked Sextus to pass on the instructions to the *vilicus* just as you said. He graciously complied. He's a man of honor."

The *vilicus* was the estate manager, the bailiff, the *mayordomo* to use the Hispanic term. In a Roman context he'd be a slave himself or possibly a freedman, but a trusted one, high-ranking and literate, with many privileges.

Josephus smiled as he went on: "An order that *your* orders are to be followed...no matter how *insane* they sound. And that replacements may be hired or bought for any labor you commandeer, at your expense. Though please, not until the harvest is finished—that should be about another two or three days at most in this district, it's warmer here, and"—he cocked an experienced eye at the workers in the fields—"it looks to be a very good one this year. Thanks and praise be to HaShem."

Artorius had noticed how even city dwellers here knew a good deal about farming and followed crops and weather closely. Josephus went on:

"And now I have an interest in the grain, too! Which didn't hurt with keeping Sextus sweet, by the way. *Salve, lucrum!*"

That meant: *Hello, profit!* Something Roman merchants often had set in mosaic at their thresholds.

"Oh, it'll take a while for us to get started," Artorius said. "Why did you grant Sextus a grace period in the first place, if you don't mind me asking?"

Josephus shrugged. "*He's* not a wastrel or really stupid, quite capable at running his family's properties in fact, he just had a run of bad luck that built on itself. Starting with him helping his brother-in-law, whose only talent was getting men to loan him money against their better judgment. And then bad weather and bad harvests."

"Which always happen at the worst possible time," Artorius observed, and they shared a chuckle.

Josephus went on:

"If I'd squeezed him hard, I'd have ended up owning at least this estate, and I didn't want that—farmland is too troublesome, given other calls on my time, and a forced sale means low prices if I just put it on the market. Land around here is well placed for selling its yield to the garrisons on the frontier, but even so it isn't moving quickly. Not these last few years."

Artorius nodded; the Danube frontier had been stripped for the Parthian war, and the barbarians across it were getting even nastier than usual. The locals didn't know the Marcomannic Wars were about to start or how devastating that would be over the next decade and a half, but they knew that the weakened defenses potentially meant raiding parties, and the work and investment of generations quite literally going up in smoke. Not to mention rape, kidnapping and cut throats. Josephus went on:

"Sextus would still be an influential man if I took land from him, and an enemy, he and his kin; there would be lawsuits and all manner of trouble and lost opportunities. This way, he's *more* influential, but as an ally I can call on. Plus I *bought* the debt at a heavy discount on its original value from someone desperate for cash who'd despaired of ever getting what he was owed. So payment in full on the principal will be very profitable, with the interest as the *garum* on top. Eventually."

"Ah, I see," Artorius said.

And thought:

Our friend Josephus keeps an eye on the long term. And apparently always has, even as a younger man.

Water glinted, shimmering in the distance to the east as they topped a slight rise; it was edged by vast reedbeds that were still intensely green in the summer-dun landscape. The lake was a big one, big enough that the eastern shore was barely visible on a clear day like this, and water stretched to beyond the limit of sight north and south. Trees fringed the inland edge of the marshes, many of them willows and aspens and hornbeams.

"It's an odd lake, shallow and a bit salty," Josephus said. "Just salty enough to kill a few of the mosquitos!"

Artorius silently blessed the scientists who'd come up with a really effective malaria vaccine a few years ago. And right now he was even thankful for the pettifogging regulations that mandated an exhaustive suite of jabs before international travel, even to safe destinations.

That had been recent too, and he'd cursed the delay and discomfort at the time. But even though he didn't have to worry about the latest varieties of Covid or monkeypox or novanilos here and now, it was nice to know that a bunch of other, older things weren't going to hit any of the five Americans.

Typhus, typhoid, cholera, rabies... they'd even gotten a shot of smallpox vaccine, he supposed because some crazed paranoid bureaucrat was terrified of terrorists with biological weapons who'd somehow stolen stored samples of the virus.

Or gotten the code and synthesized it with tweaks, in which case the vaccination wouldn't work, *would it?*

The baggage had included a small box of modern gene-tailored malaria-resistant mosquitos of sundry types, and they'd released them promptly as the instructions on the lid said they should, but God alone knew how long they'd take to spread... or if they'd survive at all. Being immune to the disease gave them a big reproductive advantage, but chance would play a role there.

Josephus went on:

"But the waterfowl are very numerous here in season, even the slaves feast on goose and duck then, and the villa smokes and salts them for sale. There are plenty of fish—the catfish here are ten feet long and heavier than a man sometimes—and the reeds have many uses. They make a very nice sweet wine here too, it's regularly exported as far as the Adriatic southward and to the mouth of the Danube and the Black Sea on the east. Now pardon me—I must make doubly sure everyone is ready for unloading and reloading the wagons."

With a grin: "Time is money!"

Artorius had mentioned that old saw a few days ago and Josephus had taken it up with enthusiasm, the way you did with a phrase that summed up something you'd always believed or known but hadn't had a precise expression for.

Josephus fell back to talk to the artisans they'd hired in Vindobona, who were riding in or walking alongside the wagons. Some with their families, too, along with a good deal else in the way of tools and raw materials... and all of the baggage the Americans had arrived with, minus most of the coin. Artorius stayed where he was, beside the lead wagon where Mark Findlemann and Paula Atkins were seated at the front, with Filipa Chang in the saddle on the other side.

Neither Mark nor Paula had ever gotten closer to riding a horse than seeing it done on a screen, and preliminary tryouts for them hadn't gone well so far. Filipa's parents—they'd both been in some arcane branch of AI in California and made very good money—had indulged her love of horses as a girl, and the skills she'd acquired in the hills north of San Francisco still showed.

Though she's probably as stiff and sore as I am, he thought. *Not that riding in an unsprung wagon on stone-paved roads is any great joy either, even* with *a folded feather mattress under your butt.*

"Did you catch that?" Artorius said to the others, in English.

They'd all been trying hard with the Latin under the lash of necessity, but their native tongue was a relief occasionally, as well as completely private. Though the locals, besides finding it foreign, thought it sounded deeply *strange*, in a way that Gallic or Germanic didn't. He suspected it was because all the languages they knew firsthand had complex inflectional syntax, and English had spent more than a thousand years stripping that out of its structure.

We're a third or more of the way back to Proto-Indo-European, he thought with a chill.

"Yeah, and I know *one* more big reason why Josephus didn't want title to the estate instead of a mortgage agreement," Mark said. "It's the slaves. Inconvenient to own large numbers long term, for a Jew who takes the basics of the Law seriously. And even if Josephus didn't personally, it would put him in Dutch with his relations if he showed it."

Paula had been brooding. That got her attention, which Artorius was glad of. One reason he was keeping everyone as busy as he could was precisely to limit overmuch thought about what they'd lost. That could only do harm . . . *did* do enough harm, anyway.

You have to sleep sometime. What dreams may come . . .

"There's some sort of prohibition on slavery in Jewish religious law?" she asked with surprise.

"Not exactly. But every seven years, in the Sabbath Year, the *shmita*, Jews have to free their slaves. And remit debts, at least to other Jews. Ummm, it's a bit more complicated than that; and technically it only applies to *Jewish* slaves. But you also can't refuse if a slave you own wants to know the Law and follow the Lord, see? Serious no-no-no. Which gives slaves owned by Jews sort of an automatic out if they're willing to convert before the next *shmita*."

He grinned and made a scissors-snipping gesture with two fingers:

"That involves a little operation for the men, too, of course. So Jews can *trade* in slaves, and owning a cook or masseuse or whatever is practical here and now, but directly owning *latifundia* like this one we're heading for with *hundreds* of slaves, that gets real awkward unless you sell it on quick."

Paula looked as if she didn't quite know how to take that. Mark went on, with the sort of grasshopper-jump non sequitur they'd come to expect from him:

"Those saddles don't look quite like American or Mexican ones," he said, glancing at the gear Artorius and Filipa were using. "Or those little English things you see in costume dramas."

Filipa laughed and Artorius rolled his eyes very slightly; it was just like Mark to notice that *now*, after days on the road.

"*I* checked that," she said.

Artorius hadn't had time, and she knew more than enough for the task. She'd also done the work of getting the horses used to unfamiliar gear, which fortunately hadn't taken long. It was actually more comfortable for them than the Roman equivalents, because the saddletree, the wooden frame, spread the rider's weight better.

"They're a traditional Spanish saddle, ordered custom made, by a company called Zaldi," she said.

"Why Spanish?" Mark asked. "Couldn't Fuchs have gotten saddles in Austria?"

"Same reason Fuchs got *Americans* who'd studied Roman history, I think," Filipa said. "He was using great chunks of his R&D money in an oh-naughty-so-bad way, stocking up on the stuff he wanted to take back here."

Mark sniggered. "Like those sacks of synthetic emeralds and sapphires and diamonds and whatnot? Cheap as dirt back . . . where . . . we came from, but no way the Romans can tell the difference. For a physicist, he sure had a sneaky side."

"Josephus was thunderstruck with those," Artorius said. "He thinks we'll have to sell them in small parcels over years, and as far away as Rome and Carthage and Antioch and Alexandria, to avoid saturating the markets and drawing attention. Fortunately he's got . . . connections."

Filipa nodded. "All the, um, *baggage* was bought in the last few months, too, and all the paperwork was stuffed in with the goods, no records hanging around for someone to read, except online. He ordered from all over but virtually nothing in Austria."

"Yeah, I noticed that with the books," Mark said thoughtfully. "No more than a couple from any seller, new and used, some pretty obscure, all done in ways that don't leave immediate tracks. He paid premium prices for speed."

"He'd have been caught eventually, but he planned to be gone by then."

"He *was* gone. Or part of him was," Paula observed dryly. "Starting six inches above the knee."

In retrospect none of them liked Fuchs, even though he'd almost certainly saved their lives; she apparently liked him even less than that. Mark looked a bit queasy. He'd lost the contents of his stomach when he saw and smelled the body up close, being nearest and having his head pointing that way when he opened his eyes.

Filipa went on: "That money in the chest? He had the fake Roman coins done in Italy, there's people..."

Her face went bleak for an instant.

"Were...will be...you know what I mean...who make 'em. Delivered the week before we...ah, left. The saddles came ten days before we arrived, thirty-five hundred euros each. They're fine, excellent saddles, just a little different. He even got the sizes right for what's available here in the way of horses."

Artorius leaned forward and slapped his mount affectionately on the neck. Roman horses did tend to be a bit small by modern standards, though there were exceptions. The riding cobs they'd bought were all thirteen or fourteen hands, technically ponies though stocky, broad backed and strong. If you wanted bigger, the price went up steeply, and few were over fifteen. Most of those went to the heavy cavalry, the *cataphracts* the Romans had copied from Parthians and Sarmatians, and their breeding was tightly regulated to prevent sale to foreigners.

He'd been raised with Western saddles, riding from the age of five or six. These Spanish models weren't all *that* different, though a bit lighter; much more similar than an English hunting saddle would have been. They had a raised curved piece at the cantle that cradled your hips, and a shorter upright pommel arch in front, no actual central horn the way he was used to, but there was a steel ring there you could use pretty much the same way. He'd had a braided-leather lariat done up, and was practicing to get the knack back when he had time. He'd been good as a teenager, before the Academy, but it was half his lifetime since he'd aspired to junior rodeo star status.

"And there's a disassembled one," Filipa noted. "That's going to be a *big* help getting more made, because they...whoever we get...can just copy each individual piece."

And you can tell Fuchs wasn't from my *neck of the woods,* the Texan thought. *This mountain of stuff...we're back in an age crawling with bandits and barbarian raiders...and not one gun. What I wouldn't give for an M-7 and a couple of thousand rounds of 6.8!*

"I wonder why Fuchs picked *this* date? Obviously from the stuff, he was *aiming* at 165 CE, or somewhere close to it."

Mark said it thoughtfully, and apropos of nothing. He often went off on unexpected tangents. He went on now:

"It's just on the verge of some really bad shit, as the Prof said in his pep talk. If he'd gone for say sixty years ago... well, ago from 165, time travel screws with tenses... it would be much more peaceful."

Artorius shrugged. "We'll never know, and he's not answering questions just now. Except to the worms. We also don't know zip about his... time machine, or how it worked or what its limitations were. And we never will."

"Frustrating!" Findlemann said.

Vandenberg had judged when they first met that Mark Findlemann was someone who regarded an unsolvable question as a personal affront and irresistible challenge. In academia that was very useful, but here it had risks.

"Frustrating if we think about that, which we shouldn't," he said. "We can't afford wasted effort, Mark."

"Oh, and Prof... what did Josephus mean about having an interest in the harvest?" Findlemann said.

Artorius grinned, which was starting to feel doable again, occasionally.

"Simple. I loaned him fifty thousand denarii for six months, at five percent, or twenty percent of the net profit, whichever was higher."

There were some gasps; that was a large chunk of the cash Fuchs had provided. They'd all had graphic demonstrations that this wasn't a society where it was a good idea to be poor. There were places in the Empire where needy citizens got what amounted to welfare, but Pannonia was emphatically not one of them.

To put it mildly. And we're just perigrinii, *Roman subjects, not citizens. Who gives a damn about us?*

His grin grew wider:

"It looks like it's going to be the twenty percent of the profits. He bought the entire saleable crop here and some other places, even before it's all cut. Then he turned around and sold it to the camp prefect of the Tenth, who he's done business with before but not on this scale."

The *Praefectus Castrorum* of a Roman legion was a senior

centurion. Usually a former *primus pilus*, the centurion who was the highest ranking of those with actual field commands. The prefect was a staff appointment in American terms, in charge of training, equipment, supplies and maintenance in the headquarters camp. That was much of the workaday behind-the-scenes management that made the legions the superlative killing machines they were.

"Unless there's a catastrophe, it looks like Josephus will come out about twenty thousand denarii up on the deal by the end of the year. Of which we get a fifth, say four thousand. Not bad, when all *I* had to do was write a letter to the *argentarius*."

"How'd Josephus *do* that?" Paula asked.

"Economies of scale, possible because of our stash of cash. Sextus and the other bigshots were willing to take a very moderate price for their grain... most of which will come back to Josephus in interest payments from Sextus, at least. And the landowners were willing to take a lower price because *they* won't have to store the wheat and sell it in bits and pieces and wagon it all over to the various points of sale themselves, *and* they get cash on the barrelhead as fast as they thresh it and turn it over at their own gates, instead of in dribs and drabs over a year or more, which is a big plus for *them*."

Findlemann glanced upward in thought. "Capital-short economy, friction from lots of little deals." He mumbled a bit, and went on: "He's buying it at, what..."

"Two sesterces the modius," Artorius said. "A lot lower than big-city prices, it's something like five or six in Rome. Three to four in most big cities, except in famine years, from what he told me."

"There's four modii per bushel, eight sestertii... four sestertii per denarius... so two denarii per bushel, twenty-five thousand bushels, bought for fifty thousand..."

"Premium for cash in hand, too," Filipa said; some of her parents' business dealings had rubbed off on her willy-nilly.

"That's the grain from a *lot* of land. Depending on yields," Findlemann said.

"It turns out Geoffrey Kron was right; yields here are surprisingly high, higher than they were again anywhere until the eighteenth century," Artorius observed. "About equivalent to England or the Netherlands around 1800 CE."

"Kron? That guy who did the chapter on food production in *The Cambridge Companion to the Roman Economy*?"

"That's the man. But the kicker is that everything's labor intensive, and the labor has to eat too. So the *surplus* is about six bushels per acre or a bit more around here in a good year, which apparently this is, after deducting seed and what the labor force and their oxen and mules eat," Artorius replied.

Findlemann nodded: "And in a bad year, no surplus so somebody goes short."

"Guess who?" Paula observed sourly. "Give you ten-to-one odds it's not the Roman army."

Mark had little money sense at the personal level, but put it in the form of a large-scale problem for analysis and he could do fine. He went on:

"And selling it at...oh, three and a half?"

"Yes, but then—"

"Yeah, you have to deduct nominal interest on the capital, and then the wagon haulage costs...hmmm..."

"Road transport's expensive as hell here even with Roman roads. Ten to twenty days depending on the gradient is as much as you can wagon grain overland and leave any profit. Call it three to three and a bit after expenses."

"Yup. That's a really good price he's getting from the camp prefect," Findlemann observed.

"But now the prefect doesn't have to haggle with two dozen landowners or hundreds of small farmers or the middlemen who buy from the peasants, or send out working parties to bring the grain in himself. He's in a hurry and has a lot of other things for his men to do, and the tax-in-kind just isn't enough. Josephus is going to run it into Vindobona as fast as it's threshed, and the landowners will get it threshed fast because that's when they get paid. And the government's credit is good here, you can sell their debts nearly at par, so working capital isn't a problem if he needs to raise some, which he probably won't."

Filipa had been thinking: "And I bet the prefect wants full granaries inside the fortress, and pronto, because if there's an attack he has to feed the city as well as the camp."

"Bingo. Josephus was grinning like a happy wolf at the way the news will hit his rivals."

"Sharp!" Mark said admiringly. "No flies on our friend Josephus!"

He waved his hand in front of his face and several of the

literal insects took to the air, a gesture Artorius had known in his youth as the *Cowboy Salute*.

"Even here," he added.

"He *is* sharp. He told me he'd been thinking of something like that for years, but couldn't get his hands on the money at acceptable interest rates to do it at scale."

Artorius hesitated for a moment and went on: "And I told him we're from the future."

All of them looked at him in appalled silence, and Mark nearly jerked the mules pulling the wagon to a stop. They glanced back resentfully, having already had a bellyful of his inexperienced hands.

"And he *believed* you?" he said, his voice cracking.

"Yup. Only took about half an hour and a look at a couple of books with pictures of Roman ruins."

He smiled. "I didn't have him talk to the chatbot, though, that would be a step too far. Then he went into a brown study, and when he came out of it, warned me emphatically not to try and tell anyone else... because we'd be accused of sorcery, and hostile sorcery's a serious crime here under Roman law. Predicting the death of an emperor, for example. Which I had, about Marcus Aurelius and Verus."

"Phew!" Paula said, and mimed wiping sweat off her forehead.

Then she really did get out her hankie and wiped her face; it was a hot day, and this low-lying area was warmer than Vindobona had been.

He was hot too, his horse was hot...

On the other hand, I'm not stuck bending over a sickle sunup to sundown with a boot to the butt if I slow down, Artorius reflected before he went on:

"A bit of a risk, but I thought he'd take my word for it. So keep that warning in mind! Things they can understand are OK, even if they're new, but no flashing electronics."

"No moving visions or disembodied voices from the air," Paula chimed in.

Artorius looked from one to the other, making sure they all nodded.

"Mark, now that I think about it, you turn your phone over. Paula, you handle it and *no* unsupervised use."

With an apologetic smile he went on:

"It's not that I'm worried you'd screw up deliberately, Mark, but you *are* absent-minded and we all know it."

"No!" Paula said, grinning. "No, no way!"

"Absent-minded? You don't *say!*" Filipa added. "Who'd a thunkit!"

She gave a comic look of astonishment as Findlemann handed the black oblong over to Paula, a hand to her face, eyes wide and mouth making a little O.

The senior man explained; he'd always believed in telling subordinates *why* they had to do something, if there was time. Things worked more smoothly that way.

"I took the chance with Josephus not least because he'd been wondering—asking—how we got to that clearing with a ton of gear without leaving tracks."

"Literally a ton," Mark said. "Almost *exactly* a metric ton. I bet that was some constraint in the time machine."

"And Josephus was worrying at it, he doesn't like an unsolved mystery any more than you do, Mark."

"What can I say?" Mark said. "He's Jewish too. We even argue with *God*, for God's sake."

"Nobody else...nobody anyone will listen to...saw that clearing before he brought the wagon and the stevedores back. And anyway, we're the goose that laid the golden eggs for him. He's smart enough to see that in the long term, our stash of cash is the least of what we have."

Just then Sarukê rode up, oiled mailcoat glistening and horsetail-plumed helmet hung on her saddlebow and her belt-slung bowcase-quiver rattling. She'd been moving between front and rear positions since they left town, and today, in the course of it, avoiding Josephus' other bodyguard as much as she could. He was a freedman and an ex-gladiator too, tall and fair like her but of Germanic origin, from near what moderns would have called Cologne and was Colonia Agrippina now. Their mutual dislike was obvious, though it didn't get in the way of doing their jobs that he could see.

Josephus is annoyed about that. Up to him to settle it, though.

"We were talking about saddles, ours and these Roman ones," Filipa said to her in Latin.

The Korean-American woman got on well with her, not least because she didn't treat the Sarmatian as a freak of nature, which was apparently something of a novelty.

Sarukê was riding with a Roman cavalry saddle; no stirrups, of course, and no *tree*, no wooden frame underneath either—

Which settles that *historical controversy! Moi Watson was right!*

—just straw-stuffed leather pads to either side and a leather cover over that linking them across the saddle blanket, and a simple single girth and light breast strap. It had horns at its corners to stabilize the rider: two behind her, nearly upright, and two in front that slanted back over her thighs, all four made of thick padding inside a leather sheath with a bronze rod at the core.

She rode superbly, as if she'd been born on horseback... which given her nomadic origins might very nearly be the case. The way she kept her legs bent back at the knee and clamped to her mount's barrel looked odd to twenty-first-century eyes, but evidently it worked.

"What use is for footrests?" she said.

They could talk by now, despite their mutual accents. Her Latin was fluent, but sometimes a bit odd, and she pointed a soft-booted toe at Chang's stirrup for an instant to show what she meant.

Filipa extended an arm. "Try pulling me out of the saddle."

She did, grabbing the offered wrist and the shoulder of Chang's linen tunic and giving a strong hard tug to the side with an experienced twist of her torso. Her brows went up when Filipa braced her foot in the left stirrup and pulled back, making Sarukê abandon the attempt to keep from being dragged over herself.

Despite being obviously the stronger of the two.

"You have to grip the horse with your legs to stay on, especially sideways," Filipa said. "With our saddles, you can use your leg and *push* back against anything that shoves you. Your arms are stronger than mine, but not stronger than my *legs*. And the stirrups... that's what they're called... let you use your whole body's strength with a weapon while you're in the saddle. Almost as if you were standing on the ground, and you can do other things too."

She cantered ahead, kicked her right foot out of the stirrup and leaned far over to the left, picking a tuft of grass free from the side of the road, and then did the same to the other side on her way back:

"Like this, you see? And it makes it easier to give leg signals to the horse."

"That would take some-some time to learn," Sarukê said, frowning thoughtfully. "Holding on to horse my way, learn like walking, when little-little. But will try, if can? Is . . . in-ter-esting. You show?"

Filipa glanced at Artorius, and he nodded; that was one thing they *were* going to try and spread around.

They passed through a long stretch of vineyards, the grapes still small and green, and then an apricot orchard on one side of the road and peaches on the other. Children from about six to twelve were working there, doing the picking and filling woven-reed baskets left in the shade while their parents got in the grain, all under the eye of heavily pregnant women, or aged ones hobbling around bent over walking sticks that they occasionally used to prod or whack slackers who didn't dodge fast enough.

He guessed that the baskets would be collected by the harvesters on their way back in the evening, some sent fresh to nearby Scarbantia for sale tomorrow and probably a lot of it dried in the sun and packed away for later.

The children were also gorging freely on what they gathered, and a lot of the fruit was apparently let fall, discarded if it looked less than perfect and left for the bugs and pigs. He glanced at that thoughtfully; it suggested some ideas.

A still for moonshine we can definitely *make and make fast,* he thought. *We've got some sheet copper, they've got the fruit for the mash, and yeast to set it fermenting. What's left will still make stock feed.*

Then Jeremey McCladden came riding up, the first they'd seen of him since he departed for here with Josephus, his bodyguard and the sacks of seed on packhorses two days after their . . .

Arrival, Artorius thought. *Got here a lot faster than we did, with no wagons. But ouch again, and squared!*

He wasn't as good on horseback as Artorius, or Filipa either, but quite competent. And he'd visibly improved since he left, as decade-old muscle memory came back.

Where he'd been raised, horses weren't as inescapable as they were on the old Vandenberg caprock ranch in the far northwest of Texas, but they weren't reserved for those with money to burn the way they were in the Bay Area either. In the Kickapoo Valley of Wisconsin, fodder and the use of turnout pasture and barn space didn't cost the earth the way they did near San Francisco. Especially if your father ran an agricultural-supply business and your house was on acres of something closer to pasture than lawn and had an old barn anyway. *And* you had older sisters who'd been horse fanatics in their teens.

But then, everything except breathing *cost the earth there in the Bay area,* Artorius thought.

He pushed aside a vision of those cities as scorched wastelands and melted glass, with the stumps of the Golden Gate's towers poking a few feet out of the dead water at low tide.

McCladden reined in and waved a greeting, stopping briefly to say hello to Josephus first. Artorius had been emphatic on the need to be polite to him, and in reminding them all that Romans were a lot more sensitive about ceremony and due address than Americans of their era.

"Hi, Prof," he said cheerfully, shaking hands all around and then waving an arm at the countryside. "This place is great! Everything we need, and Fuchs's book was right according to the locals; first frost here's usually the last week of November. I've gotten all the seed we're planting this season in and watered, and a lot of it's showing shoots already! The rest is in good cellar storage, cool and dry. They're better *farmers* than I expected. All the temperate-zone stuff will grow here, I'm certain of it. For more than one reason."

Findlemann and Atkins were looking around dubiously at their extremely rural surroundings in the wake of his wave, as if it was all even more alien than the smelly, muddy, dung-strewn streets of Vindobona.

Though they'd probably admit it was easier on the nose and stomach than a place where chamber pots were emptied through the nearest streetside window rather than bothering to carry it to a sewer opening or public latrine.

With a cry of *Coming out!* added sometimes, but only if you were lucky.

Both of them were native New Yorkers, and had gone straight from there to Harvard Yard via the Acela Corridor.

No, I lie, Mark spent some time at Yale first.

The closest they'd gotten to *nature* was probably Central Park and Boston Common. He doubted they'd seen as much country-side in their entire lives as they had in the past few days, except from airplanes at thirty-five thousand feet.

Even driving in a car wasn't the same; you still had a sense of mastering space and time. The pace of a mule-drawn wagon along country roads was much more...

Immersive, that's the word.

...down to the smells and sounds, acrid dust and jolts and inescapable *thereness* of it all. You started to feel down in your gut how *big* the world was, how a mile was a long way and twenty miles ate a whole day and left you longing for dinner and then sleep. And how much sheer raw *work* that dinner represented.

"And I know what'll grow here because I've been here before!" Jeremey said.

They all looked at him. "Honest, the year after I graduated from high school. My folks promised me a trip if I made the cut for one of the Ivies, and I did, so I took a flight to Austria and did a bicycle tour in...Christ, in 2024! Just before my first year started. I wasn't sorry to miss most of the presidential election either."

That got some sour chuckles. The uproar at the incumbent simply ignoring the third-term prohibition hadn't *stopped* him, especially after he won handily. But it had been unpleasant all 'round, with riots in many of the big cities.

Would have been even worse if we'd been living in Boston back then, Artorius thought. *Meaningless now.*

"The villa's right on the spot...far as I can tell...where this town called Rust was, and there were plenty of cornfields and sunflowers and such around in '24. Sugar beets too, at the edges, though mostly vineyards near town. I only realized the morning I got here that I'd seen the place the villa stands on, and I'm not *absolutely* certain exactly where things were up...up-time. The lake is bigger, I think. And the shoreline's different, of course."

His cheerfully self-confident face went a little frightened for a moment.

"Everything's different, except for the bones of things—those hills to the northwest, the lake, the reeds...Anyway, this way!"

Josephus came up to join them again and they turned north on another graveled lane; the one they were on led straight out to an embankment that extended through the marshy verge of the lake, and ended with a dock and sheds and boats that probably fished and hauled goods across the water.

The lane they took curved east again when the lake grew closer, running toward the water once more. That path led through land kept in sheep-cropped grass and scattered large trees, oak and ash, elm, poplar and walnut and more.

Then...

⇒ CHAPTER FIVE ⇐

Villa Lunae,
Pannonia Superior
July 15th, 165 CE

"Well, here we are," Findlemann said, and surprisingly broke into verse:

> "*The stately homes of England...*
> But make that Pannonia Superior, amigos...
> *How beautiful they stand*
> *To prove the upper classes*
> *Still have the upper hand...*"

"Noel Coward," he explained at Paula and Jeremey's blank looks; Filipa seemed to be searching her memory. "A girl I know... knew... her mom has a thing for old musicals."

"Really old, from 1938," Artorius said. "Satirical then, because the people who owned the Downton Abbeys were *all* in hock and a *lot* of them were going broke. Dead serious here."

"Truer words were never said... in Pannonia... Mark, Prof," Jeremey said. "This is the gentlefolks' entrance—lowly tradesmen off to the right. They weren't sure who or what the hell *I* was and they're real busy... busy ain't the *word*. But Josephus is big medicine here—"

He gave the man a smile and nod and translated that into Latin that already sounded a good deal better than it had when he left Vindobona, before dropping back into English:

61

"—and they're all anxious not to get on his bad side, so I got the cooperation I needed when I showed up with him, even after he went right on to Sirmium. They got even friendlier when the messenger arrived from there with orders from their boss man. I planted the iffy stuff first, of course. Pray for rain as soon as the harvest's finished; there's usually a couple of inches a month this time of year, according to the books."

"If God listened to countryfolk's prayers about rain, He'd be *real* busy," Artorius said absently.

His mind automatically fitted what he was seeing into his knowledge of archaeological digs and artist's reconstructions and descriptions in ancient literature, but with an eerie overtone that hit him in the gut again. This wasn't faked up for tourists, no matter how much it looked like the rebuilt Villa Borg in the Saarland or a virtual tour of that place in Wiltshire discovered in the early '20s.

He was *here*. People *lived* in this, and worked in it, as generation followed generation. He could smell their woodsmoke, and their roses.

Ahead were formal gardens inside a stretch of low walls framing the gateway to the *pars urbana*, the owner's residence. Walkways and low hedges of box and yew surrounded bright flower banks with narcissi, oleanders, violets, crocus, lily and more. Statues painted in lurid colors stood on plinths, heavily pruned trees and bushes grew in fantastical shapes, occasionally a pergola overgrown with roses or flowering vines stretched over a bench or walkway. There was a sort of roundabout arrangement where the road circled around a fountain playing in bright tumbling streams around a bronze Neptune with eerie colored-glass eyes that seemed to follow you.

Beyond the landscaping was a two-story stretch of building to either side of a columned arch in its center. That reached higher and was flat topped, like a scaled-down Arch of Trajan; the yellowish-white walls to either side, about the shade of thick cream, were pierced by glass windows. The small square panes were in cross-hatched wooden frames, and the roofing was low-pitched red tile. What his age had quite rightly called *Roman* tile—flat, with rows of large, separate tapered arched sections covering the ridged joins.

Something was missing...

Chimneys. I keep running into that when I see it for real; there's only those covered smoke-hole arrangements. Nothing but

*braziers in a middle Danube Valley winter. Brrr! Or hypocausts
in a few places, I suppose.*

The gates in the archway were swung back. Inside was a big
rectangular courtyard, surrounded by two-story colonnaded blocks
running backward on both sides; the columns were made of some
light fine-grained limestone and fluted. There were more flower
banks and close-clipped trees and brightly painted polychrome
statuary in the court, with mosaic on the walkways close to the
buildings and hints of murals as well; his scholarly side itched
to go take a closer look.

And also a long reflecting pool with curved sections at front
and back, where a bronze faun held an amphora that poured a
stream of real water.

The brick-paved area around the pool ended in another block
that closed the courtyard on its eastern end, with a portico
entrance in the middle of it. He knew from descriptions that
another, smaller courtyard devoted to gardens and foot traffic
lay beyond that, and then behind the villa proper a large terrace
and pool overlooking a sweep of ground down to the shore of
the lake. A four-story square tower rose from the northernmost
rear corner of the building, overlooking everything.

Josephus waved, and the other wagons headed off southward,
where the *pars rustica*—the business part of the estate—was placed
around two more courtyards that gave off the villa proper at the
right rear corner, though they were single story. Those held granaries, wine presses, workshops for carpenters and blacksmiths
and weavers and others, threshing floors, rows of cellae—small
rooms that might be storage or slave quarters, one per family—and
more, with stables backed onto those, and turnout paddocks for
the working stock beyond, oxen and horses and mules.

The *pars urbana* was stone-block construction covered in plaster and stucco. The *pars rustica* was, he thought, on a masonry
foundation, above that partly brick but mostly rammed earth or
adobe likewise plastered, and the covering was whitewash.

Artorius took a deep breath as his party went through the
central arch and across the courtyard and up to the eastern side.
Figures waited there; some at the top of a low flight of stairs,
others at its base. The Americans and Josephus dismounted (or in
Mark and Paula's case, got down from their wagon) and walked
up to the foot of the stairs.

Two women stood there, one in her fifties and one in her twenties; obviously Sextus Hirrius Trogus' sister Julia and mother Claudia, and they both had an entourage of maidservants of various kinds behind them, among other things holding parasols.

Yup, they've dropped that convention about calling women by feminine forms of the family surnames, he thought. *Yet another dating problem solved... sort of. At least for Pannonia!*

A few older men in good but sober calf-length tunics were probably the equivalents of a butler, bookkeeper and the like.

The landowner's mother appeared older than her probable age because she'd lost a lot of teeth, which gave her a witch-in-a-fairytale look not helped by a basilisk glare. The younger looked no *more* than her actual midtwenties, unlike the bulk of the population here and now.

A smooth comely face, dark-green eyes, hair a brown-russet from what little could be seen of it, and a figure just on the slim side of full. A nine-year-old girl stood beside her, like a miniature of her mother except that her hair was lighter, right down to the way she was dressed and a set of smaller jewelry, though that included a crescent-moon *lunula* protective amulet.

All three wore gentlewomen's clothing. For starters, that meant tunics long enough to brush the top of the foot, with baggy sleeves. The garments were actually two wide rectangles of fabric each, sewn together at the sides from the bottom up nearly to the top; that was left open and fastened when worn with rows of carved-ivory or precious-metal rondels secured with pins, that ran from the neck opening to the elbows. Then the garment was gathered around the waist with sash-like belts, giving a draped effect.

Both the adults had purple bands on the bottom hem of their tunics, which were green and blue respectively and of very fine, tight-woven merino-type wool. A *stola* went over that for the adults, mark of married, matronly respectability, like a second, sleeveless tunic supported at each shoulder with short straps. The *stolae* were pale pink and russet-brown silk, the fabric being a mark of aristocratic status—a century or so earlier they'd have been wool too.

The rectangular wrapped cloaks of fine colored cloth—one dark blue and the other green striped on a yellow background—they added were outside wear, which showed a certain stiff formality since they were only technically outside. Each was draped over the left shoulder, under the right arm and around the body and back across, carried by the left arm; the garments were called *pallae*. They reminded him a little of Indian saris—which word meant *strip of cloth*—and the younger woman's had a fringe of yellow tassels.

Both had folds of their pallas drawn over their high-piled hair like hoods or snoods, and their rather heavy formal makeup added to the masklike look of their faces. They also wore eye-catching jewelry, boat-shaped golden earrings, rings, bracelets and necklaces, all studded with amber, lapis, and small emeralds, down to the buckles on their openwork sandals. The jewels were polished rather than cut, but there was a certain raw splendor to it.

The covered heads inclined very slightly as Josephus made the introductions. He did so with deferential politeness. The head of their family might be in hock to his eyeballs to the merchant, but he *was* a merchant, and a Jew.

While Sextus Hirrius Trogus was a landowner, and a descendant of landowners and of generations of Roman *equites* first raised to that rank in the days of Pompey two centuries ago, when Julius Caesar was an ambitious young whippersnapper and the Ptolemies still ran Egypt. This Pannonian branch of the Trogi weren't rich or ambitious enough for senatorial rank, but below that were about as elevated as you got. There was a lot of personnel churn in the Senate, but less so as you went down the scale.

Josephus and Artorius and Mark and Jeremey were all in gentlemen's traveling gear, summer edition; essentially calf-length tunics bloused up to the knee through their sword belts, tight knee-length leather riding breeches beneath (a relatively recent innovation copied from the military), lace-up open boots and colored cloaks, with status shown by the quality of fabric and dyes. And in Josephus' case by a discreet emerald in a ring on his left hand.

And they wore round leather hats with wide brims and a center section like a low pillbox, locally known as a petasus and originally Greek. Romans generally didn't use hats except on journeys or when working all day in sun or rain. These looked a bit like a *cordobés* hat though a little more rounded on top, the type traditionally worn in southern Spain and also by Zorro in the old shows.

Which shows you some *things don't change very fast.*

Artorius inclined his own head as he removed his hat.

"*Domina*," he said to the older woman.

That was the vocative-case address used to a married woman of equal... or sometimes of superior... social status. Formal, tactful, and noncommittal. The closest equivalent in his native dialect was *ma'am*, or perhaps the way *ma'am* had been used in Teddy Roosevelt's day.

The male version, *Domine*, was roughly *sir* or *mister*.

He'd checked with Josephus, of course: his knowledge of Roman social etiquette turned out to have more holes than a lace doily. Too much of what people absorbed by growing up in a time and place didn't get into books because it was natural as air, or if it did the books that had it didn't survive. Or you could mistake truth for satire, and vice versa.

And Roman customs changed, just not as fast or as consciously as in his native time; a written description might be painfully out of date, *or* not here yet... or *chic* in Rome itself but horrifying in the provinces.

"*Domina*," again to the younger. To both:

"I am most honored by your generous hospitality and that of your son—"

A nod to the mother, followed by one to the sister.

"—and your most excellent and esteemed brother, the *eques* Sextus Hirrius Trogus, and I will strive to make the presence of myself and my associates as little of a burden as I may."

The older woman's return smile was still glacial and reluctant in a way that suggested it hurt her face, with the family's debts looming like an invisible monster hunched on her shoulder and holding clawed hands around her throat. The younger was just as composed, but he thought perhaps less hostile, and a bit intrigued by the sheer strangeness of the strangers.

Her eyes skipped back to Paula and Filipa. Paula's skin color wasn't completely unknown in the Roman Mediterranean, especially as you got closer to Egypt. But it would be a very rare sight here on the northern frontier, and even more so in the countryside. She was dressed much like the two Roman women, on Josephus' advice, except that she didn't wear a married woman's stola and her jewelry was much simpler and nothing was silk, which would be putting it on.

So her *outfit's upper-middle-class respectable, as opposed to old-money aristo swank. Of course, she's traveling without any of her male kin or even a maid, which isn't very respectable.*

Filipa's East Asian physical type was outright exotic here, and she was wearing essentially the same clothes as the males in the party, which Josephus had warned would be interpreted as...

A very assertive statement of her sexual orientation, would be the low-key, polite way to put it. Or perhaps an overly emphatic way of rejecting gender binaries? Not going to fight her about it, not here and now, and she does need to ride. Not ride pillion, either. Sarukê gets away with it, because everyone knows Sarmatian women dress in pants, a barbarian garment anyway, and she is a barbarian, so she's expected to be belch-fart-scratch-your-ass-in-public uncouth, like something in a comic play.

After the ladies retired with a few polite nothings and directions to the servants about showing them to their quarters and heating up the second bathhouse for the visiting men, Artorius caught the eye of the *vilicus*, among the others who'd been standing below the stairs to greet the strange and, in the case of Josephus, *important* guests.

He was a stocky middle-aged type with a wart beside his nose and a fringe of brown beard, in a plain good tunic and high openwork *cothurnus* boots, holding a hat like theirs in his hand and looking as if he was containing his impatience at not being out supervising things with a monumental effort of self-control. He also looked as if he hadn't been getting much sleep lately, and probably hadn't.

And he'd already been landed with a glib young stranger with a weird accent taking away some of his workers at a crucial point to plant the Gods-knew-what. Anything going seriously wrong right now would be unfixable if not caught early, and probably blamed on *him*.

"We'll talk tomorrow morning, early, about what I need," he said to the bailiff. "But for now, don't let me take you from your work. The harvest must come first. There won't be any more calls on your hands until the grain's all cut."

"My thanks, m'lord Artorio'," the man said in a rustic accent and with an air of relief, and walked off... not *quite* running.

Artorius groaned inwardly as hooves clattered at the gate; yet another interruption.

And I'm really looking forward to that bath, taken without

*as much possibly infectious and certainly inquisitive company as
in town. That dual sauna thing they do is powerfully attractive
to my aching butt. I wonder if we could introduce showers? And
individual bottom-drain tubs?*

A nondescript dark man in plain and very dusty clothes dismounted, went straight to Josephus, and handed him a diptych,
two wooden tablets hinged like a book with wax on their interiors
where you could write with a stylus. The merchant undid the
string fastener and broke the wax seal on it, opened it and read
in a low murmur, in Greek. His face changed as he did, and he
strode over to the American.

"I've been called away. My wife writes that my son Matthias
is gravely ill."

Josephus had mentioned him several times; he was ten, the
firstborn child, one of two surviving so far, and the apple of his
father's eye.

"I must go to Sirmium, and quickly."

"May he be spared! What's the problem?"

"A stomach complaint, she writes, that has taken a turn for
the worse and settled in the bowels, with bloody stool. That's
common in children, especially in the warm season."

And especially in summer in fly-swarming cities with no
concept of the germ theory and streets paved with shit, human
and otherwise; it was the downside of the dense network of towns
and busy trade the Roman economy bred. Most Roman families
lost at least one child, and it wasn't uncommon to have ten or
more births—women here married young—with only one or two
living to adulthood.

That was something that could happen to anyone, emperors
included—Marcus Aurelius and his Empress Faustina had had
more than twelve, with only four or five surviving to adulthood.
Cities in particular needed a constant inflow from the countryside
just to maintain their numbers.

The merchant's voice and words were calm, but his jaw was
tight held.

"Wait," Artorius said, and strode over to their baggage, con-
tinuing over his shoulder. "A moment only, I ask of you."

A minute later he had the large pill bottle in his hand. He
measured out six of the 100mg ampicillin capsules, wrapped them
in a cloth and handed them over to the merchant.

"Give one of these to your son to swallow as soon as you get home, delaying not an instant," he said. "Don't let anyone see, and do not speak of it, please."

At Josephus' enquiring look, he went on:

"We have only so many of these, and can never replace what we use. If it were widely known we had them and what they could do ... that would be bad trouble."

"Ah," the merchant said, nodding. "I see."

Smart cookie, Artorius thought, nodding back, then went on aloud:

"Then one more a day at the same time until they're gone or he's recovered, whichever comes first. It will probably ... very probably, almost certainly ... help. I can't *absolutely* guarantee it, but ..."

"But all else has failed. One a day, at the same time," Josephus said, frowning in intense concentration, but his shoulders didn't have quite the same degree of iron tension. "I will."

"And boil water in a covered pot, a hard boil for a quarter of an hour at least; keep it tightly covered, and when it cools, add a spoonful of honey and a small pinch of salt, sea salt, if you can, to each cup you give him. Don't let him drink anything else while he's sick. Have more ready at all times, keep it tightly covered, and have him drink as much of it as he can. No solid foods for the week after the pills are all gone, either, just broth of chicken; then soup, and regular food only when he's walking, and soft foods to start with. You *can* tell others about that; it helps those with bowel sickness, though not as much as the medicine will."

Josephus studied his face for a moment, put a hand on his shoulder, squeezed a little and said simply:

"My thanks, friend," before very carefully tucking the bundle of pills into his belt pouch.

They shook hands; then Josephus turned to his Sarmatian bodyguard:

"Sarukê, stay here and guard these people with your life. And see that the messenger is given what he needs. I'll take Kunjamunduz."

Who was his alternate, German bodyguard; the word meant *kin-protector.*

Names here in most languages weren't just arbitrary noises.

Roman names often meant something too, when you thought about it—often something like *Number Six*, or *Baldy* or *Hairy* or *Wart Face*; they'd started as nicknames and had turned into hereditary surnames.

And a good translation for *Brutus* would be *animalistic stupidity*.

Josephus went on to his clients: "All three of you may need to go back and forth between Sirmium and here with messages. Keep two horses ready at all times."

He and the tall blond Germanii headed for their mounts, vaulted into the saddle and spurred away with the bodyguard holding a leading rein with two more in tow. The messenger stood and looked nearly as tired as his horse, until Sarukê motioned servants to come and deal with them both.

"Those pills are irreplaceable, Prof," Jeremey said, his tone neutral . . . and in English.

They'd already had to use a few themselves, to halt cases of the runs before they became serious. Their immune systems had no experience with the ambient bacteria here at all. And those changed every time you moved into a new watershed anyway. What an aqueduct delivered might be safe . . . but might just as well have an elderly dead goat a little upstream.

They followed the head housekeeper into the odd-looking splendors of the mansion: more painted statues in niches, murals in a vivid style, realistic but without perspective, that showed how crude the ones in their digs in Vindobona were, polychrome marble floors or mosaics, sparse but ornately inlaid furniture and carefully calculated vistas of colonnade and garden.

"So's Josephus irreplaceable, from our point of view," Artorius said.

The middle-aged senior housekeeper went walking along proudly before them in a neat but plainer version of what the ladies had worn minus the palla cloak, and they were trailed by the more lowly maid-of-all-work types in simple but good ankle-length tunics carrying their personal baggage, with a few footman equivalents lugging the first tranche of the heavier items at the rear.

"Besides, we owe him."

It all *felt* like a procession, minus the floats and marching band. These people were ceremonious to a fault.

"Big-time," Mark Findlemann said.

Then he grinned, striking a pose, hand raised and index finger pointing at the sky, or the high ceiling.

"When trouble strikes, *who you gonna call*? A smart Jew!"

Everyone chuckled or smiled. Artorius' smile died as he looked over his shoulder after Josephus and thought:

Josephus brought two *professional bodyguards on this trip, apparently standard operating procedure. He left one with us. Every second or third male in our little wagon train had a spear or an axe along, and some had shields and a couple kept their hunting bows on hand. I should consider what that implies. This* is *the frontier of the Roman world.*

In West Texas for a long time after his ancestors arrived there, a man buckled on his gun belt when he went out the door as automatically as putting on his hat, and stuck a rifle in the saddle scabbard whenever he got on a horse. It had been common sense more than bravado, between Comanches, outlaws, range wars, rustlers and feuds with the neighbors. He'd already decided to put some serious effort into learning the sword. It might be a good idea to start developing the habit of buckling *that* on when he went out, when he wasn't in a Roman city with its gates and *vigiles*.

Where it was considered barbaric and uncouth. Elsewhere, particularly near the border...

Not so much.

≫ CHAPTER SIX ≪

Villa Lunae,
Province of Pannonia Superior
August 3rd, 165 CE

Artorius stood in the stable door, with the four...
Ex-students, he thought. *Former graduate students. Aspiring professional historians, then, God help them; talk about nailing your career colors to the mast of a sinking ship! Now ... well, we'll see. They're what I've got, so they'll do.*

... facing him; the light was bright on him, but they were more shadowed. The building was a variation on Roman cavalry stabling, but without the room behind each pen where the troopers slept next to their mounts. The Villa Lunae raised horses for the civil and military markets, but not in a really large way. The nomads who roamed the steppes just outside the Imperial frontier in what would have become eastern Hungary—someday—were known to the Empire as *Iazyges*, and spoke a dialect of the same language used by Sarukê's tribe. They had that trade more or less sewn up at the wholesale level in Pannonia.

When they don't decide killing, burning and stealing is more fun, he thought.

It wasn't an odd place to meet by local standards. Horses were high status; it wasn't an accident that the Latin term for *gentleman* translated as *horse-rider*. French and German and Spanish used ... or would have, much later ... *chevalier* and *Ritter* and *caballero* in very much the same sense. Roman country gentlemen met in stables fairly often to talk horses and do other business in the course of it; even the slaves who curried and harnessed the riding beasts had a bit rub off on them, and put on airs.

"I'm the Prof, so I'm going to give you a lecture," he said. "Now that we're settled in and know enough not to get lost between here and the villa proper."

"Except for Mark here," Filipa said affectionately, nudging him with her elbow, and everyone chuckled, including the target.

"I was thinking hard," he said, slightly sheepish. "Mind on higher things. I thought that pasture was a shortcut. Didn't know about the bull."

"You sure *crossed* in short order," Jeremey noted.

"Olympic sprinter level," Paula agreed. "And dove headfirst over the fence."

Back behind him and his companions, in the gloom of the building, horses nickered; the stables smelled of them, their wastes, the hay and straw in the loft above and the mealy smell of barley and oats kept to supplement that and the fresh grass. There were flies, but not an overwhelming number, probably because of the barn swallows flitting around snacking on them. In fact the whole thing took him back, to stables he'd known as a boy spending long summers with his grandparents. Even the heat was nostalgic, though the air wasn't as dry.

The High Plains up in the Panhandle could be an icy waste in winter when the storms barreled down the endless flat miles from Canada, but summers... the summers were long, and they *baked*.

"OK, we're trying to introduce some technical stuff here," he said. "That's our *first* success."

He pointed at a wheelbarrow resting propped up against a pillar. It was absolutely unremarkable, and could have come from any Lowe's or Home Depot in America. Except that it was nearly entirely wooden, ash poles and oak planks and a lathe-turned section of beechwood for the wheel, all held together with oak pegs. There was a shrunk-on tire of wrought iron *on* the wheel, and the pin the wheel turned on and the ring it turned *in*, and that was the sum of its metal parts.

None of that was anything the locals weren't thoroughly familiar with.

"Wheelbarrows were invented about now, in China. That's a song I'll sing more than once. We had a model; I showed it to the carpenter and smith; they had one ready in a day; now there's a dozen and in a year there will be hundreds all over the neighborhood. I'll come back to why *that* was so easy, but think of what it does. It lets you carry three or four times the load, and faster, for short distances. They're using that one to carry out manure and carry in fodder; anyone with a farmstead or a construction site will want them, just for starters."

"I've seen guys giving their girlfriends rides in them, and parents doing it for children, the last couple of days," McCladden said thoughtfully.

"Good point. That's *fun*. So are applejack and white lightning and peach schnapps...and for that, we only needed a fire, a copper pot, yeast, and a coil of copper tubing, that was the hardest part. They're bringing in fruit that would otherwise go to waste for the mash...and doing it in *wheelbarrows*. Oh, and guess what makes a really good antiseptic if you run it through the still extra times?"

The stalls on either side of the central corridor held three or four horses each, with mangers, watering troughs and straw bedding that was changed daily; the urine drained into underfloor channels and a central trough that ran to a big square area kept full of straw and leaves that was shoveled out periodically to be used as fertilizer for the truck gardens. Tack hung from pegs near the door, neatly kept and well oiled. It included some hipposandals—sort of like strap-on bootees for a horse, with an iron sole, which was as close to a horseshoe as they had here and now.

"The tech stuff's *part* of what we're going to do, and an important part. In the long run, technical innovation is the *most* important part because it sets the level of what's possible in every other field. Though in the short to medium term, war and politics are crucial, which is why we're time constrained and have to bust our asses."

"Detail on that, Prof?" Mark asked.

"Because the Marcomannic Wars start next year, and the Plague of Galen is already brewing out east, and unless we get some major traction *fast,* both those will fall on our heads like a ton of bricks. And squash us just as dead as the fusion bomb that took out Vienna would have in another second or two. But the technical things will be crucial for politics and war, too."

"That's the turning point," Mark said gravely.

When they looked at him: "Until the corn and potatoes and that wheelbarrow and that still turning out peach brandy, nothing we've done would have had much impact, unless it's quantum-chaos butterfly-flapping stuff. But those, and what we're planning today, it will *really* change things. Forever. Even a little of it."

Jeremey cut in unexpectedly:

"And it's where we find out *if* time is mutable. If you *can* change history or if something will somehow stop you if you try."

They all winced a little. If time *wasn't* mutable, something would happen to stop them changing events... and the simplest way for that to happen would be for them all to die and this area to be blotted out...

Say, by the Marcomanni killing everyone and burning everything to the ground.

He didn't think that was necessarily a big risk, since Fuchs had obviously been on the mutable-time side and he was the man who'd invented time travel, but only experience would tell.

Invented time travel very *briefly,* he corrected himself. *Which introduces a certain* un*certainty there.*

"To hell with that," Paula said stoutly. "Changes are *needed* here. Far more than they were back... home... even. Our former home. The more and faster the better. So I'll prepare my ass to be busted in a good cause!"

Artorius nodded, and also reflected wryly that the *cellae* where the slave families dwelled were rather similar to the stables, save for a *bit* more privacy, the open court in the middle, and a latrine near the kitchen.

That was probably part of what she meant, he thought. *I see her point but that's a long-term thing.*

The estate had more mules than horses, housed separately; *really* heavy work was almost all done with oxen.

And even more by human grunt labor.

Artorius went on: "None of us are engineers, which is a pity. *Scientists* wouldn't be useful here, though, because we don't have to discover things, we just have to apply them. That's still easier said than done; it's going to mean work, sometimes hands-on."

Mark shrugged and looked down at his hands and wiggled his fingers.

"I'll do my best, sure, Prof. But I'm not... well, I'm not what you'd call manually ept. Give me a hammer and I'm as likely to hit my thumb as a nail."

"You don't have to be Mr. Fixit, Mark. Look, the thing to remember is that there are two types of inventions. The wheelbarrow is a *Type A* invention, where the *idea* is the crucial thing, and you can use existing skills and tools to *implement* it. Wheelbarrows are *pure* Type A, the Platonic ideal. I gave the carpenter an idea, he brought in the smith, and I showed them a model a foot long. He had one ready after a day's work, the smith put in the ironwork, all four pieces and eight ounces, and it was ready to go; and they've gotten faster since. The *vilicus* nearly creamed his...well, his loincloth...when he saw one laborer pushing four big sacks of grain along at a fast walk with it. Because that would have taken *four* men without it, and longer."

McCladden grinned. "And now the carpenter...it's that young guy we brought from Vindobona who worked on the wheelbarrows, Quintus, his granddaddy got Roman citizenship when he mustered out of the auxiliaries...he and the smith are selling them to the tenants and neighbors at two *sestertii* a pop, with the *vilicus* taking a twenty percent cut. But give you odds that before the end of the month, someone else will be making them too."

Artorius nodded and pointed to one of the Spanish saddles, currently slung across the low plastered adobe wall that separated the horses from the passageway.

"Take stirrups, and saddles like that. Important invention, right?"

"Right," Filipa said. "And it's Type A too. There's absolutely nothing in that saddle that a carpenter and a leatherworker here can't make, maybe with a little help from a smith for some of the fittings."

Artorius nodded. "In 3500 BCE the Yamnaya culture, the Proto-Indo-Europeans, were riding horses in Ukraine...riding them to other places, too, eventually from Ireland to the Tien Shan and Ceylon. Riding bareback, or with just a saddle blanket. *They* could have made saddles and stirrups like those. Wood instead of metal for some parts, but that's not important. They just didn't have the *idea*. That's going to be dreamed up by some folks in China—again, China—in the next century or two...or *was* going to be. Or they may have copied it from the nomads north of them. It spread fast, and eventually everyone who rode horses used it, from Britain to

Japan and down to Africa and India. But for going on four thousand years, it just didn't *occur* to anyone."

He pointed again, this time to a set of horse harness hung from a peg in a wooden pillar.

"Now, that's a horse collar and draught harness, courtesy of Dr. Fuchs, and more remotely of the Chinese—inventive bastards, eh? They've got blast furnaces and cast iron *right now* by the way, and I'm major-league envious. With that harness, the horse or mule can use all the power of its body and haunches to push."

He turned his arm to another set, one sound but visibly worn by use.

"See the Roman one over there? That *was* invented by the Indo-Europeans and it's less efficient because it's derived from an ox yoke and horses just aren't shaped like oxen. Again, four thousand years and it just didn't *occur* to anyone. But they can *make* the good stuff immediately. Type A, pure form."

Mark brightened until he was practically beaming. "Oh, so you mean we just have to give them ideas! Then they slap their heads, say 'Why didn't we think of that, it's so obvious!' and they can *make* the stuff on their own."

Artorius sighed. "No, Mark, *sometimes* we just have to give them the idea. *And* convince them that there's a reason why grandpappy's way isn't good enough. Sometimes that's easy, sometimes hard."

"Going to be harder with the saddles," Filipa said. "With the wheelbarrows, anyone who has to schlep dirt and manure and bricks can see it's better right away, and anyone bossing him sees he can get more done with less. But people get emotionally attached to anything they do with horses. I certainly do!"

"Bingo," Artorius said. "There are more and more *ands* as we go along. *And* get them through the fiddly bits until they've got it working. Which is not going to be easy, because among other things they don't have a concept of technical progress as such, of research and development. They're only vaguely aware that they do things their ancestors couldn't; bronze weapons in the Iliad and they use iron, liburnians instead of pentekonters, that sort of thing. And that's the *easiest* part of what we're going to do."

"Oh," Mark said.

And then his face fell; he was so smart he knew his own weaknesses.

"Oh, shit, people skills."

Artorius nodded. "And then there's the Type B inventions, where you need new techniques and tools to *implement* the new idea. We couldn't just tell them how to make a steam engine, not even the crudest early types."

"For one thing they don't have a concept of atmospheric pressure," Filipa said.

"That's probably why they didn't *have* the idea," Artorius said.

The seminar-style dialogue was probably reassuring all 'round.

"But even with us supplying that, they don't have cast iron, dammit. Or blast furnaces. Or boring engines for the cylinders... and getting *those* good enough to make his ideas work took James Watt over a decade and a lot of money, and he had much more to start with than we do. Like machines designed to bore out the barrels of cannon. So cannon... those not right away either. They can cast *bronze* here well enough but getting the bore accurate, that would be a bitch. And very expensive, as in *you need a government* expensive.

"*But!*" he went on. "Most things aren't pure Type A or Type B. They're on a spectrum. Fuchs apparently realized that, which is odd for a physicist, even an experimental one—"

"Or some historian did, when he consulted them in a fake-speculative bullshitting-with-a-beer way. You know, *If only there was time travel, what could I do?*" Jeremey McCladden said thoughtfully.

He was good at figuring out sneakiness. You could forget how sharp he was behind that Norman Rockwell aw-shucks small-town Midwestern exterior.

"Exactly. Which is why we've not only got books and diagrams, we've got a lot of scale working models which are *really* going to help. Even model sailing ships. So, we'll decide what the priorities are, and go from the simple to the difficult. Succeeding with the simpler things like the wheelbarrow and the still, that'll give people confidence in us, which will make getting through the ones where we have to try and try again and learn from our failures easier."

He slapped his hands together and went on:

"Right! And once we *do* have something perfected, the fact that we're in an *advanced* preindustrial culture with a huge peaceful free-trade zone and relatively good communications and literacy will help spread things."

Paula had been thinking hard too. "The very first things we should do ... they should be to free up labor here on the estate. So we can use it for *other* things. Things that'll help us next year, when the Marcomanni come calling."

"Bingo again, Paula. So, Jeremey—agriculture. We can't just slap together a McCormick reaper, there are Type B problems there and the harvest's about over anyway except for carting the sheaves, so maybe next year, but what's first?"

"Planting the new seeds, but that's all done and they're doing fine."

He reached out and rapped on a wooden pillar for luck before he continued:

"Right now, a threshing machine," the Wisconsinite said confidently. "I've been looking through the books, *and* there's a model. And I've been talking to the *vilicus*, trying to get a handle on their working calendar, and beating out the grain with flails is what the field workers do from now until next summer. About a quarter of their total annual labor hours."

"It's machinery. Type B?"

"Nope, not really, I checked. The first one was built in 1786 and by hand in a farming town, no machine tools, and that's more or less what the model is a model *of*. Getting the proportions of the parts right by myself would be a bitch'n bastard, but I've got the model, and precise measurements listed so that's OK. And some tape measures, and for that matter a whole bunch of measuring gauges of different sizes, but we won't need *those* for *this*. It'll be a *simple* threshing machine, nearly all wood, but miles better than doing it with lopsided nunchakus, so we can use the workers freed up for that ... other stuff, the military stuff."

"Good. That's one bottleneck."

If you produce. If. Last time I was that self-confident, I was a new-minted second lieutenant younger than you are now and nearly got myself and everyone else in the platoon killed. Thank God for sergeants!

"And there's plowing and planting the fall grain, for instance, that's a biggie, number two after the harvesting. Got a few ideas there too. We had this museum in the town I grew up in ..." Jeremey went on.

Artorius nodded. "Paula?"

"Textiles for me, Prof, to start with. What the *women* here do is spin and weave, whenever they're not doing something else like threshing, and that's year-round. Even the *ladies* do a little now and then, sort of for symbolic virtuous-Roman-housewife slash matron cultural nostalgia reasons. So, spinning wheels, I think—spinning thread's the big labor bottleneck, we've got a model, and I studied them a little while I was an undergrad, a course called *The Distaff Side*. It would free up labor and we might make a profit on it. Then better looms. Then fulling... we'd need fuller's earth and some sort of machine to lift and drop wooden hammers. Is there a map of useful—"

"Useful minerals? Yeah," Mark said. "Lots of them, in fact. With little *x marks the spot* crosses and *pictures* of the spot."

"Most excellent," Artorius said—then felt an inner stutter, both because he was using military slang, and because he knew it was originally a translation from Russian.

This feels more like being in uniform again than being an academic. Or some weird combination of both.

He went on: "Filipa, the horse stuff? Saddles, harness, maybe horseshoes? I'll help you there."

She nodded toward the hipposandals. "They've got the *concept* for horseshoes. And we've got eight horseshoes with us already, courtesy of Fuchs. The smith can copy those just about right away. What'll be trickier than the wheelbarrows is that the smith will have to learn to *fit* them hot, and then *nail* them properly—you can ruin the hoof and cripple the horse if you do those wrong. But yeah, that's fairly straightforward, I've seen it done lots of times and I knew a farrier when I was in high school, Anna let me help, trim hooves, clinch the nails and stuff... I'll have the smith here practice on wooden models of a hoof. Take maybe, oh, a week tops."

"What about the saddles?"

"*Making* them is straightforward. Getting the locals to see why they should use them..."

She paused for a moment and went on:

"Can I get Sarukê as assistant for all this?"

"You're friends, right?"

Filipa nodded. "Sort of. We're both... deeply, truly weird... from the other's viewpoint, but we both like horses. She's already learning to use our gear, she's fascinated, I gave her pointers but she caught on *really* fast and I think she's already better than I am. As in, learned almost *uncanny* fast."

"Will anyone listen to her? She's a woman and a barbarian and an ex-slave...though now technically a second-class Roman citizen, since Josephus *is* a citizen and he bought and freed her."

"People here on the villa already know her a little, Prof, since she's in Josephus' household. They respect her horse handling too. Sarmatians have *mucho mojo* that way, and everybody knows it. Everybody in Pannonia, at least. Josephus has sent her here and other places to *buy* horses on her own with his money, now and then, the last couple of years, because he trusts her eye when it comes to picking good ones."

"Good idea; I'll write, but I don't think Josephus will mind. In fact, I'll see about hiring her full time. We're going to need bodyguards ourselves, eventually."

Mark Findlemann had been in a brown study. "Paper and books," he said.

That was related to his special field of study, which had been the *how* of Classical literature; how books were made and how they diffused.

"And printing. It's longer term, but if we cut the cost of written stuff, so every book doesn't have to be handwritten on expensive material, it would have a major impact on how information diffuses...and I think it could be a profit center in the shorter term. That's how we lost so much of Graeco-Roman literature, just not enough copies. And *we* can print books on technical stuff, eventually. That means translating the ones Fuchs sent with us...that's not straightforward either, but it's possible. Sorta."

Artorius' brows went up and he motioned the younger man to continue:

"Paper is almost exactly like papyrus from a *user's* point of view, except it's better and you don't have to be in Egypt to make it. I talked books a bit with Josephus on the way here, and he said sort of as an aside he knows a couple of guys who buy papyrus from further south and sell it around. Ready-made market we could plug into. The merchants won't care except about their margins which will be better, and the clerks and whatnot don't have to learn any new methods to *use* paper. Pulp from straw and reeds, maybe hemp and flax, or old linen rags. Biggest problem is the wire screens we'll need, but there's one in the baggage, so I can point to it and say *make more like that*. Fuchs again."

Artorius grinned. "Well, double dip me."

"That's just it—you dip the screen, it's on a pole, into the mash. Over and over and that produces a sheet of paper. Then sort of squeeze them in a press and hang them up to dry, like laundry in a '50s sitcom."

"Do that. Money we can always use, and after we get proof of concept Josephus will do the work for a reasonable cut. The guy's mentally flexible to a fault."

"And for printing, I'll need a seal cutter, that would be the ideal thing to make stamps to make molds for casting lead type. There's a book on it in one of the bundles, I'm reading it now. And a felt press like they use here is most of the business part of a printing press. We could use a cut-off stone pillar mounted on wheels, something like a kid's toy wagon, as the bed. Books cost the earth here, but they're high status. If we cut the cost, lots of people who can't *quite* afford it would buy because it puts them one up on the neighbors."

"Go for it. And you're going to get started on translations."

There was a pause, and they all looked at him, wondering what *his* pet project would be. He took a deep breath:

"Besides coordination, I'm going to be handling the 75-15-10 side—"

That was a cross between a joke and a code; those were the proportions of saltpeter, charcoal and sulfur in gunpowder.

"—because a lot of my West Point courses were relevant. I've got the materials with me, the saltpeter and sulfur are used for medicines and half a dozen other things, and they make charcoal on this property in a biggish way. But scaling up is going to be a stone bitch for half a dozen reasons. Even a little gunpowder could be useful, but a lot would be very, very ... significant."

Everyone was silent for a long moment. Introducing stirrups and paper, or maize and potatoes, would change things. Slowly at first, then massively in the end.

"But gunpowder ..." Jeremey said quietly, voicing their common thought. "Gunpowder will change things with a *bang*. Fast. Faster than in our history, because we know how to *use* it, too."

Artorius nodded. "Changes, and how. Remember what I said: the Marcomannic Wars are about to start. These Romans are no angels, the only 'law of war' here is *don't lose*, but the barbarians *are* barbarians. What they've picked up from the Romans just makes them more dangerous ones."

Paula hissed, and then said a little reluctantly:

"I've heard the slaves here talking about them. It scares them stiff when they think about raiding parties—apparently they make human sacrifices and chop off lots of heads and play spear catch with babies and barricade doors shut and burn the houses and everyone in them. Plus they rape everything that moves and if it doesn't move they shake it. I don't think... that they're exaggerating much."

"No, they're not," Artorius said grimly. "We were Americans; now we have to be Romans. We'll meet every day or two to brief the group on what we're doing and what problems we're hitting, brainstorm ideas, and help each other out as needed."

"Sounds like a graduate research seminar," Paula said, and they all chuckled.

Artorius finished: "The harvest's over, we've got all the authority we need here—let's go out and save the world!"

That got smiles, nods, apparent enthusiasm ... and Mark Findlemann doing his superhero stance again, going *whoosh* and adding a cry of:

"Behold! *Iudaeo-puer qui iter in tempore!*"

⇒ CHAPTER SEVEN ⇐

Villa Lunae,
Province of Pannonia Superior
August 21st, 165 CE

"Stop the goddamned mules!" Jeremey McCladden screamed as a crunching, splintering sound came from inside what was *supposed* to be a threshing machine.

What he'd actually said was: *damned by the Gods* mules.

He followed it with another curse—in English, and involving an invitation for the apparatus to perform an unlikely sexual act with its mother—and kicked it, hard. The only thing it had produced in the last two weeks was splinters.

Then he restrained himself; he was only going to hurt his foot if he did that again—he was wearing *caligae*, the Roman military sandal-boot with its thick soles and hobnails, but there were limits. When he looked up, the slave carpenter was white faced and trembling, obviously afraid that the foreign freeman he'd been told to obey would blame him, in a direct and physical way. Quintus, the furniture maker's apprentice from Vindobona, was looking ready to fight back if he had to.

And it would be so much more satisfying to beat something that bleeds than kicking this shitty pile of wood, he thought. *But it's bad management. And the Prof would hit the roof and I don't want the others giving me the stink eye either. We all need each other... badly.*

"Not your fault," he said to them shortly.

They were in a big shed down by the lake and the boat dock, which from the fairly overwhelming smell was usually used for salting and drying fish. Spears of sunlight came through patches where the wattle and daub of the walls had lost some of the daub; the frame of the building was made of pegged-together timber beams that rested on masonry blocks, and the ceiling was three times his own five-ten height.

He lifted the cover off the machine; this model was about twice the size of a grand piano. Then he checked to make doubly sure the mules that powered the whole thing had stopped; he most certainly wasn't going to put his hand inside this thing otherwise.

Despite having a miniature model and lots of drawings, it had been like trying to push a rock uphill on a sand dune . . . to start with, none of the Roman artisans had ever really worked from a drawing.

Maybe there were some who did that in Rome or Alexandria, but definitely not here in the sticks.

The closest they've ever come was scratching pictures of their dicks on walls or trees. And trying to get the idea of exactly through their heads, it's a choice between tears and bloody murder.

Models they could grok—

To quote Dad, he thought.

—or some of them could.

The rest had been working wood and leather and a few metal fittings. *Those* they understood.

Mostly Type A, like Glorious Prof Leader said. Mostly, mostly, mostly, that's the killer. They can do it . . . just not yet.

A stout vertical wooden shaft with two long horizontal poles attached at mule chest height provided the motive power down at one end of the rectangular barn shed; four mules waited to start walking around again pulling on opposite ends of each pole, with their new horse-collar harnesses.

Right now they were showing predatory interest in a substantial stack of wheat sheaves nearby, restrained by an occasional tap from the switch of the driver. You had to remember that livestock weren't machinery; they had their own priorities, and they weren't necessarily yours.

None of *that* had been hard, since wooden poles and draught animals walking in circles were things the locals had always done—if not put together in quite this way. The townsmen Josephus had recruited had worked on somewhat similar power systems for the big hourglass-shaped millstones used in commercial bakeries.

Here on the villa, women used hand querns to grind grain into flour with their copious spare time and superabundant unused energy, but few in a town of any size did. It was cheaper to buy bread from the bakeries anyway, since *they* could buy grain and fuel in bulk at lower prices and have their specialists work when other people were sleeping so it was ready at the right times. Only tavernkeepers and the like, and rich people with big domestic staffs, baked their own in cities. Romans had water-powered gristmills too, and one of those was on the list of priorities here if possible.

The upright shaft had an iron collar heat shrunk around the base, and turned on a smooth stone below, greased with lard; it ran up through a collar supported by a big V-shape of bracing timber running up in turn to the rafters, and engaged a horizontal pole there with a crude wheel-and-peg gear arrangement. That pole had had a bigger wheel turning at the other end, and *that* had a leather belt over it that reached down and powered the machine.

So far, so simple. And oh, thank God, thank Jesus in the foot-hills the leatherworkers could just make the horse collar without understanding it, he thought. *Slavery does have some advantages when you're Master . . . or the buddy of the guy Master's in deep hock to.*

The insides didn't look *completely* smashed up this time: that was progress . . . of a sort.

He used an iron hook and a pair of tongs and something like a crowbar to get the splintered wreck of what *had* been a grooved wooden cylinder out. The flanges were supposed to beat out the grain against a series of curved boards arranged around it in a semicircle . . . and this time the boards themselves only looked a bit battered, not broken and needing replacement.

Glad I didn't do the iron edging yet, he thought. *That'll cut down on wear . . . when we finally get this to work, that is.*

"All right, get me the next cylinder," he said.

Fuchs's baggage had included multiple sets of measuring gauges of various sizes.

The hell I won't need them, Jeremey thought bitterly. *Live and learn, you asshole: don't overpromise. Hereabouts rule of thumb means rule by thumbs. And "about the size of my thumb" doesn't cut it with machinery, even this eighteenth-century Scottish crap.*

He took the gauge and ran it along the splintered ridge.

Aha.

"Look," he said to the estate carpenter. "It broke here, in the middle. You left too much wood on there."

"But...but master, that makes it stronger—" the man began, and then took a step back.

Jeremey put a hand to his head and breathed deeply.

"That makes it *break*," he gritted out. "Look!"

A long white scratch ran down the upper surface of the ridge as he used the gauge to score the *new* cylinder.

"Now, take off the wood down to this line. Down to this line from one end to the other. Do not make any changes. Do not think. Just do it. This time I am going to watch you right to the end."

Sweating, the man ducked his head, mumbled something, and put the cylinder across the workbench, clamped it down with an awkward-looking arrangement of loops and twisting a stick to tighten them, and took up his spokeshave. That was sort of like a horizontal knife with a handle at each end.

It wasn't that he didn't know wood. His hands were scarred and callused, and delicately deft on the tool for all their size and gnarled look.

It's that he's used to getting general orders and handling all the details himself. Make a saw bench *or* make a cart, *stuff like that. So's Quintus.*

If you just told them to do something and walked away, their reflexes cut in.

"No, no, no! Right *on* the line. No higher. No lower. All the way across."

The man jumped, flushed, and bared his teeth as he over-rode years of habit. He was sweating freely as he finished and beveled the edges of the six-foot cut. He unclamped the cylinder, and Jeremey turned it to the next ridge and marked it likewise.

"Now do that again. Just the way you did the first time."

It took more than an hour to get them all done. When Jeremey snapped it back into the machine, reengaged the leather belts and put the cover back on he was grinding his own teeth. The mules walked...

And it didn't break.

Now let's see if it works. *If the ridges are too* low *they'll turn without breaking...but they won't* work. *Not too hot, not too cold, Goldilocks...you bitch. How I hate your smelly little pink pimply prepubescent ass.*

"Hand me one of those sheaves of wheat," he said.

It was prickly in his hands, and surprisingly heavy for what was basically a big bunch of long dry grass. He used his belt knife to cut the tucked-over twist of stalks that was used to hold it together and dropped the armful of three-foot lengths into the opening on the top that led to a slope-sided board chute. The rattling, banging noise grew a little muffled, and Quintus from Vindobona went down on his knees to peer underneath.

"Wheat coming out, excellent sir!" he called. "And that *fan* thing you had me make is blowing away the chaff—*just* the chaff, this time!"

Jeremey caught himself before thankful swearing involving the name of Jesus; that was illegal here. It didn't bother him in the abstract, since he'd been a closet atheist since he was twelve, coming out when he hit Boston. But it could be hard to overcome habits, and he felt self-conscious invoking Jupiter and Mars or the genitalia of Venus.

This time his touch on the machine was almost a caress.

"Get the foremen," he said. "And the *vilicus*."

"Now, you've got three ways to thresh grain," Jeremey said.

He felt tired, but *finally* it wasn't leavened with frustration. His audience of foremen who bossed the field gangs they also labored in frowned and scowled, not in hostility but concentration; the *vilicus*, whose name was Julius, had simply said *Obey this man as you would me or our master* and left.

"You beat it out with flails, you tread it out with oxen and horses and mules, or you have the draught beasts pull a sledge around on it."

There were nods; fortunately they had a high tolerance for repeating the obvious here. Roman rhetoric was chockablock with that, and apparently it had filtered down the social scale over time. They actually used flails except in emergencies, because it gave a higher yield per sheaf and a cleaner end product.

He pointed to the clumsy-looking device that was finally working.

Unless it suddenly breaks again, he thought, and used an apotropaic gesture popular here involving the thumb clenched between the first two fingers, then *crossed* his fingers for good measure.

He signaled to the man leading one of the mules, and it began to walk in a circle; so did the others. They proceeded with a resigned indifference.

Four mulepower, he thought. *A four mulepower engine, and it's the bee's knees.*

As things banged and clattered and creaked, little bits of dirt and whatever filtered down from the ceiling and its reed thatching.

Jesus. I'm saving the world *in a mud shack that stinks of fish and mule shit with a crowd of illiterate yokels who have* lice *in their hair.*

He'd originally gotten interested in Classical history because of aqueducts and big buildings with columns and gleaming marble, imperial triumphs, racing chariots, what he now knew were very bad movies, and because of gladiators. He was looking forward to sneaking off to an arena sometime, but he'd have to be careful.

A little later, after his voice broke, streaming episodes of series like *Rome* and *Spartacus* and *The Caesars* with gratuitous nudity and jiggling titties had added to the stew.

So he'd been about ten when the Glory That Was Rome struck home in his imagination and it had all been downhill from there. One thing had led to another... and later he'd been determined not to spend *his* life selling seed and feed to wrinkled old guys in billed caps...

And here I am, back on the farm standing in cow shit. Like my goddamned granddads. When the alternative's going into the stratosphere as radioactive dust, not so bad, but...

"Then we've got these grooved cylinders inside this box of planks."

He lifted off one side by a set of handles he'd specified, so they could see the innards in action, and traced the path of the sheaves with a finger at a safe distance while they crowded around and peered in. Everything was kept moving by leather straps, and the size of the wheels at each end governed the relative speeds.

"Keep the mules at that pace, over there! No faster, no slower! The grain goes in here, *you* over there, get some sheaves in the hole on top... heads first, fool, heads first! The ridges on the cylinder grab it and beat it out against these curved boards, see? Grain and chaff fall down here, past this round wooden tunnel a bit like a barrel, with the *fan* inside it...this wheel with thin broad spokes that makes a wind as it turns..."

There were murmurs and gasps at that. They knew about using wind to separate grain and chaff, but they did that by waiting for an actual wind and then tossing the mixture up with a basket or wooden paddle so that the lighter chaff blew away while the grain came down straighter. The concept of *making* a wind with anything but a lady's fan was a new one, and tickled their fancy. Several clapped their hands and laughed in glee.

And the problem there *was getting the fan so it would blow away the chaff, but* not *blow away the wheat. That little whore Goldilocks screwing with the bears again.*

"...and that blows away the chaff. Grain falls here, you scrape it off this wicker mat into baskets you put in this hole in the ground, with these boards on poles. Lift it out when it's full."

The tools for moving the grain into the baskets were like rakes without teeth. *That* hadn't been hard.

"The straw is caught by *this* cylinder with the thin iron hooks, after it crosses the grate where the grain falls through, gets pushed along this chute, and comes out over here."

Wheat straw had a lot of uses, including stuffing the more exalted slaves' mattresses. The upper classes used feathers, people at the bottom used nothing.

When the demonstration was over and the machine was working away, one of the foremen scratched his head. *Possibly* just because of the head lice that the Americans spent considerable time getting out of their own hair every couple of days; they'd all learned the origins of the phrase *fine-tooth comb.*

Paula had cut hers *really* short and tied a bandana around it with the knot over her forehead. He and Mark had imitated the Prof's military even-shorter-on-the-sides buzz cut.

Which come to think of it probably started out *as an anti-lice measure when they learned about lice carrying diseases.*

Filipa kept hers long but experimented with exotic-ingredient pseudo-shampoos and fine-tooth-combed a *lot.* She'd even gotten Sarukê to join her in mutual hair-combing sessions.

But more probably he was scratching because he was puzzled.

The gang boss hefted one of the baskets they'd put the grain into in his hands; they were of a roughly standardized size, holding about two *modii,* say thirty pounds or half a bushel. All of them were surprised at how fast the machine did the threshing, and how clean and free of debris the grain was.

"Master?" he said.

When Jeremey gave a nod he went on:

"With this engine—"

"We'll have more soon. At least three, so that two can always work if one needs to be fixed."

He nodded. "With three, we can have all the grain threshed in a few weeks, maybe four, six. But what will all the men and women"—the phrase he used was actually more graphic and rustic-earthy, referring to the respective genitalia—"do over the winter after th' plowin' 'n sowin' an' vine harvest, if they're not thrashin' the sheaves?"

They didn't use *the devil makes work for idle hands* here, but they had the concept.

Jeremey grinned. "Don't worry. We'll have plenty of work for you all. Now let's get some grain thrashed."

They did. None of them complained; the *vilicus* had made matters clear, and he thought that they mostly understood the concept that you had to learn something before you could effectively supervise someone else doing it. Once a leather belt broke, and they simply set to and repaired it without needing to be told.

It was hot, smelly, stuffy work; and very itchy, because of the little awns that broke off the dry grain and then floated to attach themselves to you, apparently making a GPS-guided beeline for the crotch and armpits.

But compared to doing it by hand this is a stroll in the park with an ice-cream cone in your hand.

After half an hour or so the pile of sheaves was vanishing, and one of them swore by Lugos—some Celtic deity—then lifted several of the baskets again, grunted again and asked:

"Master 'n lord? Are we gettin' a bit more o' the grain from each sheaf? Just a bit, mind."

Jeremey smiled at him with regal approval and whistled for a stop—during which everyone lifted the covers off buckets, plunged in dippers and drank, and the driver brought pails for the mules. Then he walked over and presented the observant specimen of yokeldom with a copper *as* from the pouch he carried at his belt.

The clodhopper scratched his head again—this time he crushed something between thumbnail and finger, which settled that question—and grinned and blushed and shuffled his feet and popped the coin into his mouth to hold under his tongue. Nobody here had heard of pockets before they arrived, though the Americans were having them added to all their tunics as fast as possible and some of the estate's upper personnel had already started to copy it.

"You're right, we *are* getting more. One part in twenty. Spread the word to the tenants, that if they bring their grain in to be threshed with this, they *pay* one part in twenty. So they'll have the same amount of grain as if they did it themselves, with a lot less work."

That brought guffaws and thigh slapping and nudges. He'd noticed that the estate slaves and the free sharecroppers who lived on the outer circle of the *latifundium*'s fields didn't particularly like each other. Not on a collective level, though they worked together sometimes and saw each other fairly often. Some of the sharecroppers owned a slave or two, and one—the descendant of a minor old-time Noric chieftain—had half a dozen field hands, a cook and a maid and a six-room house. He even owned a riding nag.

An hour later he was sure nothing was going to break right away *this* time. Jeremey turned things over to the smartest of the foremen and headed up the slope toward the *pars urbana*. It was a nice day for a jog or stroll, not too hot this time even in midafternoon, and with a light breeze off the lake.

From here, down by the water, you could see how the mansion had been built out on a low platform revetted with fieldstone, to keep the floor level from front to back. The marble-paved terrace at the rear was surrounded by fluted pillars topped with ornate gilded Corinthian capitals, with polished stone blocks on top joining them all together like lintels in a smooth U-shape. The stone ledge that made sported occasional statues, most of them gesticulating and all of them painted in colors that made them look like saints in a Brazilian Catholic church except for the nude ones. And the pool had a fountain in its center showing a nymph holding a big seashell.

The bronze nymph wasn't painted, but she had those inset glass eyes that seemed to follow you.

A drain leading to a pipe that ran out into the water sent the household runoff into the lake. Romans were *good* at handling water, as long as you didn't mind a continuous-flow system and its voracious demands. On the other hand, given the way they drained things like the pool from overflow valves at the top rather than the bottom, keeping the water turning over was a *good* idea.

So my youthful fascination with those Rome episodes and Spartacus wasn't all in vain.

He'd have a bath, a swim, and then... maybe a nap, and then...

There was a maid who'd proven susceptible to his charms... and the occasional trinket or *as*. A little charm went a long way here, when he could have just snapped his fingers and pointed at the bed and she'd have sighed and taken off her tunic and assumed the position. She had a friend who was just as flexible... metaphorically *and* literally.

A little technique goes a long way here too, he thought smugly. *Roman men just plunge away, or at least the ones they've met do. Dumb knuckle-draggers don't even know how to enjoy themselves!*

He whistled as he walked.

And so some of my adolescent dreams about Roman orgies have come true. Onward and upward! And right now, down and inward.

"Master! Master! Master Julio'!"

Which is what they insist on calling me.

What happened when they really tried to say *Jeremey* was incomprehensible, but comic. Josephus had figured out that it was ultimately of Hebrew origin when they were introduced— *Yirmeyah*, meaning "may Jehovah exalt"—and given him an odd look when the penny dropped.

The foreman came pelting up, panting, when he was halfway to the mansion. "We caught 'im! Peekin' in through the place whar daub fell out!"

I can't punch him, Jeremey thought, grinding his teeth. *Or I could, but that would be a bad idea. If you punch people who bring you news, pretty soon nobody brings you news, or they lie about it, and then the truth comes up by itself and bites half your butt and your left testicle off and it's a complete surprise. And that hurts worse than listening to things you really don't want to hear. Forethought, Jem, forethought.*

He turned around and trudged back to the big shed instead, carefully not showing his irritation. Another two of the men he'd been instructing were holding someone with a face he didn't

know, with his arms twisted up behind his back and his young-
ish, patchily bearded countenance contorted with pain.

Jeremey looked him over. No rips in his tunic, and good
sandals on his feet—most of the ordinary workers here went
barefoot until things got much colder.

"Any of you know this man?" he asked the others.

One of the older foremen scratched his head and said:

"Couldn't swear by the Gods, master, but I think he's the son
of the *vilicus* on Quintus Pollius Naso's place."

Jeremey searched his memory. That was a small estate or very
large farm north of here—about three hundred acres all up—that
he'd heard mentioned. *That* Quintus was a retired centurion of
no great importance, promoted from the ranks and he'd never
risen higher than commander of the Ninth Century. It was still
big enough to employ about twenty slaves, and make Quintus
Pollius Naso solidly middle class, in a society where the *working*
class was over ninety percent of the total.

Oh, I am so *going to kick this upstairs,* he thought.

Firmly suppressing his initial impulse to snap out: *String the
bastard up by the heels!* That could cost both money and trouble.
The young man burst out:

"I do not fear you, you wizard, you evil sorcer—"

This time Jeremey *did* punch; they had orders to firmly quash
any talk of sorcery, and the thought of rumors like that made
the skin along his spine crawl.

He figured he could hold his own with any individual Roman.
He wasn't necessarily *smarter* than any particular one of them,
Josephus for example was *scary* bright, you got that quickly. But
he had the advantage of two thousand years of accumulated
information and they didn't.

A mob afraid of magic...that's another matter altogether.

That wasn't just peasantish hick superstition here. *Everyone*
believed in it, or nearly, apart from a tiny handful of philosophical rationalists. Even they mostly believed in the Gods, they just
thought the Olympians didn't bother interacting with humans,
so you could discount them.

There was a satisfying meaty *thud* and the slave's head snapped
back. Blood ran down from his nose, and Jeremey's hand only hurt
a little while he wiped the blood off on the other man's tunic by
punching him in the stomach with a nice *Krav Maga*-style twister.

He'd learned the hard way to make sure you broke things in the other guy's face rather than bones in your fist, and done it way back in his early teenaged years before he attended his first dojo. He carefully refrained from the near-instinctive follow-up of a solid kick to the crotch.

"Fetch the lord Artorius," he said instead. "And tie this one up, and then get back to work. Who spotted him?"

Jeremey gave the one they indicated an *as*, the equivalent of a penny or nickel, and half the price of a pound of bread in most towns. If you reliably rewarded good service, you got more of it and it was more willing.

The Prof arrived about thirty minutes later, on horseback and leading a second mount; that was half an hour Jeremey would very much have preferred to spend washing and eating and drinking and screwing, or even just toppling into his bed and *sleeping* in it. Everything took more effort here...

The Prof grinned that rather annoying grin when he'd been filled in on the details.

"Let him see the engine at work," he said, and threw the reins of the second mount to Jeremey. "Then release him unharmed except for a good kick up the arse."

At McCladden's surprised look, he went on—in English:

"What's the chance of this Quintus Pollius Naso being able to make the machine from this kid's description?"

One of the infuriating things about local names was that there were only about twenty praenomen or less—corresponding to an American's first name—in common use. That made confusing people very, very easy if you relied on them. There were five or six named Quintus he'd met since they arrived at the villa. The only one he immediately remembered was the furniture carpenter from Vindobona, the sharp ambitious one he was cultivating a bit. That was one reason Romans often used two or even the full three names in ordinary conversation; though nowadays and around here at least mostly the *last* two names, the *nomen* and *cognomen*.

"Zip," Jeremey answered frankly. "I was overconfident. You need to get the proportions of the wooden cylinders right to within about the width of the tip of your little finger, or maybe Fil's little finger. And all the way along, *that* was what took so long. If they're too big even by that much even in one little spot they break off at the ridges and everything jams up and then other things break if you don't stop everything *fast*, and if that happens you can't tell what started it. And they just don't goddamned *work* at all if they're too small. Goldilocks and the Three Bears territory."

"As you say, zip chance of their getting that right without help."

Jeremey nodded: "That's the fiddly bit, and if I hadn't had the measuring gauges and the right dimensions written down in advance, it would have taken *months*. Or maybe forever. After this one I'm going to use boards pegged into grooves in the cylinders—easier to adjust with a plane or spokeshave."

"Learning by doing," the Prof said, nodding.

"We'll need three of them to handle the whole harvest, four if a lot of the sharecroppers decide to bring their wheat in. I thought we could sell the worst two or three after that, and replace them at leisure over the winter. There's some stuff in the books about how in the States they used iron pegs on the rollers when they started making these...that would take a lot of experiment."

The Prof nodded again as Jeremey swung into the saddle, then addressed the captive, looking down at the bloodied but defiant face as he shifted back to Latin:

"Boy, look your fill. Tell your master, when he has wasted enough of his substance trying to make an engine such as this, that we will teach the man he sends to us the craft of it...or sell him an engine...for one thousand five hundred denarii. In advance."

Most of those present laughed. That was the price of three or four field hands, or four to six years' income for a moderately skilled free worker.

Ah, Jeremey thought. *But with one of these, maybe Quintus Pollius wouldn't need as many slaves, so he could sell...no, it's slack-season work, he has to keep the hands—and he doesn't have tenants to fill in at peak season like the big operators, so has to bid for labor in a seller's market when the migrant gangs go around. He'll be between a rock and a hard place. Turns out there are advantages to being rich, surprise surprise surprise, I'm shocked, just* shocked.

"That was smart," he said aloud as he swung into the saddle. "They'll have to come to us and pay through the nose."

"Oh, we *want* them to start making them themselves," the

Prof said. "And the rest of the stuff. There are plenty making their own wheelbarrows in this neighborhood already—and in Vindobona and Carnuntum and Josephus' hometown, Sirmium. That's just from seeing the ones we sent as examples. And a couple of energetic types have gotten stills going. The thresher's a bit of a leap in difficulty up from that, though. We want to make money off it in the interim if we can."

"Difficulty? Tell me!"

They reined around and headed upslope, though not directly back toward the *pars urbana*; this heading would take them into the fields to the west, where preparations for the late-fall plowing and planting of the winter grains...

And a patch of canola, this year.

...were just getting started. They passed several carts heaped high with cut rushes or wheat straw as they did, heading for Mark Findlemann's paper project, which was kept at a distance because it was rather smelly.

Glad I'm not stuck with that. *Because* mash the material into pulp *is a hell of a* general *set of instructions. Devil's in the details.*

Jeremey cast a critical eye at the field where he'd planted the seed potatoes as they passed. There were a bunch of slave women weeding it with the surprisingly modern-looking swan-necked Roman hoe, the *sarculum*. In slow motion, though they speeded up automatically at the sound of riders, and they'd drop back into the slower pace when the freemen were past just as reflexively. He'd had six bushels, which was enough to plant a little over half an acre.

With no fertilizers except dung, and late planting, he thought it would produce about...

Call it a bit over half a ton of spuds. Enough for seven or eight acres planted next year... planted at the right times... minus just enough for one blowout on french fries slathered with ketchup.

His mouth watered at the thought; he was eating well, as well as the estate owner's own family and from the same cooks, but you just *missed* some things if you'd grown up with them. If there was one thing his part of Wisconsin had had in abundance, it was potatoes. God knew he'd dug enough up in his mother's garden for her to cook for the family.

Nice light loam with some sand and gravel here but a touch dry, so say a hundred and fifty to two hundred bushels yield per acre next year if the weather's not real bad, something like six tons of spuds per acre! Roasted or boiled or boiled and mashed or fried!

That was about ten or twelve times the yield of whole-meal bread per acre of wheat here, and processing and cooking it took a lot less effort than grain did once it was in the cellar. Which meant the landowner could *sell* a lot more of his wheat, which was more portable anyway because potatoes included a lot more water.

Columbian Exchange, you betcha ass.

"Thanks for bringing the horse, but what's up, Prof?" he asked.

"I want you to see that riding plow thing you've been working on," he said.

They rode on to one of the fallow fields rotated with grain; technically it was a grass ley planted with clover and such, not just weeds, part of a surprisingly sophisticated crop-rotation system they used here. There were six feet plowed with double furrows, and a wrecked piece of equipment at the end of it.

"Crap! *Again?* Crap and crapitude and shit. Not the valuable manure type of shit either!"

The Prof grinned again. "Could be worse. You could be doing the paper project. Mark just about cried when the latest batch came apart like cobwebs, plus absorbing liquids like essence of Sahara."

Jeremey swung down from the saddle. What he'd been trying to make was a two-furrow sulky riding plow, nineteenth-century style. The small-town museum in the place he'd grown up had one—something called an Oliver 23—and he'd remembered it well and spent weeks coming up with a plan to reproduce it with the modifications needed.

I have an eye for details if I do say so myself. But they were using the output of the Carnegie Steel Company's Bessemer converters to make that in a factory with lathes and boring machines, not wrought-iron scrap from the local blacksmith, he thought dourly, and bent to examine it.

The locals stood back nervously; apparently they weren't really familiar with the concept of a superior not blaming them when something went wrong. Roman slaves apparently expected a...

Let's call it a vigorous zero-fault tolerance policy *from their bosses. With a lot of hitting.*

"Unhitch the team," he said with a sigh; he didn't even shout.

They were using another innovation: three pairs of yoked oxen in a row, with the yokes pulling on a common chain—the Prof had gotten that idea from stuff he remembered about the Boer War, of all things. That hadn't been too difficult to get across, mostly one of those slap-the-head, why-didn't-we-think-of-that things.

The sulky plow, on the other hand...

The Prof and he bent their heads over it. Jeremey had kept the frame simple; a wooden beam between two wagon wheels, with a bicycle-type seat and footboard. *That* part worked fine.

The problem was with the business end.

The *plows* were fine; two moldboard types, carved out of seasoned beechwood and then given a thin hammered-iron covering carefully polished to avoid any lumps. The covering was an innovation and so was the smooth precise double curve of the shape. But Romans did have something vaguely like that for individual walking plows, used on heavier soils here in the northern provinces, sometimes with a set of wheels out front too. Though not often around here, where it was a nice light loam and they stuck with simple scratch plows not much changed for the last four thousand years.

The coulters—the things that did the initial cut in the turf— were iron wheels a foot around turning on a pin and held in front of each of the plows by a lever. *That* hadn't been a problem either, though it was new to them, as was the separate iron share on the point of the plow itself.

The problem was the iron bar that swung down with a simple lever arrangement to put the plows into the dirt or lift them out when you were finished with a row. The lever worked; the *bar* had buckled...again...into a nearly U-shape.

"And it popped one of the welds, too," Jeremey said unhappily, his hobnails clinking on the metal as he prodded the thin slanting crack. "Prof, if we were using bar-stock steel, this would work. With this shit..."

"Wrought iron's soft," the older man replied. "Steel they keep for swords and knives and edge tools because it costs the earth. And they're working from small pieces of wrought iron to start with. Ordinary hammer welding, you never know when it'll pop. Scale in the welds, probably. You'd need a powered trip-hammer to get much better."

They'd both grown up around tools and tasks and patching up and making do with what you had on hand, which was a help. Jeremy thumped the heel of his hand against his forehead.

"Look, Prof, let's think outside the box. I tried...twice... for an iron bar as the moveable swing-down support because it was metal in the one I saw back when. Why not try hardwood?"

"Not strong enough, unless you used a baulk like a rafter."

"Yeah, but *braced* with metal? Like, iron rods in grooves around the surface, held on with heat-shrunk iron bands? A lot heavier, but doable. I think!"

The Prof's pale sun-faded eyebrows went up, standing out against his tanned face, like the short new beard.

"You know, Jem, that's not a bad thought at all. None of that's really strange here, either. Use ash wood. It's strong and it's resilient as well, that's why they use it for spear shafts and tool handles."

"Hickory would be even better, but we'd have to wait twenty years," Jeremey said with a grin of his own.

They both laughed; Fuchs's stores of seed had included a number of useful trees that they'd plant next year, and hickory would grow here...but not very quickly. The closest mature hickories were on the other side of the Atlantic, which for now might as well have been on the Moon.

"Most of this is salvageable," Jeremey said thoughtfully. "I'll get the carpenter and smith on it tomorrow. Need a really strong brace for the swing-down pivots, there'll be lateral stress, that's the *next* weak point."

The older man slapped him on the shoulder. "I'll leave it in your capable hands."

❧ CHAPTER EIGHT ❧

Villa Lunae,
Province of Pannonia Superior
August 28th, 165 CE

Explaining things like this was *work*, Paula Atkins told herself. For starters, you had to control the impulse to anger.

But I'm glad the Prof talked us into saving the Roman Empire. Sort of. Because that implies changing *it. If I was just living here without that, it would drive me to drink or suicide.*

"It's a model," Paula said to the carpenters. "One-quarter the size of the real thing."

She held up four fingers of her right hand and one on her left; she thought the townsman—his name was Quintus—sighed a little, and the local man frowned and then nodded.

Explaining things like this was like teaching, but less interesting. Still, it was worthwhile . . .

"Ah, like the *unarota*?"

That was the name they'd come up with for wheelbarrows: it meant "one wheel."

"And the thing for threshing, mistress?" he said. "There was a *model* of that, too."

There was a chorus of smiles from everyone except the freeman, and he seemed to understand why they were happy about it.

Beating out the grain with flails was hard work and boring, tossing it in a breeze to get rid of the chaff was hard work and boring, scraping it up and putting it in bins and sacks and large plaited baskets and big earthenware jars and carrying and stacking them was even harder work and boring, and it took most of their otherwise-free time in winter.

In England there had been mass riots when threshing machines were first introduced, while Queen Victoria-to-be was still a princess. That was because the farmworkers had been *paid* for the hand threshing. Miserably *under*paid, but they were rural proletarians hired by the day or week or task who needed every single halfpenny to buy food over the winter slack season.

The slaves here would just have less of an unpleasant task, and get fed about the same anyway, whether they were doing something else or not. They liked things that did that, and she approved of their priorities.

It had been a good thought to do those first; it won pleased, amazed respect from the workforce here. To them, Lord Artorius and his helpers had come to lift burdens from their backs. Threshing the old way had taken up about a quarter of their total labor hours per year.

The *vilicus* approved too, because the faster the grain was threshed the faster his master got paid, since Josephus had contracted for the whole surplus and paid upfront for it as he got it loaded on his hired wagons. A small nick of several things involved with that stuck to the *vilicus'* palm, a known if unacknowledged perk.

He was probably pulling a sack out of a hole somewhere every night and smiling as he fondled it.

"Yes, like those. And it comes apart like this, see? Just make all the parts in the same proportion, but four times bigger."

Oh, if only it was that simple! From what Jem said, there's going to be a lot *of fiddling and jiggling and fitting before it functions. And that's with Type A!*

What it was a model of was a spinning wheel, late nineteenth-century style, the final refinement and oddly enough developed in Canada for backwoods farm households in Quebec. It stood on a workbench, in one of the workshops around the second courtyard of the *pars rustica* of the estate.

Adzed wooden pillars surrounded the interior of the court to leave a shaded portico, with a waist-high adobe wall joining them, but the surface they enclosed was gravel or pounded dirt or severely practical herb-and-truck gardens. There was a fountain—also plain, and women were carrying water away from it in clay amphorae or wooden buckets, gossiping as they did. Chickens pecked, dogs scratched, cats drowsed in patches of sun, children ran around shouting when they weren't corralled for chores, and work proceeded at a steady but not very fast pace.

The harvest had been a rush, working can to can't in the hottest time of year, and nobody did more than grumble. If untimely rain spoiled the grain, or delay meant it shattered and fell out of the ears, the workers would have less to eat for the next year. The interval between getting the grain in and the fall plowing and planting (and the vintage) was for catching your breath and catching up on other things you'd put off like repairs and laundry.

There was a heavy smell of sap and cut wood and sawdust here in the open-sided carpenter's workshop lit by the strong morning sun; tools hung from pegs and racks, some surprisingly modern looking, and shapes of seasoned wood were stacked up on the rafters overhead. The tools included a back-and-forth woodworking lathe powered by a bow-and-string arrangement, in turn powered by the estate carpenter's pubescent son-apprentice.

She made a mental note to suggest a foot-pedal and flywheel arrangement to replace that. They didn't have crankshafts here but didn't find them difficult to understand, and in the original history they'd have been invented in the next few hundred years.

Underneath that woody scent was what she thought of as a *slummy* smell, of body odor and dirty feet and sweat soaked into wool. Though not *too* bad, at least not now that she'd been here a while and her nose had adjusted; these people washed twice a week or even more, in a suite of baths more crowded and much more basic than the ones attached to the *pars urbana*. They didn't have enough clothes to wash them often, but they did launder them occasionally.

And it was still much better than Vindobona, because there were far fewer people packed together.

And they have that latrine with running water under it. Luxury, in a way.

There were actually *two* carpenters here; one belonged to the villa and had his son and a couple of assistants who handled the rough work under his supervision, while the other was the young freeman named Quintus from Vindobona. He'd been trained in furniture making and so was valuably good at fine joinery, but hadn't been able to set up his own shop yet before he was recruited by Josephus and Josephus' contacts.

They gave each other covert jealous looks, but they both had what would be considerable sums to them riding on this going right, which greased things. The freeman would get the tools they'd bought and be able to rent enough space to get his own shop going and marry next year. The slave would add to his *peculium*, the fund that slaves were allowed to have here. Slaves could own property, in practice if not in strict legal theory. They could also save up to buy themselves, if they were ambitious.

In fact the freeman was nodding to himself as he looked at the model and traced things with his fingers.

He muttered under his breath: "And if these catch on ... I wonder how much I could charge for one? More than I could for a good-quality table and set of reclining benches, I bet ... hummmm."

Some slaves even owned slaves themselves ... though that occurred at a much more exalted level than the *pars rustica* of an estate in a remote border province.

There was a woman present too, a middle-aged mother with a twelve-year-old girl beside her and a boychild toddler standing gripping the skirt of her tunic and sucking his thumb; he wore nothing but a string around his neck with a bead on it and had a runny nose.

Well, Ubba there is middle-aged by local standards. *She's probably only five or six years older than me, but I bet she had her first kid two or three years after puberty though she's only got those two living. She's popular and well respected here in the* pars rustica *among the other women, though, and they're the ones who do the spinning and weaving and sewing.*

The mother was standing frowning as she looked at the machine. Her hands were busy, as were those of the older daughter, apparently needing no conscious attention, spinning thread with a distaff.

That meant a stick with a big hank of—badly—bleached carded wool on it in her left hand, wool that still had bits of the spiky teasel seedpod used to comb it out in it. Her right supported a spindle dangling from the thread. She was drawing the loose wool fibers out of the distaff, deftly joining them to the end of the thread and twisting it, applying an occasional boost to the weighted spindle to keep it twirling. When there was enough thread that the spindle nearly touched the ground, she wound it onto the bobbin part and started all over again.

Paula had noted...

Just like that play of Aristophanes, she thought, blinking at the eerie thrill of it.

...that most women here who were walking between tasks, or watching children, or anything else that didn't require their hands, had a spindle and distaff going. When they *did* have to stop and do something else, they just thrust both into the rough cloth girdle that confined their calf-length tunics, and automatically resumed when they could. The distaff held enough carded wool for a full day's spinning, or two or three interspersed between other tasks.

Girls as young as six or seven did it too, with their elders correcting them at need, and old women with bent backs and a few remnant teeth often sat gossiping in the sunny parts of the courtyards of the *pars rustica* with spindle and distaff in their gnarled fingers. She'd even seen women doing it while sitting on one of the holes in the disconcertingly open-plan latrine, doing their other business too and chatting with the neighbors.

Which latrine was disconcertingly close to the *kitchens,* apparently because they both used running water.

"This spins, mistress?" the woman said, nodding at the model.

Most of the staff—

Slaves, Paula reminded herself. *They're slaves. She just called me* era, *which is the word slaves use for "mistress."*

—were born here and spoke Latin. Though except for the educated upper-echelon house slaves who'd mostly come with the ladies from Sirmium, they had a heavy local accent.

And they salted the Roman tongue with loanwords from the Celtic dialect spoken in Noricum and its neighbors before incorporation into the Empire; a fair proportion of them were descended from those folk. The others had ancestors from virtually everywhere, coffled in and ending up here at one time or another. A sprinkling had been bought from traders more recently, or had been infants whose impoverished parents exposed them in some cemetery or on some rubbish heap where they'd been snapped up by slave dealers.

Keeping up numbers was hard. There were occasional manumissions, the odd runaway—almost always a young man—and children died with dismaying frequency.

Apparently many of the free tenants still actually spoke the old
Celtic tongue, but most of them knew Latin too. Latin speakers here
expected other people to talk to them in their own language, and
not doing that could cause endless friction. Which made learning it
worthwhile even if you lived where you'd been born, and essential
if you had dealings with anyone from outside a half-hour's walk.

As far as sheer physical looks went, the coloring and features,
they looked like Central or Balkan Europeans. Shorter than in her
day, fewer living oldsters, many more kids, and nearly all wiry
slim. And maybe a bit less in the way of blonds and redheads
than modern Austrians, though she wasn't sure about that.

Except that they didn't hold themselves the same, or walk
the same, or...

The owners, the family of Sextus Hirrius Trogus, were Gallic by
descent too, as the last name, the cognomen, indicated, but long ago
Romanized. Before Julius Caesar's time in fact, and far to the west.

Slaves, she thought again with a shudder. *I don't know what
creeps me out more, just the fact, or the way everyone here takes
it for* granted. *At least it doesn't have anything to do with your
skin color.*

Her mouth quirked. A couple of times small children had
run up and rubbed a finger on her to see if the black came off
or tried to touch her hair, and been hauled away by the ear and
smacked on the bottom by apologetic mothers worried that the
odd, rich stranger staying in the *pars urbana* would get annoyed.
But that was about the sum of it.

People here knew in the abstract that people looked different
in different places, or at least the literate ones did and the rest
told fantastic stories about far-off lands where people had fur or
only one eye or foot or no heads and faces in their stomachs, but
it just didn't matter much. Not compared to whether you were
slave or freedman or freeborn, or whether you were a Roman
citizen (which freedmen who'd been *owned* by Roman citizens
were, sort of, and their children completely so), or rich or poor.

There were ethnic stereotypes here in plenty, or regional ones,
held with innocent unselfconsciousness as something *everybody knew.*

The northern barbarians were big, blond, stinky, filthy, and
dumb as rocks with murderous short-fuse tempers; Greeks were
sneaky and clever and talked too much and liked their sheep
far too much; Jews were sneaky and clever and given to fits of

religious mania; Italians were toffee-nosed, party-hearty lazy snobs; Britons were hayseed hicks on the edge of the world; and people from Syria—the Middle East—were greasy treacherous gutless-wonder lickspittles.

None of that applied to *her*. Except the ones about women, of course. But being free and rich by local standards and a guest of the family helped there. And the *vilicus* had passed the word that they were supposed to do anything she said. Up to and including stripping down, painting themselves green and then hopping about going *ribbit-ribbit*, on pain of a flogging, or for the freemen from Vindobona, loss of money they wanted dearly.

Because I'm black I'm a curiosity here, but it isn't important. *I'm black but I'm living before the* concept *of race the way we used the term was even* invented. *And* that *feels just as odd as the rest of it.*

Almost as weird as the living, breathing slaves all around her.

"Yes, it spins," Paula said to the woman with the distaff, hauling herself out of the academic temptations of introspection. "It is a tool for spinning thread, from wool or flax."

Cotton was a very, very expensive import here; unless they were maidservants to the ladies of the house, they'd rarely see it and never touch it. And the house servants and fieldworkers moved in different circles, though with some overlap.

Paula reached out and pushed the model's treadle down with one hand, repeating the motion until the parts all moved, the wishbone-shaped flyer whirling around the spindle with a rising hum as the wheel picked up speed.

"The woman using it sits on a stool here, and moves this with her foot; it's called the treadle."

The adolescent girl blurted: "She can *work sitting down* all the time?"

Her mother reached out without looking around and rapped her on the head with the end of her distaff, medium hard.

"Mistress," the girl added, wincing and rubbing the spot.

All three adults moved their lips as they whispered the word *treadle* to themselves to set it in memory, several times over.

"The wheel turns the flyer here"—more whispered memorization—"and bobbin, like this, at different speeds. That's why these little wheels the cords from the *big* wheel run on are different sizes. You hold the thread at a constant tension, feeding in more fiber from the distaff rod here as it goes. Through the hole here, then it runs over these hooks on the spinning flyer and winds itself on the bobbin. You take off the bobbin when it's full and put on another."

The explanation went easily enough. She'd actually used a spinning wheel...though not often...at demonstrations by hobbyists, just to get a little hands-on feel for it. It was a bit useful in her field, which focused on women's history; she'd only narrowed it down to *Classical* women's history since her undergrad days, that was going to be—

Was *going to be*, she thought glumly.

—the subject of her dissertation. Though she'd started on Latin in high school, and was spending some time here picking up Greek from Fil and Mark.

The woman grunted as she traced the path Paula had described with her eyes and then her finger, shoving her spindle and distaff into her girdle and pushing the treadle herself and tracing the path of the thread.

"Uh! So that...that flyer thing, some'ow it do what your fingers do with this, mistress?"

She indicated her distaff and bobbin again.

"*Sic, ita*," Paula replied, an emphatic double affirmation.

It will probably be a lot more difficult to get people doing it properly. There's parts you have to learn with your fingers and eyes, the tensioning and such, and I'm no expert.

Textiles in general and spinning in particular were generally women's work, probably because it was finicky, boring, and could be interrupted at will. Usually at a man's will, or for children.

And, surprise, surprise, it doesn't pay well, even if you're not a slave.

"Why, mistress?" the woman asked after another moment of contemplation, during which she resumed her own spinning, as automatically as breathing. "That looks tricky, that wheel thing do, and this"—she moved her hands to draw attention to the thread moving smoothly through her fingers—"is simple. Everybody knows how to do't."

Everybody female was implicit.

Paula nodded with an encouraging smile. She'd had to yell and threaten now and then, but hated it and the way it made the slaves cringe: on the other hand, positive reinforcement seemed to work here too.

Provided you didn't come across as an easy mark.

"Well, the reason is that an hour's work with this machine spins ten times as much as you do with a distaff in the same hour, and it spins very tight thread."

The estate carpenter grunted. "Like the threshing engine can thresh better an' quicker, mistress? An' th' *unarota* carries more stuff faster, an' superwine—"

He grinned and smacked his lips.

"—gets you good an' drunk faster?"

"Just so, my good man."

She showed them all a swatch of worsted wool cloth, taken from the Prof's suit jacket. They exclaimed, passing it from hand to hand, rubbing it, touching it to their faces or lips and holding it up to the light.

"This cloth's fit for the Lady Julia's stola, ev'n if it ain't silk!" the woman said. "Can we spin thread loike this wit' the wheel thing? Mostly the cloth we make here 'bouts is just f' the *familia rustica*."

Which words meant all the slaves of the estate. They grew their own food and made their own clothes—of coarse, slightly lumpy undyed woolen cloth, mostly—and shoes for winter and many of their tools, too, and their housing. There were the carpenters here, and two blacksmiths who could double with other metals, and part-time bricklayers and tile makers and leatherworkers and potters. What came in from the outside was mostly luxuries for the *pars urbana*, some of the fancier tools, and basics like bar iron. The free tenants often came to the villa's *pars rustica* too if they needed to buy specialist services.

"It's a *spinning wheel*. And no, not quite like this, but very good," Paula said.

Now for my cunning blow.

"Your masters will pay you an *as* for every ten full spindles of thread you make when these machines are ready...when you make the thread properly, it will take time to get the knack, I warn you. For every bobbin above the amount you did before with your distaffs."

The slave woman—and the slave carpenter—both exclaimed, delighted. And the freeman's brows went up.

An *as* was the equivalent of a penny, the lowest-value coin in common use, and struck in copper. There were four of them to a sestertius, the next coin up and made of brass or *orilachrium* as they called it here, and four *sestertii* to a silver denarius. A soldier in the Legions got about eight-tenths of a denarius a day; after allowing for stoppages he would make about one and a half to two sestertii. When Quintus the freeborn carpenter here had his own shop, taking slack times and others with a lot of orders together and depending on how hard and well he worked, he'd probably clear about the same.

Though the soldiers got paid regularly three times a year, and banked most of it with the unit's *signifer*, who put it in the legion's strongbox.

The owner's family wouldn't be out of pocket much making a nominal payment like that; thread was readily saleable, and with enough spinning wheels...say twenty or thirty...the estate would be producing a surplus fairly quickly, and selling each bobbin full for well over an *as* each. But rural slaves like these just didn't see much coined money at all, and Paula could see she was thinking that if the machine really did make ten times as much thread, then...

And the women *will get it,* Paula thought. *It's a small step, but a beginning.*

She looked up at the sun; she'd already become accustomed to using that, or a sundial. Their phones were just too conspicuous if you whipped one out to check the clock, and they'd all been helping each other to become conscious of it. Nobody wanted to be burned at the stake or thrown to the lions or whatever it was that Romans did with convicted sorcerers...though to be fair, apparently the law only forbade *harmful* magic, like prophesies of the Emperor's death.

Black *magician, that's me.*

"I have other tasks now," she said. "Remember, you carpenters, that there will be a denarius to split between you for every day under fourteen it takes until the first spinning wheel is ready... provided it *works.* Call on me if you have problems. After you master the spinning wheel, we will start on the *treadle-worked flying-shuttle* loom."

That model was still in her suite; it was of the type British handloom weavers had used up until the 1830s, when power looms were perfected and handweaving no longer paid enough to keep you alive.

The advantages over the local loom were even greater than

with the spinning wheel versus distaff. The estate sold most of its wool clip, well over three-quarters, and it was quite good wool from good-sized sheep, nearly as good as modern merino. The Danube's legions and auxiliaries and their dependents made a ready, steady, well-paid market. When the spinning wheels and looms were done, they could make as much cloth as they had before in one-tenth the time... or nine-tenths more, and sell it. That would finance other things.

Her next task was the *prandium*. Which was lunch.

More or less by coincidence, Romans in this period ate a light breakfast and lunch and had their main meal around sundown, the same pattern she was accustomed to. The food here was exotic but usually quite good at the level of the villa-dwelling aristocracy... in many ways like stuff from an organic health-food outfit, apart from sanitation. And she'd *still* shed some weight, slowly but consistently. No sugar except occasional honey, somewhat coarse wholemeal flour even for the aristos, plenty of veggies and fruit and lean meat—even the pigs here were usually leaner than twenty-first-century ones—and *lots* of exercise.

You didn't need to put aside time for a walk, here, and you most certainly didn't need a steppercizer; she was probably walking four or five miles a day, and they'd never heard of elevators or escalators.

⇒ CHAPTER NINE ⇐

Villa Lunae,
Province of Pannonia Superior
September 1st, 165 CE

When *we first arrived, this would have tired me out,* Paula thought a week later as she escorted two of the kitchen maids down the long path to the paddocks where the horses were trained and exercised.

They were carrying baskets with what amounted to a large picnic lunch, and each also had a big pitcher of wine mixed with water at one-third to two-thirds, as cold as a cellar could manage.

Paula didn't carry anything, because that would have upset and bewildered everyone.

As it is, it just makes me *feel guilty. I never wanted to be Scarlett O'Hara!*

It was still hot at midday and mostly cloudless an hour past noon, though there were thunderheads out over the lake that had sent the fishing boats back to shore. And just lately you could sense fall in the air at dawn, and again by midnight. In another few weeks the leaves would begin to turn. The grapes in the vine-yards were more and more juicy looking and fairly soon they'd be harvested, though there were proportionately a lot fewer acres under vines than there had been in the 2030s because everyone needed a lot of acres of wheat to be self-sufficient, much less produce a surplus for the cities and armies.

Only a few top-flight vintages like the famous Falernian from Italy were sent any distance overland. When wine could be moved in ships on the sea or boats and barges on rivers . . . now *that* was big business. It was cheaper to ship something from Syria to Sicily by sea than a hundred miles by road, even a Roman road . . . and Roman roads were better than anything mainland Europe would have again until well into the nineteenth century.

Meanwhile she was sticky and sweaty enough to look long-ingly at that wind-ruffled expanse of water just eastward. The air smelled of lake, slightly of the brackish swamps around it, more of green-hot-dusty fields, and increasing whiffs of horse and equine byproducts as she got closer to her destination, and less of the flower scents around the mansion. She was wearing a straw hat rather like a Panama today, and glad of it.

People swam in the lake sometimes, in places where you could get at the water without wading through reed swamp; for that matter, the big marble-lined pool on the back terrace of the *pars urbana* was a *swimming* pool among other things, and not a little one at that, and just for the owner's family and their guests. The problem was that nobody here had ever heard of bathing suits for swimming, any more than they'd wear clothes bathing in an actual bath, and Paula had never found nudism attractive either in theory or practice.

There were two biggish bath suites in the mansion, like cozy miniatures of the great collective ones in towns and cities: hot-dry and hot-wet saunas, hot and cold plunges, the whole nine yards . . . except that you rubbed on olive oil and scraped it off with a curved metal *strigil* rather than using soap. It worked surpris-ingly well; she still missed soap. Nice mild soap, and shampoo . . .

They know about soap but they mostly use it for cloth and laundry, Paula thought disgustedly.

She'd tried what they called *sapo,* and it was alkaline enough to take your skin off though apparently a few people washed with it, especially those with skin *diseases.* Using the town baths had been a bit hair-raising, because there *were* people with skin diseases using them, and racking coughs, and other things that made you want to launder your own skin and lungs afterward.

Someday we'll make better soap.

Currently one bath suite was for the women staying at the house and one for the men, because in this generation free women didn't strip in front of free men not their husbands or immediate family. The terrace pool was divided for alternate days for the same reason.

That was as close to a nudity taboo as they had, and even there...slaves apparently didn't count. Any more than a dog would back home. The *slaves* didn't separate the sexes in *their* bathhouse, which had been the case with most public baths once, and was apparently still true in any small low-status localized community that thought of itself as an extended family.

Takes getting used to, she thought grimly. *But girl, you ain't goin' home, nohow. Home's not there anymore and that car you came here in has been well and truly repossessed, too. So this is home now,* Rome *is home now, and you get used to smelling like olive oil and having people see everything. Damned if I'm going to start shaving down there, though. Not with* their *razors!*

There were a dozen people around a trestle table set up in the uppermost horse paddock. Most of them were men; the estate's senior horse trainer, several of the wranglers who worked with him, the carpenters and leatherworkers and *their* assistants, one of the smiths and his son, and as many visitors from outside the estate, bailiffs from other properties of various sizes, and prosperous middle-sized free farmers come to take a look at where the rumors were all coming from.

One thing her studies had gotten pretty much right was that most Romans were absolute jackdaws for useful tricks and intensely practical about copying anything that gave them an advantage, financial or otherwise. They took it, ran with it, tweaked it and made it their own.

Jeremey was there too, taking a break from his bucolic, though mostly supervisory, labors.

Jem enjoys telling people what to do too much. And those two girls he's screwing...they're happy about it from the look of things. Even putting on airs and showing off the hairpins and rings and they dance around him *like frolicking puppies and apparently they consider him a mad magical genius of sexual technique and boast about that, too. But can a slave* really *consent even if she does* say *yes?*

The table held several brand-new saddles copied from the ones they'd brought; they'd made dozens by now, besides the ones they'd sent down to Josephus in Sirmium where he advertised them by gift giving. More precisely they were copied painstakingly from the *disassembled* one provided by Fuchs. Though the complete ones had helped by showing what it was supposed to look like when finished, with sewing and lacing and gluing and nailing done.

For once, something *besides wheelbarrows worked right away and first time. Even fitting them to the horses—a couple of standard sizes handles that, usually.*

Sarukê was riding one of *her* horses with its new gear to show it off to the visitors and encourage sales; she owned four mounts herself, and treated them somewhere between a doting mother with her kids and a car enthusiast with a vintage Lamborghini.

Romans often liked horses and were usually proud of a good one. Evidently Sarmatians *really* liked horses, and accumulated them just as much as they could, as if they were money in and of themselves. Among Sarmatians, they *were*...and they were the bank you kept your money in, too, and the best of all possible status symbols.

And horses were what they really, *really* enjoyed stealing; it was the nomad national sport. Sarukê reminisced about it occasionally, like someone remembering playing soccer when they were young, only with a lot more violence.

Sarmatians collected scalps, too, and hung them from their horse tack as boastful mementos.

Sort of like blond Lakota.

Sarukê had taken to the new gear like a duck to water as well, though occasionally she visibly had to remind herself not to bend her legs back at the knee to grip the barrel with feet and shins. Right now she'd just finished a series of obstacles and leaps, and came trotting back near where the table rested; her rather hawklike face was grinning from ear to ear, not least because the trotting gait especially was so much easier with stirrups. Without them the up-and-down motion meant smacking your buttocks and other sensitive nether parts on the horse, hard, unless you kept a tight grip with your thighs and used the muscles there to cushion it.

So the Prof wants Mark and me to learn to ride. I see why. I don't think I could handle a litter with slaves. I just don't like riding. Or horses, much. Too big and strong and stupid for my taste.

With an earsplitting whoop Sarukê snatched up a lance standing point down in the dirt, couched it underarm and rode at a target, leaning forward with her feet braced in the stirrups as she galloped. Paula's eyebrows went up.

From what she'd read before and seen since getting here, cavalry here and now didn't use lances that way. They mostly used their spears in an arm-powered stabbing motion. Some of Sarukê's people did use long lances; they were called a *contus* by the Romans who'd copied them, which meant "barge pole." But they were used at moderate speeds, gripped nearly at the balance point with both hands in a thrusting motion of the arms, more like a pikeman sitting on a horse than the King Arthur tournament stuff Sarukê was doing.

This . . .

Crack!

The lance point smacked into the chest-high circle of wood on the end of a pole; it wheeled around the pivot, and she was past it *fast*, letting the lance turn in her hand to pull it free. One of the better-dressed visiting strangers—who might well be a retired cavalryman from his bandy-legged looks—shot to his feet with a complex oath, his eyes nearly bugging out of his head.

The Villa Lunae men nudged each other with proprietary smug grins. They generally got a little when a saddle was sold, and it was turning into a nice *bonne bouche*. Eventually other craftsmen would be able to copy them, but they intended to make hay while the sun shone.

Then Sarukê stabbed the point down, flipping a turnip up into the air; before it had reached the apogee of its curve she'd dropped the lance, drawn her sword and bisected it neatly on the way down, leaning far over in the saddle to reach it.

That had all the Romans watching who hadn't seen it before murmuring in surprise. You just couldn't do that with their gear, because it required throwing your weight on a foot. Then she came back at a gallop, between a double row of posts set at varying heights, each with one of the root vegetables on it, and—

What was that old jingle? She slices, she dices, she julienne-fries, Paula thought as the whetted metal blurred too fast to really see.

It was pretty, if you didn't think about what it would be like with human targets, sprays of blood and occasional detached bits flying. There were more whistles and gasps at the way the Sarmatian could throw the whole weight of her body into the cuts, not just the action of arms and shoulders, and twist whip fast from one side to another, and the greater reach.

Filipa was grinning too as she turned back from watching Sarukê, and the maids put lunch on the table. There was one set for the estate staff and hangers-on and visitors down at the other end beyond the saddles and a smaller but more elaborate one for the Americans.

Filipa's expression turned into a frown of puzzlement as the two girls winced back very slightly from her smile, lowered their eyes, did their bobbing curtsy-like thing, and disappeared back up the pathway to the *domus* faster than they'd walked down, the skirts of their long tunics flying around their ankles.

The men looked after them, mostly puzzled too. Why hurry back to where they'd be given more work? Then they chuckled at something one of the older set said sotto voce, with a stabbing motion of two fingers, and fell to dividing the goodies in the baskets. It was mostly bread and jars of oil for them, goat cheese and pickles, but with some cold meat and fruit—the ones from the estate might be slaves, but they were all above the common ruck of unskilled field labor.

Events with horses evidently bred a certain cross-class camaraderie, too, because the visitors pitched in as well. And someone was passing around a flask of *superwine*. People who'd been raised on wine tended to get a bit tiddly on first exposure to the distilled stuff, which could be useful in a bargain.

"What *is* it with the maids here, Paula?" Filipa said in English, taking out the bundle intended for her.

They'd managed to get the kitchens going on things like ham sandwiches and BLTs—the earliest tomatoes were coming ripe and they were diverting a precious few from seed production since it looked like they'd yield better than expected. Paula took one at her wave and a hard-boiled egg in her other hand, and dipped it into the little pile of salt wrapped in a twist of rag. The tomato was incredibly nostalgic.

Lady Julia had exclaimed with delight when she got a bit, too.

And this egg tastes free range, all right. Watered wine with everything, though, what I'd give for a good old Coke Zero, or a diet Dr. Pepper! And I miss mayonnaise on the BLT. Mayonnaise we could do, when we have time. A decent beer occasionally would be nice . . . we are growing hops. . . .

Filipa went on: "I swear to God, eighty percent of the maids and whatnot treat me like I've got rabies and might bite, and the others . . . am I misreading the signals? Because they seem to be *flirting* with me, or trying to in a sort of sidelong-glance, little-coy-smile, fluttering-eyelashes, sway-of-the-butt way."

Paula felt a laugh bubbling up. Filipa wasn't anything like the clueless dork at personal stuff that dear Mark was, but sometimes...

Still, we've gotten a lot closer. We're really friends now, because there's no choice. So I really do have to tell her.

"Ah...it's the way you dress, Fil."

The other woman looked down toward her riding breeks and the bloused-up green-and-blue tunic that covered them, falling to just below her knees through the sword belt.

"I *feel* like I'm wearing a housedress, or a giant's baggy T-shirt over spray-on bicycle shorts, only made out of chamois leather? Camel-toe territory, if it weren't for the loincloths, I'm glad the tunic covers things up most of the time. Buddha and Jesus on a bicycle built for two, but I miss real underwear. And tampons..."

Paula sighed; she did too. Rags were incredibly awkward and messy. The dried moss the slave women used was even more so.

And for a hundred thousand years it was just a woman's problem and therefore not important. But on to the matter at hand:

"Well, for starters, they think you're gay. Not the way they'd put it, but pretty much what they mean by what they'd say."

Filipa shrugged. "Well, I *am* gay...lately. But hell, I'm *riding* all the time. I *can't* wear what you've got on."

Her face went bleak for a second, remembering someone left behind in 2032...and under a rain of fusion bombs. Then she visibly put it aside, as Paula did the thought of her fiancé, and her parents who'd been so proud when she was accepted at Harvard...

They'd quickly developed what amounted to a taboo about discussing that.

Probably the example of our Stern, Silent Spartan Stoic Suck It When You Suffer Repression Is Good For You, You Wussie Prof Artorio' the Cowboy General. S,SSSSIWYSRIGFY,YW + SPQR.

Instead Filipa forced a smile and waggled a finger at Paula:

"And don't you dare use the dread acronyms LUG, BUG and GUG! Anyway, I thought that wasn't a big deal here? Antinoüs was Emperor Hadrian's boyfriend, and after he died the emperor went full throttle and had him declared a *God*, for God's sake. Named a city after him, too! That's only two emperors back, about thirty years. But you did the sex-and-gender stuff a lot more than I did, my area was more economics and technology and how they were conceptualized."

Paula sighed again; this time at trying to convey a specialty...
not to mention the sometimes painful modifications actually being
here had made in some of her most cherished theories.

"It's not a big deal for *men*. What's important there is who
sticks it into who, not what orifice gets used. Who's pitching and
who's catching, all tied up with the class system, age, whether or
not you're an adult Roman citizen—who only pitches, officially—
and all that good shit. The Roman Empire's an autocracy, an
aristocracy, an oligarchy, but most of all it's a phallus-ocracy.
It's the Kingdom of the Dicks, here, in *every* sense of the word."

Filipa rolled her eyes. "*Hell*, yes. It reminds me of biker gangs
or convicts in a penitentiary that way, some of the things I've
seen. The Greeks were even worse, of course, if I remember my
courses. And if the courses were on course. So, the maids?"

"So, as far as the *men* here are concerned it's not really sex
at all if there's no dick involved. What women do without them
is an icky-poo repulsive inversion of their sacred Gods-defined
penetrative role, or maybe funny, or possibly a fun kink to think
about, but it's not really *serious*. They just assume it's all dildoes,
anyway, mostly. Dick-fixation-in-operation, to get poetic."

"But why are the maids *scared* of me?"

"Well, it's the clothes again. In local terms, you're not just
signaling that you're gay, you're signaling that you're very, very
butch, too. Really, seriously, hard-ass butch. Role-playing stuff.
And from what I've heard...I talk to the women a lot more
than the rest of you do..."

"Well, they're the ones who do textiles."

"Yes, they are and they *do* talk to me now. And upper-class
stone butch types here, there aren't many but it does happen
occasionally, tend to...ummm...imitate the way their men act.
And the men here are dicks about sex, the *average* is way worse
than any but the worst back home. Especially when it's upper-
class man to lower-class woman, but maybe that's just because
the women I've been talking to are slaves."

"But why—"

Paula put down her sandwich, even the tomato taking second
place, and leaned forward.

"Fil, those maids"—she pointed to their now-distant figures—
"are *slaves*. Actual, buyable and sellable and whipable *slaves*.
You're free, you're a guest of their owners, you're connected to

mysteriously powerful people. *If you put the make on them they wouldn't* dare *say no.* So they're sending *please, please don't* vibes and avoiding you as much as they can."

"Euuw!" Filipa said, making a disgusted face and looking as if she'd like to spit out her mouthful of ham-and-cheese sandwich for a moment.

"And you're not only free and rich and well connected, you've got weird arcane knowledge too, maybe you're a sorceress who could make their hair drop out and their toenails split. The flirty ones are likely...a lot of them...thinking of what they could get out of it if they caught your eye, not your winsome charm and exotic good looks."

"Euuw all over again. Euuw, euuw. Euuw squared, cubed and to the tenth. Look, could you, just, oh pass the word that I'm *not* La Belle Dame Sans Merci and they don't have to worry?"

"I'll try."

Changing the subject, Paula jerked her chin at Sarukê as she picked up her sandwich again.

"That girl there is putting on quite a show."

"She's a natural, and she's enchanted with what she can do with the new gear!" Filipa said, probably happy to talk about something other than colliding misread signals, and showing genuine enthusiasm. "She makes me feel like I'm seven and just got on my first pony, too! I swear she can read a horse's mind and communicate with them telepathically."

A grin. "And I finally figured out who she reminded me of."

Mark Findlemann's jaw dropped as he picked up the seal cutter's work.

His office was in one of the rooms fronting the first story of the outer courtyard. That meant it was reasonably spacious, had good light, and looked out on the reflecting pool and the banks of flowers and fancifully pruned bushes, and was only a single staircase from his bedroom suite above. There was a *scent* of flowers, and he'd had a desk made and bookshelves...

"It is work that requires great skill, but now it is finished, sir!" the man said. "Twenty-four seals...punches, did you call them? In hard brass!"

He was forty or so, but looked older—and the broken veins in his nose and the slight trembling in his hand showed why he'd been willing to leave Vindobona and travel to someplace as deeply rural as the Villa Lunae. That and how gaunt he'd been when they started out, and how they'd had to pay to get his tools out of hock in a pawnshop.

Ah. And Josephus said it was sheer luck there was a seal cutter passing through Vindobona at all... and that there were only two in Carnuntum, which is twice Vindobona's size and the provincial capital and neither of them would be interested. It's a big-city skill and we were in the sticks. The equivalent of a town on the Mexican border in Arizona Territory in 1911.

The seals were actually well done, and precisely the right size for *capitalis quadrata* print on paper... except...

"I said the *impressions* the stamps made had to be reversed! So the *type* we cast in the impressions would print correctly."

His voice rose to a shout. "Like a seal!"

Seals were pressed into wax, or sometimes into lead; they were personal identifiers. That made them exactly like type-metal letters you used in a printing press. Stamps, on the other hand, were punched into soft copper to *make* the matrix for type, by enclosing them and pouring in a molten lead-tin alloy.

Spurius...

And never was a man named better!

...had managed to carefully listen to his description of what he wanted and done it precisely *backward.*

Mark had a sudden flash of picking up the inkstand from his desk, leaping over it, and smashing it into the man's face. Over and over and over and over...

He shuddered, feeling slightly nauseous. That was *not* like him.

Spurius looked at him and stumbled backward. Tears began to run down his cheeks into the grizzled stubble on his cheeks. Mark stood... which was a bit of a mistake, because the man was short by Roman standards and Mark was very tall by those same standards...

And I must look like an ax murderer in prospect. Because by the smell he just pissed his loincloth.

Spurius collapsed onto the floor, sobbing. Mark dropped his face into his hands until his breath was nearly back to normal. Then he stood, carefully navigating around the puddle of sobs on the floor, and went to the door.

The equivalent of a footman stood outside it—young and

strong looking, with his arms crossed on his chest, in a plain good white tunic. His feet were bare; servants didn't wear shoes or sandals indoors, not in summer at least.

"Master?" the man said.

I really don't like being called master *that way,* Mark thought, and composed his voice to a flat neutral tone.

"Take Spurius here back to his room. Search the room and remove any wine or superwine...oh, and his tools. Have someone stand outside the door at all times. He's to be allowed all the food and water he wants—the water should be mixed before it's taken in, no more than one-part-in-seven wine. Don't let him out unless he's dying. Bring him here tomorrow after breakfast."

Romans used chamber pots, so he wouldn't have to be let out to the latrines. And he wasn't so drunk he wouldn't be conscious and reasonably sober by then; it wasn't quite noon yet, anyway.

The slave ducked his head. "At your command, master," he said cheerfully.

Then he walked into the room and hauled Spurius to his feet.

"Come with me, please, sir," he said.

The words were respectful, but the tone wasn't, nor was the firm grip he took on the man's tunic and arm as he frog-marched him out.

A rich man's slave told to manhandle a poor freeman would do so without hesitation, and could be confident he wouldn't be called to account for it, given the way the Roman class system worked. A slave was an extension of his master's will, and hence in a sense *was* the master in relations with outsiders when obeying orders. They were often used as impromptu muscle.

It would have been a different story if Spurius wasn't a penniless pleb with no family or patron...not to mention a drunk... of course.

Mark went back to his desk and sat staring at nothing for a while. Then he blew out a sigh, and picked out the usable letters Spurius had done, the ones like A and H and I and T that were laterally symmetrical. They'd decided to use modern English textual conventions, rather than the run-together Roman style of cursive. After a number of surprised local literates had remarked on how it made things faster to read.

"Those I can use," he said to himself. "All nine of them."

They had the type metal, that hadn't been hard; lead and tin and antimony had low melting points. They could start on casting the type; you needed a lot more than one example of each letter anyway, and it would give the trainees experience.

Then he pulled a book over, opened it to where the straw he'd inserted rested and pulled two sheets of paper out of the desk drawer. At least the paper project was showing *some* progress; it was coarse and a little fuzzy, but useable, and they could refine it by stages. One piece held his transcription of the chatbot's translation of the introductory astronomy text.

The other was going to be *his* translation. The AI *could* do a good translation, if you used the term literally. *He* could read the Latin and understand it. The problem started when you read it the way someone from this century...more than a thousand years before Kepler or Newton...would read it. To them it would be mystical gobbledygook, seasoned with words that just either didn't exist or didn't mean what the chatbot thought they meant, for a basic-level AI's value of "thought."

Oh, this is going to be six times longer because I need to use a paragraph every time there's something they don't have a word for, he decided, after an initial scan through. *It's easy enough to translate the books on horsemanship...with Fil helping out... or even the ones on farming with Jem if I don't have to* explain *concepts like soil nitrogen, just give instructions to be followed... but this...*

Twenty minutes later he put the pen down, looked at his ink-stained hand, and a page of crossed-out attempts, reached for his phone to check the time...

Paula's got it, and the Prof was right—I couldn't not *pull it out without thinking.*

Instead he rose, slapped ineffectually at his tunic—there were ink stains on that, too, fruit of his learning to use a dipped split reed as a pen—and walked out into the peristyle. Being careful on marble and tile because the traction of the sandals was entirely different from the sneakers he'd worn most of the time back home and he didn't want to do *another* ungraceful sprawl. Or another painful impact on his knee.

The sundial said it was between half past noon and one.

I'm going to knock off, get something to eat, and go talk to the others. It's been that sort of day.

✧　　✧　　✧

Paula looked up. Mark Findlemann joined them after wandering down the path, finishing off a chicken drumstick.

"How's the typesetting going, Mark?" Paula said.

"It's *up*setting typesetting, that's how it's not going. My seal cutter produced a marvelous set of stamps to make the molds for the letters...and got what I said about reversing them 180-degrees wrong, so they're useless."

Paula raised her brows. "Well, the ones that are—"

"Symmetrical, yes, *those* aren't useless. But for the rest he has to do it all again...and he was drunk and made a puddle and cried, he does that a lot, but he won't do *anything* but drink unless I'm standing over him with a sneer of cold command. I've never come closer to beating a man to death with an inkstand. So I tried to take a break by doing some translation while he slept it off."

"Didn't go well?" Filipa said.

Obviously, Paula thought, making herself not smile.

"Try finding a Latin word to describe the way gravity determines orbits—"

He mimed tearing out chunks of his hair, now closer cropped, along with his beard, the better to fight off over-friendly insect life.

"And the paper?"

"Now *that's* much better. Once we get the pulp mash right, we're still fiddling with that and right now it's only *sorta* right. And once we made some wire screens with the right size holes. And once I remembered Martin Padway's great concept."

Filipa grinned, and Paula tried to remember the book. She'd read it a long time ago, in a collection of SF classics, and mainly remembered the limited female cast.

He smiled. "Use clay to keep it from being *blotting* paper. Though to my sorrow I now know not just any old clay. It's cheaper than papyrus, if we're using it for writing, but paper towels—fuhgeddaboudit, too expensive for that. And before I fuhgeddaboudit, Fil—who reminds you of who?"

"Sarukê reminds me of an actor from back in the '80s."

"You're Gen-Z like me. Born in 2006, right? Not even Lord Artorius the Nobly Brooding and Seriously Somber's been around... had been around, you know what I mean...that far back. Born around the turn of the century, wasn't he?"

"December 19th, 1999, but you were *there* for the movie and you watched it too. Remember that party—the one where they started with the new *Conan: Blood of the Serpent* movie? Well, new three years ago?"

"Oh, yeah, that was pretty decent. Much closer to the real Howard stuff than most of them. The AI effects were spectacular, too. God, those crocodiles!"

Filipa nodded: "And then they worked their way back through all the different versions?"

Mark smiled reminiscently. "Ah, the undergrad days of wine and weed...and search streaming."

"But remember the *last* one that was on? The very first Conan movie with young Arnie in a horned helmet, James Earl Jones as Dr. Stygian Evil, and the Wheel of Pain...must have been about 4:30 in the morning, most people had passed out or left, but I remember *you* were still there. Sort of there. Your *body* was there, at least."

Mark frowned, then smiled as he snaffled a honey-and-nuts pastry from the basket.

"Yeah, by then it was days of wine, weed and *cheese*. Cheesy old movies, at least. God, that one was camp heaven, the true Gorgonzola of cinema."

He sniggered. "*Thorgrim is beside himself with grief! He raised that snake from the time it was born!* So?"

"Remember the one who played Valeria, the warrior woman who was Conan's love interest and dies in his arms and then did the heroic back from the afterlife thing to save him?"

"Yes! They actually took that from Howard, one of the few times in the flick. But it was Bêlit who did that, really. Though she and Valeria were both pirates in the Howard stuff and both knew Conan in the biblical sense—"

She pulled out her phone to cut off the building monologue, carefully putting it in the empty basket so the locals couldn't see it, made sure it was on *mute*, and said quietly:

"Sandahl Bergman, *Conan*, stills."

A tall blond woman with a sword appeared dressed in arty-looking camouflage paint and not much else, flicking through in multiple poses.

Mark brayed laughter and sprayed pastry crumbs. "Showing off your private porn stash?"

Both the women rolled their eyes, and Filipa added:

"Dismiss, shut down."

They could recharge them from the solar array, but it was a strict no-no to flaunt what would look outright supernatural. And they'd wear out eventually, anyway. It was still hard to remember not to whip it out to take a picture or look something up or just to check the time.

"Sandahl Bergman!" Mark said, when he'd finished coughing up bits of hazelnut. "You're right, she was a dead ringer for our very own Spectacular Sarmatian She-Samurai Swordswoman Sarukê... of the *Steppes*! Except Sarukê's a bit shorter and she's got more muscle. And wears lots of clothes all the time, dammit, I really wouldn't mind a look at the Buns of Steel. She's a literal *and* metaphorical hard-ass. I bet she could crack walnuts with one clench—"

Paula cleared her throat and he subsided. She hadn't seen the movie; she wasn't interested in *that* sort of archaeology, or metaphorically eating fifty-year-old cinematic cheese, whether she was stoned or not.

And I don't really enjoy that *much either... maybe because the damned Millennials do, usually.*

But there *was* a definite resemblance to the face and body that Filipa had brought up. She looked up at the rider cantering back toward them, sword held exultantly aloft for a moment.

That *did* look like a still from a Conan movie, or a generic fantasy cover. That sort of literature, if you could call it that, was something Filipa and Mark shared and she didn't. They used their rationed screen time to read it sometimes, and Mark was copying some out on his new paper when the struggle with Latin and Greek vocabulary got to be too much.

And doing Latin versions. Apparently it was fairly easy to translate *that* stuff.

Mark cleared his throat. "The Prof says that Josephus can get some officers of the auxiliary cavalry to come look, maybe in a couple of months. They'll probably be impressed."

Rapid footsteps made them glance up. An adolescent from the big-house staff stopped, panting, and he'd evidently run the whole way:

"The lord Josephus is returning, and with him our honored and esteemed master and lord, the excellent *eques* Sextus Hirrius Trogus! He comes early this year! They will arrive in no more than ten days! We are all to make ready!"

⇒ CHAPTER TEN ⇐

Villa Lunae,
Province of Pannonia Superior
September 12th, 165 CE

Hail *to the Chief!* Artorius thought.

And grinned behind an impassive mask of respectful attention as he watched the master of the Villa Lunae arrive, just after lunchtime on a fair day of winds and scattered cloud.

Well, this is a demonstration of relative status in action, he thought.

The owner's mother and sister and niece and some of their attendants and the *vilicus* bailiff had turned out to welcome Josephus and his deeply strange guests. That was mostly because the head of their family was in Josephus' debt both literally and metaphorically, and they knew it.

Grant the Romans something; they do *really feel an obligation, mostly.*

But for the owner and master, the entire labor force not doing something essential—like the cook and his assistants laboring...

Like slaves, he thought sardonically.

...for the evening's feast—were there. The farm laborers and craftsmen grouped outside the outer gate of the *pars urbana,* making obeisance and giving loyal cheers and being chivvied not to stand on any of the flowerbeds by the foremen; and also by the gardeners, who'd have to work overtime to repair any damage.

The ordinary household staff did the same from the porticos around the first courtyard, throwing flowers as well, their scent strong throughout the house; the inner circle of upper-level managerial servants, and the *vilicus*, were at the base of the steps leading up to the entrance to the inner courtyard; the two ladies and little Claudia were where they'd been when he arrived, with their immediate attendants behind them...except that this time he and the other Americans were grouped off to one side, and the nine-year-old was dancing from foot to foot in delight at seeing her indulgent uncle.

Some of the house servants are probably still panting and reeling from all-night cleaning and flower gathering.

The Americans were in fairly expensive gentlemen's and gentlewomen's day dress, including Filipa this time, and she hadn't made a fuss about it. It had all been done up by the ladies' seamstresses, for very moderate bribes; that was possible only because of the basic simplicity of Roman clothing, most of which just required rectangles of cloth sewn together. A household of this type kept plenty of high-quality cloth on hand.

The dress of the two American women included jewelry bought in Vindobona and Carnuntum by proxy over the last few weeks, though it was more discreet than what the master's mother and sister wore, and Filipa and Paula *weren't* wearing the lead-based face paints.

Dress and decoration was a serious status marker here, and if you wanted people to take you seriously...

Sextus slid off his horse outside the front gate; Artorius judged he'd stopped perhaps ten minutes ago to switch into a fresh tunic and have his valet do a quick brush down and hair combing... and the saddle he was using was one of the new-made modern ones sent down to Josephus in Sirmium.

The valet appeared beside Sextus as if by magic, draping his toga over the brilliant-white tunic with the two narrow purple stripes of an eques. Sextus strode forward carefully, left hand on the toga in an attitude Artorius had seen on ancient statuary, with the immediate flunkies—secretary, clerk, and so forth—following behind him; those would all be slaves or freedmen, and carried the emblems of their jobs, tablets and pens. One had a scroll case. The other dozen came behind, with a tough-looking trio of bodyguards bringing up the rear.

In his hometown, there would usually have been freeborn clients too, lending their patron countenance. Here there was only

Josephus, a step behind at his right hand and gravely deferential. He smiled with genuine pleasure when he caught Artorius' eye, and the American found himself responding in kind. The merchant was a friend worth having, and not only for pragmatic reasons.

More sonorous formality followed; family greetings took precedence, and then Josephus did the introductions.

"My profound thanks for your gracious hospitality, most excellent lord," Artorius said eventually, which was respectful but not servile.

Lay it on with a trowel might have been invented for this culture, and their minutely graduated instinct for class distinctions made the Edwardian English look like kibbutzniks.

Sextus was in his late forties, brown haired and going gray, with a beard rather like Josephus' except without the curls. His square face was a bit jowly and he was a bit heavyset by local standards, though he'd have looked trim enough in the twenty-first century. The slight extra weight was a status marker here too, for a middle-aged man. He had most of his teeth, displayed as he smiled graciously and inclined his head to a lesser degree, and he was about average height—

No, he's a bit above *average here, around five-eight. He was better fed and got more protein in childhood than most. He's giving me the eye because I'm six feet. Which is like being six foot six here.*

"On the contrary, perhaps I am in your debt, Master Artorius," he said cheerfully, which seemed to be his natural demeanor. "My good Josephus has shown me a number of remarkable things we owe you, the saddle with footrests not the least, and the nailed-on iron hipposandals. They are *much* better, especially when you ride on stone-paved roads. Your America must be a place of wonders!"

Their cover story was that they were political exiles from a *land beyond Hibernia* called America, now torn by a terrible war. It accounted for their various strangenesses, and was reasonably plausible, since the Romans had vague accounts of Britannic legends of fantastic realms out there. How they'd gotten from there all the way to the Danube frontier was left with even vaguer stories of overland travel after landing on the North Sea coast.

Plenty of Romans, particularly the upper classes, *did* travel. It wasn't easy, but it was easier right now than it would be again until the nineteenth century. Josephus had ended up two thousand miles in road distance from the place he'd been born, and he'd said Sextus had been to Rome and Athens and Alexandria.

"And you must be a trueborn son of Vulcan," Sextus went on; lame Vulcan was the deity in charge of crafts and engineering. "The useful engines Josephus describes would require divine inspiration. I would fear he exaggerates, save that I've never known him to do that before."

"Our guest is also a devotee of the muses, brother," Lady Julia said unexpectedly.

Artorius hid a start. They'd spoken, mostly in the villa's library, but only polite commonplaces so far.

Which is certainly more than I get from her mother, granted.

"He spends his free time among the books—the histories, the poets, and some of the Greeks," she said. "And so do his clients. Mistress Paula—"

What her Latin accent did to the name made him blink. They probably talked in the bathing suite the women used. To Romans, bathing wasn't really bathing without conversation, and when you were naked and sitting in the hot room informality was the rule.

"—says that he has had to ration their time there! And his own. Many and remarkable are the things he has introduced on the estate, too, of long-lasting value."

Sextus looked shrewd, if not on first acquaintance a mental giant; that showed in the glance he shot her, and the considering one at the Americans. Romans were proud of their engineering skills, but didn't exactly put the practitioners of those arts on a social pedestal except at the highest I-am-the-patron-build-me-X level. Literary cultivation was much more upper class.

"Our scholars greatly admire your poetry, your historians and other writers," Artorius said. "And those of the older Greeks. But alas, we do not have all the books from this Roman world that we might wish. Hence your library here is a revelation to us, a source of joy."

Which is gospel, and I did have to ration people, the American thought. *Myself included.*

The library here wasn't huge, mostly accumulated in the time of Sextus' great-uncle with some Julia had brought along because she was rather scholarly herself by local standards, but it had enough to make a Classicist howl at the moon. Or possibly fall down and gnaw the mosaics while foaming and gibbering.

The lost Homeric comic poem, *Margites*, just for starters, known to later ages only from a few quotes in other authors; *Palamedes* and *Alexandros*, by Euripides; and Aeschylus' trilogy about Achilles. Filipa had nearly burst into tears when she held the compendium of Sappho's poetry in her hands; only fragments had made it to the modern era and she had had to be restrained from sitting down right there and translating it all into English. On the Latin side, the complete works of Tacitus... Mark had nearly cried too when he found Claudius' histories of Carthage (though not that of the Etruscans), part of Sulla's memoirs and one of Asinius Pollio's histories.

He *had* danced an impromptu jig.

The Americans had read out the speech given in 42 BCE by Hortensia at dinner one night, passing it around from hand to hand; the one in which she pleaded successfully with the Triumvirs for amendments to the war tax imposed on wealthy women. He couldn't remember laughing that much since...

Well, since before I left Boston that last time.

And Ovid's single tragedy, the *Medea*...

The thought of really big libraries, of what they could find in Rome or Athens or Alexandria, was tantalizing beyond words—and for that matter, if they traveled, they could *see* Rome, see Trajan's Column with Trajan's statue on the top in Trajan's great forum in its full polychromatic gaudy glory... and that would only be fifty-three years old!

See the intact, carefully preserved Parthenon and Phidias' chryselephantine Athena and his Zeus at Olympia, and a thousand other things. *That* was almost too much to bear. Perhaps someday they could all play tourist.

"The distinguished Lady Julia, your sister, is gracious beyond words," Artorius said.

The pleasantries concluded with an invitation to tonight's dinner, which made him glad he'd insisted they all take lessons in formal banquet etiquette from others of the upper servants. And that they'd introduced molded beeswax candles; they gave better light than the oil lamps, and the candles didn't stink like the local ox-tallow tapers. Infused with a little lavender oil, they were quite nice and even Sextus' mother had unbent a little after her first experience of them.

Although wax is expensive as hell here. I think there's something in the books somewhere *about how you can extract some combs without destroying the hive in a modern setup. When we get time, when we get time...*

When the welcoming ceremony—ending with a short, gracious speech by Sextus—was over, and everyone dispersed, Josephus took Artorius aside. To the American's surprise and embarrassment, he caught him in a quick *embrazo* and formally kissed him on both cheeks. He had to pull the American's head down to do it.

"Your son Matthias continues to improve?" Artorius asked.

He'd had notes to that effect, at first brief and then incredulous with relief.

"My friend, my benefactor—it's already as if he was never ill, or nearly! And...I could see the shadow of Azrael's wings on his face when I arrived. He was dying, beyond all doubt, only days from it at most. Thin, haggard and unable to move, in constant pain; he did not even know his own father. But even with just the first dose of your medicine, he began to improve within hours!"

The local bugs have never met antibiotics and turn up their toes a lot faster than our sophisticated ones.

"The fever broke, he could recognize us, and whisper a little. Each day brought more."

His face shone. "Deineira sends this to you, with my approval."

That was his wife's name; apparently women of the Hellenized Jewish community in Antioch mostly took Greek names, at least for everyday use and in the circles Josephus and his family moved in.

Artorius opened the diptych and read: the letter was written on the wax in Greek cursive, a small, neat hand and easy to read, especially since his command of that language had shed its rust and improved while he was here. He was nearly back to the days when he'd kept a copy of Xenophon's *March Upcountry* alongside Marcus Aurelius' *Meditations* in his duffle on deployments, both in the original Greek.

His eyes widened a little as he read; it wasn't fulsome, but it was heartfelt. Apparently according to her he was a man of great virtue, a true friend, and—he wasn't quite certain what the next phrase meant, it seemed to be a phonetic rendering of Aramaic or Hebrew—now to be considered among their kinsfolk in blood, one to whom they owed aid and succor if he ever had troubles, always welcome beneath their roof, and concluded with an invitation to stay and dine with them whenever he was in Sirmium which she hoped would be soon.

"I am honored," he said quietly, and sincerely.

Josephus slapped him on the shoulder in friendly wise, breaking the tension of the moment.

"I said nothing to anyone—except her—of the medicine, and she is closemouthed when it counts. I know you have only a limited supply, and cannot replace it, and you would be plagued beyond belief if any knew of it. But the other things you told me, the boiled water with honey and sea salt, the soup and soft foods—they also helped. And I did tell others of *that* part; it has the doctors in Sirmium in an uproar, but it has saved lives, I can tell you—children and adults, men and women."

Artorius felt a flush of pride; there were human beings alive now who would be dead without him. Dysentery came in many varieties, but mostly it *killed* by dehydration, and loss of essential minerals. Or by perforation of the intestines, which could be softened by some forms of the disease. If you could avoid that and just keep the victim alive long enough, recovery was very likely.

Then his face grew a little grim. *It's good I've saved some lives, because I'm working to* end *a good many others. For the ultimate greater good, but...*

Josephus caught his mood, though not its precise cause.

"Ah, I am sorry, brother—I know you had dear children and a beloved wife of your own, from whom you are forever sundered."

Artorius shook himself; wallowing didn't help.

"That is not to be altered," he said. "The will of Fate."

"The Lord gives, the Lord takes, blessed be the name of the Lord. Let's prepare for this feast—though to tell you the truth, except for the honor of it I'd as soon eat sitting up, not lying on my belly like a snake."

The Jews of Antioch were Hellenized, but apparently Graeco-Roman dining habits were a partial exception, at least for Josephus' clan.

"At least Sextus won't expect me to eat the more forbidden things. Romans..."

"Not the most tactful of humanity, no."

"And tomorrow we show Sextus some of your marvels! He's anxious to see, and...he could be very helpful with those other matters we've discussed."

It would be interesting to talk books with Lady Julia at dinner, too.

In theory senators were supposed to be above trade, living from their estates and concentrating on public service. Which meant they engaged in it through proxies, often freedmen, and often with ruthless greed. *Equites* didn't have to be so finicky, and though most owned land some were men of business as well.

Sextus Hirrius Trogus was frankly interested the next morning when he saw a barrel being wheeled by in an *unarota*. Barrels were a Celtic invention, and employed far more widely in these northern, ex-Gallic provinces than around the Mediterranean, where clay *amphorae* were still more common. Though the lighter, stronger, cheaper wooden vessels were making inroads even there.

"More of your *superwine*?" he asked, licking his lips a little.

"Just so, Lord Sextus," Artorius said. "It improves in taste with storage in oak barrels."

So does wine, but one thing at a time.

They showed him the brick vats where pulp from straw and the reeds fringing the lake was transformed into something better than papyrus at less than half the cost, and the new spinning wheels and looms set up in the portico of the *pars rustica*.

The workers in both sites—still flustered—resumed their labors at his nod and command as they left each.

"Good thread, very good, and good cloth!" he said, examining the specimens of both he'd been given.

Spinning and weaving were a standard sideline on a rural estate and in many wealthy urban households too.

"And this *charta*, it is every bit as good as papyrus. Who would have thought it could be made from common substances, rather than by the gift of the *divus nilus* as it has for so many centuries?"

"Indeed, honored sir," Josephus said. "There will be markets for the thread and cloth even as is, and with well-dyed or bleached product, still more. The *paper* should move immediately, more so if anything. Egypt is a long way away, even for something as light as papyrus, and scraped boards are poor substitutes once you have a fair text to copy onto something permanent."

Sextus was even more pleased with the threshing machine, and chuckled as he exchanged a few words with a visiting neighbor who was obviously lusting for one himself with an almost physical passion. And he rubbed his hands when the foreman there told him how many modii of wheat had already been turned over to Josephus' wagons. Every bushel...

Every four modii, Artorius reminded himself...was a little something off the landowner's debt.

"Perhaps you have also forged a bronze bull to plow my lands without human labor!" he said with a laugh as they swung into their saddles. "Like Talos!"

Then he looked down at the stirrups. "By Epona and the Divine Twins, these make mounting and dismounting so much easier, to say nothing of steadying you in a sharp turn! Or sparing your backside and balls at the trot. I'm not as lively on my feet or in the saddle as I was when I was a young man and a military tribune in the Fourteenth; then I sprang into the saddle like a Sarmatian and galloped away without a second thought."

"Not quite Talos, my lord Sextus," Artorius said; mentally he crossed his fingers. "But we have something that will help in plowing your fields, yes."

We've tested it for a week now after it stopped breaking every time we tried it, but it wouldn't be the first time the failure mode appeared out of a blue sky! Thank God the soil here is a nice medium sandy loam and there aren't many rocks. I would purely hate to try and make a spring-loaded stump-jumper version of this.

They cantered down a dirt lane, hooves throwing up a little soil; the three men and four attendants for the Roman landowner...which smallish number was a compliment in itself, though in the country more informality was permissible. The air was coolly brisk but not chilly, and the verges were green from yesterday's rain.

"If you would, good Artorius, what was your standing in your home, beyond even far Hibernia?" the landowner said.

Which was a perfectly natural question for this time and place. He'd decided to answer it when it came with a slightly edited version of the truth.

"My family had an estate of about this size...though not so blessed with fertility, and it was our sole property, passed from father to son for many generations."

Which was perfectly true; the old ranch in the Panhandle was about the same size as the Villa Lunae's roughly ten square miles, and it was one hell of a lot drier and rockier. Which meant it was distinctly subeconomic, which was why the Vandenbergs hadn't relied on it alone for going on a century, since the Dust Bowl days when half the topsoil had departed by air for the East Coast. Now that his grandparents were dead—

Forget that. Everybody's dead. *Everyone you knew.*

"Many of my line also made a calling of war. In Latin, *centurion* would be the closest translation for what we did and the rank we held."

Which made it respectable; a senior centurion was of equestrian rank, either because he was born that way or promoted into it.

"I myself commanded a double century of our troops, about two hundred men, until I was badly wounded. Then having served the State, I followed my heart, and devoted myself to home life and my scholarship; my companions, who you met, are... were... students of mine."

Sextus wasn't surprised. The city of Athens in this era made its living pretty much as a university town, sort of the Boston of Greece. With genuine scholars in plenty, and young upper-crust Romans coming to put on some polish. Even women on rare occasions, though that was considered distinctly odd, eccentric, and not at all respectable.

"That did not spare them when war and strife overtook my homeland, and alas, we are now exiles who can never return. Indeed, so devastating was the war that little may remain of our native country. Perhaps nothing at all."

Sextus looked grave and nodded; but he also looked reassured. That background gave Artorius a social standing that made him suitable to acknowledge; it was the equivalent of being an *eques* of a rank about two or three notches down from his. Of course, non-Roman rank didn't matter as *much*.

"Yours must be a wise people," he said.

"We have some useful arts that are not known here," Artorius said modestly, and nodded to a cross-braced timber framework going up on a low rise nearby.

"For example, that. It is a way of powering a mill by wind, like the sails of a ship, but made to turn by the wind in a great *wheel* of sails. That turns a wooden column—as you saw with the threshing engine."

"Like a watermill?"

"Very much, but without the need for a stream."

Sextus laughed again. "Water may be short here sometimes, but rarely a wind!"

True enough. Up in the twenty-first, this part of Austria was wind-farm central.

"And the windmill can grind grain, pump water, saw wood or stone, do the fulling and pounding of woolen cloth..."

"*Mehercle*!" the landowner said, swearing by Hercules. "That could be very useful."

"Or press oil."

Sextus chuckled at that too; he'd been getting more and more cheerful as he saw what the strangers had done with his land and workers...and very nearly for free, from his point of view.

"*Heu!* Alas! It's too cold here for olives."

Artorius reached into a pocket and brought out a twist of cloth around a double handful of seeds from the very first sunflowers to come ripe, shelled and toasted and tossed with a little salt. Sextus sampled the snack, and nodded.

"Tasty!"

"Yes, lord, but if they are crushed and pressed, they are also rich in oil. Much like olives. And we planted sufficient to get enough seed, which means much more can be planted next year like the *corn* you saw, and the *potatoes* and *tomatoes*. We call them *sunflowers*...helianthus in Greek, from their appearance when they bloom. The oil can be used for the same purposes as the oil of the olive, and the crushed pulp left over will fatten livestock of any sort—pigs and cattle best of all."

The taste *as opposed to olive oil? Well, I stretched a point there by implication. At least it's good for you, and it would do that oiling and scraping thing just as well. Or make good soap when we get around to that.*

"*Mehercle!*" Sextus said again, more emphatically.

This estate produced bacon and hams and smoked and salted pork for sale as a profitable sideline to grain, wine and wool, rather like the horses. They didn't fatten the pigs on grain, though; that would be fantastically expensive. Mostly they roved the woods, and then were finished up on waste products like pomace from the wine presses if they were given any extra feeding at all.

Romans here on the Danube used olive oil in quantity, particularly the affluent ones. But distance from the Mediterranean...

specifically from the Istrian peninsula in the upper Adriatic, which was where the oil here mostly came from...made it expensive enough to hurt a bit, and pig lard just wasn't suitable for some of the uses. The landowner looked over at Josephus.

"I think there could be a large market for the oil, lord," he said judiciously. "And it is a late crop, from what our friend Artorius says. Planted at the right time it will be ready after the wheat and before the vine harvest; then the seeds can be stored in baskets or sacks, and the oil in barrels, for sale later. The oil keeps well, and the seeds even better, so it can be pressed at leisure when other tasks permit. Cattle and pigs can be grazed on the fields after the seed is taken, manuring them. While the new grain, the *corn*, can be planted so as to ripen *after* the grapes."

Sextus laughed again. "Better and better!"

One of the drawbacks of slavery—from the owner's point of view—was that slaves ate every day whether you had anything for them to do or not; you couldn't turn them off and park them in a shed like a tractor and save on running costs. And agriculture was necessarily seasonal, so anything that stretched out the harvest season or found another profitable product that didn't conflict with the labor needs of established lines was *highly* desirable.

They came to one of the big square fields; this one was in fallow, more or less...but many Roman landowners and farmers including Sextus sowed lupins and medic, clover and alfalfa into such, following the advice of the agricultural writer Columella, who'd penned as much in his *De re rustica* a century ago, which was a compendium of best-practice advice.

There was a well-used scroll set of it in the library, and the *vilicus* had read it. The title meant: *Of Country Things*.

That gave the field a certain look of scraggly fertility, and provided both good grazing and an increase in the yield of crops when it was plowed again because of the nitrogen which legumes fixed from the air. Fortunately the ground here usually had limestone in its makings, and was about neutral rather than acidic, which let clover and its relatives flourish.

Romans wouldn't know soil nitrogen if it nibbled on their toes, but they're pragmatists, and they can be observant. You don't have to know why *something works, though that helps. Just that it does work.*

Jeremey McCladden was there, looking only slightly nervous

as he stood beside a broad strip of plowed land, smooth and harrowed as well, amid a small clump of estate workers and the *vilicus.*

The visitors swung down from their horses and walked over to him, the earthy-damp smell of the turned soil growing stronger, with a tang from the manure spread on the field before the plowing to feed the next crop of wheat or barley. Birds were flying over it, stooping to strike at exposed earthworms. The stems of lupines and clover and alfalfa...and grass, and weeds...stuck out of it like patchy morning stubble on a man's face.

A triple yoke of oxen were there too, and a piece of equipment that looked like a two-wheeled cart at first glance. It did have two spoked wheels, joined by a piece of timber, which sported a bicycle-type seat on a pole and a board to rest the feet. A simple lever arrangement lifted or lowered a thick bar of metal-strapped ash wood, and on that were mounted two moldboard plows, made from blocks of carved beechwood covered in thin iron beaten to shape and polished, and preceded by iron disks turning freely on projecting straps and pins.

"Take it away, Jeremey," Artorius called.

Jeremey called an order to the man at the head of the ox teams as he mounted the riding plow. Sextus was already looking interested, because the draught team's rig—six oxen in three successive pairs, with each yoke pulling on a common chain—was little known here, where pairs of oxen on either side of a yoke pole were far more common. When Jeremey engaged the lever, and the plows—which looked absolutely nothing like the standard simple ard type used on the light soils around here—sank into the soft moist earth and left twin furrows in their wake, his attention became very keen.

"*Mehercle!*" he said for the third time, and the most emphatic of all.

And his eyes went wider as he realized just how *fast* the two-furrow riding plow was going compared to what the simple instruments he knew could do, the oxen striding along at what the lumbering beasts used as a brisk pace. They virtually bulged when the disk harrow nearby swung into the plow team's wake, chopping the rough furrows into a good seedbed.

All much faster still with mules or horses, but one thing at a time. Even this way, it's at least three or four times faster than the same number of oxen the way they used to do it by cross-plowing, and it only takes two men instead of six. Call it seven or eight times the productivity per ox and per worker. Ditto for the seed drills compared to broadcast sowing by hand, and nice neat rows mean you can weed the growing crop with animal-drawn field hoes, so higher yields too.

Plowing was the most fundamental of all agricultural tasks here, and a symbol for all the others. Getting it done in timely fashion was absolutely crucial to yields, and after harvesting it was the most expensive single operation of the crop cycle in labor and gear.

"By Ceres and Demeter the Mother!" he said. "Though...alas, already it is possible to sow more grain than can be reaped."

Artorius bowed his head, letting a little of his inward grin leak out. They'd decided that McCormick reapers weren't doable right now, though the very first one had been built by hand by a blacksmith...a slave blacksmith in Virginia, at that, owned by McCormick the elder in the Shenandoah Valley almost exactly two hundred years before their...departure.

But—

"Your laborers don't use scythes to cut grain, do they?" he asked.

Scythes were another Celtic invention, and used more here in the north in lands formerly Gallic than they were further south, where the growing season was longer and animals didn't need as much stored fodder over the winter. Down there even cutting grass and clover was usually done with the short blade.

Sextus raised his eyebrows. "No, scythes would leave it scattered, like grass cut for hay. You can rake grass, but raking scattered grain stalks would lose a good deal of the yield from wheat or barley. Far too much to be practical."

"There is a simple and easy way to remedy that," Artorius said.

And described a cradle scythe. Which was simply a scythe with three or four light wooden fingers the same shape as the blade, fixed in a framework above the iron. They caught the cut stalks and the harvesters just tipped them out in a neat row to wait for the binders.

Sextus grasped the concept quickly, obviously visualizing it.

Type A again, Artorius thought.

"This is faster than the sickle, I suppose?"

"It takes more strength, but a good scythesman can harvest between two and three acres of wheat or barley a day with such, depending on how thick the grain stands. I have seen it done myself."

Only at county fairs and living-history exhibits, though, he thought. *It's* pure *Type A, even more than wheelbarrows. With a couple more weeks we could have done it* this *year, and it'll be easy to get enough made by next summer. Even if we have to buy or make more scythes, it's not rocket science.*

"By all the *Gods,*" the landowner said, glancing upward, obviously making mental calculations.

"You will need to train more of your workers to the scythe over the winter, though, excellent Sextus."

Who was obviously liking what his figuring told him. A good hand with a sickle could do a quarter to a third of an acre of grain a day. The difference gave the cradle scythe an advantage of nine times or better. And there was only a two-week window here to get small grains cut; any longer and every day increased the risk that either the stalks fell over, or the kernels fell out of the heads. Or more likely both. In this area, rain in harvest time was an occasional threat too, unlike the lands around the Mediterranean.

"This... all this... will increase the revenues of this estate by at least a fifth part! *And* lower the expenses. I can put more land in vines... the sweet wine made here sells very well..."

Josephus cut in. "And you have not seen it all yet, Lord Sextus. Perhaps you can increase the total by more than a third, when all is done, *and* reduce expenses by a similar amount."

At the landowner's questioning look, he amplified:

"You won't have to hire any harvest labor gangs, you can do it all with your own slaves or them and a few of your tenants working estate fields when they're not needed at home."

Hired harvest workers got high pay; two or three denarii a day and a small share of the crop as well as their food. And you needed a lot of them because the grain harvest meant your labor needs were suddenly five times what they were at other busy seasons; this estate usually hired over a hundred and fifty. That was a major outlay in cash and kind, the biggest single expense of whole crop cycle.

"And it could all be copied on your main properties near Sirmium, as well. That would take a few years, but..."

"But I would be the first to use all this!" he said, turning to Artorius and seizing his hand in both of his. "How can I reward you, my most welcome guest? I thought Josephus here was making an imposition at first, when he asked me to bid my *vilicus* obey you in all things, but instead he was conferring a great benefit!"

Then his face fell a little. Artorius spoke with intention to soothe; the man *was* cash poor right now, and he had to spend in a way appropriate to his family's standing to keep up appearances. Which was vital unless he wanted the sharks to scent blood in the water and close in.

Although Josephus was going to give the Americans a cut from the faster payments on his loan Sextus could make now, and a one-third interest in the paper workshop he'd have running near Sirmium by the spring, with workers from here as cadre—they'd be freedmen there. Artorius would be loaning him the money for that, too. His nephew Simonides was here learning, and would manage the new plant at first.

"I could not accept coin from you, noble Sextus Hirrius Trogus, after your kindly hospitality to me and mine in our bitter exile," he said, and saw a flicker of relief. "Your friendship, your favor, are all that I could ask."

"Spoken like a man of true antique virtue! They are yours," Sextus said heartily.

Josephus coughed discreetly, as he and the American had planned if things went well.

"Artorius and his followers *are* exiles, their homeland fallen and forever lost," he said. "I think that they might feel greatly reassured if Roman citizenship could be . . ."

Sextus smiled; that was something he could do with pull, not cash.

"I think that this can be arranged; I am an aedile of Sirmium, after all. There are other magistrates, yes, and legates, and this new provincial governor himself, who will listen to the words of the Trogii with respect and attention."

Meaning, I have favors I can call in; in Sirmium and with the provincial governor in Carnuntum, which is closer to this villa. He'll like doing a favor for an influential man, especially if it doesn't cost anything.

Citizenship wasn't as important now as it had been in the age of the Republic, but it was still far more important than it would become in a few generations, when it was extended to all free subjects of the Empire. Right now only somewhere between a tenth and a fifth of the total population held that status, much higher in Italy but rather lower here in the wilds of Pannonia. Except around the military bases where so many veterans settled; legionnaires were citizens to begin with, and auxiliaries were raised to that status on discharge, along with their wives and children.

Artorius thumped his chest with his right fist, a bit of histrionics that would be well received. Roman rhetoric relied heavily on gesture, and Josephus had been coaching him last night.

"I speak from my heart when I say that I and mine would feel the most profound gratitude for such a grant, noble Sextus Hirrius Trogus. Lasting gratitude."

Sextus made a gracious gesture. "Consider it done!"

"I will strive to be worthy of the honor, and to fulfill the duties and obligations of a citizen of the *rēs pūblica Rōmāna*," Artorius said.

"And speaking of which," he went on smoothly, after an exchange of further mutual compliments as the two-furrow riding plow grew smaller in the distance and the four-disk harrow followed in its wake, "you are … of course … aware of the deplorable banditry and menace of the Marcomanni and Quadi? My friend Josephus has told me of their lawless defiance of all decent behavior and their own sworn word as Roman allies, and how it threatens us here in the rich and valuable province of Pannonia Superior. Us and our neighbors."

Sextus' face flushed. "Yes!" he snapped. "The emperors were … were *badly advised* to strip the Danube frontier of so much of its garrison!"

Hastily: "But the troops of our province … and our neighbors … have fought with valor and skill in the east, and Imperator Caesar Lucius Aurelius Verus Augustus will doubtless win still more victories, and the detachments will return covered in glory to chastise the barbarian scum."

Josephus and Artorius nodded gravely; that was ass covering, of course, but they'd anticipated that Sextus, like most of the local landholders, was deeply unhappy that the defenses of Noricum and the two Pannonian provinces and Moesia near the Danube delta were being cut to the bone. From an emperor's perspective the problem was that nearly all the Roman army was deployed to frontier provinces facing threats. To reinforce one place, you had to withdraw men from others where they were also needed. Or raise fresh units, which was slow and cost heavily.

Artorius spoke soothingly:

"I can see that our divinely favored emperors have no more loyal follower than you, Lord Sextus."

Which translated as: *We won't fink you out to the Frumentarii.*

Who were the Roman Empire's combination of the CIA and FBI, with a bit of KGB thrown in; headquartered in Rome and run by the *Princeps peregrinorum,* a high-ranking officer of the Praetorian Guard, but with widespread agents and tentacles. Whispered rumor made them even *more* widespread, of course.

"But it is the duty of every citizen—a status which is now assured to me and my followers, praise the Gods and your generosity, noble Sextus!—to assist the State. I have something here that is rather more important in that respect than better plows and looms or mills driven by the wind. Or even better saddles and nailed iron shoes for the cavalry."

Sextus blinked—he evidently hadn't thought of the military implications of better horse gear yet—then narrowed his eyes at the promise of something *more.*

"Indeed?"

"Yes. We have kept this in the forest of the hills, to still wagging tongues and shield it from prying eyes. There are rumors in plenty already."

"Sir, we must ask you to come alone. Only your eyes should see what is to be seen," Josephus said.

He looked at the merchant, and then nodded with his eyes narrowed and told his escorts to wait here.

They rode northwest toward the higher ground; the cool shade of the forest closed over them after a half hour, and yellowed leaves scattered before the horses' hooves.

In a clearing nearly a mile into the woods were a dozen sheep, bleating uneasily because they were tethered to stakes and they could smell predators. Among them were German-style shields propped against scarecrow figures also wearing helmets. Some of them were also draped in mail shirts, though those were expensive. And in the center, on a thick stake driven into the soil and rising to waist height was a bronze sphere about the size of a man's head. A cord rose from a plug in the top, and dangled down the side.

"First, let me assure you that there is nothing here that smacks of sorcery," Artorius said.

Josephus nodded vigorously. "My lord will know that my people's Law and our God, blessed be Him, strictly forbids any such," he said. "Even something as innocent in the eyes of others as taking auguries is forbidden to us."

Sextus glanced between them and nodded slowly. Jews *were* forbidden such, though of course not every one of them was averse to breaking those rules.

"Certainly nothing I have seen so far is more than skill in the mechanic arts," he said.

Behind an earth bank about sixty feet from the stake holding the bronze sphere was a table, and on that were a number of objects covered in cloths. They dismounted, and Artorius glanced up at the sky.

No rain today, thank God, he thought; though there were clouds, and the dry part of the summer was coming to an end soon.

"Here we have saltpeter, sulfur and charcoal," the American said, indicating bowls and removing the covers. "These are taken in a certain ratio. Then they are ground very finely while damp, mixed together, and pressed into cakes to dry, which gives us this."

The result looked like a slab of shale about the size of a candy bar, or dark chocolate itself.

"That is then broken and ground and sieved—very carefully! The result is this, which my folk call...thunderpowder."

It was heaped up in a bronze bowl, like coarse black cornmeal, about enough to half fill a teacup.

A candle in a perforated brass holder burned not far away, with a pile of splints beside it. Artorius lit one, and offered it to Sextus.

"If you will drop this into the bowl, most noble sir...at arm's length, and please, step back rapidly..."

WHUMP-WOOSH!

Sparks and flame shot into the air with a hiss. Sextus jumped back further in alarm, brushing at his tunic where specks smoldered. At first he looked stunned, then he smiled in delight.

"That was like the volcanoes I've heard of!" he said. "And I can smell the burnt sulphur, yes, just as you said."

Then he looked quizzically at the American; he knew he hadn't come to this remote spot to be shown an amusing novelty.

"But this is a weapon, you said as well? Something we can use against the Germanii?"

"Yes, lord. See here."

He indicated two bronze half spheres. They were lined with lead balls the size of double-ought buckshot or an 8mm pistol bullet, held in a matrix of dried resin.

"These halves are crimped together and the powder is poured in through this hole at the top, and tamped down. When the sphere is nearly full, finer powder goes on top, and then a plug is inserted—"

He held it up.

"With this special linen cord, soaked in dissolved saltpeter and dried, the inner end long enough to bury itself. It will burn at a steady rate...more or less...so you can calculate how long it will take; that is why the cord is marked at set intervals, so that you may select how much time until it burns through the plug. When the thunderpowder is contained, if it burns it presses with great violence against the inside. Shall I show you, noble Sextus Hirrius Trogus?"

"By all means," the man said.

"I must warn you not to look over the earthen bank after the fuse is set alight," Artorius said. "I will light the fuse, as the cord is called, and then I will retreat here with all speed."

He took a burning splint and walked around the earth bank and toward the ball on its wooden plinth, covering the flame with his other palm. One of the sheep bleated at him with an appeal in its eyes...

Look, you dumb wooly bastard, you were getting the chop anyway this fall, he thought. *This will be quicker than the usual way.*

He touched the splint to the match cord, then retreated sharply; he could see the two men looking over the top, their heads hidden below eye level. When he'd vaulted over the top he grabbed them both by the backs of their tunics and hauled them down and jammed his forehead into the heaped earth.

CRACK!

Sextus opened his mouth to protest, but the whine of lead bullets overhead stopped him, and he gulped slightly as he realized what had chewed at the dirt and thrown some on him. Then he walked slowly around the little berm and over to the circle of destruction. The sheep were all dead; those closest to the explosion had *spattered*. The landowner was a hunter, and used to dead animals there and on his estates; for that matter, he'd been going to gladiatorial shows all his life too, and he'd seen some field service as a tribune. The savagery with which the lead balls and the blast effect had ripped into the carcasses still shook him a little.

He examined a shield, riddled in half a dozen places, collars of white splinters standing up around each hole in the planks on the inside. Then he quietly took up a helmet from fifty feet away, pierced likewise in three places, and a tattered shirt of mail.

"You are right, Artorius," he said in an even tone, showing suitable *gravitas*. "This is a weapon of terrible power! How could men fight with such?"

"I was wounded by something similar," Artorius replied. "My closest comrade, dearer to me than a brother, had his legs torn off by the same...we call them a *bomb*. I myself was six months healing, and it was a year before I could walk without a limp."

Sextus shook his head. "If I hadn't seen what was left after a raid by the barbarians, I could *almost* pity them," he said. "But I have, and I do not, for they are a plague upon Earth's bosom. So perish all Rome's enemies. *Parcere subiectis et debellare superbos!*"

That was a quote from Virgil, and summed up the Empire's operating code: *Spare the obedient subject and beat hell out of the proud rebel.*

Then that practical shrewdness returned to his gaze.

"But how will you...oh! A ballista could throw these!"

"A *carroballista*," Artorius said.

That was the name of the light field catapult. Most legions had scores of them.

"Of an improved type. I would need perhaps six veterans used to the making and using of such engines; the rest of the crews I could recruit here, from the tenants, or freeing slaves as needed, for which of course I will pay market price."

Sextus nodded. Employing freedmen in things military was unusual but not unprecedented in times of emergency. Doing it with slaves would be much more likely to arouse hostility...and due to the innovations, he suddenly had something of a labor surplus here.

"And I will need fewer hands here next year, anyway," he mused. "Unless I put them to something new."

"If the Marcomanni and Quadi stay on their side of the river, nothing further need be said. If they do not...well, by next spring, I could have perhaps half a dozen ready, with many such thunderballs to throw. Have I your permission, sir?"

Sextus nodded firmly. "Yes. Yes, you do. This province is my home, the home of my family and my kin, it holds the ashes of my ancestors for many generations, the temples of my Gods, and the hope of my descendants. It is their inheritance. I will not see it put to slaughter and the torch if it can be prevented—and this is the very gift of the Gods to defend us. You have my patronage and my protection in this."

He shook himself. "I will stay for the *vinalia*, but I will write immediately to secure what you need. As you say, there is only so much time between now and next year's campaigning season."

The *vinalia* was the celebration of the wine harvest, held considerably later here than in Italy, and sacred to Venus and Bacchus.

"You and I and good Josephus here will consult on what is needed; the wine festival will give me a reason to linger here if any ask."

"*Taubrą!*" Gunþiharjaz spat behind the hazel bushes that concealed him.

Which meant *sorcery* in their language.

His companion reached over and clamped a hand over his mouth, then hissed softly in his ear.

"*Silāþiz!*"

Which meant *we must be silent*, spoken as a command.

He was obeyed. Alarīks was the elder of the two brothers, with the right to tie his hair in the warrior's knot on the right side of his head, having killed his man. Gunþiharjaz was just old enough to carry a spear...though in fact they both had their long light-brown hair in plain single braids falling down their shabby tunics right now, like mere peasants, and their legs were bare, like thralls.

They had crossed the river to scout, wandering and doing what work came to hand like poor gangrels and listening for news that might have meaning for the war band. He had some Latin, his brother less, but they both spoke passable Gaulish, learned from their mother who was of an old Boii chiefly family. People just assumed they were wanderers from some backwoods farm in the Roman province where folk still spoke that old tongue, as many countryfolk did.

The troll stench of the magic weapon drifted their way. The Romans, the fat landowner and the Jew and the evil wizard—who he noticed immediately had the look of a dangerous man of his hands, as well, something you could sense—talked for a while, then mounted their horses with the odd-looking saddles and rode back down from the hills.

Alarīks led his brother over to the place the lightning flash had struck, and the stench of burnt sulfur was stronger. Stronger than when Thunraz's hammer struck ironstone, which he'd whiffed once or twice—that was thought to be lucky. He didn't think this was. The sheep looked as if invisible spirit wolves or bear ghosts had ripped them apart.

"*Skōhslō!*" his younger brother said. "Evil demons!"

"*Wirsistaz taubrą!*" Alarīks replied in agreement. "Most evil sorcery! But rumors of sorcery were the reason we came here to this steading, remember. The Romans have many wizards."

"The *bragz* Ballomar our uncle must know of this," Gunþiharjaz said.

Alarīks looked at his brother's beardless, eager face.

If I send him back on his own, he won't travel two days without getting into trouble, getting into a fight, getting killed, he thought. *Perhaps...*

"We will ask for work here," he said. "That we may see more of this *wikkô*, this wizard, and bear word of it to the prince our kinsman."

It was the first time they'd tried that on a *villa*, as the Roman lords of broad lands called them, as opposed to ordinary farms.

"I have heard they hire outsiders, and they are starting to gather their grapes now," he went on.

His brother made a face. "I do not like working beside thralls," he said. "It is not honorable."

"You've worked beside the thralls on our father's steading often enough," Alarīks pointed out. "This harvest just past for one, and I worked beside you."

"That is different," the younger man grumbled. "That is cutting grain, the stuff of bread, and on family land."

"This is cutting grapes—which make wine, as barley makes

beer," Alarīks said. "Besides, we are scouting, so many things are honorable that are not otherwise."

He grinned, and smacked his lips. "We will *drink* wine, too—as if from the ever-giving hand of our kinsman the prince."

Gunþiharjaz laughed. Much of the trade across the Danube was in wine, which chiefs and lords and their handfast men drank because it showed wealth and your chosen lord's open-handed ways as a giver of gold...and because of the taste and the greater strength of the wine spirit, to be sure. There had been rumors that some sort of very superior wine of redoubled strength was made here.

"Let's get our bundles and get going," Alarīks said. "Before they send a cart to collect the dead sheep."

Gunþiharjaz shuddered and made a sign with the first and last fingers of his left hand.

"Who would eat of beasts slain so?"

"Roman thralls eat what they're given, like hogs being fattened," Alarīks said. "So let us go and make sure the free Folk of the Border—"

Which was what *Markōmanniz* meant; the folk of the border, the People of the Mark. The ones who had faced the Roman-kind along the great river for a century and more, and got nothing but knives in the back for thanks from kin further away from the point of the pilum.

"—do not face that thralldom."

⋙ CHAPTER ELEVEN ⋘

Villa Lunae,
Province of Pannonia Superior
October 10th, 165 CE

People with swords...don't look odd to me anymore, Artorius thought. *Which is passing odd.*

Josephus and his big German bodyguard—the man was six feet two, and outweighed Artorius as well, with not an ounce of fat—were joined by the five Americans and Sarukê for the...

Ceremony, I suppose, he thought, inhaling the damp, almost-ocean smell of the nearby lake and the once-more familiar scent of warm horse. *An open spot like this is the right setting for it.*

There wasn't much problem getting privacy, because at the end of the first week in October the vintage was at its peak or just a little past it. In the late afternoon most of the estate was hard at work, even some of the mansion's domestic staff out cutting bunches of grapes with little curve-bladed knives or doing the dance-like crushing as they trod out the juice. Not to mention every set of hands...and feet...they could hire.

It wasn't *quite* as intense as the grain harvest, but everyone was working hard and even Sextus Hirrius was out watching over things. Most of the Americans' special projects were suspended until the grapes were in, except the plowing and sowing. And that took less labor this year, with the new plows and harrows and seed drills. Which let the *vilicus* throw more hands at the vines and cut the time needed, and *that* reduced the risk of damage from bad weather *and* meant they could plant all the grain at the optimum time.

Vines were a much smaller part of the villa's operation than grain, but a much higher proportion of it was *sold*, rather than being consumed on-site.

They'd picked an out-of-the way spot, on the far end of the paddocks below the stables. That put them fairly near the lake. Trees rustled, their leaves turning dry, but the damp breeze was still comfortable; the endless whisper of wind in the reedbeds was a constant. Bees murmured, and overhead a wedge of geese were heading south, their honking cries a faint lonely sound. Not far away was the field where Jeremey had sown the corn in late June; it stood in neat rows more than man high, and the leaves and the tassels atop the stalks and at the tops of the ears were starting to turn dry, making a papery rustle as they moved. It looked like their gamble on that would pay off, since they could probably expect another thirty days of frost-free weather.

Six acres this year, maybe three, four hundred next time 'round, with four times the yield. And now Sextus wants to plant corn and sunflowers and the rest on all his estates. So will the neighbors, when they hear he's on board and see the results.

Josephus stepped forward, put a hand on Sarukê's shoulder and said:

"I release you to a new patron, Sarukê *dhugatêr Arsaliôn*, one who is friend, partner and ally to me as well. You have served me well and bravely; let no blame at this parting attach to you, as all present may witness. As recognition, I give you this gift in farewell."

This gift was a bridle and bit in the new style, done with dark tooled leather and a few silver studs.

"I thank for gracious leave, lord," Sarukê said in her turn as she took it and then hung it from the fence to one side. "You good lord, honorable. Save my life, free me from slavery. I no forget."

That ended his part of the formalities; he and Kunjamunduz stepped back. Sarukê turned and faced Artorius; she was in her native dress, but the fanciest version of it she had, crimson jacket embroidered with running wolves and stooping hawks, baggy blue pants, polished soft boots secured with silver-buckled straps. And every trinket she'd managed to acquire, including gold bracelets with garnets and sapphires and a necklace of coral beads; that was a way of saving as much as swank, compact wealth that could be turned into coin at need.

Her strong-boned beaky face was grave as she drew her long,

ring-hilted sword and knelt, offering the burnished, pattern-welded steel across her palms.

"Lord Artorius, take this sword mine. With steel and blood I serve you, to death. You enemies, mine, you friends, mine. For you and yours I kill, I die."

This part of the ceremony was a mix of Roman and her people's.

"I accept your sword, Sarukê daughter of *Arsaliôn*. Carry it in my service. As you keep faith with me, so I shall with you, unto death, yours or mine. I will stand by you in any fight"—under Roman custom, that included a patron seeing to a client's needs in a lawsuit, but he didn't think that was exactly what she had in mind—"and avenge your blood if you fall."

She rose, and he slid the long straight blade into the scabbard at her side and clapped both hands on her shoulders for a moment; they were springy-resilient under his fingers.

"Take then these gifts of me."

That was a dagger of fine Noric steel in a tooled sheath with golden studs, a knee-high stoppered amphora of the Villa Lunae's finest sweet wine, and a halter—attached to a leading rein, and on the muzzle of a fifteen-hand black mare with a white star and fetlock. Sarukê smiled as she bent and touched the handles of the amphora, more broadly as she slid the dagger out of its sheath for a second and tested the edge with a thumb before she tucked it in her sword belt, and most of all for the horse, stroking its neck and breathing into its nostrils and feeding it dried apricots from a newly installed pocket.

The last part was wholly Sarmatian, and involved thrusting her long sword into the earth and then making a libation to it, a small fire made smokey with hemp, passing hands and steel through it, salt and a little blood from both of them mingled in a cup of milk before they drank from it.

Sarukê said something in her own liquid, archaic North Iranian tongue, repeating it as she faced the four quarters with hands and arms upraised, then clapped her hands together and bowed to Artorius with palms pressed together and fingers under her chin in a gesture that looked oddly Hindu.

No, Artorius thought, with an eerie thrill.

It's Aryan, original vintage, and survived in India all those thousands of years. And on the steppes where they came from in the first place, evidently; she's descended from the ones who stayed there when the others went south and ended up in the Punjab and became something different.

Then she grinned, as she shook hands with the four younger Americans.

"Now we serve same lord," she said. "Josephus good man. Brave, honest, clever yet no cheat. But I better serve warrior."

Seriously, she added to him: "But you need more bodyguards, for you and yours. One not enough, you travel outside cities, carry wealth."

He nodded back at her. They hadn't had any blood trouble yet . . . but that was probably because they hadn't traveled without enough people visibly ready for it.

"I will think seriously of that, Sarukê."

Hmmm. And she probably has the connections to get them for us.

Filipa Chang watched the ring of dancers around the fire from a distance, herself leaning against trussed hay in the darkness. The light of the flames caught the vine leaves woven in the dancers' hair, accenting the autumnal colors of red and gold. A statue of Venus with gilt hair and pale skin and opal eyes presided over the merriment from a plinth, and flowers and grapes lay before it in offering.

The noise was getting louder and louder. At the Vinalia, you drank your wine neat, and dozens were already lying in various nooks and crannies around the *pars rustica* and within it, not necessarily alone but often unconscious or nearly. This wasn't quite the Saturnalia, but it did allow a degree of license—it was watched over by wild Bacchus and by Venus *Obsequens*, Venus the *Indulgent*.

The smell of roast meat—sheep, pigs, and two large oxen— lingered on the air with the tang of the fire. The feast had had the workers loudly blessing the generosity of Sextus Hirrius Trogus, even when they were drunk enough to be careless of what they said about their master. It was one of the rare occasions at which they could eat their fill of meat, and have plenty of other provender too, and drink to repletion, with the two main harvests of the year safely in and the plowing going fast.

Though since they raised the beasts themselves, how generous is it to let them eat some of what they produced?

The last of the vines had given up their fruit to the feet of the treaders yesterday, though after they'd stomped there was a lever press to get the rest of the juice out and that was *not* an innovation of the newcomers.

Filipa chuckled a little to herself; the Prof and Paula and Mark and even small-town Jeremey had thought the last bunches were spoiled. In a sense they were, but it was noble rot—*Botrytis cinerea*. That required just the right combination of rain and sun, humidity and timing on the picking, but if you got it *just* right the fungus concentrated the sugars to make the wine strong and sweet...and as far as her nonexpert but Californian-from-a-family-of-wine-fanciers Bay Area eye could see, they had.

"Some of this you would like?"

Filipa looked up, smiling; Sarukê had the jug she'd gotten as part of the...

Weird ceremony, Filipa thought, nodding with a smile.

...in the crook of her arm.

The Sarmatian sank down beside her, sitting cross-legged, took it in an expert grip with one finger through the handle and the body over her forearm, and drank deeply. Filipa took it next and let a mouthful trickle between her lips. This was a Botrytised wine, sure enough, probably last year's vintage.

"Do your people have festivals like this?" she asked.

"Not for pick grapes—though we drink Roman wine, yes, much, when can get it! Or fermented mare's milk, or millet beer, and we sit in a tent around fire and drink smoke of sacred hemp. But festivals yes, dance, drink, feast. At four turnings of the year, and for victories, or birthdays, or coming of chief or birth of heir. And we wail at funerals, but then dance and drink to help spirit make way for to—"

She pointed up at the stars and bright moon, then took the jug back, and sipped this time.

"Or before raid. I that see in here, in head, the last. My—"

She used a word in her own language, then frowned for a moment and translated it into Latin:

"Sister of sword? Lover, friend, comrade. She with me. We pledge on swords then to marry—"

"Each other?" Filipa said, slightly surprised; that sounded more than a bit modern for the year 165 CE.

Of course, Sarmatians may be completely different. Nobody knows...knew, uptime...all that much about them. Our only written sources were from people who hated and feared and despised them.

Sarukê looked at her, puzzled too.

"No, how so? To marry same man, so we together always, our children sisters, brothers. We raid for dowry first; need many horses for marriage of worth, other things."

A sigh and another drink, and she leaned back against the truss and stared upward too.

"But she die by my side, I hit on head with sling-bullet, dead too if not helmet. Now exile, here. Never home more, no see sea of grass, no ride forever beneath high holy heaven."

"I'm an exile too," Filipa said. "I also left a friend, a lover—she died. I can never return."

It seemed very natural when they kissed. After a few moments more, Filipa chuckled and said, holding the other's wrist:

"That would be nice, but not here. I have a perfectly good bedroom."

Sarukê rose on an elbow and looked at her. "You invite me to your bed, beneath tent...that is, say you, roof?"

Evidently that meant more than a—literal—roll in the hay to a Sarmatian. Filipa decided she didn't care about that, rose, and extended a hand. Sarukê came to her feet with a lithe movement that didn't use her hands...though she hooked her finger back through one of the handles of the jug, first.

The festival went on into the night. Filipa bowed before the smile of Venus as they passed with fingers entwined.

"That was quite a blowout," Artorius said.

Mark belched slightly and patted his stomach. "Serious puppy-fed python syndrome," he said, smiling a little foolishly.

The strong sweet wine that was the Villa Lunae's specialty was to his taste; he said it reminded him of Manischewitz, but much better. He went on:

"Man, the Romans take to your Texan BBQ sauce like Russians getting their first taste of vodka, though, don't they?"

"Weeping as they munched, but that didn't stop them," Paula noted.

"We've got enough tomatoes and chilies once we extract the seeds," Artorius said. "I'm just glad they yielded so well. Good work, Jeremey."

He looked around the lamplit second-story corridor overlooking the peristyle. They'd put all the Americans along this stretch here: it was guest rooms, and probably not used much before they arrived. He'd gotten the distinct impression that Lady Julia was a bit *infra dig* by the local gentry's standards because of her husband's rackety life and sordid dead-broke death, though her brother was invited around ceaselessly.

Not that we have anything to complain about.

The plastered walls were painted in Pompeiian-red upright rectangles bordered in black, with gold-colored wreaths beneath the ceiling and trompe d'oeil engaged columns with occasional painted *putti* peering out from behind them. The floor was a type of white-and-pink marble he recognized from visits to Vienna back when he was stationed in Europe and Mary and he felt a need to take in some culture.

They each had a suite—his was four rooms—and the house staff put up with their eccentricities, including their reluctance to use chamber pots even when it was a long chilly walk late at night to the continuous-flow latrines. Oddly, the Romans had different and gender-specific shapes and names for the ceramic utensils.

The air was slightly fruity from the alcohol lamps, with woodsmoke and cooking smells from the big bash outside. And...

"Where's Fil?" he said, concerned. "The party was getting a bit wild went we left."

Like, with naked guys playing Bacchus surrounded by naked nymphs in masks and more guys with goat hair on their legs pretending to be satyrs playing flutes and things getting very NSFW. Naked except for vine wreaths and bunches of grapes. And the free tenants were just as enthusiastic as the field hands. I think this is a real let-your-hair-down occasion, no questions asked afterward. Including nine months afterward for most people. I noticed the ladies Claudia and Julia only made a brief appearance at the beginning to offer to Venus.

Jeremey chuckled—almost snickered.

"I'm not the only one locally hooked up anymore," he said, and pointed a finger down the hall toward the stairs, where Filipa's rooms were first on the right. "She retired early—holding hands with a certain Sarmatian. Who she told us awhile ago reminded her of Sandahl Bergman in *Conan the Barbarian*, by the way."

Ah, I saw that once on Amazon Prime, back in the early '20s, before I left the service, Artorius thought, after searching his memory.

It had been one of those evenings you spent in a warehouse on an air base, the whole company waiting to deploy and nothing better to do than watch old movies on a laptop if you couldn't sleep, after you'd field-stripped and cleaned everything one last time.

Quite a fox... back in Dad's salad days... and come to think of it Sarukê does look a lot like her. Not quite so tall and willowy, though.

"No accounting for tastes," the young man from Wisconsin said.

"Like you'd turn her down if it was on offer, Jem," Mark said. "Envy, much, do I."

"I wouldn't *dare* turn her down! Have you seen her shooting geese on the wing with that bow?"

"I bet *Fil* doesn't have to hand out any *jewelry* to get some," Paula said snidely. "And on that note, goodnight all."

Artorius laughed with the rest, saw that everyone was safely ensconced for the night—there were a pair of slurred giggles and a call of: *Hello, man-bull!* and *Have some of this, O stallion!* from Jeremey's rooms when he opened the door—and turned to his suite.

It was all a little like being in an undergrad dorm.

Except that I'm the dorm monitor.

He reached out a hand toward the door to his rooms. That portal was a handsome slab of worked beechwood with inlays, like most Roman doors turning on a pivot pole set into sockets above and below rather than on hinges... they *had* hinges, they usually just didn't use them for *doors* inside houses, for some reason.

And it was slightly ajar.

And I left strict instructions the door's to be kept shut and nobody's to enter unless I'm there... and the ordinary staff here think I'm a magician and they wouldn't dare *disobey.*

According to Paula they thought he was a *good* magician, come to bless and protect them, but it was still major mojo.

A chill cut through the glow of the BBQ and wine. He'd taken to wearing the sword Fuchs had sent back with them, to get accustomed to it. Now he let the cloak slide off his shoulders, wound the dense wool length around his left arm and drew the twenty-inch blade—which was good twenty-first-century steel. Then, very carefully, he raised one foot and nudged the portal open.

A figure in a plain brown tunic dropped down into it—obviously he'd been braced between the stone lintel and the ceiling. Equally obviously expecting to land *on* Artorius heels-first as he came through.

Artorius lunged; there was a knife in the man's hand. He was cursing the meal and the wine all the way, and felt as if he was wading through glue.

The... the word *assassin* flashed through his mind... didn't waste any time going *huh?* and wondering where his target was. Definitely a fighting man's reflexes.

He let the fall drive him into a squat, and dove forward into the room, rolling three times, turning and bouncing back at the man he wanted to kill like a rubber ball.

Artorius had just enough time to draw back into his own defensive crouch; it had been years since anyone made an up-close and personal attempt to kill him, and it was just as unpleasant as he remembered. He skipped back and cut at the man's knife arm at the same time, the honed edge just kissing the skin above the wrist, as the seven-inch dagger came uncomfortably close to his stomach.

Keep him at a distance, I've got the longer blade, drifted through his mind; not really a conscious thought, since he was already doing that.

Glad it's a short *sword. Too cramped here for anything longer. And the* winner *of a knife fight goes to hospital...*

The lunge-and-twist left them both in the corridor, with the assassin's back to the staircase a good distance behind him. Artorius raised his voice and shouted, only remembering to use Latin at the last instant:

"Bandit! Armed bandit, bring weapons, quickly!"

Another lunge. The man was young, beard still patchy, but nearly as tall as he was, long armed, and rattlesnake quick. A flurry, a twist and the knife went past him—slicing into his tunic and scoring his left side with what felt like a line of ice. He wasn't in position to stab or cut back, but he clamped his left arm down to hold the assassin's right immobilized for a moment. In the same instant he hammered the beech-and-brass ball pommel of the short sword down on the other man's shoulder with vicious strength and tried for a knee to the crotch at the same time.

The man was used to dirty fighting, youth or not, and blocked with a twist so that the knee hit the inside of his thigh instead of its target. But he grunted with pain at the downward strike despite the muscle that cushioned his bones. Roman infantry swords were *short*, but they weren't *light* at all. He hadn't been able to make the stroke very long, but there was weight behind it, and desperate strength.

The young man backed rapidly as Artorius shouted again and went back into stance, ignoring the hot trickle of blood down his side.

If he doesn't kill me right away, I win when help arrives.

The young man hesitated, snarled anger, spat a curse in a language Artorius didn't recognize, something like *skitiz*, whipped around and ran full tilt with his injured arm clutched against his side.

Didn't drop the knife, though, dammit!

"He runs! Be careful! Take him alive!" he yelled aloud.

Because I want to ask him some questions, went though his mind, more than half a snarl as he put his hand against the cut. *Not too deep...*

The last door before the stairs opened before the assassin reached them. They opened inward; what shot out was a long white leg, at shin height. The man yelled, slashed desperately, and went flying forward as he tripped, tumbling downward into the stairwell in a half-controlled fall.

Sarukê burst out of the door with her shield in one hand, her long double-edged sword in the other. And nothing else on her athletic frame but a sheen of sweat, some scars, curvilinear tattoos, and a pair of strategically placed hickies. She lunged after the fleeing man, and Artorius shouted again as he followed:

"Alive! I want him alive!"

He was on her heels as she went down the stairs, vaguely conscious of some of the others following him—Filipa, wrapped in a blanket and with a reversed candlestick in her hand as an improvised mace, and Jeremey behind her, in his ragged Fruit of the Loom underwear and a plausible replica Louisville Slugger baseball bat in one hand. He'd been teaching some of the villa folk the game in his spare time, being an ex-Little Leaguer and Red Sox fan.

A shouting brabble came from the courtyard below. When they ran out, a crowd of servants and field hands were struggling

with what couldn't be seen well by torchlight but was probably
the fugitive. A shout, a man staggering back clutching a cut arm,
and half a dozen of them had him, one holding him by his long,
braided hair, a pair on each arm, and one with commendable
presence of mind kneeling and hugging the man's knees. The
sixth was punching the man enthusiastically.

"Good," Artorius panted, looking at the ones who'd thrown
themselves on an armed killer because he told them to do it and
memorizing faces. "Thanks, I won't forget this. All right, enough,
don't kill him!"

Sarukê had a light cut on her left leg that was dripping, more
slowly than his side. She grinned at him:

"We shed blood together, fight against same foe, lord," she
said, which apparently meant something special to her. "And I
tell you twice, need more guards."

"You're right," Artorius replied shortly. "You're in charge of
that. Get five, good ones."

"Tomorrow, we talk it."

The young captive's face was contorting, as if in a rictus of
agony. Then he opened his mouth...

And his severed tongue fell out, bitten through at the base.
A gush of blood followed as the slaves dropped him in swearing
amazement and disgust. He choked out something unintelligible—
probably to anyone who knew his language, too—and went to his
knees, then his face, coughed in spasm a few times, and went limp.

Sarukê bent over him for an instant, then nodded.

"German," she said. "Marcomanni or Quadi—" Her sword
tip prodded the knot of hair on the side of his head. "This new,
but real. And I know some words—he say bad-bad thing about
our mothers. And last word, that their god. *Wōdinaz*. God of..."

She paused for thought, frowning.

"God of fighters. God of good warrior death, leads warrior
dead to halls of Gods. Man dumb-dung-head, but brave. No talk
now!"

More people were arriving; a shocked-looking Sextus Trogus
still carrying a wine cup with a wreath askew on his head, Josephus and his German bodyguard, a growing crowd.

Artorius sat on a bench, incongruously conscious of the scent
of the last roses from the bushes around it, mingled with blood
and his own sweat. That prompted an order of his own.

The results arrived at the same time as Sextus' plump Greek doctor, who examined the cut in Artorius side.

"This needs stitches, *Domine*," he said briskly.

A glance at the slave nursing a cut arm. "So does that."

And at Sarukê: "She doesn't, just a bandage."

He began to extract things from a bag he'd obviously snatched up, kept ready for emergencies. One of the slaves had fetched what Artorius called for, in the form of a large jug. The doctor looked at it and sniffed.

"You may have a drink, *Domine*, but I have poppy syrup for the pain."

"This isn't for the pain," Artorius said, as the man produced a pair of tweezers to pluck fragments of cloth out of the wound on his side.

"It *causes* pain," he said, putting a hand on the doctor's wrist.

In fact, it would be like having the raw flesh bathed in fire.

"But it also prevents infection. Pour some into a bowl, wash your hands, instruments and the catgut for the stiches in it, soak some cloth in it and use that to wipe out the wounds first. Then apply more when you bandage."

He looked at Sarukê and the injured man. "For you, too. It makes cuts heal cleanly. Don't argue, Doctor, just do it—I'm not in the mood. Yes, the tweezers too!"

Next morning, Artorius could tell the *vilicus* was both angry and frightened as he talked to the master's mysterious ... and now injured ... guest. He also found the presence of the armed and mailed Sarukê standing behind the stranger's chair a bit intimidating, from the glances he cast that way.

He's made a good thing out of our being here and he's afraid of losing that, too, Artorius thought. *Let's put him at ease, a bit. It really isn't his fault.*

You got angry after a fright and fight like that, no way around it, especially if you got hurt—and no amount of superwine would have prevented an agonizing death if the blade had been a few inches further right and gone into his gut. The antibiotics *might* have.

But it was important not to take the anger out on anyone who didn't deserve it. People who did that got bad reputations *and* less honesty and cooperation from everyone around them, often at times they badly needed both.

One of the cases of virtue being its own reward, literally.

"My apologies—" the estate manager began.

Artorius waved a hand. He didn't particularly like the man, he was a bit more free with the whip than was necessary, but he was intelligent and observant.

"No need. Sit. There's wine and water in the jug, have some if you want. Just tell me the facts."

The small shrewd eyes blinked a little, and the man sat on the stool on the other side of the stone-topped table; they were in a medium-sized room off the ground floor of the *pars urbana's* outer court. Artorius had been using it as an office and there were bookshelves, and diagrams pinned up on boards attached to the walls. Out of the window Artorius could see housemaids on their knees scrubbing at the place the young Marcomanni had died, trying to get the bloodstains out, and a couple of gardeners gossiping animatedly as they raked up leaves at the steady but slow pace most nonurgent work here went by.

The room was warm on a chilly day, and only a slight haze gathered under the ceiling from the brazier glowing with fine charcoal in a corner, and a faint indefinable smell of scorched bronze from it. That was one reason they made a lot of charcoal here; an open wood fire would have turned this into a gas chamber.

Sarukê's scent of oiled mail, leather and horse sweat was considerably stronger than the smell of the charcoal burning, though she'd adopted Roman habits on bathing. What Sarmatians probably smelled like on their native ground was best left to the imagination. Especially when it was too cold to jump into streams and rivers.

The coals weren't why the vilicus was sweating, though.

Blame runs downhill, and he's worried.

"I hired them both, lord," the man said in a neutral tone. "They claimed to be poor countrymen looking for work, by the names of Tinkomāros and Katurīx. Grand names for vagabonds, and they looked better fed than most, but they were strong and willing to work and we don't ask questions at harvest times. They did talk Gaulish—I can follow it myself, and speak it for simple things. How was I to know they were *Germanii*?"

"There were Gauls across the Danube before the Germanii came there," Artorius said. "As there were here on the southern shore before Rome came."

Gauls who conquered the previous inhabitants, and so it goes. As the old saying runs, all title deeds are written in blood; the sole difference between one place and another is how long it's had to dry.

The Marcomanni leader making trouble there was called Ballomar, which was a Gallic name too—meaning *Mighty Arm.* They and the Quadi had invaded and settled in the lands of the Celtic-speaking Boii up north a long time ago. That was the tribal name which was the source for "Bohemia"; the Germanic conquerors had mostly though not completely absorbed the Celts by now, but obviously the influence hadn't been all one way.

"They kept close to themselves, brothers they said, and from their looks they were, but they worked well enough. The older one was gone by the time I was told of the attack last night. *And* he stole a good horse, and one of the new saddles!"

"Nothing you could have done," Artorius said, with a shrug... and a wince at the way that pulled at the stitched wound.

So far, no complications, which spares our supply of antibiotics.

There wasn't much more the man could tell. When he was gone, Artorius looked at Sarukê.

"How long?" he said.

"Day, night and quarter day to Carnuntum, lord," she said cheerfully, walking around to his front. "Then I go to *ludus*, find out things, ask around who needs work. Have friends there."

A *ludus* was a gladiatorial school, sort of an instructional academy-cum-spa-prison-camp for the damned; Carnuntum was the provincial capital, southeast of Vindobona on the great river and more than twice its size. It had a *ludus*, and an arena that could seat fifteen thousand, most of the free adults in town. Fights were a regular feature there, usually the home team against those touring the provinces.

Not every gladiatorial combat ended in a death, since that added to the price, but enough did or left men maimed that it wasn't a healthy profession. Most but oddly enough not *all* were slaves, though he wouldn't have wanted to meet the volunteers in a dark alley. Their oath of initiation included:

I agree to be burned, to be bound, to be beaten, and to be killed by the sword.

"Still know some there."

He wasn't surprised that she did; there were certain trades

that you could only really talk over with people who'd been through the same mill. He'd have thought fighting in the arena was one. Even more than soldiering, in a way.

"Get five men?" she said. "Take, oh, four days, maybe six. Then ride back here, not so fast as I go. Take horses and food, but for gear, weapons, should buy all stuff there. More and better, cheaper."

Then she added in a warning tone: "Get good men, need pay good."

Artorius nodded again. "Filipa will go with you. I will not part...sword-sisters, is that your word? Not without real need."

The Sarmatian smiled at that; for itself, and because it was a respectful acknowledgment of their relationship, which pleased her even more.

It wasn't *that* out of line here. Romans had their own prejudices about sex and what people of various types did in bed. In spades, and unlike his native century the majority were utterly unbothered about who they offended with them. They were just weirdly, wildly *different* prejudices than those a Westerner from the 2030s would be personally acquainted with.

For example, here and now pederasty was OK, between grown man and adolescent youth, but sex between men who were the same age and social equals was a degrading perversion for at least half of those involved. You had to be careful about your unconscious assumptions and *think* about things if you hadn't been raised here.

The past is another country, and they do things differently here. Think lest things rise up and bite you on the ass, he thought. *For example part deux, most Romans wouldn't be strongly morally disapproving of her and Filipa being lovers. Some would find it funny, others repulsive. Mostly they just wouldn't take it seriously or give it much respect, because it's two women so it can't be important. She's glad I do.*

"Our banker there knows Filipa's name and she'll have a letter authorizing her to draw on our account, so you won't be short on funds. Get it done fast, but done well—you understand? Good fighters, but *reliable* ones, that's just as important."

"Yes, lord. Not many gladiator *like* arena. Them do are—"

She made a brief gesture that involved tapping the knuckles of both hands on her temples rapidly and rolling her eyes upward and sticking her tongue out of the corner of her mouth; it self-evidently meant *complete loons* or *barking mad.*

"Get *rudus*, become *rudiarii*"—a *rudus* was a wooden sword given as a symbol of freedom to those who survived the arena— "what do, get food? Some sit down, drink until they dead ones, maybe cut wrists, jump in river from bad dream. But guard work, yes, for others not—"

She made that gesture again.

"I lucky—Lord Josephus give me home. We treat well, give honor, pay well, kick ass sometimes, work pretty good. They know me. Victories I have, some trust, some...respect. Tell I you is good lord, strong man who made knife stabber to run, worth respect, they believe I."

"They won't have jobs already?" he asked.

Carnuntum was bigger than Vindobona, but it wasn't large enough to have all that many ex-professional gladiators. On the other hand, any gladiator who lived uncrippled long enough to get the wooden sword was going to be tough for certain and probably smart and assuredly very good with weapons and *most* certainly have steady nerves.

She gestured out the window at the turning leaves. "Winter, bad time—few merchant travel. Not so many need guard, all things *slllllooooww*," she said, drawing the word out dolorously. "Some hungry by spring. Get work through winter, they want it. How much I say?"

"Six *sestertii* a day, plus food, gear and a place to sleep, for good service and obedience," Artorius said.

That was about what a worker in a migrant harvest gang got, very good wages indeed for steady long-term employment.

"Guaranteed until...hmmm. Until at least a year and six months. Then we'll see. In any case, they may keep the gear they get when they leave, and a month's bonus if I'm satisfied."

Her teeth showed white in her tanned face. "With that, no trouble, lord! Get four certain, five maybe."

She departed in a clink of mail, looking cheerful; this was a promotion for her, too.

And until she and Fil get back with the hired blades, we're all going to be very, very careful, and I'm going to step up the combatives training no matter how much Mark and Paula bitch and moan. I don't know where the brother of that youngster with the knife has gone. Whatever he's doing, it won't be with love toward us in his heart.

⇒ CHAPTER TWELVE ⇐

Villa Lunae,
Province of Pannonia Superior
December 20th, 165 CE

I *suspect my nickname here is Nervous Nellie,* Artorius thought, glancing up at the gray clouds and the smell of damp chill.

Looks like rain... again.

The storage shed for the gunpowder was out in a hillside pasture northwest of the main villa complex; the nearest house was a tenant cottage half a mile away. It was laid out like a comb, with a covered wooden corridor in front, and individual storage chambers dug back into the hillside and roofed over, each with six feet of solid dirt between it and its neighbor and four steps down to the wooden shelves where the kegs were kept. With underfloor drainage pipes.

There wasn't a piece of iron in the whole construction, now that the metal-edged shovels of the digging crews were out of the picture.

Sparks... he thought. *Sparks are seriously contraindicated, by God!*

What really gave him the willies was that the only source of artificial light here was open flame. When you combined that with the tendency of gunpowder to shed near-invisible mists of finely divided particles...

"Hades eat you, don't throw those things around!" he barked. "Stack them gently!"

And backed it up with a medium-hard boot to the backside.

The problem was that the villa's slaves were _used_ to having people yell at them; eventually the yelling man went away, and the work continued in their own way and pace. Sometimes you had to use kinetic aids to really get their attention. And nobody here had any idea of what the word "explosive" really _meant_.

The man gripped the little barrel harder and ducked his head, and went into the tunnel. The light was fading...

"All right, everyone finish up and pack up!" he said.

Then he turned and gaped for an instant. Over at the filling table a worker was pouring measured quantities of sieved powder—the grinding and sieving operation was a long way from here too—from clay containers through funnels into the little barrels. At the call he stooped to pick up some sort of bundle at his feet...

"No!" Artorius screamed. "Cover the jug first—"

The man halted, gaping, with the lit oil lamp in his hand. Artorius checked a lunge toward him and went down to one knee instead, and ducked his face into the crook of his left arm.

WHUMP!

A flash of red light and a pillow of hard, hard air struck. The experience of being knocked back by an explosion was eerily familiar; so was the savage pain in his arm. It took him moments to break the hold of shock, and to realize he wasn't lying waiting for the medevac.

Artorius flogged himself back onto his feet. His left forearm was bleeding, and a patch of the skin was red and cracked, and he bit a yell back into a hiss between clenched teeth.

That's why I'm not blind, he thought grimly.

The worker who'd lit his oil lamp without securing the lid on the container of powder was lying on his belly halfway between the shattered wood of the table and Artorius. His face was relaxing from an expression of shocked surprise into slackness, and his back looked...

Chewed. Chewed and smoking.

Several large fragments of the amphora stood out of the blackened flesh along with splinters, welling red blood and shattered pink-white fragments of spine and ribs.

Sarukê was galloping toward him; so was Filipa, with a snatched-up first-aid kit. The Sarmatian drew rein and leapt out of the saddle running. Artorius was glad of that shoulder to lean on; his legs felt a familiar weakness. Though all the fingers moved, and he didn't think any bones were broken.

"Disinfectant and ointment," he said to Filipa in English; she was gulping and carefully *not* looking at the fresh corpse tumbled not far away.

He raised his voice for the foreman's benefit as he switched to Latin: "Get everyone here!"

There was nothing like visual aids...and a stink of scorched flesh...to get across exactly what *explosive* meant.

Consider it a learning experience. Death is a greater professor than me!

Two weeks later he reflected that this might be a warm part of Pannonia, comparatively speaking, and they might be at the peak of the Roman Warm Period, but the climate could still be perishingly *cold* when you were well into the darkness of late December. Cold, wet, more cold, more cold rain, more slush, and then snow.

All good for the crops next year, all unpleasant now.

Artorius sank into the chair, feeling for once fully relaxed, and took up the scroll with careful pleasure. It was old, and the papyrus was a bit brittle and more brown at the edges. The left forearm still hurt, but he'd had plenty of experience with ignoring that from healing wounds.

A long day's work in the cold, yes, he thought.

But the snow that beat against the small panes of the window behind him had held off for the day and a good deal of it had been spent near the forges. *Carroballistae* had iron frames, not wood. Between the veterans who'd spent their lives working and repairing the weapons and the smiths here, they were managing.

And then a—careful—bath, a good dinner with the four who were his friends now, as well as assistants and students...and now some delightful reading, and then sleep.

Hopefully, dreamless. Not getting the nightmares nearly as often anymore, especially the ones about Mary and the kids. Some of those were...really bad.

There was a wine cup on the table beside him, whose round marble top was upheld by three elongated bronze fauns, and a narrow-necked clay jug on a stand, filled with double-distilled superwine. That wasn't for drinking, or as a disinfectant this time. A circular linen wick went into the liquid through a plug, and burned above with a bright blue flame, better light by far than the oil lamps and diffused by a modified glass jug acting as a chimney.

And it still smells a little of peaches, he thought whimsically. *Which goes well with old paper, and beeswax from the furniture, and that old-stone-building scent. And that doctor was really impressed that all the wounds healed without any infection. Sextus said he wrote to his friends about it, too.*

Across the library a fire crackled pleasantly on the andirons in a very new fireplace, behind a screen of repurposed fretted bronze; above the mantle were the figures of a pair of *Lares,* carved in low relief on a slab of marble and picked out with paint. The protective domestic spirits were crowned with leaves, dancing and holding a cornucopia and wine jug and flanked by small columns, with a snake painted beneath them.

He raised his wine cup in salute to the little Gods of the Hearth, and took up the scroll. Occasionally he murmured a phrase aloud, hesitantly; it was old, and in Classical Athenian Greek, but worth the effort.

The whisper of a sandal on the marble tiles made him look up. It was Lady Julia; he rose and inclined his head. A maidservant, her personal lady's maid, stood quietly behind her; he noted idly how much her face resembled her mistress's, though she was a few years older. It was the sort of bone structure that aged well.

"I will withdraw, if you would prefer, *domina,*" he said.

She shook her head and sat on something that looked like a folding stool fantastically elaborated that swept up on either side to waist height; only the fanciest Roman chairs had both backs and arms, for some reason.

Around them shadows danced, on shelves for scrolls and a few codex books, which had been an innovation when this building rose on the shores of the lake and were still much less common than the older form. There was a faint musty bookish scent, part familiar but not quite like anything he'd smelled before, and *she* came with a waft of verbena. He sank into his own seat once more.

I don't even notice the smell of olive oil on human skin any more, unless I specifically think about something connected with... personal scents.

Julia was dressed for indoors, in winter; two long tunics, both of fairly thick wool and the undermost with long sewn sleeves, knee socks—with a separate big toe so she could wear sandals, and also of woven and sewn cloth since nobody here had heard of knitting until the Americans arrived—and a shawl draped across her arms. Her hair was put up and confined by ribbons as befitted a Roman matron, for whom it came down only in intimate situations.

"I understand you are to be congratulated...Lucius Triarius Artorius."

He'd chosen that *gens* name—the middle of the three, the *nomen* that originally indicated your clan to Romans, though that didn't necessarily mean much by now below the uppermost aristo level—with malice aforethought. All five of them were saddled with it now; it also meant *old soldier* in Latin. He thought she'd guessed that little bit of linguistic play too; she was definitely rather smarter than her brother, or perhaps just more subtle and observant.

"Yes, the *libelli* for all of us have arrived."

That was a brief, witnessed official document; a bit prosaic compared to the folded and sealed bronze copy given time-expired auxiliary soldiers, but fully legal. Eventually a copy would wend its way to Rome, into a rarely consulted archive.

Except by the rats who eat the documents, I suppose; you could call that *consulting the records.*

"It's good to be a citizen...again," he added, and raised his cup: "Your brother is as good as his word, lady."

"Yes, Sextus will always do the right thing...eventually," she said dryly.

He turned a whole rich man's villa over to you...far from your native city and isolated with your joint dragon of a mother, Artorius thought. *He* will *do the right thing, but sometimes rather obliquely. Still, I owe him and he's not a bad sort at all, for a Roman aristo. Witness the way he gets on with Josephus.*

She inclined her head toward the fireplace. That had a pleasant blaze of seasoned beechwood, which burned long and hot with few sparks.

The Americans had copied a late eighteenth-century model... invented by an American named Rumsford, and invented in Europe because he was a Loyalist and in exile after the War of Independence. It had a cunningly angled shallow hearth, air space behind, and a slanted plate of iron—cast in the originals, welded wrought iron here—at the rear of the blaze to absorb and cast the heat outward more efficiently.

The *thought* had taken the bricklayers aback, but they'd had no difficulty *doing* it, with a little initial fumbling due to the fact that a chimney wasn't simply a long brick box but needed a flue liner and other touches. The limiting factor was the amount of bricks on hand, especially after the first few in the kitchens gave them experience, but the estate's brick kiln was working every day now, instead of now and then. Workers who *weren't* beating out grain with flails *were* digging clay and cutting wood.

Type A again, he thought.

Julia smiled slightly as she held out a hand to enjoy the warmth.

"My mother felt it was undignified to ask you to have such as this installed in her rooms. It not being part of the *mos maiorum*, the customs of our ancestors, you understand...though I pointed out to her that our *Roman* ancestors lived in a country where it was never cold enough to kill an olive tree. And our *Gallic* ones were savages who nailed their enemies' heads over the doors of their thatched huts and kenneled with pigs and cattle."

They'd become much easier with each other since her brother's visit; and oddly, since the attempted assassination.

Now she turned up her nose and sniffed; Artorius chuckled, because that was old Lady Claudia to the inch. Julia went on:

"Now she visits me more often, to sit before *my* place of fire. And my daughter plays and sits before it even more often. The winters in this house were hard on her."

Artorius smiled at the thought. The little girl was active and seemed healthy, but she was also rather thin in a gawky shooting-up way.

"In our land, it is a winter custom to sit before the fireplace"—*ignis locus* was what the Latin speakers had instantly and spontaneously decided to call fireplaces, logically enough—"and tell our children stories."

His parents had done that, and his grandparents even more often, in the old ranch house. He had himself, the last little while.

Braziers just weren't the same.

"That sounds very pleasant. Perhaps I could bring little Claudia here, and you might weave some of the tales of your homeland for her?"

It wouldn't do for him to visit *her* rooms for that, of course.

He had a sudden vision of her naked on a sheepskin rug before a fire, smiling and making a come-hither gesture with a forefinger, and blinked in surprise before he pushed it aside.

"That would be a pleasure, Lady Julia," he said gravely.

Josephus had seen the first fireplace working on a visit during an early cold snap, and bought two of the slave bricklayers on the spot for a quarter again the usual price. He'd taken them back to Sirmium with him and promised them emancipation as soon as they'd trained six more, starting them with installing four fireplaces in *his* house.

They were now freedmen with a flourishing business financed by their ex-master and current patron, and by the freedman manager of Sextus' brickworks, which was profitable for all parties concerned as the fashion swept the largest city of Pannonia Inferior as fast as weather permitted.

And Josephus had had them visit Vindobona and install two in the rented house the Americans had stayed in right after their arrival. The camp prefect of the Tenth had seen it on a *casual visit* with his grain supplier on a cold day, and immediately set about equipping the legionary fortress with them, starting with the hospital and his own quarters...and the farmhouse he planned to retire to.

"Much more heat than a brazier, and no smoke making you cough and dulling everything with dingy vapors. And much less hungry for fuel than a hypocaust!" Julia went on enthusiastically.

Hypocausts were the system the Romans used for heating parts of a wealthy man's building, or the public baths; channels under the floor and in the walls to carry hot air...and smoke... from a fire. It worked well, but it was so extravagant that only a few rooms here near the bath suite had it, even in a house like this, one of them the formal dinner chamber. And the baths themselves did, of course, or they'd have been unusable in the cold season. Even the one in the *pars rustica* for the slaves did.

"Ours was a cold land in winter, for the most part," Artorius said.

He thought he saw an ironic twinkle in her hazel eyes, but wasn't sure.

"On my family estate—"

He imagined his grandmother snorting at that description of

the hardscrabble Vandenberg cow-calf operation, one that occasionally gambled on some wheat sown and reaped by contractors. Which paid off slightly more than half the time.

"—the summers were very hot, hotter than here, but the winters were much colder too. We Americans have used the *ignis locus* for a long time."

Julia nodded. "And how do your veterans suit, the ones secured by my brother?"

Well, found by Josephus, secured by Sextus, and helped along by the prospect of three denarii a day plus room and board and lots of girls impressed by their glamor, or at least by their pay, Artorius thought.

Not all time-expired Roman soldiers spent their discharge bonus wisely or had a worry-free civilian life.

She went on: "They seemed very...very *martial*, when I saw them."

In fact they looked like a collection of villainous aging pirate thugs, with scar-seamed faces and bodies to rival the ex-gladiatorial bodyguards, with whom they got on well. Still strong in middle age but with the occasional hitch in their movements which told of old broken bones that twinged in the cold. He'd found them all competent, even if some were a bit too fond of the jug, but they'd all been suitably impressed by what they called Jupiter's Thunderballs, or just Jupiter's Balls.

A few friendly wrestling matches—using US Ranger–style combatives—had won him a degree of personal respect. He was taking sword-and-shield lessons from them too, as well as their new bodyguards, just as he and Filipa were from Sarukê in mounted bladework.

All his teachers thought he was doing reasonably well and had native talent, though they also thought he should have started much earlier and that it would take a long while to make him solidly competent.

In my copious spare time. At least I don't complain about it the way the others do—except Jeremey, to be fair, and Filipa only now and then.

"They'll do nicely," he said aloud. "Another three...or four or five...months and the teams for the new-style *ballistae* will be ready; we're aiming at six of them."

And nothing in them that a local workshop couldn't do with a model to work from, just bronze and iron, wood and ox sinew. Though the elevation and traverse screws have to be hand-filed, which is just...frustrating. And the built-in pulleys, that's taking time. How I wish the Romans had metalworking lathes! A project for another year.

"Though I'd prefer to have more time. Making the ammunition goes slowly."

Charcoal was no problem, sulfur not too difficult if you could pay, but saltpeter was the bottleneck and it was the largest ingredient. It was like trying to scale up production of some medicine people took in teaspoon doses to industrial levels. He'd taken to just buying the scrapings from under manure heaps all over the district: then it had to be refined...and people wondered what the Hades he was doing with it, too. Rumors had started to spread.

It's a good thing we don't plan to keep this secret indefinitely.

He flexed his left hand, feeling the healing scar under the newly changed bandage there on his forearm. That had been a flash rather than a real explosion by the time it got to him... but close enough. When it wasn't wet, loose black powder not in a sealed container smoked off dust that hung invisibly in the air; and then the slightest spark...

What did Filipa say? Yes, that I was supposed to be blowing up the enemy, not myself. There's a reason powder mills used to be put way out in the boonies with berms around everything. Even du Pont did that. It's distracting, too.

"If the Marcomanni remain on their own side of the river, there will be plenty of time. But I am afraid they will not," Julia said gravely. "You labor for the State and for our safety."

She certainly had that Roman emotional control down pat, what they called *gravitas.* If that war did happen, if the barbarians came over the Danube and she couldn't get to someplace with good walls and lots of Roman soldiers in time...well, they did use that saying here: anything that could happen to anyone could happen to *you.* She'd already had graphic proof that a pair of Marcomanni *could* get this far.

"No, I also fear you are correct, lady. Hence this is work of importance to which I must devote my time, when I would rather—"

He waved a hand to indicate the library, and sipped at his wine; it was the sweet style that was a specialty of the Villa Lunae, and since he was only planning on one cup, it was unwatered. There was a pleasant silence for a few moments, before she asked:

"What is it that you were reading when I interrupted?" she asked. "I heard you, and usually you *legere tacite*, without making any sound at all. Like a scholar indeed."

Most people here at least muttered the words as they read or wrote; he thought it might have something to do with the way they usually ran all the written words together without a space between them in the cursive form. Reading silently was a rare skill, and associated with great learning.

He leaned forward and passed her the scroll. She read the title: *Iphigeneia en Aulidi.*

"We have...we had...no complete copy of this in America," he said. "Only something incomplete, and corrupted by scribal errors. And now all the libraries there may well have burned, leaving nothing. As a favor, would you read it for me? My understanding of Greek is greater than my command of it, particularly the old Athenian dialect: and with Euripides, the sound and the sense complement each other closely."

She gave him a long considering look, and then smiled in friendly fashion. Nearly all men of her class could speak and read and write Greek; it was a less common skill for women, but not *very* rare and she had it.

"Very true. I will begin where you left off, then:

> "Aye, but that is where
> The danger comes;
> And ambition, sweet though it seems
> Brings sorrow with its near approach..."

He closed his eyes and let the majestic words flow over him... and he was probably hearing it spoken closer to the original than any modern ever had.

There are *positive points about this.*

The news that a Marcomannic host had crossed the Danube, burning and killing, came by an exhausted messenger on a lathered horse almost exactly five months later.

The Americans and Josephus set out in a party more than seventy strong, including the six catapult crews and their machines, each drawn by six horses in the new harness, each of the two-wheeled *carroballistae* clipped to its two-wheeled ammunition limber by the trails. Everything shiny new, down to the gear their crews wore. Nineteenth-century-style buckboard wagons pulled by mules hauled gear and food, tents and tools that included a little portable anvil and forge, to keep the new horseshoes in order.

Two days later on a bright spring morning a little south of Vindobona the equipment looked a *bit* more worn, and so did the people—he'd been pushing everyone hard, over twenty miles a day. The air was pleasant, and the sky clear save for a few fleecy-white clouds, with that slightly bleached Fragonard look European skies often had to American eyes. The last rain had been three days ago, though the air was full of the scents of damp turned earth and fresh growth as well as horse and mule and hard-worked sweating humans, and the birds were loud in the roadside trees. The leaves there had that new-minted, crisp-cut look leaves did right after they got to full size too.

Well, I don't think *I have to worry about the crews deserting*, he thought, looking around the open farming country; scraggly and weedy by his standards, prosperous by local ones. *Hmmm. Wheat's coming along well. And not much livestock, and a lot less people than there should be.*

Slightly to his surprise, countryfolk here tended to live either in single farmhouses or tiny hamlets; the Villa Lunae had around two hundred in its *familia rustica* and was about as *nucleated* as rural settlements got in this area. He suspected the Roman peace had something to do with that, though people said big villages were common a little further south and east.

A lot of the houses and hamlets here they'd passed since they started out at dawn looked stripped and deserted; yesterday they'd passed a good many rural types heading out and driving their cattle and sheep and goats...and pigs, when they could... before them, with everything moveable piled onto their little oxcarts or on their backs.

There had even been a few pushing wheelbarrows.

Last night he'd bought a sounder of pigs to roast from one party delighted to turn the surly, dangerous beasts into nice portable cash, and gotten news as well for no more than letting them have a meal from their own former porkers. The BBQ sauce had been a hit, as usual, from the smell it gave off while it was cooking and on through the eating. He'd yet to meet a Roman who didn't like it after the first bite made them hop and swear, from Sextus Hirrius Trogus and his mother and sister and niece and on down to his kitchen maids and scullery boys; so far that seemed to be a pan-Imperial predilection. And letting people taste it was low-cost advertising for the tomatoes and chilis.

The refugees said the Marcomanni crossed northwest of Vindobona and that the legion was going to sortie to meet them. We'll hit the river there today, if we don't run into Legio X Gemina *first—most of them are definitely out of Vindobona. Hopefully they'll be in a mood to take any help they can get, understrength as they are.*

The catapult crews marched along proudly beside their machines down the Roman road, here gravel on a deep foundation of packed rocks between stone-block edging, amid rolling farming country cleared save for the occasional woodlot on a rise. The closer you got to a city or town here, the more intensive the cultivation.

About half the crews had been recruited from the free tenants on the Villa Lunae *latifundium*, and the rest were new-minted freedmen because they'd volunteered. Arming slaves was violently illegal, though not unknown in really serious emergencies, so they'd gotten their manumissions ten minutes before they officially joined up.

Arming freedmen was problematic too though not as much so. As was a private citizen arming *anyone* beyond a few bodyguards; the Roman government at all levels was touchy about its monopoly of armed force. Sextus Hirrius Trogus' written permission—he was an *aedile*, a senior magistrate in Sirmium—might or might not do some good, or might just get *him* in trouble too.

To his credit, he didn't hesitate to put his name to the...paper, now. Anyway, we'll probably either be live heroes or dead goats, in a day or two, he thought grimly.

And touched his left hand for an instant to the spot over the healed knife wound. Not his first scar, but it had been the first in quite a few years.

Hell, the Marcomanni have already *tried to kill me. I seem to have a trophism for getting into situations where lethal intent runs free.*

If the freedmen did well the wives and children of those who had them would be freed too. And they were all getting three sestertii a day plus their keep...and after all, this province was *their* home too. He'd leaned on the fact that they'd be defending their homes and kin in the departure speech.

Each had on a thigh-length sleeveless mail shirt with doubling flaps on the shoulder over a padded leather *subarmalis* jerkin, the type most auxiliaries wore, a short sword and dagger at their belts, a flat oval shield over their backs, and a plain bronze bowl helmet with a neck guard and hinged cheek guards. The veterans he'd recruited had the same, and they were riding on the left front horse of every team, not marching—for a number of reasons, starting with practicality and working on through middle-aged knees.

They were also getting three times the pay.

He'd winced a little at the price of the gear, which Josephus and Sarukê had rustled up through various sets of connections, especially when put on top of the compensation he owed Sextus for the slaves. It gave him a slightly different perspective on the parsimony of quartermasters he'd cursed in his own military career, and drove home that armies were *expensive*.

Having them paint the shields olive-green with a white American star had assuaged the feeling only a little.

By the standards of most people he'd met since he got here, he was rich; even a big landowner like Sextus thought he was moderately affluent...though Sextus didn't know about the bags of synthetic gemstones. But back in the warlord era at the end of the Roman Republic, someone had written that to be considered *really* rich, you had to be able to raise and pay a complete legion for a year from your own resources, without straining.

He'd have had to successfully sell most of the synthetic jewels to do that, and Josephus had only been able to move half a dozen of those to date.

Bless him for that, though. "Wealth is always relative." That's still just as true in 166 CE as it was in 2032, he thought. *I was rich in the twenty-first on a professor's salary...compared to a peasant in Burkina Faso.*

An hour before noon, they saw a column of smoke off to the left. He reined in and flung up a clenched left fist; the column all came to a halt in good order...which was a welcome development.

Should have done more on march discipline, but that would have been very conspicuous on the roads.

"Sarukê," he said, and pointed. "Scout that."

"Lord!" she said, and put her heels to her horse.

Filipa went with her, and came back ten minutes later, looking distinctly green.

"Sarukê says you'll want to see this," she said. "No danger."

Then she added, with feeling: "No physical danger. I don't want to see anything like *that* ever again. Not if I live to be a hundred."

Filipa clammed up tight after that.

But that lets me know roughly what to expect, he thought, as he ordered the column to swing off toward the evidence of arson.

"*Pedicabo me!*" he swore less than ten minutes later.

The first hint had been a man in a shabby peasant's tunic lying by the side of the rutted lane, with half his face sheared off by something like an axe and two ravens quarreling over the remaining eyeball. The big birds hopped off resentfully and glared at the passing humans and beasts; a cloud of flies buzzed up from the great fan of black blood on the dirt where he'd died. The wound had dried thoroughly, but the flesh hadn't shrunken much and there was only the beginning of a stale-meat whiff, so it couldn't have been more than a day this time of year.

They've all toughened up at least a bit, he thought. *But it's an ongoing process.*

Jeremey was back on the Villa Lunae—ostensibly because the greatly expanded corn and potato planting needed to be overseen, and the sunflowers and so forth, and the new horse-drawn three-row cultivators and riding plows for the spring crops. Privately, Artorius had given him instructions on what to do if Germanii were seen in the neighborhood, and thought it was *fairly* good odds he'd do it rather than just heading south on a fast horse with the cashbox.

Paula and Mark were here, and both looked disturbed as the wagon they were driving rumbled past the corpse. Nobody else paid it much mind, and the veterans and ex-gladiator bodyguards none at all besides a casual glance. This wasn't a culture where you could live your life without seeing a dead body, unlike the way twenty-first-century America was for most of its inhabitants.

Here people didn't go away to hospitals to die; it happened at home, or near it. With the whole family watching, and usually in pain. And plenty of farming accidents were just as gruesome as this, in a trade that involved moving heavy weights and swinging large sharp tools and managing large, strong, heavy animals with minds of their own.

For that matter, Artorius himself had seen a man trip and fall under the spinning teeth of a big field-grade rototiller himself, before he'd been nine. A brief scream and a *big* spray of blood and . . . bits.

The steading under the pillar of smoke had been a fairly prosperous one in rich-peasant terms, which was probably why the raiders had headed for it. They passed a small vineyard and a little orchard of mixed fruits, a well with a tall, pivoted sweep to raise the bucket, and closer to the center several thatched sheds and outbuildings, a circular mud-brick granary, and a couple of small cottages for the help.

They were where the smoke was coming from. From the stink, either livestock or people or both had been inside when they were set on fire. A long, low rectangular adobe farmhouse with patchy whitewash hadn't burned, probably because it had a tile roof and the Marcomanni weren't used to buildings that were resistant to having a torch tossed on top.

What had happened to the rest of the inhabitants was unfortunately completely obvious.

Four women—or females at least, one couldn't have been more than ten—lay with their legs spread open and their tunics around their necks, dead either from the gang rape or spear thrusts in the gut or neck. The rest of the farmhouse household were crucified to the mud-brick wall with hardwood stakes through their wrists, or in the case of one, barely to toddler's age, through the stomach. Barbarian whimsy had put two dogs and a chicken down at that end of the line, treated the same.

From the looks, some of the others had still been alive when foxes or something similar came to gnaw at the guts dangling from their slit bellies. That argued for knowledge and some care on the part of their killers, although the victims wouldn't have seen anything, since their eyes had all been carefully put out with burning sticks. All the wounds were crawling with flies.

"*Pedicabo me*," he swore again, and spat.

Josephus looked grim, and muttered something in a language the American didn't speak.

Artorius recognized it anyway.

"*Yit'gadal v'yit kadash sh'me' raba.*"

That meant: *Magnified and sanctified be His Great name.*

Artorius murmured: "Amen."

Josephus looked at him, a little startled. Artorius nodded gravely and added:

"B'al'ma di v'ra chir'ute."

Which translated as: *Throughout the world which He has created according to His will.*

"Amen," Josephus replied quietly, then looked a question.

"I learned that for the funeral of a man I commanded . . . in America," he said quietly. "Take your guard and ride scout, my friend. We don't want to take chances. I'll send Sarukê to join you in a minute."

He and his hulking ex-gladiator reined around. They were used to working with the Sarmatian and would do a good job of it, which was one less worry.

I've seen some very bad shit in my day, but this takes the cake, the American thought, returning his gaze to the farmhouse. *Especially for things done by hand, personally.*

The smell was memorable already. Paula and Mark had been looking more and more apprehensive as they came closer to the house; once there they took one horrified glance, tumbled off the seat of their wagon and puked noisily in unison with explosive heaves. They weren't the only ones, either: though the ex-gladiators were mostly blank faced except for one who whistled softly, and the Roman army veterans just shook their heads or swore at the Marcomanni.

One looked at the ammunition limber of his catapult and showed his teeth in what might have been a smile . . .

Sarukê was a little off to one side, her eyes moving purposefully on the surroundings and an arrow on her bowstring. She had a prisoner lying before her horse, his arms tied behind his back at wrist and elbow. An arrow through one calf helped explain how he'd gotten there; he was a squat man, a northern tribesman of no particular rank from his shabby wool trousers and shirt, nondescript and with a mousy-brown shaggy beard.

Wish I could show some of those noble-Nordic enthusiasts this, Artorius thought; he'd run into a few in his time. *I also wish I hadn't had to see this. My head just doesn't need more interior decoration like this. Nightmares coming, with mix-and-match incorporating this, too.*

"This one here, asleep, drunk I think, lord," the Sarmatian called to him. "Others gone by sunup from way ashes of fires are. They leave him, he try run just now."

"Gnaeus!" he barked, and the senior veteran turned to look at him. "Unit front and center here!"

The crews fell in, each behind the veteran acting as NCO. Still in the saddle, Artorius pointed to the wall and its burden:

"This is why we're off to fight, to keep this from our homes and families," he said, catching their eyes. "Does any man want to run rather than march with me? Speak now if you do."

Nobody did, though a fair number were looking green and gulping. They were a lot harder grained than an equal number of random rural Americans would be, but this wasn't the sort of thing that happened very often in their peaceful corner of the world either. It had been a long time since enemies threatened the Villa Lunae.

And if I have anything to say about it, it'll be another long time after this.

"We are those who put our bodies between our kinsfolk and the war's desolation," he said firmly. "Remember that!"

He turned to the veteran. "Gnaeus, get people organized, get the bodies down, build a pyre...no, we'll use the house, lay them out inside, put the coins on their eyes. And do it fast."

The man nodded soberly and said:

"Animal for the sacrifice, sir?"

That would satisfy the religious sensibilities via an offering to Ceres. Cremation was the usual Roman rite anyway. Artorius silently jerked his thumb at the wounded Marcomann, and the veteran smiled thinly and nodded. Artorius went on:

"Sarukê, bring me that Marcomann. We need to make him talk," he said.

She did, dismounting and tying her horse and dragging the man over by locking her right hand in a fistful of hair, his legs scrabbling to push him along as he moaned and whimpered.

She threw him down at Artorius' feet as he dismounted.

"You go and join Josephus and his man until we're through here. I don't want any unexpected guests," he said.

"Lord," she said, and swung back onto her horse with a lithe skip that made nothing of her gear.

"Dablosa!"

That was the senior-most of the bodyguards under Sarukê, a stocky quick-moving Dacian of about his own age, with close-cropped reddish hair and beard. The ex-gladiators were all mounted, and none had gotten out of the saddle.

"You'll be taking Lord Marcus—"

Which meant Mark Findlemann.

"And Lady Paula to Vindobona. Get them inside the wall, and put them up at a good inn. Assign one man to stay and guard them, and then rejoin us with the other three on the road from the northwest gate—and incidentally, if we're alive tomorrow by sunset, all of you get a month's bonus. You'll earn it, too, one way or another."

"Maybe I'll need to pay the guards to get inside the wall, sir," Dablosa said; the others were looking pleased. "Looks like things are rough around here right now and they'll be jumpy."

He shrugged. "Townsfolk, you know how it is, sir. They scare easy."

His Latin was accented, but much more fluent than Sarukê's. Dacia had been a province of the Empire for fifty-odd years now, since Trajan's conquest back around the beginning of the second century. If he had family, they'd be among the ancestors of the Romanians.

Or would have been, except for us.

Artorius passed him a handful of silver coins, which ought to cover everything.

"You two get into the saddle," he said to the Americans; they had plenty of spare mounts along. "I'll see you tomorrow or the day after, probably."

If we're not dead didn't need to be said aloud, and he thought they both picked up on it; a few hours of fast riding wouldn't kill them though it would leave them sore.

Live and learn.

"No argument, Prof," Paula said, unusually subdued.

Mark nodded after rinsing out his mouth from a goatskin bag of watered wine and spitting.

"Fil, get them horses, saddle them up and ride with them down to where the lane joins the road. Fast. You stay there when they and the guards head for town, keep an eye out and we'll rejoin you, or you can come up when you see the funeral pyre lit. You *don't* want to come back right away if you can avoid it. Stay alert."

Paula and Mark were keeping their eyes carefully averted from the farmhouse. So was Filipa, looking at the clouds.

"Right, Prof," Filipa said tightly, and shepherded them off toward the remount string.

Artorius waited until they were a little distance off up the laneway to the north, then called to the crews about their grisly tasks:

"I need someone who can speak Marcomannic!"

One of the veterans barked: "You two! With me!"

He trotted over with his helpers. Artorius wasn't surprised they had a bilingual. They didn't have AI translator earbuds here, and the man had spent twenty-five years with the Danube legions. Sometimes you had to be able to communicate with the people you fought, might fight, or were preparing to fight.

As he passed one of the wagons, the veteran stopped for an instant and pulled out a sledgehammer, hefting it as he walked over with a brisk stride with a hint of a hitch in it when his right foot came down. He was a stocky man in his late forties, like most of the half-dozen ex-legionnaires, and his arms bulged with stringy muscle roped with visible veins. A scar drew up his upper lip over one yellow tooth, and the tip of his nose ended in a small blob of scar tissue, probably from the same fight.

This was almost certainly *not* his first field interrogation, either. He showed that when he arrived, kicking over an empty barrel and telling his assistants:

"Put him over that... no, with the backs of his knees on it, you fools, not ass up. I want to ask him questions, not bugger him! I'm picky where I put my dick, not like this piece of barbaro-shit."

Then he briskly swung the sledgehammer, smashing the man's left knee to bleeding pulp with a crackling sound that put the American's teeth on edge like fingernails on a blackboard.

After the first shrill screams, he turned to Artorius, smiling.

"What do you want to ask him, sir?"

"Where the host crossed, how many, when."

The veteran chuckled. "The usual. Ah, that takes me back!"

Then before he dropped into the rhythmic, buzzing sounds of Proto-Germanic:

"All right, Hermann, let's get on with it—"

➢ CHAPTER THIRTEEN ➣

Banks of the Danube,
North of Vindobona
May 20th, 166 CE

"Lēgāte, *futui sumus*," Centurion Lucius Sextius Caelius, the First Spear of the Tenth Legion Gemina, said to its commander.

He was standing on the ground by the legate's right knee, as the senior officer sat his charger, resplendent in muscled cuirass, scarlet cloak and official sash of the same color. When the man looked down, the eyes under his crested, heavily decorated helmet were fixed and staring in a way that made the senior centurion suddenly realize his commander had come to the same conclusion as he had about their situation.

And had no earthly idea of what to do about it.

The tribunes were all out somewhere trying to shore things up, except for the highest-ranking one, the *tribunus laticlavius*. Who was a young second cousin of the legate and was having a very permanent nap over yonder, where he'd stopped a slingstone by head-butting it.

Lucius went on, hoping to get through to the man:

"These Hermanns, there are just too many of them, sir, and they're not stopping for shit. Sir."

Lucius wiped a cloth at the blood running into his eyes from the cut on his brow; he could taste it, mixed with the even more familiar salt of sweat running down and under the cheekpieces of his helmet. It wasn't the first time he'd tasted his own blood in twenty-three years with the Eagles, or the twenty-third for that matter, but he didn't recall ever feeling such a conviction of impending death along with it.

Plus the usual aches and stings, a feeling in the muscles of his shield arm that reminded him he wouldn't see forty-four again, the throbbing headache you got from wearing a helmet all day (and getting thumped on it occasionally), and a thirst so complete that even gulping down a full canteen on his way here from the left flank hadn't cut it much.

He'd been making payments on a snug little villa south of Vindobona for his retirement for years, and his woman of twenty years and their children lived there. They'd already been drawing up plans and an invitation list for the *official* wedding when this last hitch was over at the end of next year, *gregarius miles* style. His eldest boy Marcus was just about old enough to enlist himself, and champing eager to do it, the young fool.

What a waste of money I could have spent on drinking Falernian and screwing fancies and betting as much as I felt like on slow charioteers and clumsy gladiators.

He felt as if he was chewing on brass strips, coated with bitter alum. Dying in battle himself was one thing. It surprised him to wake up alive some mornings and he hadn't really expected to make it this far. This was the biggest *battle* he'd ever been in, but there had been plenty of *fighting* on this frontier even during the ostensible peace of Antoninus Pius' reign.

But if this monumental buggering *cladis* went the way he thought it would there would be nothing left of the Tenth but the detachments sent to the Parthian war. The countryside would be burned out all the way south to Sirmium ... or even further. The Marcomanni host had already shed a dandruff of raiding parties who found pillage more attractive than a pitched battle, and there were pillars of smoke to the west and south marking their progress.

"We're in some difficulties, yes, *Primus Pilus*," the legate said stolidly.

Lucius fought down an impulse to scream and hack the man's leg off; it wouldn't do any good. Neither would replying:

Some difficulties, yes, and the Alps are likely to slow you down a bit, you blue-blooded filius meretricis!

They were about a mile southwest of the Danube here, and on a long low slope facing northeast. There were woods on the other side of the road behind them, both a bit further upslope still, but the command group had an excellent view of the engagement over their own troops' heads.

Here the Romans were, their line running from a little west of north to a little east of south; there the Hermanns were, right now in close contact. It was painfully obvious that the Marcomannic line was a lot thicker than the Roman, though the terrain features securing the flanks meant they couldn't overlap, and they didn't have enough discipline to rotate their front rank with rested men. Which was probably why there were still Romans alive on this field.

Not just Marcomanni and Quadi. Long-beards, Vandalii... odds and sods from all over the sodding Barbaricum.

The battle would have been mostly amid fields of barley that would be ready for harvest in summertime, if thousands of men hadn't been trampling—and killing and dying—across it since an hour before noon. Now it was looking to be a red sunset in a few hours, of which the only good feature was that now the sun was in the *enemy's* eyes. Dust was heavy on his tongue, and the stink was thick enough to cut into chunks and burn like peat.

It would also have been a very good position, if the Tenth was at full strength, putting the enemy in the dubious position of fighting uphill, with a big deep river at their backs. The lowest parts of the slope were...had been...in young fruit trees and pollarded willows, which slowed and broke up German attacks a little. The Roman right wing was secured on a low wooded hill, and their left on one that was bare, but steep on its eastern side.

Cavalry and reserves had been stationed behind, to contain any breakthrough and pursue once the barbarians lost heart. Pursuit meaning cavalry and auxiliaries taking the heads in their usual fashion, and chasing the rest into the Danube to drown, and with luck leaving some prisoners to sell.

Except that the reserves had all been committed, and then chunks of cavalry had been dismounted and pushed into thin spots, and now the line was nothing *but* thin spots and the men were starting to look over their shoulders and it was hard to blame them.

"Sir, if we were full strength, we could have done this. But we had five thousand three hundred and twenty-two men to start with as of the morning roll call, that's counting every ass-wiping piece of sponge from the auxiliaries. We're half strength, with the detachments off east. I know it, you know it, and that *spurcifer* Prince Ballomar over there knew it when he started this, and we just can't hold them here anymore. If we pull back now maybe we can get *some* men back to Vindobona—get the standard away, at least."

The Eagle of the Tenth stood not far from where the legate sat his horse, swept-back golden wings outstretched with the *aquilifer* carrying the staff proudly, lion's head on his helmet and the guard from Lucius' own cohort around it. His face was impassive; you had to be unmoved by death, your own or another's, to get that position.

To the First Spear's eyes the golden wings shone with holiness and dread. The divine Julius Caesar had bestowed it, when the Tenth was raised for the conquest of Gaul more than two hundred years ago. The Tenth had carried it from one end of the world to the other. Legionnaires would die for the standard as they would for Rome—the Eagle *was* Rome.

And there were many times their number of Germans down there, all of the barbarians ready and eager to help them do just that sort of heroic self-sacrifice. The Tenth had come out here expecting a really big raiding party...

And found a giant army of nothi Germanici *burning and plundering and killing and molesting the sheep.*

It wasn't like granddad's day, either. It wasn't naked savages with clubs, or a metal point on their wooden spears if they were really lucky. Though there were still plenty of madmen possessed by *Wōdinaz*, bare-arsed save for their holy bearskins...and you had to cut them to ribbons before the frothing-mouthed bastards would decently die, as well.

But far too many of the Marcomanni and Quadi and other border tribes had done hitches in the *auxilia* by now, or their brothers and fathers and grandfathers and cousins had, and brought back what they'd learned to pass on to youngsters. The chiefs and their handfast men had mail coats nowadays, and good helmets and shields and *some* idea of how to fight in groups.

Even a lot of the ordinary farmers the chiefs called up to fight had at least metal-strapped leather caps and boiled cowhide breastplates and a reasonable spear and sword—Roman merchants would sell them gear in exchange for their cattle and pigs and furs and sometimes for their neighbors, and their own smiths kept picking up tricks.

The legion was still killing them two or three to one...

But there's always a Hermann irrumātor *number three and four and five,* he thought, despairing. *All right, now he tells me to go back to my post, and I do, and we all die. Kill a few Hermanns first, and at least I won't have to live with the shame of losing our Eagle.*

Hooves clattered behind the command group and his head twisted around automatically, but the party coming down from the road were obviously Romans, you could tell that at a glance. For that matter, they still had *some* cavalry covering the flanks and rear, enough to raise the alarm if not block any move in force.

Romans, but civilians and therefore useless, he thought.

The legate's mounted guard detail swiveled their horses and brought spears down in an X as one of the newcomers broke away and rode close, but Lucius recognized who it was. Josephus ben Mattias, the merchant—a Jew, a citizen, moderately rich until recently and then somehow much richer, well known along the frontier as a hard bargainer but one who kept his deals fairly and to the inch. What he was doing here, the Gods only knew. He had a German bodyguard with him, an ex-gladiator like most in the trade, though not that weird Sarmatian she-devil he'd used to drag around.

"Hail, most noble *Legate* Sextius Lollius Tiberianus," the Jewish merchant cried formally, saluting.

He was in helmet and mail shirt himself, and his Latin had only a little of the characteristic lilt of someone who'd spoken Greek first and learned the Roman tongue later.

"Let him through!"

Josephus preempted questions: "As a loyal citizen of the *rēs pūblica Rōmāna,* I have brought my household, my friend Lucius Triarius Artorius and *his* household"—even then, Lucius' eyes narrowed slightly. There were rumors about a newcomer of that name, wild ones—"and a new weapon of great power to your aid on this bloody day," he said... or declaimed.

He pointed to the left wing, the northern wing, where the First Cohort had been doing its best since it was sent to contain a breakthrough an hour and a half ago, and where a column of Germans was obviously getting ready for a final push. Screaming and stamping their feet and hammering swords and spears on their flat plank shields, with various crude-to-bestial standards and banners swaying and chiefs giving pep talks. Some of them were doing it while standing on shields held up to shoulder height by their followers.

Six oddly harnessed six-horse teams from the road behind the Romans were heading to the hill there at a slow trot, their wheeled burdens bouncing behind them as they took the slope. On the western side that rose gently, until it ended in a near cliff facing the foe.

"They are going there. Have I your permission to act to support the emperor's loyal soldiers?"

"Yes, yes," the legate said.

The oddity seemed to jar him a little out of his funk, if only in the sense that an irritating fly you had to brush out of your face would.

"*Primus Pilus*, see to it on the way back to your cohort!"

"Sir!" Lucius said, and signed his *optio* forward with his horse.

The First Spear leapt creditably into the saddle, very nimbly for a man in his early forties, wearing armor and after a very hard day.

"What the *caca* is going on, Josephus?" he asked the Jew as they cantered along behind the line. "What are you doing here? New weapon? What does that mean? You've got Hercules' club or Jupiter's thunderbolt with you? Or Mithras is dropping in for a drink? Your Jew God throws thunderbolts too, doesn't he? I'll take anything I can get right now. Including Wōdinaz and Thunraz and Balðraz if they were on my side."

"He smites in any way He pleases, honored senior Centurion, with fire or plague or flood," Josephus said. "The Lord gives, the Lord takes, blessed be the name of the Lord."

They were far enough behind that no stray arrows or sling-stones were likely to impede their passage; if the First Spear was going to die, he intended to do at the head of his own personal command. There wasn't much wreckage or detritus or many bodies (except for the laid-out Roman wounded being attended to) either, because the Roman force had been falling back slowly over the past hour. The whatevers the Jew had brought looked a little like *carroballistae* now, though he couldn't see any details.

Any of those would be welcome; usually a legion had about fifty of the mobile dart throwers, but the detachments sent to the Parthian war in the east had taken nearly all of them. The

country was more open there anyway, and they were very useful against cavalry hanging on your flanks. The Parthians had
forts and walled cities too, though their field armies were mostly
mounted archers and cataphracts. Most of the fighting *here* had
been against small raiding parties for nearly a generation now.

The bolt casters had been sorely missed in a biggish set-piece
battle like this. Fifty of them showering four-foot darts through
two or three men at a time, shield or armor or no, would be
just what was needed to discourage the Hermanns now whipping
themselves into a frenzy around Prince Ballomar right opposite
his own First Cohort. And obviously intending to punch through
and roll up the line; just the spot to send your reserves, if you
still *had* any reserves.

*Which we don't. Six catapults... six will be six better than
none. Not enough, but some help.*

The distance behind the line also made it possible to talk
at something less than a complete scream, because it gave them
a slight distance from the waterfall roar of combat. Battle cries
and screams of agony and rage, metal thudding on shields and
occasionally clanging iron on iron, the whicker of arrows and
the whistle of javelins, bellowed orders and the sound of *cornua*
and *tubae*.

He noted absently that the merchant was using one of those
big new-fangled saddles with rests for the feet on straps, but
didn't have enough time to comment on it as Josephus went on:

"And I meant just what I said, *Primus Pilus*, a new... a *novel*
weapon," Josephus said with a tight smile. "You won't believe it
until you see it and hear it anyway. I didn't," he added mysteriously.

A few hundred paces ahead of them the six-horse teams were
wheeling half a dozen *somethings* into line abreast on the hill that
anchored the Tenth Legion's left wing. That had a barely perceptible
slope up from the road, but a really sudden, steep drop-off ten
paces high or a bit more toward the river eastward. You could
climb it from that direction, but you'd need to use your hands,
or a spear butt, and you couldn't do it quickly.

Now he was close enough to see that the machines looked a
bit like ordinary field catapults, but mounted differently. On two-
wheeled carriages, not just carried in a small cart. The two-wheeled
arrangement had been linked to another two-wheeled cart by a
pole, and the second vehicle apparently held ammunition. Now

they were being unlinked and the ammunition carriers opened up and when the pole was dropped to the ground the catapult was at throwing level.

Clever, he thought. *Faster to move around a battlefield.*

Josephus smiled, looking almost smug despite the massed German mad-dog killers less than long bowshot away.

"It's not the catapults, though they've some good new tricks, it's what they'll be throwing," he said. "Hail and fare you well, *Primus Pilus*! May we meet and drink together to victory after the battle! Oh, and beware—there will be very loud noises."

He spurred his horse toward the hill, looping around to take it from the easy western side. Lucius turned right, down the slope to the Roman position, slid off his mount as someone took the reins and strode forward to his position beside the cohort standard—a tall spear with two scarlet tassels hanging from a crossbar at the top, and the crowns and disk medallions of unit decorations below.

His *optio* handed him his shield and he settled the nearly twenty-pound weight of laminated wood and leather and iron by strap and handgrip, ignoring another sharp twinge in his shoulder. He'd been hefting it, or the double-weight training version, since his enlistment—and before, when his own father, who'd been a promoted ranker, put him through his paces.

So I can use it today until the Hermanns kill me, which shouldn't be long. You can rest when you're dead.

The next-senior centurion shouted into his ear; they were only three ranks back from the front and the noise was like the end of the world.

"What orders?" Lucius heard bawled into the side of his head.

"Stand and die, what else?" he screamed back. "Let's take some of the fellatizing Hermann bumboys with us."

The noise ebbed just a bit as the Germans in actual contact on this flank backed and then trotted away to join the mass forming for the next attack, snarling and roaring and throwing things that banged and rattled on the Roman shields like hail on a tile roof as they went. One rock slammed into his own upraised shield, rocking him back on his heels and making him thankful for the pain in his shoulder. It beat having the stone slam into his *face*, beat it all the way to the River Styx and back.

The Roman troopers took the opportunity to switch ranks at

the centurions' orders, or in some cases the *optio*s if the century commander was dead; the frontline men stepping sideways and then walking backward between the files in a clatter of armor as the next rank stepped up, then switching to the rearmost position, leaning on their shields and gasping, gulping water cut with raw issue wine that was nearly vinegar until they coughed, and tending to hurts too minor to send you back to the *medicii*.

Everyone was tired, though. A lot of the faces beneath the helmet-brims were gray, a lot of limbs had rough bandages of rags around them.

"What's that?" the other centurion asked, pointing to the hill on their left.

Lucius glanced that way. The catapults were in position ten paces up and a hundred and fifty north. They looked ready for business; they had an unusual arrangement of two metal shields on either side of their throwing trough, hinged to the vertical bronze tubes that contained the sinew springs, and thin lines of smoke were coming up from behind them.

Maybe the *new weapon* was flaming bolts, which might impress the Hermanns. Though they wouldn't kill them any deader than dead. Setting your target's chest hair on fire after skewering his gizzard was gilding the lily.

"It's that crazy Jew merchant Josephus, brought us some *carroballistae*, says they're improved types and heap big bad news," he yelled. "Got a friend with a spooky reputation with him. Can't hurt, and I've got to grant him guts."

"I'll buy him a long drink and a thousand years with the best whores in the afterlife," the other centurion shouted, grinning. "With the ghosts of Helen of Troy and Dido of Carthage in his bed at the same time, if I get a big enough pension from Hades."

Lucius nodded. "No *brains*, since he's come to join in this cluster buggery, but *guts* to spare, I grant him that."

He shrugged armored shoulders: "Jews, what can you say?"

It was commonly known that Jews were crazy; the number of doomed rebellions they'd launched against the Empire was solid evidence of that, if refusing to eat delicious ham wasn't proof enough of madness. Detachments from the Tenth had fought Bar Kokhba's uprising in Judea when his own father was a new-minted *optio*, just thirty years ago now. And from the old man's stories it had been pretty much like fighting rabid Germanii drunk on Wōdinaz, except extremely quick and tricky ones instead of lumbering ox-stupid dolts foaming at the mouth.

"Now let's push your century to—"

The first of the catapults on the hill cut loose with the familiar *tunng-WHACK*, though much louder than you'd expect from a light *carroballista*. It was throwing some sort of round projectile, not a dart, and it blurred through the air trailing smoke…

As the little column came off the road Artorius reined his horse aside and pointed.

"There!" he shouted, pointing at a hill on the north end of the Roman line. "Set up there, a bit back from the edge of the slope down eastward, and angled back from the right to take the enemy in defilade!"

Filipa Chang nodded, Sarukê saluted, and the six…

Engines, he thought.

Six *engines* of the battery headed that way across the trampled grain stalks of the field, bouncing a little as the wheels hit furrows. Sarukê and Filipa were in the lead, the Sarmatian to manage the teams with her near-supernatural talent for handling horses, and Filipa to site the catapults and oversee their operation. He'd discovered she was very good at estimating ranges, and that was a valuable talent now that tracking lasers were nostalgic memory.

None of the crews were trying to run away screaming, at least, though the freed slaves and tenant's sons looked to be feeling a combination of fear and exaltation as they ran along beside the catapults. The scar-faced grizzled veterans riding on each lead left-hand draught horse were mostly grinning, or at least snarling in a contented sort of way.

They knew what their new toys could do, and were willing to risk German spears to see it happen with live, but soon to be dead, targets.

The hill had a gentle slope on the western side, and dropped off more sharply on the east, which was perfect. Josephus peeled off with a wave to talk to the legate, since you had to at least make a gesture toward the chain of command; Artorius waved back, then ignored him and concentrated on his part of the job, heeling his horse into a gallop after his command.

He pulled up just as the teams wheeled to put the business end of the engines toward the enemy, each one to the left a bit further forward, following the line his left arm cut as they'd been trained.

"Dablosa!" he called to the chief bodyguard. "Get your men about ten yards in front of the engines. Deal with anyone who comes up over the lip of the hill."

The Dacian nodded and sorted his three men out—one was still in Vindobona with Mark and Paula.

The battery were about twenty feet up above the rest of the battlefield here, which would help a bit, and he could see a massed enemy formation forming into a blunt wedge—what the Germans called a *swine array*, named for its resemblance to the head of a wild boar.

Obviously someone on the other side, probably Prince Ballomar himself, intended to snap the Roman line at the end and roll it up.

These aren't like field guns, he thought, not for the first time, looking at his soon-to-be-no-longer-secret-weapons. *Think of them as field* mortars, *but short ranged. Those bombs have about the same punch as a heavy mortar round. But we never got targets like this. Like firing into a subway platform in New York at rush hour!*

They were about two hundred yards away from the enemy, and the ground between the Germans and the Tenth Legion's line of battered shields was littered with broken weapons and dead men—the dead mainly Germans, many with the Suebian hair knot above their right ears, but scores of armored Romans too. Each deposit of corpses or twitching, moaning wounded ran in wavering north-south lines across the slope.

"Like waves on a beach," he murmured to himself. "Washing higher and higher each time."

The smell was pretty bad; he'd been close to ripped-open bodies before, but not in thousands-strong masses like this, and it was as if a major blood bank had slashed all its containers and let them flow into an open sewer, and then the sun heated it all until it steamed. Battles in this age were concentrated, not like the twenty-first century, when you dispersed to survive.

Concentrated in time and space.

Here you fought close enough to see a man's eyes and smell the stink of his breath. Such safety as there was meant standing shoulder to shoulder with your comrades; it was just as deadly as the fighting he'd done in his younger days, but less lonely.

The noise was a white blur at this range, but a snarling beat was growing from the German swine array, the individual screams and howls settling into a unified:

"*Ha*-ba-da, *Ha*-ba-da, *HA!*-BA-DA, *HA!*-BA-DA . . ."

And then they broke into a screaming, pounding run with the standards of their chiefs—often topped by the skulls of men and horses, bears and wolves—leaning forward with the war leaders and their sworn men grouped around them. Prince Ballomar's own flag, an antlered man with a spear painted on cloth and hanging from a crossbar, was toward the point of it. Artorius . . . who rarely thought of himself as Arthur Vandenberg any more . . . pointed to it and shouted:

"Filipa! That flag is the aiming point!"

She didn't look up as she dashed from one catapult to another, but she waved an arm without turning. They'd mounted the weapons on something like Civil War Napoleon twelve-pounder carriages, except that they had split trails—the recoil was low enough that you could do that, and each trail had a big spade's-head thing on the end that dug into the ground. As the trails were drawn apart the horse teams wheeled around to face away from the business end of each weapon; a man ran back with a rope and hook and hitched it to the drawbars.

The horses pulled, with the drivers yelling and urging them on . . . and a ratcheting sound came as that force went through pulleys to draw back the curved iron throwing arms. Each was run into a slot in a bronze column full of twisted ox sinews, one each on either side of the throwing trough. A six-horse team could exert a *lot* of force and the pulleys they'd rigged used mechanical advantage well. The draw weight was in multiple tons and it didn't take long to cock the action, seconds rather than minutes.

He was close enough to see the fixed grin of tension as the nearest catapult team brought a round bronze ball from the limber; they knew what it could do, and they were only *just* convinced that the foreign magicians could keep the evil spirits under control. It was the size of a man's head, sheet metal soldered and crimped together from two halves beaten into shape around a wooden ball. The all-up weight was twenty-five pounds or so, with the powder and lead shot inside.

Filipa bent behind the sights of the first: "Range two hundred—up . . . up . . . left traverse . . . that's right!"

Then: "Light the fuse!"

The crew chief opened the top of a perforated brass candle-holder and applied the flame inside to the loose end of the long string. That ran from a wooden plug through the bronze sphere that sat ahead of the cable linking the throwing arms. The fuse was woven hemp soaked in saltpeter solution and carefully dried, and it caught with a sputter and shower of sparks. A moment's wait to be sure it had taken, and—

"Shoot!"

Tunng-WHACK!

The curved four-foot arms whipped forward too quickly to actually see; they seemed to jump from full back to slamming into the rope-wound rests without crossing the intervening space. The ball wasn't quite as fast; it was a blurred streak leaving the throwing trough, but you could follow it once it was a hundred feet away, and it was trailing a thin plume of smoke and sparks.

The Germans reacted; they knew about catapults even if they didn't use them. It would be a rock, traveling fast. It might kill one man, or two or three, and cripple more. That didn't mean much to them, not with victory in front of their eyes ... and the eyes of sworn lord, comrades, kinfolk, neighbors and oath brothers on them, to witness their honor or their shame.

Arrows or spears or stones from a sling could kill just the same, after all, and a man who died facing the foe feasted with the Gods forever. A bubble of space shaped like a teardrop opened where a practiced eye could see the shot would fall; they wanted to kill before they died if they could, to have slaves in the afterlife.

Artorius levelled his binoculars, a taut grin on his face as he rode to the crest of the hill nearest the enemy. They'd all seen what the spray of raiding parties spun off from the Marcomanni host thought was a pleasant day's exercise in the fresh air.

These guys have it coming. Oh, so much.

The bronze sphere struck the newly cleared space, bounced head high and spinning, visibly bent out of shape, and—

CRACK!

A snapping flicker of red light, instantly hidden by the puff of dirty gray smoke. Black powder made the *fog of war* more than a metaphor—in fact, he was pretty sure that was what had given rise to the proverb in the first place. Scores of men opened out from that center like the petals of a flower—an incongruous image for limbs torn loose, blood and bits of flesh and sharp fragments of bone spattering twenty yards, brains cracked open like hen's eggs by lead balls traveling too fast to see.

Thirty-yard kill radius, he thought coldly. *Quite a few of them within thirty yards.*

One *severed* head arched up, still covered in a helmet that had a gilt boar as a crest, seemed to pause for a second, then fell back into the smoke. Beyond the circle of dismembered and the dead were a penumbra of figures that shrieked and writhed and crawled. The harsh fireworks stink drifted toward them on the westward breeze.

And the Marcomanni swine array froze in place—jerkily, by blobs and sections and individuals, looking back over their shoulders or craning around to see what the thundercrack meant.

"Battery—shoot!" Filipa shouted.

She'd been at that farmhouse too.

Tunng-WHACK! Tunng-WHACK! Tunng-WHACK! Tunng-WHACK! Tunng-WHACK!

That curiosity meant none of the Marcomanni were looking up when the next five bombs arrived; they mostly hadn't realized the catapult had anything to do with the big noise yet. And then right on the heels of the sound of the catapults:

CRACK-CRACK-CRACK-CRACK-CRACK!

Like a ripple of monstrous firecrackers in a string, by malignant luck landing nearly down the middle of the swine array. Artorius grinned savagely as the whole formation vanished amid a fivefold ripple of red flashes and clouds of smoke.

When that began to clear a few seconds later, overlapping circles of dead and wounded lay, or moaned and screamed and whimpered and writhed and tried to crawl or tried to stuff guts back into bodies.

The fringe at the rear was running—he trained his field glasses and saw men limping, or with faces blood splashed and distorted by terror looking over their shoulders... And he saw unwounded warriors throwing away shield and spear and dashing for the Danube, heedless and witless and howling in bug-eyed terror, with tears running down their bearded faces. By then the second volley was ready:

CRACK-CRACK-CRACK-CRACK-CRACK-CRACK!

"Cease fire!" he shouted.

They only had enough for twelve rounds from each catapult, and that made his back teeth ache from clenching. That wasn't enough to actually kill off many of the enemy as a share of their total numbers, which were huge. Even with the dense-packed formations there just wasn't enough ammunition or enough launchers.

It would have to be a mental gut punch or kick in the crotch, alien and incomprehensible and terrifying even to hardened killers.

That seemed to be working, though the unfamiliarity would be gone after this. There weren't many Germans left around the area that they'd selected as the launching ground for their final attack, and most of those were running. They were probably screaming that *Thunraz* of the Thunder had aimed his hammer at them, which from their point of view was a perfectly rational explanation. They lived in a perceptual universe alive with spirits good or bad, the barrier between world and otherworld thin as cloth.

Which all meant that right now *Wōdinaz* wasn't with them after all, they weren't going to win, and evil spirits would eat their souls if they didn't get out of Dodge, pronto.

The grin died as he saw that Prince Ballomar's standard was still up; and there were about sixty or seventy warriors with him, hale or at least still standing. The barrage had landed not where he was but where he'd been a few seconds before, probably unavoidable and providing him with—living—shields to absorb the lead shot.

A tall man in armor of gilded scales, with a rearing serpent or dragon on the top of his helmet, stood beneath it. Artorius focused his glasses; the man's face was covered in blood, probably mostly other people's, which made his teeth more white by contrast as he shouted—and pointed his sword right at the hill that bore the catapults.

Oh, shit, Artorius thought, startled into English. *Why can't enemies* all *be conveniently slow on the uptake?*

Ballomar started forward, swinging the sword around his head in a flashing glitter. The standard-bearer followed, and then men by ones and twos and then groups. Even with ears battered by the explosions, Artorius could hear their shrieks—mostly on the lines of:

"Slahadau!"

Which was the imperative form of the verb "to kill." It was

one of the first things you picked up in the Proto-Germanic of this century. Fuchs had packed a book on that ur-language, too.

"*Kill!*"

"*Slahadau ubilôz wikkaniz!*"

"*Kill the evil wizards!*"

"Oh, *shit*," he said.

Then he dismounted and ran for the nearest limber. Filipa was standing frozen—she'd seen what he had, and knew they couldn't depress the catapults enough to bear on *this* threat. Sarukê was beside her, mounted and reaching for her bow; Sarmatians were nomads and didn't have a hang-up about retreating, but she wasn't going to leave her friend, lover and sword-sister. Josephus and his bodyguard were galloping up from the base of the hill to the west; the Jew was drawing his *spatha*, face set.

Sarukê looked at Artorius as he grabbed a ball out of the rack in the limber, turned and ran back toward the edge of the slope.

"Get the shot!" he screamed. "Light the fuses short!"

There were about as many of his followers around the catapults as there were German warriors with Ballomar, but they mostly weren't really trained to sword and spear—it would be like ducks trying to fight wolves, or at least foxes. The veterans were highly skilled but past their best, there was Sarukê, and the four other ex-gladiators...

And I'm no Miyamoto Musashi with the sword yet, either.

His example did more than his words, as he ran toward the edge of the slope leading down to the battlefield. Sarukê moved first, and Filipa a moment later, both snatching round bombs out of the closest limber and dashing after him. The Sarmatian woman even had the fuse on hers cut short by the time her horse arrived at the edge, because she'd caught the cord between her teeth and trimmed it with her dagger as she rode.

Artorius copied her, and noticed Filipa doing so too; it was a three-arm job if you wanted speed. He pulled something he'd just had made for the battery out of his pouch; a brass tube full of the new distilled naptha, with a flint and a steel in the form of a wheel, beside a wick running down into the reservoir, all covered by a hinged lid.

Not quite the Ronson granddad had in Vietnam, but it'll do, he thought, as his thumb spun it.

A nearly invisible flame touched the end of the short-cut fuse.

He hefted the twenty-five pound weight overhead in both hands and stepped to the edge of the steep drop, a knife-sharp break here. That gave him eyes on Prince Ballomar not twenty feet below, toiling upward by chopping the edge of his big hexagonal shield into the ground to brace himself from slipping. Some of his followers *had* slipped, tumbling and sliding back down.

"*Dawi, wikkô!*" Ballomar screamed.

In German, or the proto-language, that was the imperative of the verb *to die*; another term you picked up.

"Eat this, *filius canis!*" Artorius...or Vandenberg...shouted back, and threw it hard at his face.

Then he threw himself back from the lip of the steep slope, twisting in the air and landing facedown, arms over his head. He'd seen Ballomar in the beginnings of a frantic duck too, but *he* didn't have any place to hide.

CRACK!

This time he was close enough to feel the hot wind from the explosion, and hear the whine of a few lead balls.

Filipa lit and threw hers a second later; Sarukê did the same, wheeled her horse, leaned far over, snatched Filipa up and had her slung across the saddle and safely a few yards distant when—

CRACK! CRACK!

The last explosion seemed to push the final group of Marcomanni over the lip of the slope; one was smoking all along one side, and fell over limply. Prince Ballomar wasn't limp, though the thin bronze of the serpent crest on his helmet had been cut through and dangled to one side, and his shield arm was drooping. He panted like an overburdened hound, and blood and spittle ran from his broken teeth and sprayed out ahead of him and down his reddish-blond beard.

The ex-gladiator bodyguards were all sprinting in his direction, but they'd need a few seconds...

There were no words in the barbarian prince's scream as he charged, sword high. Artorius waited; no point in trying to leap to his feet wearing a mail shirt, that would just trap him halfway up.

Instead he held himself motionless until the long blade passed the top of its arc and started to drive down.

Let him think the evil wizard is paralyzed with fear of his heroic manliness, he thought.

That was probably how it usually went in their sagas or songs or whatever.

Never hurts to be underestimated in a fight.

Then he jerked aside just enough at the very last instant. The steel plunged into the soft dirt beside him, spraying some into his face. His left hand snapped out and caught the sopping-wet sleeve of Ballomar's right arm and pulled hard.

That gave him extra leverage as his left leg came up, knee bent, and then straightened with all the strength of his thigh to drive the heel of his boot into the other man's crotch below the short mail shirt. There was a hard *thump* and the feel of things crushed flat and ruptured between the hammer of the hobnailed leather and the anvil of Ballomar's pubic bone.

Even through the berserker fury, that went home. The other man froze, eyes bulging, mouth open and working but unable even to scream. Artorius flicked himself upright with the Marcomannic chief as a lever and kicked again, a side-thrust kick into the side of the prince's knee.

There was a tooth-grating crackle; not bone breaking so much as tendons snapping as the joint was suddenly punched sideways in a way not suited to the design or construction of knees. Ballomar toppled, still trying to scream and instead making small mewling noises. Artorius scooped up the Marcomannic sword, put the point at the base of the other man's throat, leaned both hands on the hilt and pushed.

He was panting as if he'd run two miles in full kit, and he staggered slightly as he wrenched it free. Fifteen feet away, Josephus was in the act of bringing his sword down on a Marcomanni in a mail shirt . . . but who'd lost his shield and helmet somewhere. His German bodyguard had just topped a head like a boiled egg, which made Artorius blink even now. Three more were being dispatched with businesslike efficiency by Dablosa and his crew.

Just then an arrow whickered past Artorius' neck, nearly close enough to brush the feathers against his skin, and there was a meaty *thock* sound. His head whipped up, in time to see a tall warrior falling back with the arrow in the center of his face, dropping the heavy spear he'd been about to drive home.

Sarukê shot again, into the chest of another spearman not more than ten paces from Artorius. The Marcomanni looked down, coughed a sheet of blood, and collapsed. Artorius looked at her; Filipa had slid down and was holding herself upright by clutching at the stirrup leather of the new-style saddle, staring as the catapult crews swarmed forward and joined Josephus and Dablosa in dealing with the Germans still moving. Ganging them under three and four to one, with the veterans giving advice and sometimes stepping forward to drive home a blade.

The Sarmatian looked down and said to Filipa in her rough Latin:

"You know, Germanii-man think-say so how bow is *unmanly* weapon."

Artorius started to laugh. The Sarmatian followed suit.

Filipa bent over and puked her lunch out on the horse's hooves.

⤳ CHAPTER FOURTEEN ⤎

Banks of the Danube,
North of Vindobona
May 20th, 166 CE

CRACK-CRACK-CRACK-CRACK-CRACK!
Lucius, senior centurion of the Tenth Gemina, felt his mind stutter and gibber. One minute he'd been preparing for death...and now there *was* death.
CRACK-CRACK-CRACK-CRACK-CRACK-CRACK!
Death for the *Hermanns*, in great job lots.
When the sulfur-smelling smoke cleared in a few seconds he could see hundreds of them dead in the formation that had been about to punch through...annihilate...his beloved First Cohort. Hundreds more were wounded, and a thousand or more were simply running away, throwing their weapons aside to run the faster.
His head whipped to either side. His own men were staring in slack-jawed astonishment; there was fear there too, and it could build. That snapped him back to the present moment. He strode forward, the signifer and the signaler beside him. A moment's echoing silence had fallen, not complete but close enough after the roar of battle and then the cataclysmic bangs of...whatever it had been. Something to do with those new catapults, certainly.
"Men of the First Cohort, Tenth Gemina!" he shouted. *"Jove's thunderbolts fight for us!"*
He pointed with his sword to the hill. Heads turned; that let them see the clot of three score or so of Hermanns around Prince Ballomar's standard clawing their way up the steepness.

Three more of the bronze balls arched out, thrown by hand this time, trailing smoke, and...

CRACK! and a very brief pause, then: CRACK! CRACK!

More of the Marcomannic warriors died, with the Romans watching; some of them...or parts of them...flipped all the way back to the base of the hill. A breath of wonder went through the watchers, and he could hear a building excitement in it. To the south, the German line was beginning to unravel; a lot of them could see what was happening too, and rumor would fly like thought, magnifying it.

Battles could turn on their heels sometimes, like a chariot rounding the *spina* in an amphitheater.

Then the last few Marcomanni fell back over the lip of the hill...or the crews of the catapults up above showed up there, waving severed heads and dancing with glee.

"Prepare to charge!" he shouted, with decades of experience in projecting his voice behind it. "Cohort will wheel to the right and advance! For our Eagle, for the Emperor, for Rome! Signaler, sound charge!"

There was a sound from the men as the curled brass instrument sang; first more of a rasping croak: "Jupiter!"

Then a massed bull-chested bellow: *"IUPPITER OMNIPOTENS!"*

Who was now definitely, demonstrably with *them* and giving the Hermanns what they deserved.

Then a crashing double bark, as the far-right century marched in place and the far-left double-timed out, the whole of the 372 men still on their feet performing as if this was a parade:

"ROMA! ROMA!"

The First Spear of the Tenth Gemina chopped his blade forward.

Shields up under their eyes, short swords held hilt down for the gutting stroke, hobnails treading down the dirt and the dead, the living walls of Rome began to walk.

When the legate and his command group cantered up the easy western slope of the hill, Artorius came to his feet and stood beside the heavy Marcomannic battle spear rammed butt-first into the dirt. The veterans chivvied their crews into line and stood to attention as he drew his horse to a halt, and the bodyguards grouped around Saruké and Filipa.

The American saluted, in the palm-out, arm-vertical Roman

style. The legate returned it, his eyes traveling across the catapults and their crews, stopping a second where Sarukê stood helmetless with her arm around Filipa's shoulders, passing on to the scatter of two dozen dead and mostly headless Marcomanni...and then up the spear to the head of Prince Ballomar, mouth gaping and flies swarming for their feast, his mutilated helmet still on his head.

The Roman commander obviously recognized it, probably from previous diplomatic meetings, and gave a slow smile and a satisfied nod.

Josephus slid down from his horse, stepped up beside the American and bowed, indicating him with a sweeping gesture of one arm.

"Behold the maker of this mighty new weapon, my lord Legate," he said. "And the man who slew Prince Ballomar in single combat, and brings his head to the most noble Legate of the Tenth Legion!"

"Commendable," the Roman noble said, then turned back to the American. "This man deserves well of the Republic. Name yourself, that you may receive the thanks of Rome."

Artorius bowed, catching Josephus' eyes as he did so and getting an almost imperceptible nod.

Meaning, he told Centurion Lucius to remind the legate that the Emperors will be getting independent reports about all this from their agents—probably by something tactful along the lines of What wonderful reports the Frumentarii will be sending to Rome, sir! *So don't try to hog all the limelight or you'll look bad.*

"My name is Artorius, most noble Legate," he said firmly. "Lucius Triarius Artorius. My thanks for your generous words."

By now his Latin bore only a faint accent from his native tongue. It was also still, by second-century Roman standards, a bit archaic, in the style scholars and men of old family cultivated. In fact it was quite similar to the legate's diction.

The legate looked up at the head of the Marcomannic prince again, and sighed with the happiness of a man reprieved from death...and worse, from failure and disgrace that would make death attractive as an escape.

"You shall have more cause for thanks. The Emperor in Rome shall hear of your service to the State."

He motioned to a clerk and began dictating a report, still glancing up at the spear and severed head.

⇒ CHAPTER FIFTEEN ⇐

Palatine Hill,
Rome
July 15th, 166 CE

Imperator Caesar Marcus Aurelius Antoninus Augustus entered the room with a slight internal sigh behind a suitably impassive face. He would have preferred to confer with his advisors in the old way, strolling through a garden or a peristyle, as the great philosophers he admired would have done. He was in hard good condition for a man of frail constitution in his forties, ate sparingly of fare as simple as an Emperor could—no great hardship given his frequent stomach pains—and drank only well-watered wine. But his daily duties didn't give him as much exercise as he'd have liked.

And he would have liked to do the walking and conversation in one of the villas near the city, if only because the summer stink of Rome's million-strong population wafted even up here to the Imperial palaces, despite all that the world's greatest net of sewers and aqueducts could do, even to flushing the wastes that piled up on the paved streets into the river in man-made miniature floods. For that matter, the Tiber stank all year 'round for many miles downstream of here, halfway to Ostia.

Everyone in the city who had a country place was there by now if they could, in the hills or at the seacoast.

Still, duty is more important than sweet smells, even the scent of cut grass and flowers. Though those are aids to thought, I find.

His predecessor, uncle and adoptive father Antonius Pius

215

had preferred to hold such meetings sitting down, especially in his later years. And he'd stuck to Rome and a narrow area around it for the whole of his long reign, letting his proconsuls and procurators and legates handle everything else, unlike his energetic and widely traveled predecessor. That had been a sign of the peace, the peace of strength, that the soldier-Emperors Trajan and Hadrian had established.

It looked as if Marcus' reign, and that of his co-Emperor Verus, would be far more...active. Verus was in the east, winning victories...or at least his legates were...but the Parthians weren't giving up just yet despite the sack of their capital, Ctesiphon, though it couldn't be long now.

This news of trouble on the Danube was deeply unwelcome; there had been serious incursions in Upper Germany and Dacia too. The whole barbarian part of Europe seemed to be seething. Everyone knew that transferring three entire legions and large detachments from the others away from the northern frontier to the Parthian campaign was a calculated risk; the problem was that Rome's other enemies knew it too and apparently intended to take full advantage.

The details of the reports from Pannonia Superior were increasingly *bizarre*, as well, even though they told of a Roman victory that was very welcome indeed. For now he'd continue the custom Antoninus had established and discuss it around a table with his *comites*, his close advisors and the men in charge of important parts of the government.

The room was quietly sumptuous, with *opus sectile* marble work on the floor in patterns of gold and green edged with black and red and a rendering of a naval battle—it was Actium—on those walls that didn't open through pillars onto a broad ter-raced balcony with pruned trees and flower bushes in pots and troughs of polished stone.

Some remote part of his mind noted critically that Queen Cleopatra was shown in the mural as a beautiful but evil Egyptian sorceress in the middle of casting a spell. Though in fact she'd been a big-nosed Greek of nearly pure Macedonian descent and a hard-headed, intensely clever politician.

Ruling Egypt didn't make you an Egyptian. In *fact*, she'd been the first of her Lagid dynasty in three hundred years to even bother learning how to *speak* Egyptian.

Braziers with incense joined in the flowers' struggle to make the air sweet.

Praetorian guardsmen came to attention and saluted with a clank of pilum on shield boss as he entered; the half-dozen men around the table rose and bowed slightly. Those not in military dress were wearing togas; by way of contrast the Emperor was in a rather plain tunic, with only the Imperial purple and a little goldwork to mark it out, and a diadem wreath on his head. He slept on a simple pallet too—he was indifferent to luxury, as a Stoic should be, despite being raised at court.

He strove not to be puffed up about it, either, which was more difficult than skipping nightly banquets which his stomach couldn't take and beautiful courtesans or mistresses who did not move him to desire. Plain living could be as arrogant as extravagant luxury, if approached in the wrong way.

Marcus Aurelius winced sometimes in retrospect at how priggish he'd been about it as a youth in the first flush of his love affair with Stoicism.

Insisting on sleeping on the ground in a cloak until dear Mother talked me out of it. Insufferable!

He'd have preferred a retired life of study and thought, in fact. He'd been adopted by his uncle the previous *princeps* when still a young man, only seventeen, and had never *wanted* the purple. One of the few good points about monarchy, considered in the abstract, was that someone born to a throne wasn't *necessarily* obsessed with power for its own sake the way someone who plodded through the whole of the *cursus honorum* had to be.

But duty comes first, always.

"Gentlemen," he said, after their greetings were done.

Those were kept as simple as possible as well. Emperor Domitian had insisted he be addressed as *Dominus et Deus*—Master and God. Besides the absurdity of it...

The slave who empties the Imperial chamber pots knows better, he thought.

...Marcus reminded himself frequently of what had happened to Domitian in the end.

Such a small difference, between Domine—

Which was the standard address for a respectable Roman citizen from those who didn't call him by his praenomen, his first name.

—and Dominus; *only the vocative and nominative cases of the*

same word, but Domitian found out in the end that a declension can be a matter of life and death!

Octavian, the original Augustus, had scrupulously respected the old Republican forms in public... and unlike Julius Caesar *or* Domitian, he'd died old and in bed of natural causes, not under an assassin's knife.

He took his seat at the head of the gleaming stone table; his chair was the only one with back and arms, and it was slightly raised as well, on a one-step plinth. The others remained standing until he had seated himself.

"So," he said.

Leaning forward and coming to the point; ceremony was something he endured when necessary and seemly, not one of the pleasures of his life. A clerk took station behind him, stylus poised over the wax on the polished ebony tablet, ready to take notes. Another from the office of the *Ab epistulis*, the chancellery that handled the Emperor's correspondence, stood ready to pen drafts of any decrees and orders.

The Emperor went on: "What do we *know* of the events in Pannonia? Know with reasonable certainty, that is?"

The Praetorian Prefect was here, the commander of the Guard and a number of other functions; Sextus Cornelius Repentinus was a dark hard-faced man whose family were prominent landowners near Carthage in the Province of Africa. His bright white military dress tunic had the two narrow purple stripes of a knight; that was an equestrian position, mainly because it would give a man of senatorial rank too much power.

With him was his subordinate the *Princeps peregrinorum*, who managed the *Frumentarii* throughout the Empire: they had started as commissary agents, but by now were news gatherers, spies, and at need assassins.

The spymaster spoke:

"Imperator Caesar Augustus, I have three separate reports of the battle on the banks of the Danube between *Legio X Gemina*, its auxiliaries, and a considerable host of Marcomanni, with numbers of Quadi and smaller contingents from several other tribes joining them. They all agree with the legate of the Gemina's claim that the barbarians were defeated with enormous losses, and their remnants chased into the Danube, along with many thousands of living prisoners taken for sale."

There was a chorus of relieved nods around the table. The Emperor nodded too.

"This is most welcome."

Which was an understatement. He frowned in thought, then looked at the clerk from the correspondence chancellery.

"To Legatus Augustus pro praetore Sextus Calpurnius Agricola"—who was the current governor of Britannia, an ex-consular and hence a senator, and from Cirte in Numidia originally, in the central part of northern Africa—"notifying him that he is unlikely to be required to send *vexilliationes* from his three legions to the mainland, and hence he will not be required to withdraw forces from northernmost Britannia as was planned."

If you could read between the lines, Sextus Calpurnius had been *very* unhappy when that was proposed; he'd been in charge of the advance from Hadrian's Wall to the shorter one further north known as the *Vallum Antonini*. He'd also had a distinguished career and hated the thought of an inglorious retreat. This should mollify him...and he was a man whose opinion was respected in military circles.

The clerk's stylus moved over the wax. The spymaster took a deep breath and continued:

"And the reports all agree—in substance though not in every detail—on how this victory was won, sir."

There were nods at that too, this time half unconscious; any intelligent man of rank knew that no two accounts of the same happenings were ever identical unless someone coordinated them. Suspicious uniformity was one of the ways you could tell that an underling was selectively editing what got through to you. Then, of course, you had to wonder if someone was doing that...but was clever enough *not* to make the reports suspiciously uniform.

"Legionary Legate Sextius Lollius Tiberianus underestimated the enemy, and marched out from Vindobona with a force of less than six thousand men, more than half of them auxiliaries, and only realized when engaged that he was facing five times his own numbers. At least five times. The position he assumed was good—on the advice of his *primus pilus*—but by the afternoon of the day of battle and after about six hours of combat they had suffered loses of one in eight or nine killed or seriously wounded, there were no more uncommitted reserves and they were facing

defeat and slaughter. Which would have left the whole province
open to devastation and ruin. Then..."

He swallowed. "Then a party of civilians with six *carroballistae* of a new pattern intervened. Under the leadership of one
Lucius Maecius Josephus, a Jewish merchant, and a newcomer
to the area named Lucius Triarius Artorius, who was granted
Roman citizenship late last year together with four of his clients,
who arrived with him. Arrived from outside the Empire's borders,
and not from any of the client kingdoms either—they claim to
be from an island realm in far western Oceanus."

"Hibernia?" the Emperor asked in surprise; he hadn't heard
that part before.

Hibernia was a proverb for squalor and backward savagery,
full of chanting robed Druids making human sacrifices and tattooed, head-hunting lunatics with lime-bleached hair, still driving
war chariots to battle.

"No, sir, west even of Hibernia; they call it *America*. The
ballistae set up on a hill at the extreme left flank of our position, just as a large Marcomannic force was about to break the
line, and...and here all the reports become very strange, Caesar
Augustus. They speak of...

The man halted, obviously reluctant to continue.

"Go on," Marcus said gently and evenly. "You are speaking
of reports you received. You cannot vouch for them personally
because you were not a witness to these events."

"They speak of, of thunderbolts like those of *Iuppiter Fulgur
Fulmen*, and of the barbarians slain in huge numbers in the blink
of an eye with flashes of red light and smoke smelling like Hades.
And of Prince Ballomar, the Marcomanni leader, being slain by
this Artorius in single combat and his head put on a spear; that
most definitely. Then the First Cohort of the Tenth counterattacked
through the gap the...the thunderbolts...created and it was a
slaughter. The barbarians were demoralized, they ran, and our
men killed until they were too weary to lift a blade; if we had
had more cavalry on hand, not one would have escaped. All of
the German raiding parties were cleansed from our territory over
the course of the next week after doing relatively light damage."

Though unpleasantly heavy *to anyone who fell to their spears,*
the Emperor thought. *Still, it could have been much, much worse.*

The spymaster concluded: "Probably no more than a third

of the barbarians returned alive across the Danube. Those who ran first and fastest."

He looked around the table. "All the reports from my men... each of whom was unaware of the others' presence... and the official report of the legate agree on this. As I said, only differences of detail and emphasis."

Silence stretched, and Marcus was aware of the eyes on him.

"And what of this Artorius?" he said.

"He was first seen, with four companions—two men, one a Jew, and two women of very unusual appearance, a Nubian and one with the looks of those from the furthermost east—"

"I still await the report of the embassy I sent there two years ago," the Emperor said, staring into the distance. "No matter. Continue."

"—in Vindobona in June of last year, in company with Josephus the Jewish merchant. Then a few weeks later they traveled to an estate named the Villa Lunae south of Carnuntum, property of—"

He checked the page before him. "Sextus Hirrius Trogus, an *eques* of old family and of some wealth by provincial standards; he owes Josephus a large sum of money, but they appear to be on friendly terms nonetheless."

"Another magical miracle!" one of the men at the table said, and subsided when the Emperor glanced his way with a frown.

"There Artorius introduced many changes and improvements, some of which have already been copied by others in Pannonia."

"Improvements?"

"In horse gear, farming gear and methods, and the manufacture of new products such as, ah, superwine, a new and superior form of papyrus somehow made from local reeds and ordinary straw, a method of having an open fire in a room without problems from the smoke, and others. Some saw this as evidence of sorcery."

There were snorts from around the table, except from a few of the notoriously superstitious, who touched amulets or made apotropaic gestures for protection. Sorcery *did* exist, no doubt, but the commons saw it under every rock and behind every bush, and it was not a view limited to the illiterate.

"These novelties enriched both Josephus and Sextus Hirrius Trogus; Josephus also used funds borrowed from Artorius to buy considerable quantities of grain and rush it to Vindobona, where it was bought by the camp prefect of the Tenth to fill the fort and city granaries. On the Villa Lunae Artorius made the car-roballistae and their ... well, whatever it is that they throw, over the winter past, and was able to use them at the battle in May."

He looked up again. "Artorius and his companions were at first thought to be barbarians themselves, for they spoke Latin with a heavy, unfamiliar accent on their initial appearance, but more recent reports say that they now speak it very well. In fact, in a scholarly way, like a rhetorician or a senator. They certainly read it, and several of them are also fluent in Greek, including Artorius himself."

"Nobody can improve their command of a language *that* quickly, not *de novo*," the Emperor said. "Hmmm."

Then he tapped his fingers on the right arm of his chair.

"Unless they already knew Latin well, but only from books ... that would be possible. With respect to Greek, it happens some-times with students from the farthest western parts of the Empire, Britannia or Lusitania or the German provinces, for example, who go to Athens for the schools without much contact with *spoken* Greek. They also often improve very rapidly. And they also often speak Greek in an old-fashioned way, having learned from books written centuries ago. But where would someone from the West learn *Latin* only from books? Hmmm. A puzzle. But continue."

"They were granted citizenship by the provincial governor, Marcus Iallius Bassus, immediately after his appointment, at the urging of Sextus Hirrius Trogus."

Marcus stroked his beard. Bassus he knew well, and it seemed the man had done a routine favor to a locally prominent man, granting Roman citizenship to the provincial grandee's favored clients. An effective governor had to be firm, but also to keep the respect and support of his province's men of influence, which usually meant the larger landowners. He'd appointed Bassus late last year, as a man able to deal with the threatened emergencies.

The Emperor stroked his beard again, and sighed. If it weren't for these multiple reports of thunderbolts and strangers with odd powers, he'd be inclined to remain in Rome, where information was most easily available and orders moved quickly. This new pestilence in the east was very worrying, each report of it more alarming than the last as it spread. But as it was—

"I will go to Vindobona myself," he said, and the men looked at each other, recognizing the tone of a decision made firmly.

"The northern frontier needs the attention of an Emperor and it cannot wait. The *Barbaricum* is stirring; the *other* border incursions prove that. One reverse inflicted on the barbarians, even a bloody one, will not see the end of this, so we'll be campaigning north of the Danube next year. And the matter of this battle in the spring must be looked into. With this degree of agreement, something... something truly extraordinary... must have taken place. It is imperative that we know precisely what."

He turned to the Praetorian Prefect. "I will take as many of the Praetorians as can be spared, commanded by yourself, Prefect Repentius; prepare them rapidly. Also, the legates of the *VII Gemina*, *IX Hispana*, and *II Traiana Fortis* are to be informed that they may be called on for *vexilliationes* on short notice, unless it proves possible to divert forces from fighting Parthia, which Mars and all the other Gods grant. Send enquiries to my colleague Imperator Caesar Lucius Aurelius Verus Augustus"— which actually meant to his legionary legates and governors—"as to what forces can be immediately marched back to the Danube frontier without endangering his victories or giving the Parthians new heart."

Clerks scribbled frantically. Verus was regrettably given to putting his own pleasures first, but he would of course be informed at the same time. He wasn't a total wastrel, just... not as dedicated to duty as he might be.

"And set preparations in hand for raising more regular troops," he said. "A full legion, and as many new auxiliary units. Legate Fronto, I will put that in your capable hands."

One of the financial officials actually whimpered slightly; two extra legions, *Legio II* and *Legio III*, both named *Italica* because that was where they'd been recruited, had been commissioned early last year under Fronto's direction. They were in the later stages of their training, and could fight now at a pinch; next year they would be as ready as men could be without actual battle experience.

"We will dispatch the second and third *Italica* to Pannonia, immediately," the Emperor added.

Fronto nodded, his sun-browned hawk face pensive. "They can be there in... to be pessimistic... no more than sixty days from the date of departure. Possibly a few weeks less. A good long forced march will help finish up their training," he added thoughtfully. "So will a winter in a field camp they build themselves, and some skirmishing would be excellent. They'll be ready for field service by next campaigning season. But the new legion *won't*, sir," he added warningly.

Raising new legions was a hideously expensive proposition, besides adding to the standing army that ate at least three-quarters of the Imperial revenues every year.

"We will call the new unit *Legio IV Italica*," Marcus Aurelius said, nodding. "Begin preparations immediately. It will be fit for garrison duty by next year? To relieve an experienced legion for field service?"

"Certainly, sir; frontier garrison duty will help with bringing them thoroughly up to scratch quickly. If I might suggest..."

The Emperor nodded permission to go on.

"...early next year we could send the new *Italica* unit to relieve the Ninth Claudian Legion at Durostorum; the *Claudia* would then be available for Pannonia, especially if the detachments fighting the Parthians can be returned, since it isn't far from Durostorum to Pannonia Superior...and it's closer to the east, too, which would help with getting their cohorts back quickly. They could be shipped by sea from ports in Syria and thence through the Bosporus and to the mouth of the Danube. The *Claudia* is first-rate. We wouldn't want more than two newly raised legions in a field army anyway."

Recruiting legions wasn't just a matter of money, or even finding good recruits; you needed a solid cadre of tried and tested centurions, *optios* and *capidoctores*—instructors in all the arts a soldier had to learn. Which included but were not limited to drill in maneuver and weapons skills; a legion had to be able to build when it wasn't fighting, and supply specialists for a dozen arcane trades.

Durostorum was on the lower Danube, near the Black Sea. And Fronto had commanded the *Claudia* himself late in Antoninus Pius' reign, not too many years ago, so he'd be a good judge. He'd commanded successful actions against the Parthians, too, governed provinces well, and done a good job with the new units; and his family were reasonably prominent in the Senate.

Decision firmed.

"Excellent suggestion, Legate Fronto; make the arrangements, and you will join me in Pannonia with the *Claudia* next year as my second. Keep me closely informed of progress on this matter."

Fronto nodded briskly and stood to salute, with the hint of a carnivore grin if you knew how to read men's more subtle expressions. That would give him a command even more prestigious than the one he'd held early in the Parthian war, and a chance to shine directly under the Emperor's eye.

Marcus Aurelius raised a hand: "You may leave, gentlemen, and prepare for this movement. I wish to depart personally for the north within no more than seven days, and make the journey with all practical speed."

Nobody looked cheered by *that* thought, particularly the ones who'd be going with him. Some Emperors traveled in what was effectively a mobile palace; he was not among them. The fiscal officials, on the other hand, were *always* unhappy these days. Wars were expensive.

Not as expensive as defeat, he thought. *Not as expensive in money, and not in the lives and goods of those it is our function to protect. The State exists for its citizens, though of course all individuals must be ready to sacrifice for it.*

"Galenos, please remain," he added, shifting effortlessly to fluent and accentless scholar's Greek, and the physician did. The clerks left too, at a wave of his hand.

Some of the others gave Aelius Galenus—the Latin form of his name—from Pergamum covert glances as they left, despite how inconspicuous he'd been. Suddenly becoming a court physician, and discussing philosophy with an Emperor known to have a lifelong fascination with it was one thing, but being invited or commanded to attend a private meeting of the Emperor and his *comites* was another. A completely private audience afterward... that was even more so.

Fronto and the Praetorian Prefect Repentius and several others were deep in conversation by the time they reached the door; they'd be extremely busy now, as an explosion of messengers and aides went out from Rome. Legions would march, and many, many lives be forever altered, because of what he'd just said.

A sobering thought. But what must be done, must be done. Not to act is also to act...and badly, generally speaking.

When they were alone, Marcus leaned forward and went on:

"And what of *your* recent correspondence with this mysterious Artorius, oh man who loves wisdom?"

Galen lifted a leather container from beside his feet, set it on the table, unlaced the cover, and took out various objects. The Emperor suspected he'd remained in Rome last year mainly *because* the man Artorius had written him, but he'd brought it to the attention of the Imperial court quickly as well, and they had become friends thereby. And it was always best to have multiple sources for important information.

"First, *kyrios*," he said.

Using the Greek for *lord*, which Marcus preferred to the usual Greek translation of Imperator as *Autokrator*.

"There is the covering letter that arrived with the packages; it is from Artorius himself, and written in his own hand. Which is a good one as I have noted before, but with some odd turns of phrase and even odder...ways of writing."

"Ways?" the Emperor prompted.

"His use of *capitalis quadrata* like those on an inscription in a cursive text, for the first letter of certain types of words... personal and place names, a few others...and for the word at the beginning of a sentence; at the end of the sentence he places an interpunct, not in the middle of the line but at the lower right of a word. And his constant use of a uniform *spacing* between words...which incidentally I find makes silent reading much easier. It is not simple error, it is far too consistent in all his letters and the wording itself too fluent. My guess would be that he is using some at least of his native language's... habits of text."

"Which would imply that his native tongue is not Latin, nor Greek, and that it also has a written form," Marcus Aurelius said thoughtfully. "One similar to ours...using the Latin alphabet, perhaps...but with differences too."

Galen nodded. "This letter is on the new papyrus, and there was a bundle of fifty blank sheets with it for me to examine, as I had requested. It is of more uniform quality than even the best Egyptian scrolls, takes ink better, and apparently is much cheaper. Now to the letter itself."

Galen read it aloud. Marcus closed his eyes in thought.

"So, he claims in response to your doubts that he will prove all his assertions, and as an example invites you to use the therapies he outlines."

"With details of each under separate cover, lord."

"And he is...rather blunt. Grammatically fluent, very much

so, quite scholarly. But abrupt to a degree odd in a man of such obvious education."

"Yes, lord. He outlines two new therapies; the first for wounds, which as you know I dealt with extensively as physician to the gladiators in my native city of Pergamum. The second is for inflammations of the bowels which induce diarrhea. In both cases, he said that I should establish two groups, one to receive this new treatment, and the other not, but to be cared for by doctors using the best standard methods. He calls the latter a *control group* or *reference group*."

"It seems a clever way to quickly assess these new methods without as much time-consuming trial and error as one would normally expect."

"Yes, lord, it is—and possibly of more general application, I think, for testing *any* new treatment, because it isolates the *new* elements and so clarifies cause and effect. In both cases I put ten in one group, ten in the other, assigned to one or the other by throwing dice. And the results were *just* as Artorius predicted. In those suffering wounds or requiring surgery, far more infections in the . . . the control group, where my standard therapies were applied. The treatment for the second group of wound patients involves the application of *doubled superwine*, which came with the letter."

He put two corked glass containers on the table. One was full of a pale yellow liquid, the other of something more nearly colorless.

"Superwine—the yellow fluid here in this bottle"—he tapped the colored one with a finger—"is made by a process of concentration involving heating and then the condensation of vapors."

"But the active spirits of wine are not thickened or concentrated by boiling, if I remember correctly," Marcus Aurelius pointed out.

"Indeed, *kyrios*. Boiling drives them off; but apparently the active element is evaporated at a lower temperature than water, and they may be separated by this. The process catches the vapors in a coil of copper tubing cooled by water, and is called *distillation*."

That was obviously the past-participle stem of *distillare*, "to trickle down in minute drops."

"A clever coinage," Marcus Aurelius said approvingly; skill with words was at the heart of a gentleman's education.

"The initial material can be wine, or other fermented substances, in this case peaches but any sweet fruit would do, possibly even a grain mash such as is used to make beer. I have sampled it; it merely makes you drunk much faster than an equal quantity of unwatered wine, and gives an especially vile hangover."

"As always, immoderation carries its own punishment... eventually."

"Yes, lord. The other, he says, is the result of doubling and redoubling the process. Applied as he specifies, with the other measures, involving boiling of water and surgical instruments and thread to close wounds cleansed *in* the boiling water, cleansing of bandages by high wet heat and drying in a protected container, repeated washing of hands with *sapo* and doubled superwine or the boiled water before touching the patient, careful removal of all foreign matter, and so forth, it reliably prevents infection in a large majority of cases. No or very little pus, laudable or otherwise. No spreading rot or gangrene in *any* of the cases, as opposed to several in the... *control group*."

"Remarkable!" the Emperor said.

Usually some pus was inevitable if there was a deep cut or serious crushing, or if it was necessary to perform surgery.

"Yes, lord. This is a treatment of possibly enormous worth. It would cut wound fatalities massively, and enable surgical interventions with far less risk."

"And the other? The diseases of the bowels?"

Those were always common, particularly in warm weather, in cities, and among children, though anyone could suffer from them and the elderly were almost as vulnerable as the young. Travelers often fell ill with them too, which was among the many miseries of voyaging far afield.

"The treatment for dysenteric illness involves strict bed rest, and the use of a decoction of boiled water—boiled in a covered container—then amended with honey and sea salt, and the mixture administered in large doses. Followed by a regimen of the same gradually combined with broth, then soup of soft materials, then regular soup, and then solid foods boiled to softness. The results are not as absolute as with the wound treatment, but they are definitely not random. The rate of fatality is cut by more than half, and recovery in those cases is usually much swifter than normal."

"*Why* do these treatments give better results?"

Galen smiled thinly and bowed in his seat. "I have no idea, *kyrios*," he said. "None. But I would very much wish to learn!"

Marcus Aurelius nodded slowly. "There seem to be many secrets this man...and his equally mysterious companions...possess. But he is ready to share them, and use them for the benefit of Rome and the State. Or the general good of humankind, in the case of the medical methods."

Galen nodded, and his mouth twisted. "I confess I felt anger at his brusque manner at first, at being treated like an ignorant child...until I remembered how the physicians of Rome attempted to destroy *me* when I arrived here a few years ago, and demonstrated better treatments that had nothing to do with their auguries and superstitions. Treatments I had deduced from empirical study, not merely from *a priori* assumptions! Then I subdued my conceit, as a lover of philosophy should, and accepted my own ignorance—that being, as Socrates said, the beginning of wisdom."

He sighed and turned the letter over. "And he says that if—he repeats that *if*—the new pestilence in the East is what he suspects it is, then he knows of a preventative treatment that will infallibly preserve people from falling ill with it. Though it will *not* cure it if already in progress."

"There is a strange *modesty* to this man's claims, odd though that seems," the Emperor said thoughtfully. "For one reputed to throw thunderbolts like a God! Yet, he makes *limited* claims, with careful caveats laying out alternative possibilities and even admitting the possibility that he is in error or that in some circumstances he will be helpless."

Galen nodded again. "Yes, lord, I had noticed that. And for those we can *test*, his claims are borne out just as he predicts, neither more nor less. Either a very clever deception, leading us by the nose somehow I cannot imagine, or he is simply telling the truth."

"At least *part* of the truth," the Emperor said thoughtfully. "Which can, itself, mislead."

"Indeed. And if his secrets can smite armies and win battles, they are of...of sovereign importance, Caesar."

A glance went between them. There had been no serious civil wars or usurpations in the Empire for more than seventy years, a long lifetime. Not since the assassination of Domitian and the providential succession of Nerva, which had not caused strife of the sort that had given Domitian's father Vespasian and elder brother Titus the purple nearly a century ago.

That didn't mean such times as the Year of the Four Emperors *couldn't* come again. In essence the Divine Julius had been a successful warlord, after all, and also his successor, adopted son and great-nephew Augustus. The Emperor's chair rested on spearpoints; everyone had known that from the first Augustus' time, however much he'd tried to disguise it himself with soothing talk of restoring the Republic.

If an ambitious man secured the favor of enough troops... a man who had someone wielding the thunderbolts of Jupiter at his back, for example... he might be tempted to strike for supreme power himself.

"And this Artorius offers to lay all his secrets at my feet," the Emperor mused. "You will accompany me to Pannonia, Galenos. And you will take exhaustive notes."

≈ CHAPTER SIXTEEN ≈

Near Vindobona
August 30th, 166 CE

Filipa Chang sat her horse and gestured Sarukê forward, doing her best to look aloof, mysterious and powerful as she remained with the Prof and her friends and the Sarmatian cantered forward, her tall horse stepping high and effortlessly controlled despite its spirited gait.

It was a bright summer morning on a broad dusty field taken over by the Imperial army as a maneuver ground as the reinforcements arrived. There was a smell of wood fires in the air from the tented camps nearby; also of men and horses and their sweat and wastes.

One huge camp showed infantry from the newly arrived *Legio III Italica* swarming like disciplined ants as they built field fortifications topped with rows of sharpened stakes. When the temporary fortifications came down and the tents disappeared, some farmer or landowner was going to get well-dug-over and abundantly dunged fields out of it.

In the middle distance one luckless soldier was trotting in a wide circle around the whole parade ground with his *lorica segmentata* held at arm's length—no easy feat for any long period, since it weighed over twenty pounds—shouting:

"*Rubigo!*"

Which meant: *Rust!*

—at the top of his lungs every second stride, while a gimlet-eyed

231

tesserarius with a face like a hobnailed boot leaned on his staff and watched him sweat.

From the sidelong glances the three-hundred-odd troopers of the recently arrived *Ala I Thracum Victrix*—the First Cavalry Regiment of Victorious Thracians—were giving the Americans, Filipa thought her think-of-me-as-a-Goddess act was working. Or *something* was.

The reputation of Artorius the War-Wise and his four companions had lost nothing in the telling since the victory won in the spring. Some were calling him a God, anything from Hercules to Mithras, and the rest of them were rumored to be demigods or spirits of wisdom who'd taken on human form.

More and more troops had been arriving, too. Not rapidly, the Roman Empire was too big for that, when feet and hooves were the fastest means of travel and the armies were mostly dispersed along the frontiers of a territory that covered nearly two million square miles, going on for two-thirds the size of the continental US.

But steadily.

Units arrived in good order, according to schedule, fully equipped, their numbers close to the duty rosters sent on ahead, and well fed. Arrangements made locally were much the same. Everyone was slotted into a prearranged position, and pitched uniform camps. Even supplies of firewood arrived on schedule.

A bit intimidating, really, when you think of what they have to work with. The Roman central government is surprisingly small and it isn't very bureaucratic... except the Army, and that is, and very effectively so. An army with a government attached, was the way the Prof put it.

The cavalry troopers were in ranks by squadron, each thirty-one troopers and a decurion, and standing by the heads of their mounts, except for the command group and the standard-bearer, who stayed in the saddle. The regimental flag was the bronze open-mouthed head of a snarling dragon, carried on a pole, with a hollow silk body behind it cased in shimmering gilded scales. It stirred and writhed and rustled in the breeze from the river, looking almost alive, amid a hissing noise.

This was a standard cavalry unit, not the cataphracts whose head-to-toe armor and armored horses and long *contus* spears imitated Sarmatian or Parthian lancers, nor wild Numidians riding bareback. They were equipped with spatha swords and spear and oval shield, the troopers wearing short mail shirts and helmets with broad neck guards and cheekpieces.

And they would all speak Latin. Many people in northern Thrace and Moesia—what she thought of as Bulgaria, though neither the original Turkic Bulgars nor the Slavs who took their name and absorbed them were anywhere near it yet—did these days, and professional soldiers most of all. It was the Army's command language, and the Army pumped out a steady stream of Latin-speaking veterans and their families every year. Which made Army bases constantly spreading pools of Latinity and *Romanitas* over the generations.

Saruké cantered up in front of the cavalry and brought her horse to a stop with a shift of her body, not bothering with the reins, and rested her hands casually on the pommel of her saddle before she spoke. She was in mailcoat and her native garb; the voice and the blonde head revealed with her helmet off didn't leave much doubt of her gender, though.

The Sarmatian woman's voice carried well—projecting it over distance was a necessary skill in her homeland.

"I am Sarmatian. Your word. We say *Aorsi* in tribe mine."

There were nods at that; everyone in the Roman cavalry knew the reputation of Sarmatians, as light horse archers and armored heavy cavalry both. Sarmatian amazons were not unknown either, though not as frequent as they had been once. Certainly they'd all have *heard* of them.

"In tribe mine, I was...we say...*wirapta*."

She smiled unpleasantly, a curving of her lips away from her teeth.

"Means in Roman tongue, *interfector hominum*."

Which translated as: *killer of men*.

"Then on raid captured—sling-bullet—became *gladiatrix*—"

Which was the feminine of gladiator. Again, very, very much less common than the male variety and considered unnatural and scandalous by some even allowing for the arena's raffish standards, but not *vanishingly* rare either.

"—of sixteen combats. Five victories in death fights."

She smiled again. "Two of them with men, so still *wirapta*, eh? Now free. Retainer of Lord Artorius."

She pointed to him.

"You know him-of. Master of war, war-wise, slayer of Prince

Ballomar of Marcomanni. Taker of his head! I there, fight for him there, I see that. Artorius fight Ballomar bare-handed against sword and shield! Then take his sword and with that"—she drew a bladed palm across her own throat to illustrate—"cut neck."

There was a stir as the cavalrymen looked over at Artorius. They would have heard a great deal from the others now based here in the week since they arrived, some of it embellished. They probably believed most of it, too.

"Lord Artorius wise in all way of war. Horse-war, too. You horse now iron shoe."

There was a murmur, this time pleased. Roman roads had been designed for infantry in hobnailed *caligae*, the military sandal-boot, and Roman infantry could do a bit over twenty miles a day on them, day after day, in anything but a howling blizzard in February. But unshod hooves on hard stone, or gravel over stone, were a perennial problem, chipping and cracking. So were horses getting splints because the paved surface was a strain on their forelegs. Both of those were why you rode on the roadside verge when you could.

That wasn't always possible. It hadn't taken long—usually no more than one route march over the roads—for the merits of horseshoes to be fully apparent, and for the regimental smiths to eagerly learn their mysteries from the instructors sent around. Bar iron and blacksmiths weren't hard to get.

From simple to complex, Filipa thought. *Build confidence from the bottom up. The Prof was sure right about that! And I'm saving a* lot *of poor horses from going lame. They* don't *volunteer for the cavalry.*

"Lord Artorius give iron shoe! He also give new saddle. I learn, I use. I show now to you."

She did, in a routine she'd developed that...

Would have wowed them at rodeos, Filipa thought with pride, and warm fondness. *Even Prof the Glorious Cowboy Leader is impressed. And it's mostly things you just can't do at all* with *Roman... or Sarmatian... gear, no matter how good a rider you are. They know it too, I can see they're gaping.*

It ended with her putting on her helmet, tying off the cheek guards under her chin, then snatching up one of a pair of lances standing with their butt spikes in the dirt.

By then the men were murmuring, pointing out the way she was doing things, and keenly interested—they were professional horse soldiers after all, and proud of the skills that kept them alive and their enemies dead.

The lance had an ash-wood shaft about nine feet long, two feet longer than the type the Thracians were carrying. It also had a ball of leather on the end, tightly stuffed with wool, rather than a spearhead.

She used it to prod its twin.

"Beat me with spears, get one hundred denarii and promotion," she called. "Who?"

She rode up and down in front of them, whirling and tossing the lance in circles like a baton in a casual display of skilled strength.

"Who can fight like woman?" she taunted.

There was a boiling, and then one man leapt into his stirrupless four-horn saddle and galloped out, snatching up the other practice lance with an effortless motion as he went by. Behind him the Roman centurion who was *Ala praefectus*—regimental commander—cursed and stopped himself from grabbing at the man. Roman cavalry were disciplined, but not with the machine obedience legionary training aimed at.

Oh, I do hate this *part,* Filipa thought.

This wasn't the first demonstration she'd attended.

The modern saddle's a big advantage and she's the best rider I've ever known...even the best I've ever imagined...but still... What did the Prof say? You always meet someone better than you are, if you keep looking long enough?

The two figures trotted away from each other until they were a hundred yards apart, then turned and charged at a pounding gallop, amid rhythmic cheering by the Victorious Thracians for their champion. The horse hooves—both sets shod—tore gouts of dirt and clumps of grass out of the light sandy-loam soil.

The trooper of *Thracum Victrix* rode well, his oval shield slanted across his body and up under his eyes, spear held ready in the overhand grip, though he'd been a bit puzzled by the way it thickened toward a weighted butt spike.

There was a murmur from the regiment too; probably bets being laid. Then a rising buzz as they saw how Sarukê was holding her weapon, not two-handed as Sarmatians wielded their great *barge poles*, but not overarm either, instead with the rear of the shaft right under the armpit.

Sarukê brought the boxing-glove-like head down level at the last minute, clamped the lance under her arm with her hand only one-third of the way up from the butt, and leaned forward with her feet braced and her own griffon-blazoned shield up.

WHUMP!

The padded end of the lance struck the cavalry trooper squarely in the middle of his shield, well before *his* spear was within reach for a thrust. Sarukê was slammed back against the raised cantle of her Spanish-style saddle, and her horse stumbled for a half pace before she brought it back up.

The trooper of the First Thracians catapulted back over his horse's tail, spear and shield flying in opposite directions, turned a full heels-over-head circle in midair and landed with a bone-jarring thump facedown. His horse galloped on for a few yards, slowed, then stopped and looked around with a visibly puzzled—

Where's the boss? *Where did he* go?

—running through its equine mind, followed by:

Oh, there *he is!*

Filipa suppressed a giggle and thought:

It looked like a kid's cartoon! Perfect!

The Roman saddle's rear horns gave you *some* protection against getting knocked back ass over teakettle, but not anything like the degree of support you got from the combination of stiff frame and cantle and stirrups. Which was why the couched lance technique hadn't been developed until a *long* time after this. When you used a lance like that, you weren't stabbing with your arm muscles, you were using the entire momentum weight of horse and rider traveling better than thirty miles an hour. Over sixty, if it was against someone galloping toward *you.*

It made a *big* difference in the weight of the punch behind the business end.

The cavalry trooper wasn't unconscious, not quite, but there was blood over his face when he raised it groggily, and the chin strap of his helmet had snapped, leaving it lying a few yards away. The Sarmatian woman turned her horse in its own length, then leaned over and rapped him sharply in the face with the leather-covered business end of her practice weapon. The man flopped down limp, open mouth drooling spit-diluted blood.

Sarukê raised her lance, and pointed with her rein hand at its head as she pitched her voice to carry to his comrades:

"This be iron, he"—she jerked a thumb over her shoulder—"be dead man. Any else? Any want hundred denarii?"

There was an echoing silence, in which the slap of the ala commander's callused palm on his own forehead could be plainly heard, along with several horse snorts and the stamping of ironshod hooves.

Sarukê grinned, just visible behind the cheekpieces of her helmet, and the horsetail plume atop it bobbled in the wind.

"When he wake up, I send him bottle of superwine for ache in head. That too from Lord Artorius!"

That got a couple of laughs; the troopers had probably all tried the new brandy in the week since they'd arrived.

The ala commander glared those to silence and jerked an equally silent thumb as he ground his teeth. Two troopers from the beaten man's *turma* led his horse back and tossed him across the saddle and strapped him in, before the entire unit mounted, turned and cantered off at trumpet signals. Many of them were looking back over their shoulders, and Sarukê waved in friendly fashion.

Besides giving these object lessons in why the new gear was being introduced, she was also helping to supervise saddlers learning to *make* it, and various target devices for learning how to handle a couched lance. She'd more or less developed that herself, from hints and pictures Filipa had provided.

The provincial governor wanted all the horsed units to be reequipped by the time the Emperor arrived, with a convert's fervor. But first she trotted back to the Americans, removing her helmet and hanging it at her saddlebow.

"Work to do, lord," she said cheerfully, saluting Artorius and nodding respectfully to the others.

Then she leaned in and gave Filipa an enthusiastic kiss; garlic and wine, the smell of horse sweat and oiled metal and leather.

"Later, sword-sister."

Mark grinned as she trotted off. He could ride now, in the sense that he could stay on as long as he didn't try to go very fast, or turn quickly, and they picked a horse with a good sense of plodding docility. Paula was mounted too, wearing very full loose trousers that looked more like the skirt of a woman's tunic when she was on the ground.

Filipa had to admit they were practical and got her fellow American far fewer hostile and puzzled what-is-this-weirdo-who-disrupts-my-categories sidelong glances, but she'd decided to tough it out. Being around Sarukê most of the time helped with that.

"Fil's in *luuuuuuve*," Mark half chanted.

"You know, Mark, someday you'll be older—emotionally speaking—than a bratty eight," Filipa observed. "It's sort of like dog years with you, but in reverse. Yeah, I am. So?"

Am I really? she thought. *We don't have much in common... can I actually be in love with someone who doesn't know how to read or write, when so much of my life has been books? We weird each other out fairly frequently. And gross each other out occasionally. I do like her quite a lot and I'm massively, massively in lust with her, which is very nice too... let's see how this goes.*

The Prof smiled. "Fil could do worse," he said. "Unless we take up with each other, we'll all be in that boat sooner or later."

"Or in that bed," Paula said... rather sourly.

She didn't think Roman men were much of a bargain, on the whole.

I agree, but—lucky me—that doesn't apply. Poor Paula!

The Prof nodded: "This is where we have to live all our lives. And that's part of life.

"Even," he added softly, "if you feel for a while like the capacity has been... taken away."

"Each other? Sorry, Fil, but you're just not my type," Paula added with genuine amused regret.

She'd confessed once in the baths—the habit of gossiping and chatting in the *caldarium* was contagious—that she'd found by dismal experiment that she was straighter than a surveyor's set square and that was that.

Artorius turned to the others who'd travelled a one-way trip in time with him:

"And there's a lesson here for us. We can't do all of what we want to do by ourselves. We need help, lots of it. And ideally, the people who help us should know why, and *want* to do it."

Jeremey nodded. "I've got to admit your girlfriend is *very* persuasive about anything to do with horses, Fil. Saves us a lot of time and aggravation with the cavalry. We may have the legate of the Tenth and the provincial governor on our side now, but some of the others... Romans understand foot-dragging and slow-walking and yes-of-course-sir-whatever-you-say-but-but-but just fine when they want to."

"*Obedezco pero no cumplo,*" Mark said; that was an old saying from the Spanish colonial empire about orders you didn't like from far-off Madrid, many months distant across pirate-haunted oceans and bandit-frequented mountains.

It meant: *I obey, but I don't comply.*

"Showing not telling helps," Artorius said. "And that Sarukê's a woman, even if she is Sarmatian, drives it home."

Filipa grinned, an evil expression: "It drives the Roman cavalry...well, Thracian and whatnot...batshit *crazy* when she does that *who can fight like a woman* thing and then knocks whoever volunteers clean out of the saddle."

"Always some macho idiot to fall for that one," Mark said, grinning in his turn. "Even when it's obviously like trying to fight a six-shooter with a flintlock on a wet day. And I thought *our* jocks were dumb."

"Then once they've had their faces rubbed in it they can't wait to get the new saddles so they can do all that stuff too and don't feel *emasculated* anymore," Filipa said.

"Oh, God, do they ever think that way," Paula said wryly. "Dicks with a dick fixation."

"And the Germans think that way, and Thracians and Greeks and Gauls and Nabateans and Phoenicians and—" Mark pointed out, ending with: "No! Don't hit me, you two! I'm harmless!"

"Which makes them *want* to do what we want them to do," Jeremey added thoughtfully. "And on a personal level, Sarukê's absolutely gorgeous in a big, healthy, athletic, outdoorsy, strapping country girl, horsey sort of way, yeah, Fil. But it would be too much like going to bed with a leopardess for my taste. That woman is *dangerous*. No, really. She's a killer."

Filipa gave him a long, chin-out, eye-slitted smug feline smile before she said judiciously:

"Well, I don't notice *your* girlfriends...plural...doing anything for the Noble Cause of Civilization but interrupting *your* sleep."

And yes, it is *a bit like sleeping with a leopardess. A truly affectionate, very* horny *and* hot *leopardess. And* she likes to just cuddle too, which is something I've really missed.

"Wait a minute, wait a minute," Mark said suddenly. "Did anyone else notice?"

"Notice what?" Jeremey asked.

"We're having this conversation in *Latin*. I was *thinking* in Latin."

Filipa checked her memory of precisely what she'd been saying.

"Christ and Buddha on the same skateboard, we were!" she said—in English.

The Prof started to laugh, and then his face grew grave. "We're five drops of ink in a really, really big tanker-truck of milk," he said. "Let's say we all live another forty or fifty years. How much time will we spend talking in Latin, or thinking in it, by 210 CE? Or 963 AUC? By then, it'll be *our* language too."

Hooves thudded. Artorius looked up; it was a legionary on horseback, and one who actually knew how to ride well—every legion had a small cavalry unit, to carry messages and provide the legate and tribunes with escorts. The trooper saluted—though technically he shouldn't, since Artorius didn't hold any formal Roman military rank—and handed over a message on a diptych.

"Well, playtime's over," Artorius said, returning the gesture and reading. "The Emperor is arriving within the next week."

"That's pushing it!" Jeremey said, and whistled.

They'd all gotten graphic—sore-muscled—lessons in how hard getting from A to B was here. The just-arrived *Legio III Italica* had done it in about a month...but from their training camp in the vicinity of Aquileia, east of where Venice had been in their home century. Rome was a good deal further, and meant crossing the Apennines as well.

"He's not a dawdler. And we're to hold ourselves ready to meet with him—a public thing, the victory parade for the Tenth Legion, then we're invited to dine. Which is a major honor, by the way, and don't forget it. OK, let's get as much as we were scheduled to do today done as we can, and at dinner we'll meet to prepare how we handle this. I hope I don't have to tell you how crucial it is."

He heeled his horse into a canter. Paula snickered in good-natured mockery as he rode away.

"Fil, Jem, I'll give you odds you're not the only ones who're going to be locally hooked up soon."

At their looks she went on: "Have you noticed how Lady Julia tends to gravitate to the library back on the villa when it's the Prof's turn for his rationed time with the books? Actually the scrolls, mostly. When it got warm enough, walks together in the peristyle and the garden. Carrying scrolls, sitting on benches reading together, playing with her kid..."

Jeremey laughed. "Don't tell me they're making out among the priceless lost works?"

Paula rolled her eyes. "Get your mind out of your crotch, Jem."

"It's not nearly as interesting a place as you think it is," Filipa put in.

Paula snorted and went on: "It's all discussions of literature and history so far and reading poetry to each other and talking about her daughter and the stories he's telling the kid, which incidentally are mostly cribbed from Grimm's with a soupçon of Disney but a lot of them are new here. Little Claudia thinks the sun rises and sets on him now. There's no way the Prof and Julia could keep any hot stuff secret in that little village setup and I'm plugged into the gossip circuit there. Besides, there's always someone else with them; her lady's maid, mostly. Who incidentally is her half-sister, which everyone knows but nobody talks about."

Filipa asked, interested: "How do you know it's not just a we're-friends thing?"

Paula smiled. "Because Julia's been asking me questions about him, mostly in the baths. About his wife, and children and his family and his career and all that good shit."

Mark frowned. "That's a sign of romantic interest?" he asked.

Filipa, Paula and even Jeremey stared at him.

Paula explained: "It's an *infallible* sign, oh Mr. Oblivious... though I don't know whether *Prof* Oblivious *realizes* she's interested yet."

Jeremey snickered. "How did he manage to end up with kids?"

"He married his high-school sweetheart a month after he graduated from West Point and I doubt he ever strayed or even thought much about it in the ten years after that," Paula said. "I checked around for safety's sake when he contacted me for the ... trip."

"The man's not *human*," Jeremey replied.

"Just sort of old fashioned and ... steady. Also a respectable country-bred Texan."

"But we're not on the villa anymore," Mark said.

Paula's smile got wider. "They're exchanging letters, too. He smiles this slow smile and puts it in his pocket and pats it when he gets one."

"Oh, yup," Filipa said. "Got it bad whether he knows he does or not."

"Yeah, probably," Jeremey agreed.

"No bout adoubt it. Though it could be awkward. From Sextus Hirrius Trogus' point of view, we're all seriously déclassé. Honor of the family stuff, and he's her legal guardian, their father died a while ago, so she needs his consent," Paula agreed.

"You mean the Prof's not rich enough and not high-status enough?" Mark said.

"Well, yeah, wasn't that what I just said?" Paula said, exasperation in her tone.

Mark Findlemann surprised Filipa by laughing knowingly.

"Oh, *that* can be taken care of. Probably will be. Highly probably. Highly probably very soon."

"How?" Filipa said.

"Not how, who."

Jeremey started laughing too, before he spoke: "By Imperator Caesar Marcus Aurelius Antoninus Augustus, of course."

Filipa nodded. "If it isn't *off with their heads* at the parade."

"Oh, if this was *Domitian*, or *Nero* or *Commodus*, yeah, maybe," Mark said confidently. "Not *Marcus Aurelius*. Haven't you read his *Meditations*? We won a battle for him. We protected—"

He waved a hand around him.

"He takes that seriously."

I hope he's right, Filipa thought, who *had* read the *Meditations* and had found them rather platitudinous. *You know . . . suddenly I realize I do have a lot to live for. And we're all young.*

Mark frowned. "Though . . . he hasn't actually *written* the *Meditations* yet. He did that during the Marcomannic Wars."

❧ CHAPTER SEVENTEEN ❧

Vindobona,
Province of Pannonia Superior
September 5th, 166 CE

The Emperor of Rome had taken over the municipal council building on the marketplace forum of the civilian part of Vindobona. It wasn't anything as grand as a proper basilica, not in this small provincial border city, but it would do for now. It had sufficient space, the local officials could work out of other buildings for the nonce, and the Praetorium in the Tenth Legion's fort was crammed to bursting right now anyway. A cot in a cubicle was good enough for sleep, and a vast improvement on the forced-march pace of getting here, which had brought his stomach pains on badly; this plain plastered room with a window opening on the courtyard to let in the afternoon sunlight was quite sufficient for indoor work.

Even the smell wasn't too bad on this pleasant summer's day, only moderately warm by Italian standards, despite how crowded the city was right now. The builders of the fort had done well, two-thirds of a century ago, in laying on water and sewage.

Though if I'm here any length of time, I'll see to having more of the streets paved. The mud here is memorable, and bottomless.

Right now he had a tricky bit of political balancing to do. The two men standing in front of him on the other side of the table were the beginning of it.

They made their greetings after the Praetorian guardsmen at

the door settled back to parade rest with a clank, silent as statues, menacing as the scorpions on their shields and embossed in low relief on the cheekpieces of their helmets.

One of the newcomers gave Galen only a fleeting glance; the physician was inconspicuous on his stool in the background, and he probably took him for a clerk, given his writing tablet and stylus. The other sent a slight nod in that direction, respectfully polite in a noble-to-commoner sort of way.

The greetings to the Emperor were politely deferential but not sycophantic; Marcus Iallius Bassus would have warned the other man to keep it simple, since he and the Emperor had known each other for many years. Bassus was of a senatorial family from *Gallia Narbonensis*, a spare man of around the Emperor's own midforties with thinning brown hair, an ex-consul and as such a *nobilis* and member of the Senate himself; he'd also been a legionary legate and governor of Pannonia Inferior east of here, before being appointed to Pannonia Superior late last year.

Loyal and capable, the Emperor thought. *Not brilliant, but intelligent and solidly competent. I wonder why he looks so nervous? Though he hides it well.*

"*Salve, Legatus Augusti pro praeto* Marcus Iallius Bassus," Marcus Aurelius said to the provincial governor of Pannonia Superior, who was in a toga and tunic with the broad senatorial stripes, though his office entitled him to military garb. And:

"*Salve, Legatus legionis* Sextius Lollius Tiberianus," he added to the commander of *Legio X Gemina*.

Who *was* in full military fig down to the knotted scarlet sash around his muscled bronze breastplate, with his crested, relief-worked helmet under his left arm. That was perhaps a little ostentatious.

Since his own military talents *nearly produced a disaster.*

"First, congratulations on your great victory over the barbarian invaders in May," he said.

Quite sincerely; it had saved everyone between here and Sirmium at least, and quite possibly between here and the Adriatic— there simply hadn't been any forces available to plug a gap torn in the defenses of the frontier. Not in time; he could have been fighting the Germans hundreds of miles south of here, trying to drive them back while they burned everything to the ground and left devastation for him to remedy as best he could, even if...

when...they were expelled. Citizens of Rome expected Rome to protect them from outsiders.

And rightly so.

"We passed several caravans of prisoners a little south of here. The people of the provinces celebrated this evidence of the triumphant valor of your troops."

They'd also tried to attack and lynch the captives being marched off to the slave markets and the mines and the arena, a sign of both relief and lingering fear among the populace. The military escorts had had to beat them back with shields and the shafts of their spears, or the clubs they carried to deal with recalcitrant captives. That wouldn't be a problem further from the frontier, where people would regard them as so much saleable mobile meat.

"A feast of celebration is being prepared in your honor, and wine and food will be distributed in the city."

The Emperor indicated two ornate scrolls on the table in front of him.

"You have both also been voted the thanks of the Senate and People of Rome, and the *ornamenta triumphalia*."

That was a memorial to how worried the Senate had been. Those were the ornaments of a triumph, as close as anyone not an Emperor or their close relative could come these days to an *actual* triumph through the streets of Rome. Both men looked pleased, and the commander of the Tenth gave an almost audible sigh of relief.

Yes, you will not be called to account for nearly destroying your legion. A privilege of rank, but one only granted since the legion was not in fact destroyed; on balance, a positive outcome. And if it had been destroyed, you would probably at least have had the grace to die with it.

"And you have my own thanks. Not only for the victory, but for your actions since—with respect to Lucius Triarius Artorius and his following and the invaluable knowledge they seem to possess. What the cavalry can do with the new *Pannonian gear* has made a great impression on me, and you two have been most active in procuring it. I look forward to a demonstration of the other...novelties."

Hmmm. Bassus is still nervous; Sextius was very nervous, but now is not. So my good Bassus is not apprehensive about my opinion of his performance as governor. Which has in fact been about as good as could be expected, given the antics of the Tenth's commander.

"Sextius Lollius Tiberianus, it further pleases the noble Senate to recognize your services to the *rēs pūblica Rōmāna* by appointing you proconsul of Hispania Baetica, as of the kalends of next January."

It pleased the noble Senate because the Emperor had spoken *under the rose* to several senators, but there hadn't been much argument, even though Hispania Baetica was a senatorial province and a plum appointment and someone's cousin or nephew was going to be very disappointed. Everyone who paid any attention knew there had been a battle and a victory here, and a badly needed one. Most *didn't* know the details yet, except for wild rumors about divine intervention.

Baetica was the southernmost part of Hispania, taken from Carthage more than three centuries ago; its rich valley lowlands had drawn many Roman colonists then and later. Nowadays it exported massive quantities of oil and wine, wool, grain and garum, and the silver and copper of its mountain mines, all over the Empire. It was also so thoroughly Romanized that it might as well have been in Italy. The Emperors Hadrian and Trajan had both come of families settled there, and so did many senators; he had kin there himself.

And it needed no garrison except for a few auxiliaries to serve as, effectively, *vigiles*. That meant police who patrolled against the bandits who were an occasional annoying problem nearly everywhere, including the rougher parts of Italy.

Which was precisely *why* it was a senatorial preserve; Octavian, the first Augustus himself, had established the precedent that the *princeps* directly controlled any appointment that involved significant numbers of troops. Nobody was going to start a revolt and aim for the purple from peaceful Baetica, amid the warm, sleepy vineyards and villas and olive groves and bustling, ship-thronged port cities.

Sextius beamed; he'd been rewarded with a choice appointment, far more desirable than a governorship on this cold northern frontier if you didn't care about the chance of military glory... which right now he probably didn't. One where you didn't have to take risks or overstep the conventions and unspoken rules to end your term in office wealthier than you began it.

But it also signifies that he will never again have a military command, Marcus Aurelius thought. *No matter the politics, I will not have Roman soldiers under the control of such as he. He's no danger to me, but he would be to the troops he commanded and therefore to the Empire. How I wish I could always promote men on ability alone!*

"Perhaps you should begin to gather your household for your new position," the Emperor hinted. "To be ready after the victory parade; it's a long way to Rome, as my backside bears witness, and then there's preparation and the trip to *Colonia Patricia*."

Sextius beamed at the mention of *Colonia Patricia Corduba*, capital of his new province, bowed, drew himself up and saluted with his fingers pointing at the ceiling.

"Hail, Imperator Caesar Augustus!"

"Sit, Bassus," the Emperor said after the man was gone; an attendant poured them both well-watered wine. "Your opinion?"

"Probably as good a solution as any, sir, given his status and family connections," Bassus said. "He's not a fool and he'll govern Baetica reasonably well, and will be satisfied with the usual perquisites of office. He's just not suited to a field command, or to governing on the frontier in a time of troubles. Which, alas, this seems to be."

"Granted, and alas indeed. Now—Artorius, the man of the moment," Marcus said. "Your appraisal of him *as* a man? No need to speculate on his origins just now; I want your opinion of his *character* before I meet him myself."

"Very intelligent, learned in many respects but with curious lacunae—well, he is a foreigner by origin. Forceful, brave to a fault, as he showed in his fight with Ballomar, and daring. But *sensibly* daring, so to speak, not reckless."

"Ambitious?"

"Not without ambition, but I think—curiously—genuinely devoted to the cause of Rome, as much as anyone born in the Empire or even birthed on the Seven Hills in the shadow of the Forum. And to your person, sir: he seems to be something of a Stoic himself, familiar with the philosophers from Zeno on and I would say that he admires you. Not least because he does *not* loudly proclaim any such sentiment. I speak of the implications of what he *does* say about other matters."

He frowned and went on: "Devoted to Rome...but in an odd

way. He has praised the *Pax Romana* in my hearing, the trade
and prosperity it brings, and our law and the discipline of our
armies. But he praises them like a man who has...it's difficult
to express what I mean, sir...as if he had observed it all from
a great distance, as something of interest but only to the mind.
Like you or I discussing Alexander of Macedon, or the character
of Socrates."

Bassus shook his head. "For the rest, he is a fine horseman in
this new fashion, and knows a variety of the *pankration*"—which
meant all-in unarmed combat—"that has impressed men skilled
in such. Oddly, he knew nearly nothing of the sword when he
arrived, but has learned quickly. I have the impression that he is
a countryman by rearing and inclination, and he says his family in his homeland were landowners who dwelt by preference
on their rural property when not doing military service, which
I believe. Even a small and tidy city such as Vindobona seems
unclean to him, though he does not complain loudly. For that
matter, he and his followers are all *very* particular in matters
of cleanliness. Even by our Roman standards, much less those
of any other folk I have seen. Or even of whom I have heard."

"And those followers? The four who arrived here with him?"

"Difficult to say; I've had less to do with them. The Jew,
Marcus, is extremely intelligent but otherworldly and strange, as
if he were not quite on the same plane of existence as the rest
of humanity."

"I have met scholars like that, including some fine ones," the
Emperor said. "If my birth had been otherwise, I might have
been such myself."

"Yes, sir. He has overseen the making of the new papyrus,
and has constructed a very odd engine that can reproduce writing
quickly, which I have only seen this last month. An extraordinary
thing. I watched for an hour, and an *entire book* was written
down on the, ah, *paper*. And done *perfectly*."

Marcus Aurelius' eyebrows rose. A whole scriptorium of busy
scribes couldn't do that, and there were always errors that crept
in as one copy after another was written down.

"The other young man, Julius, now he is *very* ambitious,
I would judge; he's also knowledgeable in agriculture and the
management of estates in a way which may create much wealth,
things unheard of by Varro or Columella, and new crops of many

uses and strange appearance—apparently from this America place, brought as seeds. I've already written to the *vilicii* of my own properties to use some of his innovations, and bought examples of his engines and pledges of the seeds, once they are harvested, to send to them. The women—"

He shrugged his shoulders. "For starters, they're both formidable scholars too."

"Odd, but not completely unknown," Marcus observed.

"The one called Philippa, who has that look of the very far east, is a *tribas*."

They both shrugged their shoulders this time; not a matter of great importance to a man of the world. Some found such things amusing, others unnatural and repulsive because it usurped masculine attributes in a way that the usual love of man and youth did not, but not *important*, no.

Though consider my divine predecessor Hadrian. He was a very capable Emperor, but the depth *of his infatuation with that Greek boy Antinoös exposed him to ridicule. Some things should be kept private, and one should avoid immoderate passions. Though remember to be moderate even in moderation!*

"And she is an expert on horses and horse gear, oddly enough. Though appropriate to her name!"

Which meant *lover of horses* in Greek.

"So are many Sarmatian women, the writers say."

"They speak truly. One of Artorius' retainers is a Sarmatian amazon, and she is one of the best riders I have ever seen."

Marcus Aurelius made a gesture, spreading one hand palm up.

"*Nomos* is king of all, but he wears different masks among different nations."

That Greek word *nomos* meant roughly "law," or perhaps "local custom," if you used Herodotus' reuse of Pindaros' poem as an example. Bassus nodded in acknowledgment and went on:

"And she also has deep knowledge of *mathematics*. She has expounded a new system of arithmetical calculation and notation which allows for very rapid multiplication and division, and my man of business tells me a number of merchants have taken it up, along with what she calls *double-entry bookkeeping*. Together these simplify their dealings and their records remarkably, and make it easier to understand the more arcane aspects at a glance."

The Emperor's brows rose; that *was* unusual for a woman.

He would have to look into it; mathematics were an essential part of philosophy, and had many practical uses elsewhere too.

If these new methods are useful to merchants, they might well be of service to the servants of the State, as well. Keeping and transmitting accurate records is always a struggle.

"Paula, the one of Nubian appearance, has introduced innovations in spinning and weaving. My man of business also tells me they will eventually be a source of great riches to anyone with properties producing flax and wool, and they are already being widely copied. Faster than the mathematics!"

They both smiled at that.

"And she has also introduced novel ideas in midwifery. These seem to work as she claims, judging by the news from the Villa Lunae. Far, far fewer mothers dying of childbed fever."

Galen shifted on his stool, and the Emperor nodded permission.

"Do they involve the use of boiled water, frequent handwashing in *sapo*, and lustration of vulnerable or injured parts with double-refined superwine, excellent Governor?" the Greek said.

"Yes, they do. She and the others have tried to persuade the army's field physicians to use similar methods for wounds, but there has been resistance and I hesitated to override it amid so much else."

Galen nodded as a man did when his thoughts were confirmed, and spoke to the Emperor:

"Lord, this would be similar to the wound treatments I outlined in Rome and have tested further on our journey here. Childbirth often leads to ruptures and tearing of tissues, and it is logical that the same treatments would work in both cases."

The Greek thought for a moment, and said slowly: "Deaths by childbed fever are common for mothers, and not unknown for children too, as everyone knows, lord. Between one in twenty and one in a hundred births. Fewer if the labor is easy and swift, more if it is prolonged or difficult, still more in the case of a breech birth even if the child is successfully repositioned by the midwife. If this treatment works as well as the one for wounds, that would mean..."

His face went still, looking upward a little as he thought.

"...a reduction of more than half, shall we say, in the proportion of women dying soon after bearing. Possibly even more than that. Which would mean more women surviving to bear more children later."

"More hands to work and fight, eventually, then," the Emperor noted. "The Empire's strength is in its people. And less grief for the families and husbands of the unfortunate women."

Bessus leaned forward on his chair. "Should I have been more forceful with the military doctors, sir?"

Marcus Aurelius shook his head. "I do not think so. Galenos?"

"Recalling the response of the doctors of Rome to *me*, I don't think it would be productive to attempt to make the military *medicorum* listen to what they will think is a mere midwife and weaver of cloth, lord. However *right* she is, frustrating though that might be in an abstract sense."

Marcus Aurelius smiled; he wasn't a man who laughed easily, or often, but he was pleased now.

One thing I like about Galen is his lack of intellectual arrogance despite his undoubted genius, he thought. *He tries steadily to see the world as it is, not as he wishes it might be. He fails sometimes, as we all fail, but he does not cease to try because of that. That is a rare quality, and one I struggle to possess myself. It is a failing of philosophers that we often fall in love with our ideas and become blind to their true merits. That is vanity.*

"But they will listen to the Emperor's physician from Rome," he said aloud. "See to it, Galen—you have my full authority in any medical matter here, and may tell anyone so if they question you. You may also tell them that I will be severely displeased if it becomes necessary for me to intervene directly to sustain your authority."

He turned back to Bassus. "Your overall advice in the matter of Artorius?"

"Reward him and his, and do so lavishly, Caesar. In wealth and also in public praise and office."

"Your reasoning in this matter?"

"First, it is right because he deserves it. Without him, we would have lost the Tenth...all except the *vexilliationes* in the east...and Vindobona at the very least would have been sacked, and the countryside around it burned out. I would simply not have had enough force to remedy the situation, not if I were Alexander of Macedon or the Divine Julius come again. Which I am not, though I am not a fool in battle either."

Unlike Sextius Lollius Tiberianus went unspoken between them.

"This is true, and I had thought as much myself," he said,

making a mental note to talk to the procurator of the *res privata* in this province, the Emperor's private estates. "Good to know that our thoughts still run like a matched team, Bassus. You implied there is another reason?"

"Yes, sir. Two more. There are many rumors about Artorius, each wilder than the last, some attributing divine powers to him, some casting him as a sorcerer. If you are seen to reward him and he is seen to gratefully take reward from your hands—"

The Emperor raised his brows in question, and Bassus qualified his remark:

"Which it is my strong impression that he will, it is then plain that he is *your* man, *your* retainer, *your* client and loyal supporter. Then the rumors and the awe they generate rebound to Caesar Augustus' benefit; which is to say, to the benefit of the State."

"Cogent," the Emperor said. "And frankly, I had not thought of that...though I should have."

An Emperor had to maintain his prestige to retain *auctoritas*. History showed that a well-meaning fool or even a vicious clown could rule Rome...but not for long, and without *auctoritas* catastrophic disorder could spread so, so easily. It was not just a matter of the Emperor suffering what he deserved, but the Empire itself and its people suffering *with* him.

For disorder means civil war and the ruin of lives; burning, wasting, lost trade, famine, barbarian invasions.

"And the third and last?"

"That he and his are men *worth* cultivating, that they are among those whose loyalty and counsel will be of great advantage. Advantage in ways both obvious now, and those at present unseen."

"That had also occurred to me. And now," the Emperor went on, "let us prepare for the victory parade; it is one of the more pleasant features of my position that I can reward the worthy. And prepare for the exhibition of the thunderballs. It is important that the troops gain a realistic knowledge of their capacities."

He wasn't looking at Bassus, but he noticed a twitch. "What is it, Bassus?" he asked.

"Sir..." the man said.

Ah, this is what he was nervous of.

"Sir, I have beheld the thunderballs before. I believe Artorius' explanation of them—that they are a simple combination of well-known materials, with no sorcery involved. I have seen the thunderpowder made at each stage of the process. And I am a man of sufficient courage, I think my record shows that. But . . . something about them makes my bowels turn liquid."

"No shame in that," Marcus Aurelius said. "You have mastered your fear and do not let it affect your actions or prejudice your thoughts. That self-mastery is all that can in justice be expected of any man. The more credit to you if it requires an admirable self-discipline, then, my good Bassus."

⇒ CHAPTER EIGHTEEN ⇐

North of Vindobona,
Province of Pannonia Superior
September 7th, 166 CE

"Now *this* is a new experience," Artorius murmured.

As they waited while the troops marched—or rode—past the other side of the reviewing stand well up the long slope.

"What, meeting a bigwig, Prof?" Jeremey asked.

The hard tramp of thousands of hobnailed *caligae* covered anything they said, as long as they didn't turn their heads. The noon sun was bright overhead and it was a fine summer's day with a scattering of fleecy clouds in the pale washed-out blue of a central European sky, and the Danube glittered behind them to the east. By no particular coincidence, the reviewing stand was on about the same place where the command group of *Legio X Gemina* had positioned itself during most of the battle with the Marcomanni that day in late May.

With the barbarians expecting a crushing victory and rich booty and murder-and-arson fun, Artorius thought. *Which is precisely what they'd have gotten, if it weren't for us. They would have made it as far as Italy, if it weren't for us. That farmhouse we saw repeated a thousand times and more.*

The battlefield had been cleaned up and it didn't even smell of death anymore, only the frowsty-musky, sweat-leather-oil-metal-dirty-socks scent that massed troops had in this era. But the unit standards and the Eagle of the Tenth Legion had been placed roughly where they'd been during the battle too, stretching behind the timber construction draped in purple cloth where the Emperor and *his* bigwigs waited and which put them ten feet in the air. Mostly they were military, but with a scattering of his *comites*, his close advisors and the equivalent of the Cabinet.

"Meeting bigwigs? No, I've done that before."

Artorius and his companions were here in a clump downslope toward the river; behind them were Josephus and Sextus Hirrius Trogus. Behind *them* were the families of both, who'd at least be able to watch the formalities from a good vantage point.

The Tenth Legion itself led the parade, marching northward along the highway that ran from Vindobona, then swinging off it toward the river and passing from south to north before the reviewing stand. After it passed the Emperor, the legion marched all the way to the bare hill that had anchored its line during the battle, looped around in a 180-degree turn, and the units each took up the places they'd had on that day.

Minus the dead and crippled, of course, Artorius thought. *Quite a few of those.*

The long line of armored men kept marching, each unit halting when it reached its standard, until the last cohort came to its station on the south. Then the *tubae* called, and the whole mass did a right turn to face the Emperor with its standards to the fore.

Close order drill really means *something in a fight, here,* Artorius reminded himself. *"Their drills are bloodless battles, and their battles but bloody drills,"* as the man said.

"Plenty of generals, and the President, once," Artorius went on after a pause.

The other troops, about six thousand, followed and formed up behind the Tenth. That put more and more helmeted heads between the Americans and the platform, but the slope gave them a clear view of it, helped by the fact that a wide clear path was left stretching to the steps on the eastern side. The men on the platform simply had to turn to face the troops when the last had passed before them.

Silver spears glittered there behind the Emperor, and a great banner fell from a crossbar on a pole topped by an eagle; the crimson silk had a golden fringe on the bottom, and the main part of it was occupied by an embroidered wreath of golden leaves, the image of the one the Emperor himself wore around his head.

Within it were letters in *capitalis monumentalis*:
SPQR
For *Senatus Populusque Romanus*. The Senate and the People of Rome.

He shook himself back to the question: "No, it's not that. It's not that Marcus Aurelius is a panjandrum," Artorius said quietly.

The President had pinned the medal on him, in fact. He hadn't much liked or disliked the man, unlike the usual passionate reactions he generated, but he'd appreciated that. As much as the pain and drugs allowed.

"It's that I've met plenty of Romans by now, but this is the first time I'm going to meet one I've really *studied*," he said. "As an individual. Someone whose life and death I've gone over in detail for years. Someone whose *book* I've read!"

"Prof, you are indeed a *Prof*, even now," Paula said, and Filipa snorted under her breath.

"No, he's right, that's—" Mark began, and then gave a muffled yip as someone kicked him in the ankle.

They had guards, columns a century strong on either side. They'd been Praetorians originally, but those had marched off as part of the ceremony. Now they were from the First Cohort of the Tenth, and considerably smaller because both centuries were understrength more than half, between casualties and detachments sent east. The legions had high standards, and it would take six months of hard training before the first of the replacement recruits fully joined the Tenth's ranks; they'd go into the lowest-ranked cohorts, bumping men upward until some got into the elite First.

Primus Pilus Lucius Sextius Caelius was at the head of the century on the right, mail glittering; the medallions on his chest that showed his record and his valor polished to an even brighter finish, and his vine-wood swagger stick was oiled and gleaming. The red transverse crest of bristling dyed horsehair across his helmet moved slightly in the cooling wet breeze from the river, and his scarred, brutal-looking face was impassive as he muttered at his men, something clearly audible to Artorius too:

"We got this job instead of those mincing Praetorian *fungos* from the city, and the Emperor is watching. So, you pantomime clowns, let's get this *right*. Or by Mithras and our Eagle, you'll wish the Hermanns *had* killed you!"

When Artorius looked back at him for a moment, he could have sworn Lucius gave a hint of a wink.

Reminds me of some lifers I've known, he thought.

When the last unit was in place, scores of curled *cornua* and straight *tubae* beside the platform sang; it was in a complex pattern, but basically meant *commander present* and *attention to orders.* Marcus Aurelius stepped forward to the edge of the platform, raised his right hand high and called:

"Soldiers of Rome!"

His voice was a medium tenor, and it carried very well.

Well trained, Artorius thought; public speaking and upper-class Roman education were very closely linked.

Then he started very slightly: every soldier on the field—over ten thousand of them—shouted in chorus:

"ROMA! ROMA! ROMA!"

It was like the voice of a God or a giant, loud enough to numb the ears for a second or two, a little blurred but thudding and rumbling in your chest. None of their escort seemed surprised; evidently this was an everyone-knows part of an address.

By the Big Panjandrum, he thought.

Artorius caught most of what followed, and was mildly surprised at the tight focus and the way it said what these soldiers wanted to hear and could understand, without many rhetorical flights. This man had a long-lasting reputation as a philosopher and writer, but apparently he knew how to temper the words to the audience. There was a faint murmur in the distance, as designated men repeated what he said for those too far away to take the words in directly.

In essence it amounted to:

The barbarian filth crossed our border and attacked our people; we're going to make them suffer to show them what messing with us means, put a boot on their necks while they squeal and beg, and take everything they have.

He didn't quite promise "rape and pillage/in every village," but that was the general direction of things, and there was a tense growl.

Then the troops reacted as one, a chant of:

"AVE! AVE IMPERATOR!"

The word had become "emperor" in English and a dozen other languages, from Lithuanian to Portuguese, with variations on

"Caesar" as the alternative—the German version even sounded very much like the way Romans he'd met pronounced it, hard and clipped. Probably because they'd borrowed it early and it hadn't changed, that was common with loan words. Here and now *imperator* meant something halfway between that and its original Latin sense: *Victorious leader*, with overtones of *fit to command Romans*.

Roman emperors didn't just use "imperator" as a title and part of their official names, they counted the times they'd been acclaimed *as* imperator by the troops.

Marcus Aurelius went on: "We are also here to celebrate the valor of the Tenth Legion Gemina and the loyal *auxilia* who fought with them. From the time of the Divine Julius and the first Augustus, the Tenth Gemina has fought with courage and skill. On this field, it showed its mettle once again, never wavering, against great odds. Today I award it this *phalera*, to be carried below the Eagle!"

The legion's *aquilifer* with the lion's tanned head on his helmet and its skin falling down his back took up the Tenth's eagle and marched—strutting just a little—to the platform and up the steps. The Eagle dipped, and a polished golden disk about the size of a dinner plate was affixed, showing a low-relief rendering of the bull's-head symbol of the unit and the date and place of the action. Slightly to Artorius' surprise the standard-bearer and his escorts stayed there, behind Marcus Aurelius and with the *twin* Eagles now looming above him.

A rolling cheer went down the Tenth's ranks, along with a rhythmic thunder of spears beaten on shield bosses. It fell into silence again as he raised his hand.

"And to the honored name of *Legio X Gemina*, I add—*inexorabilis*!

That meant "unyielding strength." The cheers this time were even louder.

"And every soldier who was on this field in that great battle will receive a donative of one third of a year's pay."

Now, that's a real cheer, Artorius thought ironically. *The crowd goes wild! The auxiliaries are cheering as loud as the legionnaires.*

The other units here would want to get the same, the recognition and the bonus as well, and would fight the harder for it.

The ceremony now went into particulars—individuals were called up to receive decorations and rewards; the *primus pilus* of the Tenth had a shiny new medallion on his harness, but unlike the others he remained on the platform, near the Eagle of his legion and in the equivalent of parade rest.

At last the Emperor said:

"Let the man whose timely aid turned the tide of battle approach! Approach, Lucius Triarius Artorius, to receive the thanks of the Senate and the People of Rome!"

That was the signal for the whole party waiting between the two centuries of the Tenth to move forward. They did, the legionnaires at a slow march so as not to leave the civilians behind, then halting to line the immediate approach to the stairs.

I've got some sense of what to expect, at least, given this getup.

A tunic had been delivered by one of the servants of the Emperor's aides that morning, carefully wrapped. It had turned out to be of dazzling white wool, beautifully woven from fine thread, with narrow purple stripes down from each shoulder. That was the garb of an *eques*; Sextus Hirrius Trogus was wearing the same, beneath a toga, as he came up on Artorius' right. So was Josephus, on his left, and he *hadn't* been an *eques* any more than Artorius. The other four Americans were in their best Roman clothes including togas for the men, and came directly behind Artorius; the other two men's families were a bit further back.

Artorius was conscious that Julia was in that group, and that she'd given him a long smile when she saw the new tunic. Though he himself had been told *not* to wear a toga.

Theoretically, they were now of the same class . . .

Damn, but that's one fine *woman,* he thought. *She deserved better than that creep her father married her off to. Though their little Claudia is a pleasure, bright as you could want, cute as a bug's ear, and she has beautiful manners, for a nine-year-old. Julia's smart, she's good-looking, and I think she's good—not sappy, but good. The staff at the Villa Lunae actually like her, as opposed to the way they put up with her mother, which is significant. She could treat them any way she pleased, after all, and she had reason to be irritable, sent into quasi-exile with that harpy.*

They all walked up the steps of the purple-draped platform, except for the families, who waited to either side of the risers. That was a privileged position in itself, of course.

His first close-up view of Marcus Aurelius was a slight shock, because he was so *much* like the portraits on his coins and the faces on statues seen eighteen hundred years later.

A little older, possibly, or simply more worn.

A long face, curling dark hair and beard with a few first gray hairs, over a very slightly receding chin. The eyes were deep brown, and—

Tired, he thought. Not physically, but he's tired. That's the look of a man doing his very best on a job he doesn't like. And you can see thoughts there, like fish in a deep pool. Definitely someone there, there. Remember that; you have more information *on some things, but there are no flies on this one at all.*

The Emperor of Rome was about a decade older than he was, or a little more; shorter, but not by much, about average height for a twenty-first-century American, tall here. He looked vaguely Mediterranean, with light-olive skin and hair that was a very dark brown but not quite black.

Like a Tuscan or Sicilian or someone from Spain. Surprise! And they call me Prof, but he looks a lot *more like one,* Artorius thought. *And when you're looking at his face you don't notice the diadem and the purple tunic and* toga picta *and the standards and things behind him.*

The Americans and their companions bowed and stood waiting. Surprisingly, Marcus Aurelius' attention went first to the local landowner and the Jewish merchant.

"Lucius Maecius Josephus, Sextus Hirrius Trogus, you both gave aid and support to Lucius Triarius Artorius upon his arrival here, and not only when it was to your advantage, and hence contributed to his great deeds. Therefore you are also deserving of the thanks of the State. Sextus Hirrius, you are hereby freed from all taxation on yourself or your lands for the remainder of your life; and the Imperial *fiscus* will immediately pay all your debts."

He turned his head to Josephus. "Lucius Maecius Josephus, you are hereby elevated to the Equestrian Order...whose property qualification I understand you *now* meet."

Artorius kept his face impassive, but he couldn't suppress an inward grin; he thought from his eyes Marcus Aurelius was smiling inside too. The Emperor had just given two different men large gifts with the same money; Sextus went from deeply indebted to debt free in one fell swoop, probably doubling his disposable income by eliminating the interest payments and his taxes, and Josephus got his biggest single investment back all at once and quite a bit *more* than doubled from what he'd paid for it, vastly increasing his cash reserves.

Both men stepped back, leaving Artorius and the other four Americans behind him facing the Emperor. The sovereign placed a hand on Artorius' shoulder for a moment before he stepped back, and there was a slight murmur—that was a signal of honor—and a sort of huge, muted sigh from the watching troops.

His brief grip was firm, a strong hand but one with nothing to prove.

"This man," he said, pitching his voice to carry, "is one to whom we owe a great debt. Next to the unyielding strength of the Tenth Legion, it is to him and his followers that credit goes for the victory won here. He has given to me the secret of his great weapon, and given it freely, without request for reward. Yet rewards he shall have."

He made a sweeping gesture toward the American:

"I hereby elevate him to the Equestrian Order, and confer upon him the rank of *tribunus angusticlavius* attached to the Imperial headquarters."

That was roughly equivalent to being a divisional staff officer, something like a staff colonel or even brigadier-general, though the Roman concept of rank was deeply alien and less definite. It was considerably better paid than the American Army's equivalent, though, about the same as a *primus pilus'* sixty thousand sesterces a year.

"That he may maintain the dignity of his new state and rank, I hereby grant him sufficient estates from the *res privata*, for himself and his heirs."

Artorius felt a moment's surprise as a rolling cheer went through the assembled army. Starting with the Tenth, almost all of whom knew perfectly well what he'd saved them from, but spreading to the reinforcements as well. Artorius the War-Wise was genuinely popular with the troops, for the good and sufficient reason that he'd made it much more likely they would win victories...and much *less* likely they'd be killed or crippled doing so.

Now I'm a landed aristo, junior grade. Not bad, after arriving...well, moderately rich and with a nosebleed.

Emperors tended to guard the *res privata* jealously because it provided a large chunk of their revenues without the unpopularity of general taxation, but they could tap it for rewards as well. And it was enormous, something like twelve or fifteen percent of all the farmland in the Empire, not counting mines and urban land.

An aide handed the Emperor a scroll, and he passed it ceremoniously to Artorius, who bowed as he accepted it with both hands, then tucked it into the crook of his left arm in the gesture that Romans used carrying this type of writing.

That would be his copy of the transfer deed. Others—handed over by the aide, not the Emperor—went to Mark, Filipa, Jeremey and Paula... or to Marcus, Philippa, Julius and...

Paula, he thought. *Some things don't change even with the fall of empires. Probably they're getting a fair chunk each, enough to live comfortably for the rest of their lives, and pass on something to their children if they have them.*

"Now behold the weapon he brought to the fight, his gift to me and to the Senate and People of Rome, who now hold this godlike power!"

Orders rippled down the massed formations, and they did an about-face. So did everyone on the platform who wasn't already looking that way.

At the base of the long slope toward the Danube, in the location where the Marcomanni and their allies had massed for the initial advance, was a forest of stakes supporting scarecrow figures rigged out in German war regalia, including helmets and mail shirts for many, and the banners topped by skulls bestial and human that the barbarians had borne.

A large flock of sheep had been driven in among them and confined with wicker hurdles. They were grazing on the sprouting barley and weeds and grass and ignoring everything else with the idiot concentration of their breed. They didn't understand humans, and unlike dogs or cats they didn't try, either.

Gear captured after the fight, on the scarecrows, Artorius thought. *I'm glad I managed to talk them into using sheep instead of German prisoners. Of course, the prisoners fetch a higher price than sheep... and once the sheep are dead, you can eat them.*

Then the *carroballistae* came bouncing onto the field, the six he'd made over the winter, and twelve more they'd gotten functional since, with the help of the governor and the Tenth since the battle, all moving at a brisk canter. Having official backing for the collection of saltpeter had been a big boost too.

Getting people to be careful around stored gunpowder... or

thunderpowder ... was coming along too. Not without several gruesome accidents, but after those they started listening to his warnings.

And to getting the concept of explosive *into their heads. Odd to meet people who just don't have the* idea, *but they don't. Didn't.*

They deployed smartly about three hundred yards from the targets; he'd used his original crews as cadre, getting special permission from Bassus to enlist the freedmen who normally were barred. There was a tense silence as the trails were spread and the horse teams pulled back the cable that cocked the throwing arms; only the Tenth had seen the bombs in operation before, and most of them hadn't been really conscious of it at the time. The army was going to see it all, now.

The rest of the Tenth were sort of busy, Artorius thought. *The First Cohort got a good look, though.*

The reinforcements who'd come in over the last few months had only rumors.

Mental fingers crossed. I really hope this comes off smoothly!

The horse teams spanned the mechanisms with a ratcheting clatter; it was clearly audible, because the troops still kept silence as they waited to see what rumor had spoken of. The string—thick and strong, another cable really—linking the arms on each machine through a hardwood block carved into a cup went back ...

And now the moment of truth. I think *I got it through all their heads about not lighting the fuse too early.*

"I wish I could see this more clearly," the Emperor said quietly. "For it will be an experience unique in my life."

Artorius was wearing a *balteus* and a sword, the gladius on his left hip in the officer's position. He'd been told to bring the belt and weapon; the reason was obviously the military rank he'd just been granted, which was also the reason he wasn't wearing a toga.

That was explicitly civilian dress. The bleached white tunic was just what an officer wore, especially on special occasions.

He'd kept one of the sets of cased field glasses from Fuchs's treasure trove on the belt as well; they were the older type with no electronics, but well kept. Nobody objected, since Roman uniforms and gear weren't all that uniform; they tended to be more-or-less similar, not identical.

"Sir, try these," Artorius said, uncasing them. "Put them to your eyes and move the screw between them with your thumb, until things become clear."

Marcus Aurelius did; then he started a little as the distant targets became clear...and close.

"How is this accomplished, Tribune?" he said.

And he does *pronounce the final* -us *and* -um *sounds,* Artorius thought, unable to resist academic curiosity even then. *It's like people here in Pannonia speak Old Deep Texan and he's J.R.R. Tolkien at Oxford.*

"If you put a stick in water, or look through water in a clear glass cup, you see things bent and distorted, sir," he replied. "That is the materials bending light, the light that gives us sight. There are glass circles in these...we call them field glasses, for their military uses...that are ground to careful shapes. Depending on how they are made, they can magnify the small, or bring that which is distant close."

"Aristophanes and Seneca both remark on how a round glass jar of water can make things appear larger. Another secret... can you do the like? These would be very useful to officers and scouts, and I would like to train them on the heavens!"

"Perhaps, sir, but not very soon and not easily. I know the theory, the explanation...but producing glass of the right purity, and shaping it...that would require much trial and error. We might use rock crystal of exceptional clarity..."

"One thing I have noticed in your letters, and now in your speech, Tribune Artorius, is that you do not boast and make grand promises that cannot be fulfilled. This encourages me. And now..."

He raised his arm, and chopped it downward. The centurion in command of the ballistae was watching, tiny at this distance. He saluted in the arm-up style, then barked an order which couldn't be heard from here.

The distinctive vibrating-smacking impact of the throwing arms could and was:

Tunng-WHACK, repeated eighteen times. Then—

CRACK!

A first flash of red fire, and a great puff of dirty-gray smoke.

CRACK! CRACK! CRACK! CRACK! CRACK! CRACK! CRACK! CRACK! CRACK! CRACK! CRACK! CRACK! CRACK! CRACK! CRACK! CRACK! CRACK!

A broad swath of the targets disappeared, hidden in the

smoke. The *carroballistae* were reloading even as the breeze from the river wafted the burnt-sulfur firecracker stink over the massed spectators.

CRACK! CRACK! CRACK! CRACK! CRACK! CRACK! CRACK! CRACK! CRACK! CRACK! CRACK! CRACK! CRACK! CRACK! CRACK! CRACK! CRACK! CRACK!

Another eighteen bombs burst, and another, and another. The volleys continued, until nearly a hundred bombs had been launched. It was good theater and the target zone looked as if it had been under hot steel rain, but Artorius' teeth clenched.

Because it's also half the ammunition I've been able to get made since that little show with Sextus last fall.

When the volleys ceased, a goodly proportion of the scarecrow figures were down, and the sheep had been butchered like...

Butchered like...why, like sheep in a pen! he thought mordantly. *Not that men in the same situation wouldn't be ripped to pieces too. With sheep ghosts cheering from the sidelines, probably.*

The murmuring of the troops grew; then the horns and trumpets sounded again, and it died away. A man from each century and *turma* came forward, and walked through the area of devastation. The Emperor returned the field glasses with a rueful smile.

"You are more likely to need these in the service of Rome than I, Tribune," he said.

Then slightly wistfully: "Though if at some time you can make more of them, I would like a pair. That was like being a young man again, and with the eyes of an eagle. Mine were never so keen."

"Sir."

I am impressed, Artorius thought as he nodded soberly. *There aren't that many men who could be supreme autocrat of, from his point of view, virtually the whole civilized world, every third member of the human race, and who would still do that. The problem is that men like Marcus Aurelius are rather rare, and ones like the disaster his son Commodus will turn into are distressingly common.*

Artorius refocused the field glasses; evidently the Emperor was shortsighted. As he'd suspected, the sheep were all dead or badly wounded, a couple of hundred of them...and the soldiers were looking thoroughly impressed. He focused the field glasses on one poking the tip of his dagger through the hole in a helmet, another doing the same with a mail shirt and his little finger, and a third picking up a shield...and standing with a piece of it in his hand as the rest dropped in fragments at the toes of his hobnailed *caligae*.

Still another—a Middle Eastern-looking auxiliary archer in a chain-mail shirt over an ankle-length tunic and with a spired helmet on his head, long bearded and hook nosed and dark—bent over an eviscerated sheep, and gave it the mercy stroke with his knife, then wiped it on the wooly hide while he examined the wounds.

The trumpets called them back. When they'd returned to their centuries and squadrons the brass spoke again, and the whole formation did another about-face.

The Emperor stepped forward again. "This weapon can do nothing—nothing—without your good swords, strong arms and brave hearts. But *with* those swords, those arms and hearts *and* this weapon and others still to come, Rome will have *imperium sine fine*."

Which meant something like *rule without limits* or *eternal Empire everywhere*.

"Rome! Rome forever! And all the world under the protection of the Roman peace, beneath the wings of our Eagles!"

"ROMA! ROMA! ROMA!"

The chant went on for some time, and the booming thunder of weapons drummed on shields. When it died down, the Emperor spoke again:

"There is one more reward to give the excellent Artorius, but it is not mine to dispense."

Artorius blinked; nobody had told him about *this*. Marcus Aurelius went on:

"Lucius Sextius Caelius, carry on!"

The *primus pilus* of the Tenth Gemina kept his face grave, though Artorius had the distinct impression he wanted to grin like a hungry wolf. Instead he stepped forward, his ceremonial scarlet cloak swinging from his armored shoulders, and spoke to the soldiers—specifically, those of his own legion—in his parade-ground bellow.

"Legionnaires! Soldiers of the Tenth Gemina and the auxiliaries who fought by our sides! Generals give crowns of distinction and armbands and medallions of reward to soldiers. But there is one crown that is given only *by* the soldiers to the man who saved them."

His *optio* came up beside him, a scarlet cloth over his hands. On it rested a wreath, a diadem—but made of grass and twigs and shattered stalks of barley from this very field.

"Fellow soldiers! Shall I give this crown of grass to the noble Tribune Lucius Triarius Artorius, as we recognize our debt to him?"

"*Ave, Artorius!*"

The cry grew louder and louder as more of the 2,738 armored troopers of the Tenth present today and the auxiliaries who'd fought with them took up the cry. The rest of the field remained silent—this was a matter between those who'd been present at the battle.

The senior centurion waited until they were all shouting it before he took the wreath between surprisingly gentle fingers and marched three steps to stand before Artorius.

"For you, sir, the *corona graminea.*"

Artorius swallowed, suddenly moved far more than he could have expected. That was the highest and rarest of all Roman military decorations, not awarded more than once a decade even in times of war and sometimes not for generations at a time.

And by the men to the one who gets it. For saving them from death.

He bowed his head so that the centurion could reach it, and felt a prickle on his scalp as the rough material touched it; Lucius was an inch or so below average height for a Roman of this era, though stocky and troll strong, which meant he'd had some sort of pull to be allowed enlistment. Then he led Artorius to the edge of the platform, and the men cheered again.

A sudden thought came to him. He raised his arm. Silence fell, a little slowly.

"Soldiers of Rome!" he called, thankful that the accent was mostly out of his Latin.

Not that there aren't plenty of accents here today, and I doubt one in a hundred of these men have ever even seen the City of Rome. Maybe less. Most of them would have been born on the frontier, even the ones who are Roman citizens by birth. The Roman Empire's a bit like a lobster: these are the claws and armored shell that protect the soft, yummy-tasty interior. North of the border . . . there's no interior. No area of peace.

"Our Caesar Augustus has rewarded me beyond my worth, and so have you."

He turned slightly, toward the great eagle-topped banner and the man who stood before it and saluted:

"To Imperator Caesar Marcus Aurelius Antoninus Augustus... *Ave, Imperator!*"

The whole assembled throng barked it out in a chorus that echoed from the road and forest to the river and back.

"AVE, IMPERATOR!"

Marcus Aurelius acknowledged it, and made a gesture. The curled *cornua* and straight *tubae* sang again, a single long note for silence. Then another volley of orders. The formations faced left and marched, swinging along in a perfect order that would leave the Tenth—the newly decorated Tenth, with a new title to be inscribed on their banners, and a hundred *denarii* burning a hole in their belt pouches—in the lead on the road back to Vindobona and celebration.

The Emperor and his inner circle waited until the last were on the road.

Marcus Aurelius spoke, when the earthquake rumble of thousands of boots and hooves died down enough for him to be heard speaking in ordinary tones:

"Great changes will come of what you have brought to the Empire, Tribune."

Artorius smiled to himself, and said:

"Sir... *What can take place without change? What then is more pleasing or more suitable to the universal nature? And can you take a bath unless the wood that heats the water undergoes a change? And can you be nourished, unless the food undergoes a change? And can anything else that is useful be accomplished without change?"*

Marcus Aurelius looked at him quizzically, then smiled more broadly than Artorius had seen before.

"You echo my own inner thoughts on the matter, Tribune, but I had not yet reduced them to so compact and eloquent a form."

No, I echo your own book that you haven't written yet, Artorius thought. *Talk about stealing a man's credit! But I* do *think that's* true.

Aloud he went on: "Caesar Augustus, I am glad your inspiring speech included the words: *and others yet to come* when you referred to the new weapons."

Marcus Aurelius smiled, this time a more typical very slight curve of the lips, as much a matter of eyes and the way he cocked his head slightly to the side as anything.

It was the commander of the Praetorians, Sextus Cornelius Repentinus, who spoke. There was an underlying guttural accent in his polished Latin, probably something regional:

"How so, Tribune?"

"Sir, if the Germanii or other enemies face us the way those scarecrows and sheep did"—he pointed eastward—"we'll give them exactly what the targets got, and what Prince Ballomar got in the battle here. Then our troops will butcher any who live long enough to run away."

"Good work for the cavalry," the commander of the First Thracians said. "And with the new gear you've gotten us, Tribune Artorius, it'll be a grand old day chasing them. Spearing them in the buttocks with the new couched-lance style and betting on how high they can jump."

That got a general laugh, though not from the Emperor.

"They're barbarians, but not necessarily stupid," Artorius said. "They'll realize that. Perhaps already, certainly after a few more lessons like the one they got on this field. Then they'll try other tactics. Falling back before a Roman army, harassing, ambushes, rushes from cover, attacks on supply trains. They'll try to do as much damage as they can without giving us a massed target."

Marcus Aurelius nodded. "Quite likely."

Repentius grinned, a coldly unpleasant expression. His dark olive face had scars on it that showed as lines of white through his dense black beard, and he had two narrow purple stripes on his white tunic—command of the Guard was an equestrian post.

Whatever else the Praetorians might become...

Might have *become, in a history that now will never be. Who knows what* this *future holds? I don't know, any more than anyone else on this piece of purple-draped boards. The more we change things, the less use our knowledge of* that *history is, at least the political details.*

...they were still elite troops here and now. Their commander went on:

"Very likely, that's a shrewd prediction. I can see you've led men on campaign before, Tribune. But Romans have seen the same before from tribes who don't dare to face us in open battle and abide the results. We have an answer to it that always works."

And he continued with a single word:

"*Vastatio.*"

That meant *to lay waste.* In the sense that you left nothing human behind you except ashes, bones and chained coffles heading for the slave markets and mines. And when the Romans set their hand to something, they tended to do it very, very thoroughly and usually with any amount of patience necessary.

Marcus Aurelius nodded.

"That is sometimes necessary, Prefect Repentius," he said. "Remember though, that the Gaulish chief Brennus burned Rome once, and the Divine Julius fought for eight hard years to sub-due Gaul itself—sometimes employing *vastatio*, yes. But now... Marcus Iallius Bassus here comes from the land of the Helvetii, who the Divine Julius fought and defeated. And he is a senator of Rome, a commander of legions, a man of culture and virtue who has governed provinces well. Carthage was our great enemy. Rome destroyed Carthage and sowed the city itself with salt. But now Carthage is a great *Roman* city... and the former domains of *Punic* Carthage have given us men like you, Repentius. All human beings are of one creation, all men brothers *in potentia*; it is the great task of Rome to make that potential real. Some-day the descendants of today's barbarian Germanii may be loyal Romans as well, speaking our tongue, working and fighting for Rome. I certainly hope so. *Imperium sine fine*, eh?"

He turned to Artorius again. "You and your clients... and good Sextus Hirrius, and you, *eques* Maecius Josephus... are bidden to dinner with me tonight. It will be a small affair, and humor me that we may dine sitting upright; no slight is intended, but such is my inclination and what I take to be the fruits of philosophy."

Artorius inclined his head. "No slight taken by me, sir. In fact, lying down to eat is one Roman custom I have found hard to acquire. Swallowing takes more effort without the food's weight assisting you."

Marcus Aurelius departed amid the semiscandalized chuckle that got, a valet taking his toga before he mounted a horse held by a Praetorian at the foot of the stairs... one that had the new type of saddle, Artorius noted. So did the *Equites Singulares Augusti*, the select horse guards who formed up around him. The rest of the party went down the stairs with a smooth juggling of rank and precedence that was next to instinctive in Romans who moved in these circles; Artorius was a little surprised how far forward the position he was subtly nudged into was.

At the foot of the stairs strict precedence yielded to a more ordinary order. Paula spoke...in English:

"You know, that entire ceremony...did you get the impression there ought to have been rows of searchlights around the whole thing? *Imperium sine fine*, yup."

"Hey, everybody who makes wheels makes them round, and that's how you get guys fired up to fight," Jeremey observed. "Us good, them bad; us tough, them wimps; kill-kill-kill. Sure seemed to *work*, didn't it?"

"And that Repentius...I think *they make a desert, and call it peace* was coined for people like him," Filipa added.

"Well, he's not going to win any sensitivity contests, yeah," Jeremey said cheerfully, unconsciously patting his new title-deed scroll. "No lashings of universal empathy, nosiree Bob. It's sort of scarce around here, just in case you hadn't noticed."

"But keep in mind what Prince Ballomar had in mind for the area. And not in the cause of anything but fun and profit," Artorius added. "*Fun* being defined as what we saw at that farmhouse."

"There is that," she admitted, grimacing a little.

"And the Emperor did do the *all men are brothers* thing. Sort of," Mark replied.

Paula snorted: "Yeah, brothers...once they've been clubbed, cuffed and kicked into *Romanitas*."

Mark chuckled, or almost giggled. "Rome—the seven-hundred-pound green alien amoeba of civilizations. *Shloop*—Rome absorbs the sofa! *Shloop*—Rome absorbs the dog! *SHLOOP!* Rome absorbs *you*."

"We're committed," Artorius said. "And we all got tangible evidence of the Emperor's appreciation."

Paula looked dubiously at the scroll in her left hand, barely showing past the fold of her *palla* draped over that arm:

"I don't think I'm the plantation-owner type, lolling on the verandah sipping a mint julep and watching the...um...pinkies...at work."

Artorius grinned. "You don't have to be. Imperial estates are rented out to contractors and subcontractors and so on down to the tenant farmers of various sizes. Not much management required if you don't feel like taking it in hand. You just get the rents sent to your banker instead of the provincial procurator who's doing it for Caesar Augustus. You could live in Rome... or Alexandria...and have them sent to you. No need to do more unless they drop off without a good excuse."

He shifted back into Latin as Sextus and Julia came up to them; their mother was still on the Villa Lunae, feeling—quite genuinely—indisposed and cursing her own bowels for keeping her away from a massive status boost.

And I didn't offer her *ampicillin.*

"Greetings, eminent sir," Julia said to Artorius, with that wry expression he liked in her hazel-green eyes.

Her curtsey-bow gesture was subtly mocking, but in a friendly way.

"As you told the Emperor with such eloquence, change is constant! A year ago you had a terrible accent in your Latin and didn't know how to wear a toga! Now...an eques, a tribune on the staff of the Emperor himself, recipient of his largess...given the Grass Crown, the first to receive it in many years! And all for throwing around a few bronze balls full of everyday ingredients that can be bought from street vendors and apothecaries!"

Artorius laughed. *Just what I needed to bring me down to earth,* he thought.

Her brother laughed too. "Fortunate was the day Josephus came to ask for the loan of the Villa Lunae!"

"Fortunate was the day I...met Artorius on the road," Josephus said.

Said *carefully.*

"Many the gifts that that chance and he himself have brought me. Some of high price; others beyond all price."

"I'd like to speak with you of two things, if you would, Sextus, Josephus," Artorius said, a final decision crystalizing.

I'm going to go through with it. Life's too short for much waiting when you don't have to.

"Matters of business. And no, Lady Julia, please stay too; this concerns you as well."

He handed the title-deed scroll to Josephus. "What do you make of these properties?"

Josephus read, moving his lips without much sound, closed his eyes for a moment in thought as he consulted the files in his memory about the neighborhood of his hometown, and shook his head.

"Caesar has been generous! Very! These properties are just southwest of Sirmium. Fertile land of the highest quality, and well placed to deliver valuable produce to the city by road, or by river barge on the Savus"—which would be the Sava river in Artorius' birth century, and was a tributary of the Danube—"to more distant markets as well."

"What would you say of their value relative to the Villa Lunae?"

"Easily three times the value," Josephus said promptly, and showed the transfer document to Sextus. "Even allowing for the, ah, recent improvements."

The *eques* pursed his lips in thought. "Yes, that's fair," he said, after a moment. "I know that land."

"I would like to propose a contract between us, Sextus my friend," Artorius said. "A portion of these lands equivalent to the value of the Villa Lunae plus . . . say five parts in one hundred . . . to be yours, in return for title to the Villa Lunae. I will also give you a first share of the seeds for the new crops, and examples and instruction for your smiths and other craftsmen in all the new engines and methods for the improvement of the estate, now and in the future."

Sextus was a little taken aback, but his eyes narrowed as he looked at the deed again.

"These are closer to Sirmium and to my other properties; the Villa Lunae is inconvenient in that respect. Yes. Yes, this an excellent proposal, my friend. At least from my point of view. Indeed, I would hesitate only because my debt, my debt of honor, to you is already so great."

"I've come to a fondness for the place," Artorius said.

And I really have, he thought. *For a number of reasons.*

They shook hands, a firm pump. "I'll have the documents drawn up?" Sextus said. "Wait, why don't we have Josephus do it, yes, and specify *which* of these lands will be transferred. If I would trust any man on earth to do so skillfully and fairly, it would be him."

"I agree," Artorius said promptly. "None better walking the earth to do so, for wits and honesty both, as you say."

"Flattery from both of you balances out," Josephus said. "With honored Sextus, it's probably relief at having no more payments to make."

"You were a prince among creditors, and will be a credit to the Equestrian Order, my friend," Sextus said to him. "But yes, I feel as if I am Sisyphus...but I've finally managed to heave that boulder over the top of the hill and I now watch it bounding away, crushing all my critics as it goes!"

Well, that's an easy adjustment to the change in relative status, Artorius noticed. *He's already treating Josephus as a near equal.*

Aloud he went on, clearing his throat to cover a sudden dryness in his mouth:

"Which brings me to my next proposal. I would like...like very much...to receive your permission to pay court to your sister, the lady Julia."

This time Sextus *was* surprised. With virtually no property of her own, only a brother cash-strapped until today to provide a dowry, already burdened by a daughter who'd need a dowry herself in a decade or less, and by Roman standards distinctly old for marriage at twenty-six, Julia had little prospect of a good match.

A man in Artorius' position could do much better in terms of wealth and useful family connections. The Emperor's favor was with him, after all, and with Sextus only *through* him.

"You ask for her hand?" the Roman said, a delighted smile breaking through his frown of puzzlement.

Artorius looked at her and shook his head. "No. I ask your permission to ask *her* for her hand."

Sextus wasn't shocked at that. As her legal guardian, he could refuse, or technically in strict law grant her hand regardless of her wishes, though it had been centuries since that was actually commonly done. But even in the upper classes where weighty matters of property were involved, it had long been customary to allow women widowed or divorced far more latitude in making their own marriage choices than young maidens.

"What of her daughter Claudia, my niece?"

"*If* the lady Julia accepts my suit, I would adopt Claudia as my own, and give her the shelter of my name."

Which was fairly easy under Roman law. Adoption was simple, quite common in the upper echelons of society, and conveyed pretty well all the rights of the equivalent blood relationship.

As witness the way the last four Emperors came to the purple.

Effectively little Claudia would be exchanging a dead deadbeat father who she scarcely remembered anyway for a living one with excellent prospects.

"And I would guarantee her an equal inheritance with any

children of the union," he said. "I have become very fond of her in any case, as if she were my own blood in truth."

Which is gospel, he thought. *Great kid!*

"You are my friend and my benefactor, and the savior of this province. You are an *eques* now, and a wealthy one, and you have the Emperor's favor and will probably go far. And you are also a man of virtue, whose word is good and who I trust to give my sister all due honor, and the mutual gift of heirs, uniting us in blood. Though I admit my own father was wrong in his judgment with her first husband, for all *his* ancestors! You have *my* blessing," Sextus said.

That was a tactful way of saying: *Hot damn, I get an Imperial favorite as a brother-in-law!* while snapping his fingers over his head like castanets and dancing a fandango.

"But as you say, it is in Julia's hands now," he added.

Julia was smiling. "You ask permission to pay me court?" she said. "You ask for my hand in marriage, but give me leave to consider the matter as it suits me, rather than in familial obedience to my brother?"

"Yes, lady."

Her smile grew. "You, Lucius Triarius Artorius, are a man of unmatched courtesy...and even sweetness...but also a peerless warrior—the Grass Crown!—and a fine scholar. And courtship is, I think, what we have been doing since the end of last year, though under other names. Life with you would never be tedious, even if it will be strange. I accept."

Artorius felt his own grin break loose, and he was only vaguely aware of the other Americans pounding him on the back.

Then he gestured them aside and cleared his throat. "Lady Julia, among the people of my birth it is the custom for the man proposing a marriage to offer a ring to the woman, and for her to signify her acceptance to the world by accepting it, and wearing it on the third finger of the left hand."

"Why, we have exactly the same custom!" Julia said, and the Romans all nodded.

"Very civilized, these Americans!" her brother murmured, beaming. "They might almost be Roman!"

"Yes, but it is offered in a particular way. May I?"

She put her hands together before her throat—not quite in a clap—and said:

"By all means!"

Artorius reached into the pocket he'd had hastily installed in his new tunic. The little box was there, and he pulled it out and went to one knee. Her brows rose, but she kept smiling.

Then he offered the open box. The ring within had one of Fuchs's synthetic diamonds in a setting of braided gold. There were a few gasps from the Roman spectators. Partly because it was a diamond at all; they knew about them here, but they were few and all imported at vast expense from India. They weren't used to symmetrically faceted ones either, but the hard glitter was unmistakable.

And Julia smiled with unaffected delight—not so much at the gem, he knew, but at the thought. In his long *naturalis historia* Pliny had said they were the property of royalty.

"For the queen of my heart," he said very softly.

Josephus was *very* impressed; *he* knew that if this jewel could have been sold at all, it would fetch at least as much as all the coins the Americans had landed with.

Sextus had some idea of that, if a less exact one, and started to say something, then subsided as Josephus touched him gently on the arm. Behind him Josephus' wife Deineira smiled and wiped the corner of her eye with a fold of her *palla*.

"Lady Julia, will you do me the honor of becoming my wife?" Artorius said gravely and formally, for all to hear.

"Lord Artorius, I will, and gladly," she replied with equal solemnity.

He put it on her ring finger, and when he rose their left hands stayed clasped as Artorius formally said to her brother:

"*Spondesne?*"

Which meant:

Do you promise?

Sextus extended his hand and clasped Artorius' right.

"*Spondeo!*" he said heartily, giving it a firm pump:

It is promised.

"We shall be kin," he added. "Our children will be cousins!"

Then his happy face fell very slightly; glancing sideways, Artorius met his fiancée's eyes and knew they shared a thought.

He just realized he's going to have to find a home for his mother again. Because she is most certainly not staying with us! Not for long, at least!

⇒ CHAPTER NINETEEN ⇐

Villa Lunae,
Province of Pannonia Superior
September 25th, 166 CE

Josephus smiled broadly.

"This is the first time I've seen a wedding combined with a real-estate transaction on the same day and *as part of the ceremony*," he said quietly, in the atrium of the Villa Lunae.

Josephus had been delighted when Artorius informed him of the American custom of the *best man*, and agreed readily once it was clear it didn't mean he had to take part personally in any pagan rites. He wasn't bothered by *witnessing* them as a nearby nonparticipant, though Mark had told him that was a relaxed attitude by contemporary Jewish standards.

"It occurred to me when you described Roman wedding rituals for me," Artorius said.

I'm happy. Nervous, but happy...was the first time too, if I remember rightly. Maybe a bit less nervous this time?

He had that sense of Mary watching again, and smiling.

I wanted the ceremony here, but by God it turns out to be convenient all 'round, he thought.

The Latin language had several terms for a wedding. *Nubere viro* was from the woman's point of view, which meant "to put on a veil for a husband." From the groom's, it was *ducere uxorem,* "to lead a wife home."

For strictly legal purposes, Roman wedding ceremonies were more a marker than what *made* you husband and wife: you were married though a public declaration of intent and making a wedding contract before witnesses, followed by cohabitation. Witnesses usually signed the contract, if it was written. The ceremony was customary, and leaving it off would be shocking, but in law the witnessed public declaration was what counted.

Especially for the commonest form of marriage, *sine manu*, which this would be.

So the wedding ceremony itself started in the bride's house, with the paterfamilias—that would be Sextus here, since their father was dead and he was head of the Trogi—bringing the bride out. Then there was a procession to the groom's house. In this case...

The Villa Lunae is technically still Sextus' until he hands me the deed of transfer. Once he does, it's mine. So—

"Time to go," Josephus said, taking a glance over his shoulder.

"How do I look?" Artorius asked—not for the first time.

"As if you were going to a very important party," Josephus said. "Distinguished...dashing...handsome...any woman's dream."

In fact, Artorius was in a white tunic with equestrian purple stripes, and a good white toga with another narrow purple stripe on its edge. He had a flower crown of roses and some yellow wildflower...

And I'm not embarrassed by it. Well, not much.

...and moderately fancy sandals. Basically what he'd have worn to a classy dinner party, just as his friend said. Traditional Roman clothing in general was extremely simple though it could *look* quite splendid. And very comfortable in good weather, once you were used to it.

Except for the toga.

They walked out together into the inner courtyard in the bright sunlight of a fall morning, with a few golden leaves from the trees fallen since the final sweeping. Then across its flower-and-statue splendor, through the building and the *second* courtyard and out into the walled enclosure of the formal entrance garden. As with Sextus' arrival—

Just about a year ago! Artorius thought, a little dazed. *How time flies!*

—the whole *familia rustica* had turned out for this, besides quite a few guests, both neighbors and from the Imperial entourage.

He thought the cheering from the *familia rustica* was more wholehearted than it had been then. Paula told him that Julia was popular with the staff, and that he was too—nearly everyone liked the changes he'd made here. Work had gotten a bit lighter and a bit less tedious, and there had been a spate of manumissions covering about a tenth of the whole slave population of the estate.

The projected village of cottages so that each family could have its own hearth and yard was regarded as too good to be true... but *possibly* true because he was a divinely aided miracle worker.

Plus the staff were all getting a three-day blowout and barbeque with only essential work done and those doing *that* getting a hefty bonus, which meant they'd all be getting a big party before *and* after the vintage. This year there was plenty of BBQ sauce and salsa, too, and a fair try at pizza which had also turned out to be wildly popular; the tomatoes and chilies and peppers and whatnot were doing very well. The French fries were generally well received too.

Right now I seem to want everyone in the world to be happy. Humbug perhaps, but it's a happy *humbug.*

His recently acquired status reflected on *them*, too, and there were rumors that there would be still more manumissions. True ones, in that the *vilicus*, his wife and children, and Julia's maid Tertia had all been emancipated as a kickoff for the celebrations and a sprinkling would be done afterward. The others would follow later, gradually, to avoid shocking the neighboring landowners and big farmers excessively.

The cheering was accompanied by a few thrown flowers from children, followed by scolding from their elders; that was supposed to come in the *next* stage. Artorius grinned and waved to signal that no bottom swats were necessary. Romans had about the same attitude to that that his grandparents did when he was growing up, and casual smacks were common as dirt. His own background made him considerably less upset with that than the other Americans, or at least Mark, Paula and Filipa.

He suspected that Jeremey's parents had been over-enthusiastic corporalists, though.

They halted by the fountain and statue of Neptune outside the gates, amid a scent of flowers and water. And that wonderful smell of old leaves and cut grass and mellowness he associated with fall, which was his favorite time of year, what he privately thought of as *the golden season.*

The leaves turning here were pretty but not as spectacular as it could be in parts of North America—New England, for example. Not as far as trees were concerned at least, but the *vineyards* had turned into a massive carpet of gold, crimson and orange; enough had been plucked to make wreaths for most of the estate's spectators. There were plenty of them here. And not far away a century of Praetorians was at parade rest.

"Now all we have to do for a while is wait," he said quietly.

"In fear and trembling, my friend, as before the Lord," Josephus said with a smile. "I remember how *I* felt that the earth might open and swallow me...very vividly. At least you and your bride have met before the day, which Deineira and I had not! But I have a small flask of superwine beneath my toga, fully a year old in the oak—there is none better! Call if you need it to avoid a fainting spell. Your reputation as a mighty warrior is at stake!"

Artorius nodded; the badinage was relaxing, though his gut kept trying to clench again. He could see what was happening in the house vividly, with his mind's eye—there had been enough rehearsals over the last week. Her mother and aunts and the attendants would be decking Julia out in ways that ministered to the Roman love of tradition. Her hair—

That beautiful russet-brown color, he thought. *So soft...*

—would be parted ritually into six braids by a tiny ceremonial spear called the *hasta caelibaris,* then fastened by wooden bands. The piled hair would be topped by a crown of flowers—roses and marjoram—and covered with a ceremonial yellow-silk veil. Her long embroidered tunic would be white silk, cinched with an intricately knotted belt, and she'd wear special yellow shoes.

They'd be taking auspices—they had a professional in from town for that who could be relied on to find no bad omens—making a sacrifice to Venus and to Juno of incense and sprinkled wine, and to Vesta of the Hearth and the *Lares* and *Penates* of the household...

And technically I sacrificed the oxen and pigs and sheep and lambs for the feast over the past couple of days, to Ceres and Jupiter.

Though that mostly consisted of being present and making certain gestures and speaking the ritual words. He'd been present at plenty of nonreligious stock slaughter as a youngster, of course. That part of it was quite familiar, even nostalgic.

Come on, come on, he thought. *I'm going to start dithering and dithering in a toga is very undignified.*

Then he heard the rising cheers again. Sextus came first, also in his best and wearing a wreath, with Julia behind him in a more elaborate floral crown, her face a suggestion behind the yellow veil. The elder Trogus moved a step ahead.

"I hereby deliver this deed," he said formally. "As those here may witness."

"I receive it," Artorius said, and held it up so that it could be seen...before handing it off to Josephus, who tucked it into *his* toga.

That capacious garment had many uses.

"As those here may witness."

Now the house was no longer that of Julia's family. Having left *her* house, the wedding procession would now go to *his*.

Julia's mother and aunts and nieces and nephews were there behind her, along with some respectable neighboring matrons; even little Claudia was. Among the troop of guests behind *them* were the Emperor and the provincial governor, and some of their higher-ranking hangers-on; the elder Claudia was positively glowing at the rain of status her family was receiving.

Julia was serene, ignoring it all as her elder brother took her hand and deposited it in Artorius'.

He thought he saw her mouth twitch very slightly behind the veil as everyone roared out:

"*Talassio! Talassio! Talassio!*"

Which was a *really* obscure cry, probably referring to the abduction of the Sabine women by Romulus and crew. There were times you could tell the Trogi had been equestrians since Pompey, two hundred years ago, even if this particular branch of the family were big fish only in a small provincial pond.

And I'm lucky that there's always been room in Rome for a novus homo, apart from some sneers. Hell, I'm just damned lucky. So far. Be careful. The dice have no memory.

The couple who were the center of the ritual turned and walked back toward the entrance of—now—the bridegroom's house. Half a dozen torches were lit, and put in the hands of children old enough to be trusted with them—mostly of Julia's aunts, but including little Claudia. Now the cheers were deafening, from the *familia rustica*, the free tenants, and assorted guests. Flowers flew toward the pair, and nuts as well—a symbol of fertility.

Artorius ignored them, which was easier than ignoring the bawdy words of encouragement and risqué songs, the *Fescennines*. Some of those were in a very archaic dialect of Latin—evidently trotted out for weddings, and they went back a long way, to ancient rustic rituals...judging by the one that called him a *garlanded man-bull* or a *ewe-tupping ram rampant*, or *behold the eques—what a stallion!*

That was a bawdy pun on the relationship between the Roman *knights* and the beasts they rode. Originally *equites* had been meant literally—it was the class who came to the war levy on horseback, when Rome was a glorified village squabbling with neighbors a mile or two away.

Things got more anatomically specific from there; the songs and chants were *supposed* to embarrass the bride and groom.

At the doorway he paused. One of Julia's attendants—her unacknowledged half-sister, now a freedwoman with the Hirrius cognomen, but still her personal maid—handed her a vial, and she solemnly anointed the doorposts of the entrance between the green garlands that decked them.

"What *is* that?" he muttered.

"Rendered fat from a she-wolf," she said, as quietly. "A lot of people just use lard or olive oil, but this is a family tradition. To remember the Capitoline she-wolf who suckled the twins."

"Smells like dead dog," Artorius said.

Josephus heard that, and smothered a snort as he stepped past to throw open the tall doors, while Artorius accepted a coin from Julia and in turn gave her the key to the door.

"Now *I* have something to do," Artorius said, and swept her up in his arms to avoid the remote chance of an unlucky stumble.

"Very pleasant armful," he said into her ear; she was. "Pity we have to waste time on a feast."

"Oh, you ram-pant stallion of an ewe-tupping garlanded man-bull," she whispered back, and giggled. "Remember to water your wine, or your boasts will be as slack as the wineskin!"

When he put her down the courtyard was crowded; free guests were in the forefront, but everyone was here.

Being *public* was the point of the procession. More nuts flew. Josephus stepped forward, taking a diptych from one of the Emperor's clerks—although what was inside it was paper now, not wax.

He ceremoniously presented it to Marcus Aurelius with a bow. Even then, Artorius noticed how the two hard-faced Praetorians behind him—in civil garb—tensed ever so slightly and slid their hands into the folds of their plain plebian togas.

Marcus Aurelius noticed him noticing, with a very slight wry twist of the lips. Their eyes met, and shared a thought:

And yet men actually strive *for this position!*

Another clerk offered a pen and held an ink bottle. The Emperor of Rome signed his name at the head of the list of witnesses with a firm flourish: legally there had to be ten, but there would be considerably more before the diptych was closed, bound with cords and sealed. Putting your autograph on the same page as Caesar Augustus gave you boasting rights.

When it was done a few moments later, Josephus took a symbolic step back as they exchanged fire and water, Julia lit a symbolic torch, and they made a joint sacrifice of incense before the statues of the family *Lares* set in a niche, with the usual serpent to embody the *genius* of the household below their feet done in bronze inlay. A scrap of food in the form of a breadcrust went into the fire as an offering to the *Penates* of the house; they had originally been guardians of the pantry and storeroom. Many families did that before every meal, an equivalent of saying grace.

"Now this house is yours," Artorius said formally, as he'd been coached. "Be a stranger here no more; here you are *materfamilias*."

"And here I thought the house looked remarkably familiar from my last few years, oh *paterfamilias*," Julia said gravely.

The Emperor laughed aloud, which startled some of his followers, adjusted his purple *toga picta* and said:

"This marriage is now legally binding, Tribune. I suggest you kiss your new wife."

Antonius did; it was decorous, but enthusiastic. There were more shouts of bawdy advice, and this time the chant was:

"*Feliciter! Feliciter! Feliciter!*"

Josephus joined in that, then stepped back again when the crowd broke into a hymn to Hymenaeus. When the song subsided, the newlyweds faced each other with clasped right hands.

"*Ubi tu Gaius, ego Gaia*," Julia said: *Where you are Gaius, I am Gaia.*

"*Ubi tu Gaia, ego Gaius*," Artorius replied.

More torches were waved as they crossed the courtyard; tables were being set up there, for the guests who would overflow the usual banquet room. The crowd grew less formal; many garlands were sported, and Marcus Aurelius quietly switched his Imperial diadem for one.

Walking on Artorius' arm while the torch-bearing youngsters danced around them, Julia inclined her head to him. "My thanks, sir...you have made my mother very happy."

"Which ain't easy," Artorius muttered...in English.

But it was true; Lady Claudia was virtually—for her—beaming amid her coterie of sisters and nieces and nephews.

The Emperor grinned, which earned a few double takes from *his* entourage.

"Thank *you*, Tribune, Lady Julia. This is as close as a man in my position may come to being *just* a man, enjoying a festive occasion with his friends. Much joy to you both!"

Julia chuckled. "And you have given our cook a reason to boast for the rest of his life."

Galen was there, a spare man in his thirties and inconspicuous as usual, though in a Greek chiton rather than the toga which his Roman citizenship entitled him to.

"I advised the cook on which dishes suit your humors, Caesar Augustus."

"You are a true friend, Galenos!" the Emperor said, with a trace of fervor.

And how! Artorius thought.

The physician would impose a certain degree of simplicity, in the name of the Emperor's delicate stomach.

I like Roman cooking, except when they try for ultimate haute cuisine. Then it gets deeply weird. I even like garum a bit, sometimes. It's not much stronger than kimchee, *and granddad always trotted that out on special occasions, in memory of* his *mother the war bride from Seoul.*

"Though after your new treatment, Galenos, I find my stomach pains have abated somewhat, and now I look forward to dinner!" Marcus Aurelius said happily.

The physician exchanged a look with Artorius.

That treatment is newer than you think, the American mused. *Long life to you, Emperor of Rome!*

The feast was winding down several hours later—the bride's friends and attendants had taken her away to prepare her for the bridal chamber, amid much hilarity—and Artorius was preparing for the rather more raucous and physical male version.

And we Harvard alumni are proving where we come from,

in more senses than one, he thought, standing in a corner and sipping his—well-watered—wine amid the shadows cast by the flickering oil lamps.

While listening to the four ex-grad students discussing the rituals of the wedding, and comparing them to twenty-first-century historical reconstructions.

Mark stopped in midsentence, frowned and said: "Y'know, speaking of religious rituals, there are *Jews* here in the Pannonian ass-end of Roman nowheredom. Not many, only Sirmium around here even has a *minyan*, but enough so you notice 'em. Still, I haven't met a *Christian* yet? People hardly even mention *them*."

The other three stopped and looked at him; by now they were used to his grasshopper leaps and non sequiturs.

Jeremey shrugged. "Christianity's illegal—enforcement's spotty, but they keep out of sight, I hear. Why would anyone invite trouble and the roving eye of the *Frumentarii* by 'fessing up to someone like us? Since we're people with official connections?"

"True enough. There are probably a few in Carnuntum and a few more than that in Sirmium," Artorius said judiciously. "Christianity's an urban phenomenon at this date, and it's just moving away from being a Jewish heresy... mostly spreading among people attracted to Jewish monotheism but not the ritual entanglements. But that's mainly in eastern cities—Alexandria, Antioch... and there probably aren't more than, oh, a hundred thousand or so in the whole Empire. Give or take fifty percent! As opposed to a million or more Jews."

Filipa looked thoughtful. "As opposed to five, six million Christians when Constantine comes to the throne a hundred and forty years from now."

"That's not certain," Mark said, his eyes lighting at the taste of a scholarly ding-dong. "Peter Heather made a convincing argument it was a lot less than that in *Christendom: The Triumph of a Religion*, back a decade ago... well, a decade before we left... and *I* say the research supports him—"

Artorius cleared his throat. "Either way, the third century was the period they really took off, especially after Alexander Severus is assassinated in 235. Will be... would have... time-travel tenses again."

"When the third-century disaster really hits the edge of the cliff and topples over it and windmills down screaming to the jagged rocks," Paula said thoughtfully. "Though... if we succeed in what we're trying, the next century won't *be* a disaster, right? We're *aiming* for a Golden Age. Peace, prosperity, progress in medicine and science, reform. Think that'll affect things religion-wise if we pull it off?"

Artorius spread his hands. "I have no idea," he said. "I'm a historian, not a prophet!"

Then he switched to Latin:

"Ah, is it time, sir?"

"Nearly," Marcus Aurelius said. "By the way, I admit those *forks* you use make dinner . . . tidier. I may have a set made up for my own table! But the next part of the wedding festivities is a trifle . . . undignified."

Artorius shrugged. "We have a saying, sir: When in the *Imperium Romanum*, do as the Romans do."

The Emperor chuckled quietly at another example of the Artorian wit.

"Very wise!"

"We were discussing details of the religious rites here," Artorius went on.

"True scholars!" the Roman replied. "What are your American rites like in comparison?"

Artorius chose his words carefully; he didn't want to actually *lie*.

"Fundamentally not much different. We have many religions. Some worship your Gods—those of Greece and Rome—with very similar rites. Some follow Gallic or German cults."

"My family followed the Way of the Buddha, sir," Filipa observed.

The Roman frowned for an instant as he searched his well-stocked memory, then nodded:

"Yes, that Indian belief that has some parallels with Pythagorean teachings!" he said.

"Our policy was to tolerate all forms of worship that did not do violence to public order; the founders of our Republic laid that down. And we have . . . had . . . Jews and Christians."

All of which is, well, gospel *true, in a way,* Artorius thought. *Perhaps with problems of emphasis.*

"Sound policy!" Marcus Aurelius said; Josephus was at his elbow and looked as if he was biting his tongue a bit. "Though Christians . . . they can be troublesome. Did you have no difficulties with them?"

Mark choked into his wine cup, and Jeremey hid a grin by thumping him on the back. Paula rolled her eyes very slightly.

"Occasionally," Artorius said gravely. "But extending our policy of toleration to them proved to be practical, sir. I recommend it, in fact—they would be *less* troublesome if you did so, I believe."

Marcus Aurelius shook his head dubiously. "Yet they unreasonably refuse participation in harmless symbols of public allegiance—sacrifices to the guiding genius of the Emperor and the Goddess Roma."

"Sir, that could be dealt with, as it has with those of the Jewish religion," Artorius said. "For example, if they were permitted to pray *for* the spirit of the Emperor, publicly imploring their God and His Son to favor the ruler and uphold Rome, and to send him inspiration that will help him act with wisdom and justice? And those who did so were then allowed to practice their rites in public rather than in secret? Without secrecy, there would be far fewer unfortunate rumors."

Marcus Aurelius frowned. "The ones concerning cannibalistic feasts?" he said. "Many believe that."

"Well, sir, I know little...nothing...of the way Christians worship here. But if they resemble the ones in my former homeland, they have a feast in which they drink wine and break bread together, both blessed by their priests, which blessing makes the two substances *symbolically* represent the blood and flesh of their prophet which were sacrificed for them. Sanctified by his suffering and resurrection from Hades, which prefigures everlasting life for his followers at the end of time and their entry into an eternal paradise."

The frown cleared. "Truly? Why, that makes sense...in fact, it reminds me of some Orphic beliefs, or those of the Eleusinian Mysteries, of which I am an Initiate!"

"Truly, sir, and is it surprising that men seeking to grasp the Infinite will find common aspects of it? You can see how garbled rumors, combined with malice, would lead to...unfortunate misunderstandings."

"Yes, yes, that makes good sense. As you usually do, Tribune... we should speak more of this later!"

Well, Mary, I'm doing my best, Artorius thought, and imagined her smile.

Persecution of Christians was occasionally deadly, but very sporadic up until now. Possibly it could be avoided completely from here on...

An uproar followed, as Sextus Hirrius Trogus and others

headed in their direction, waving wine cups in the air and wreaths askew on their heads.

Though a couple of them are waving pieces of pizza in their other hands, which is probably a first. As I told the Emperor, what's accomplished without change?

Paula and Filipa ducked away—they'd be part of the bride's party in a little while.

Artorius sighed as Mark and Jeremey and Josephus stepped forward and helped the others grab him, strip off the toga, and hoist him overhead like a star surfing the mosh pit.

Marcus Aurelius stepped back with a smile; it wouldn't do for him to participate in this, though his benevolent-spectator role would be noted.

When in Rome, Artorius thought fifteen minutes later, as his friends—still including Mark and Jeremey, this was an all-male part of the ceremony—stripped him naked, heaved him into the bed and retired with detailed good wishes, some of which would have confounded a sixteen-year-old's capacities.

He'd had an American-style king-sized bed made up, albeit with what he considered the rather gaudy standard Roman decorations, gilded bronze heads of cats and satyrs at the corners and wood inlay. But there was a fair facsimile of a box spring under the mattress; brass did well enough for the coil springs, though it was expensive.

The lamps are just *enough. No, don't have another drink, fool,* he told himself, snatching a nervous hand away from the blue-glass decanter. *You're just elevated enough, you don't want to go to sleep, for God's sake!*

Then there was a chorus of women's voices singing outside the door, and laughter, and then it was opened. The female part of the party—including Paula and Filipa—didn't carry Julia in bodily, but they *did* launch her in, so that she staggered laughing as the door thudded shut behind her.

Then she removed the veil and started toward the bed, dropping one item after another behind her until she was close enough for him to untie the ceremonial *nodus* in the band around her waist...

Considerably later, Julia's eyes fluttered closed. He only heard her last sleepy murmur because her lips were near his ear:

"Dear husband, you are the most *considerate* man..."

⇒ CHAPTER TWENTY ⇐

Municipium Aelium Carnuntum,
Capital of Pannonia Superior
November 5th, 166 CE

"Drippy!" Jeremey McCladden said cheerfully, as their horses plodded down the street.

The sound was a wet plock-plock-plock; this stretch wasn't cobbled, except with garbage thoroughly wetted down by the cold drizzle and trodden by feet and various types of hooves and wheels into the nameless mix of smelly mud. The horses' heads were drooping, and occasionally one would let out a blubbering equine sigh with a flutter of lips. It was around thirty miles since they'd set out from Vindobona in a cold predawn, and they'd done it at a quick walking pace most of the way, stopping to rest, feed and water the horses occasionally.

It wasn't far enough to justify a string of remounts. Not quite.

A mangy-looking dog huddled disconsolately against a brick wall with peeling, dirty stucco. It growled at them, head down and eyes sidelong, then cringed and ran as one of their escorts prodded at it with a spear butt.

Roman towns, especially ones founded as adjuncts to military bases or *colonia* built as homes for retired veterans, often had a few broad straight paved streets, and a grid plan. Unfortunately they also had lots of lanes and alleys and narrow side streets, rarely paved in a provincial backwater like this. It didn't have *sēmitae* either, which was Latin for sidewalks; those were a luxury for the stone-paved main drag.

The climate's *totally different, but these Roman towns here sort of look a bit . . . Mexican,* Jeremey thought. *Not all the details, but the overall impression, and from what people say, it's like that over most of the Empire. Like real backwoods old-style parts of Mexico, that is. The Prof thinks so too and he spoke the language and spent time down there, missions against the cartels. I suppose the Mexicans got it from the Spaniards and the Spaniards got it from the Romans when they* were *Romans, and didn't change some of the basics of how they built houses and towns for a long, long time.*

"Bad as New England," Filipa said morosely.

The wide hood of her *birrus Britannicus* cloak was drawn forward, and looked a little strange since she had a hat on underneath it. He had gotten the impression she'd enjoyed studying at Harvard, but not the local weather there.

"Californian! Which is to say, wimp! You should try the Kickapoo Valley this time of year. This would be a drought and a heat wave there," Jeremey said, with continued and deliberately annoying good cheer.

Which is also an exaggeration of my hometown weather for rhetorical effect. Slight *exaggeration.*

"Bah, humbug," Paula said. "People there in Deep Flyover Country have fur . . . had fur . . . whatever . . . anyway, and lived in caves, and wrestled with bears for fun. Wrestled bears in a *sexual* way. They didn't bite them, though, because they usually didn't have any teeth."

"Humbug bah-bah-bah," Mark agreed; he was a New Yorker too. "Good day to stay inside with some hot cocoa, and here we spend it riding all the way from Vindobona."

"All the way . . . all thirty immense, endless miles. I *love* horses but I *miss* cars," Filipa said.

"Maybe hot cocoa with some rum. Maybe a cappuccino—"

"Jesus and Buddha on a tandem bike, Mark!" Filipa said dolorously. "*Don't* bring up hot cocoa! Or coffee. I'd be so, so *sad* when I finished slashing you to death for reminding me!"

"Remember caffeine withdrawal?" Paula said hollowly, and they all winced.

Carnuntum was easily twice as big as Vindobona. Besides being the provincial capital, it was the headquarters of *Legio XIV Gemina*—the *Fourteenth* Legion of the Twins, currently much depleted by detachments, like its namesake neighbor upstream; its *castrum* was east of town.

And it was the headquarters of the *Pannoniorum classis*, the Empire's river fleet on this stretch of the Danube, and had been for a little over a hundred years. The civil settlement was within a substantial wall of its own—this *was* on the frontier—and had better than fifty thousand people. Plus most of what second-century Romans considered the modern conveniences: public fountains fed by an aqueduct, for example, and lots of public baths.

And there was a big arena to the south of town and outside the wall, with seats for fifteen thousand, and an attached *ludus*, a gladiatorial school. The locals constantly boasted it was bigger than many in Italy, and smacked their lips over the shows the gladiators put on.

"Yeah, here we are, back in the big city, civilization with a capital C," Paula said sourly, obviously thinking of those displays of mass sadism, and other things like the slave markets. "Look, I need a drink, maybe a snack. Still a long time to dinner."

It hadn't been the sort of a day where you stopped to do lunch by the side of the road, and it had been a long time since breakfast. Which had been light, because Roman breakfasts usually were. The staff on the Villa Lunae had learned to do bacon and scrambled eggs and hash browns or a passable cheese-and-ham omelet; nobody in Vindobona did yet.

"That's a cantina, isn't it?" she went on.

She'd actually said *taberna*, the local equivalent; even when they spoke English now, they salted it with Latin.

Only five English speakers on the planet, and about ten, maybe fifteen million who speak Latin from the cradle, which is one in every . . . oh, less than one in ten, but not much less, of the human race, Jeremey thought. *So it's inevitable. Natural. And hell, learning Latin* literally *saved my life. So* Latine loquor OK!

The street was more or less straight and typical of a non-fancy, nondestitute lower-middle to working-class neighborhood in a Pannonian town important enough to have a wall. Which put space inside at a premium but not enough of one to breed *insulae*, big apartment blocks like Rome or a few others of the great cities in the southlands.

Single-story artisan shops fronted this street, built of brick or stone and surfaced in rather spotty painted stucco. They rose to two stories a room's width back to provide apartments over their work for the shopkeepers and workmen, and all the roofs were topped by red Roman tile. The one across from the *taberna* was a fulling-and-dyeing establishment, and somewhat aromatic even on a day like this given that the Roman clothworkers used pounding in stale human urine...pounding by human feet... for fulling. That meant degreasing the wool and then working the cloth to make the fibers knit.

"Thank God I *discovered* fuller's earth," Paula said with a snort.

"Amazing how helpful a map with little *x* marks is for prospecting," Filipa said. "Once you learn how to read a map."

Paula nodded. "And all that good Girl Scout shit. Now to spread the know-how around."

Fuller's earth was a special type of clay that did about the same thing as the stale urine and *didn't* stink nearly as much. It had come into use along with mechanical fulling mills in Europe around a thousand years from now. They had a pilot plant on the Villa Lunae now, with the first windmill working wooden hammers to beat the cloth. When it wasn't grinding grain, but number two windmill was under construction and going much faster.

"Spread it *soon*," she qualified. "Sometime before next summer, preferably. Can you imagine what this would be like in hot weather? Talk about pissed off!"

But they'd all become case hardened to stinks. It was dark enough on an overcast November day that many of the buildings had oil lamps lit inside, light leaking out through shutters. There were few glass windows in *this* part of town, of course. Hypocausts didn't go this far down the scale either, though some prosperous upper-middle-class types had a room or so equipped with them for special occasions.

"Yeah, a drink and snack sounds good, and it's a couple-three miles more to the *castra navalis*," Jeremey agreed. "It's going to be slow work through town, too. Fil, Mark?"

"Yup," Mark said, looking a little less semiconscious.

"Twist my pinkie," Filipa said, and extended the digit, adding to Jeremey:

"Ooooogh, brutal torture, you win!" when he pretended to grab it.

They all swung down and hitched their horses; the guards took nose bags off a packhorse one of them had on a leading rein and slipped them over the animals' heads. The horses munched doggedly, glad to stop even in the wet and even gladder of the chopped green oat fodder that was like chocolate truffles to them.

Sarukê jerked a thumb at one of the bodyguards. Bossing them was her job by general consent, since she'd recruited them in the first place; none of them argued with her.

Not twice, at least, he thought.

Jeremey had done martial arts himself for quite a while, but...

But Christ, she's fast! Of course, she was in the arena for years and came out alive and compos *mentis... sorta. Those places are like asylums for the criminally insane, only run by trusties recruited from the inmates. If there's a better school for all-in dirty fighting, I haven't heard of it. And flunking out there means death.*

The guards were ex-arena types like her, hard and tough and scarred, cold eyed and quick as cats. They all had mail shirts of the type a lot of the auxiliaries wore, thigh length with doubling straps over the shoulders, and wore swords and daggers at their belts. They had shields and helmets as well, three carried spears, and the other pair had bows like Sarukê's, cased now against the damp.

A real armored brute squad, but they like *working for us. Good pay, nice perks, and we* don't *treat them like something you scrape off your shoe, unlike a lot of elevated types here. If there's anybody it's dumb to treat like that, it's a bodyguard!*

The unlucky guard on first watch hitched his cloak tighter around his shoulders, drew the hood further over his helmet, and prepared to keep an eye on the horses without more than a token grumble. He crowded up against the wall to get a little shelter from rain and wind under the porch-like overhang of the roof, too; all the houses had that.

Anyone unwisely trying to steal a horse or put sticky fingers into the saddlebags would get the full brunt of his discomfort. Given Artorius' status, the part-time amateur town watch, the *vigiles*, would only object if he left a body for them to dispose of, and a couple of sestertii for *buy yourself a drink on us, good folk* would take care of that.

That and the capacious, all-forgiving Danube.

Woodsmoke trickled out of covered holes above him, adding something more agreeable to the general urban pong.

Sarukê looked unfazed and even fresh, but then she'd spent the first twenty years of her life on the Pontic steppe well northeast of here, riding constantly in weather that made *this* look like a promenade by the beach in San Diego. While living in tents and felt-lined wicker huts on wheels through Russian . . . or Ukrainian . . . winters to boot.

They all had cloaks tightly woven from *un*-fulled wool, with the natural lanolin grease still in it. The best were a British export . . . from the province of Britannia, at least . . . and shed water very well, though they smelled like wet sheep while they did. The guards had been delighted to get a new one each as a free perk; anyone who traveled any distance or did outdoor work and could afford it bought them.

Shed water very well . . . for a while, he added to himself.

Jeremey was acutely conscious that *a while* had passed them by on the road some time ago, and both the tunics he had on underneath were damp and cold if not sopping and chilly, along with the tight leather riding breeks and the knee socks under his boots—the latter newfangled knitted types, another thing Romans hadn't heard of. They'd all toughened up and he flattered himself he'd started out tougher than any but the Prof.

But this is ridiculous.

The Sarmatian opened the door and stuck her head into the *taberna,* looking around conscientiously, then said:

"*Caupona*"—which translated as *hostess,* or tavernkeeper-with-a-feminine-ending—"we take two tables. One back there, one out by door."

They all crowded in, shaking out their cloaks and hanging them and their wide, round Zorro hats of waxed leather up on pegs, in the dim flickering light of a couple of oil lamps. It was warmer inside, especially farther away from the door and the shuttered window. Mostly because the long L-shaped slate-topped bar at the back had several pots sunk into its surface, and a fire underneath one of them, leaking smoke and much more welcome heat and an appetizing tang of fresh bread just out of the oven and ham-and-bean soup.

The bread oven's bricks still radiated heat, and a grill over a bed of glowing charcoal did more. For something *done* on the grill, customers usually brought the raw materials themselves and paid to have it cooked. There were baskets and bowls of raisins, walnuts, prunes and green onions set out on the counter for snacking; the ceiling was blackish with long-accumulated soot.

In the standard fashion a steep stairway led from behind

the bar up to the apartment above, blocked only by a curtain of coarse cloth. The wall there was shelves with various food items in rodent-repellent containers; the floor below the lowest shelf had amphorae—basically big elongated pots—leaning against the wall.

A small barrel of what the locals amusingly deluded themselves into thinking was beer rested on an X of poles, and there was a stack of firewood beside it.

Smoke hung under the blackened beams above their heads, slowly trickling out through a couple of holes whose exterior covers kept leaks to a slow drip. Nobody had the novelty of fireplaces and chimneys here yet, obviously. It would probably take at least a generation for them to filter this far down the social scale. No matter how enthusiastically the upper classes of Pannonia and the local military officers were taking to them.

Especially now that word had spread about how Marcus Aurelius had ordered their installation wholesale in the Palatine palaces back in Rome. Mark had done up a set of instructions with woodblock illustrations, too, and a cadre of experienced Pannonian bricklayers would make a very well-paid trip. Many of them would probably *stay* in Rome too, and make a good thing of it career-wise if they survived the giant city's mephitic breath.

If the Emperor wears a beard, everyone wears a beard, he thought, stroking his own close-cropped light-brownish-yellow one.

The last four *had* worn beards, and it had become a fixed habit Empire-wide.

Mind you, shaving here is a pain the ass and dangerous, so three cheers and one cheer more for Da Boss Beard.

There were only three other customers, all at one table. All were ordinary-looking townsmen in multiple layers of tunics and scarves, cloaks and legging-like knee socks of woven, sewn wool under the straps of their thick-soled sandals or in one case closed shoes. That was the garb that greeted the onset of cold weather, for people who were traditionalists about not submitting to the barbarian degradation of trousers. A lot *did* wear pants through the winter.

All of it looked moderately clean apart from the odorous mud on the socks, because it would be washed and put away in spring and kept in the drawer until needed in late fall, around now. By next spring, they'd *really* need washing. People didn't stop going to the baths, though; but two of them smelled in spite of it, evidently from the fuller's shop across the way, and the elder of those was giving the bodyguards appraising looks in a way that marked him as a veteran. Roman garrison towns were lousy with those.

People kept bathing, if only because those were the only really warmly heated buildings in town, at least ones that people at this social level could get into.

The tavernkeeper behind the bar was in her thirties and a bit worn looking with a chipped front tooth, though rather attractive in a slim, high-cheeked dark Mediterranean way. The other woman there was probably her slave; one of the things that had surprised them was how far down the social scale slave ownership went. About like owning a car in Henry Ford's early Model T days, not universal but fairly widespread above the level where people were focused completely on the struggle to buy that day's loaf.

She was younger than the *caupona*, looking about their own age to the ex-graduate students' American eyes and therefore probably at least two or three years younger than that. She was buxom and had a vaguely Germanic appearance, pale skin and blue eyes and dark-blond hair. And she was dressed in a much more stained and threadbare tunic that looked like a hand-me-down from her mistress, not least because it was rather tight. She was also obviously not wearing a *strophium*, the long cloth breast band that was the Roman answer to the bra.

Wowza! Jeremey thought, giving breast and hip and backside a look.

Roman high fashion thought the ideal woman's figure was small busted and wide hipped. One thing you could rely on, apparently, was that whatever the local ideal of beauty was, most people wouldn't have it.

But I have more rational tastes. And she looks tasty!

One thing he *did* like about the second century was that you were *expected* to ogle. She preened a bit when she caught him at it.

And he noted the full lower lip and blue eyes wandering lazily over the new-come...and visibly affluent...men. Even the bodyguards were modestly affluent by this neighborhood's standards, since they got a denarius and a half a day *and* their keep too.

Scrub her down, and that's quite a fox! Better than a hot-water bottle on a cold night...or any other day of the week!

There were two children as well who were obviously the

caupona's, looking bored on a day when they couldn't go out to play. One was a boy about eight or nine, with a wooden toy legionary's short sword in the belt that confined his grubby undyed brown-gray tunic. He was tossing dice idly on the brick floor, while his five-year-old sister played with a wooden doll, though they both stopped to gape at the newcomers.

Sarukê put the four guards on the table nearest the door, and told off one to spell the man with the horses in a quarter hour, then settled down herself with a rustle and chink, undoing the under-the-chin thong that held the cheek guards of her helm closed and setting it on the table before her with them folded in.

She automatically nudged her sword scabbard out of the way with her left foot as she did, in a manner that left the bone-and-rawhide-covered hilt accessible. Two of the other guards produced dice of their own and started tossing them, betting lightly. That was the local equivalent of playing music or a game on your phone to while away the time.

The *caupona* was gaping at *her,* too. Blonde hawk-faced Sarmatian women five foot nine tall, in mail hauberk and helm and with a long ring-hilted straight sword and dagger and a covered bowcase-quiver on their belts, weren't a common sight here. To put it mildly.

Though they've heard *of Sarmatians, and probably seen them now and then, here selling horses. And heard* stories *about Sarmatian amazons, though they're not all that common even back home north of the Black Sea and I doubt many of* them *were ever here.*

She gaped even more at Paula; voluptuous *black* women with skin like polished ebony and West African features weren't everyday here either, even in the provincial capital. And most of all at Filipa—Korean features were much *less* common, vanishingly so, and she was in male clothing. Which was extremely unusual and severely frowned on. Though not technically illegal the way it would have been in, say, Victorian-era Europe or America.

Though by my *standards, everyone here including* moi *wears a baggy Mother Hubbard sack dress—the women just have longer skirts on theirs. Mine would come to my calves if it wasn't pulled up through the belt.*

You could see her blinking too at the fact that all four of the civilians were noticeably taller than average; the women five-four and five-five, Jeremey at five-ten. And Mark Findlemann was a hair over six feet. Which made him basketball-player towering in the Roman Empire of 166 CE, though when you saw him move his gawky frame you wouldn't mistake him for an athlete. Jeremey and Filipa wore spatha swords at their belts, too, as was common for well-to-do travelers in the frontier provinces but *not* for female ones. They all had belt knives at their hips, but those were standard.

Jeremey stepped up to the bar. "What's your best wine?" he said. "How much?"

"Wu-wu—" the *caupona* stuttered.

Then she mastered herself: "Ah has Falernian, sir," she said, and listed the price—which was steep, in local terms. "Th' gennuwine art'cle."

Her Pannonian accent was fairly thick, the local equivalent of a mountain-an'-holler hillbilly twang. And her eyes widened again when he tossed three denarii down on the counter, the silver ringing sweetly on the slate. A place like this wouldn't see anything but copper and brass most days. Money and formal, bookish diction both marked *him* as upper class, as surely as the bodyguards and his clothes.

The pocket sewn into his tunic where he kept his change was an innovation too.

"Falernian for us and our guards, then, good *caupona*—watered half and half, and a second when we're finished."

The locals only drank unwatered wine when they were drinking strictly to get drunk. He went on:

"Bread, oil, cheese, and bowls of that—"

He indicated the thick bean soup simmering with a slow *pop* of bubbles in one of the big pots set into the stone counter. The others contained varieties of the local wines.

"—for our whole party. Just the thing on a cold day and it smells good! Make change when we leave, if there's any left."

"Yessir. Julia, stop gawking an' move!"

Julia the probable slave girl had been staring at the silver with a delighted smile. She turned it on him and upped the wattage; he gave her a smile back, but shook his head.

Jeremey snagged a handful of raisins and went back to the table. Mark was nearly asleep now that he was motionless and warm, or at least less cold; he could ride by now, but only after a fashion and he still detested it even with more than a year of

Prof-enforced practice. Paula was shifting uneasily on her stool, and probably longing for the hot room at the baths and a long soak. She was better on horseback now than her fellow New Yorker, but despite the way she'd trimmed down and toned up, it was still an aching strain for her to put in hours in the saddle. Especially in this miserable weather.

Even he and Filipa, who'd ridden a fair bit as teenagers and much, much more since they got here, were tired. It was different when you had to ride to *get* somewhere, instead of doing it for fun.

They all paused for a moment to warm their hands on the pottery bowls of hot bean soup an eager Julia brought out, returning with a tray of fresh bread, cheese, bowls of oil, onions and a little loose salt in a clay cup to be administered with fingers and thumb. Nobody had heard of saltshakers here either, though the upper classes used elaborately *chased* and *decorated* little bowls made of silver or gold. The *caupona* herself poured out the strong white—actually sort of amber—Falernian, mixed it and brought the big cups out.

"What do you think the Prof wants us all for?" Paula asked, sipping and giving a sigh. "Eat your soup before it goes cold," Paula added to Mark gently, with a firm pat on the shoulder that was half wake-up shake. "It'll warm the rest of you right up."

He blinked himself back to consciousness and plied his spoon.

The *caupona* returned to the bar, where she kept looking at them out of the corner of her eye. Julia served the table with the bodyguards, laughing and joking as she set out their food and drink and casually slapping off wandering hands, though she seemed a little wary of Sarukê.

Don't worry, blondie, she's utterly monogamous, Jeremey thought.

Paula had spoken in Latin, because they made that a habit most of the time, unless secrecy was necessary. English attracted attention by its sheer foreignness even if nobody could understand it. There wasn't anything much like the sound of English on the entire planet; there just *weren't* any Indo-European languages with its stripped-down analytic form yet, and that strongly affected the way it hit the ear. Latin and Greek and Celtic and Proto-Germanic...and Sarmatian and Middle Persian and the Prakrits they were talking in India now...were still all first or second cousins by contrast, as close as French and Spanish or English and Swedish had been up in their native time.

They'd been arguing about the summons from the Prof since it arrived, of course.

"Probably *another* emergency on the 75-15-10 side of things," Mark said, as his eyes came open under the stimulus of the soup. "An interruption for our work, in other words."

Jeremey snorted with a sound that was half a chuckle; he thought it was funny to use the formula for gunpowder as a code for the military part of their project. The Prof probably intended irony. Paula rolled her eyes. She didn't find it either amusing or ironic, though she reluctantly admitted the necessity. A little experience with the Marcomanni from across the river went a long way. Seeing a farmstead after their raiders had passed through . . .

From Grandma to the toddlers, according to the descriptions from the guards, and I believe them—more so as Fil and the others wouldn't talk about it at all and started gulping their wine if I asked, so I stopped asking them *about it,* he thought. *With the guts hanging out too. Got to admit, that gave* me *the incipient heaves even at secondhand and I'm not squeamish like these big-city types. Before we got here they* thought *chickens hatched headless, bloodless, gutted and in sealed plastic bags. And pigs turned into pork chops by magic. Not the Prof, of course; he's even more of an old-style country boy than I am.*

"I don't really mind," Mark said, then qualified it: "Except the riding in the rain part. But the paper thing's out of my hands now until the *next* round of innovations—the guys we've had on it from the beginning know it better than I do now, we did a lot of trial and error, and Josephus' little factory in Sirmium is going great guns and he's expanding it fast and talking about a branch office in Rome run by one of his younger relatives. That Simonides kid going partners with Josephus and his own dad now that he really knows the moves. Big market there, what with all the upper-crust types and government offices. A couple of years from now in Egypt they'll start wondering why orders for papyrus are falling off a cliff. And the printing's really coming along."

"Finally," Filipa said dryly.

"Finally," Mark agreed, unbothered and yawning hugely. "One man trains two, two train eight, so it goes. There's a big market here for less expensive books, too. And frankly I'm glad for a break from trying to *translate* books into a language that just doesn't have the vocabulary to express a lot of the *concepts.* Though I think Galen will be a big help, especially with the medical stuff. Zeal of a convert and he's smart as a whip. I think newsletters in the bigger cities would pay, too..."

"Yeah, well, Sarukê and I—"

Filipa gave a glance and smile at the Sarmatian; the tables weren't that far apart. She got one back, too, as the *wirapta* lounged at her ease, alert and relaxed as a cat with her wine cup in her right hand and a hunk of bread she'd just dunked into the soup in the other.

"—aren't really needed with the horse stuff, not any more. The new gear is spreading fast now. The Emperor just ordered horseshoes and saddle samples and instructors from the units here sent to every single cavalry *ala* between Eboracum and Nisibis."

Eboracum to Nisibis meant from northern England to southeastern Turkey, in twenty-first-century terms. Marcus Aurelius had been *impressed*. And what the cavalry had by this time next year, everyone except the absolute backwoodsmen would copy in the next decade or less along with the horse-collar harness and newstyle wagons the military logistics train was adopting wholesale.

The Romans were calling it all *the Pannonian gear*. Jeremey sniggered every time he thought of the elaborate theories historians a few centuries from now would probably spin out of that. All of them more believable than time travel...

"The gospel of positional arithmetic's coming along too," she added. "Besides being useful, some of the philosophical types find it fascinating. The Emperor and his court doc, Galenos, had me drilling them on the times table for a while. They spent twenty minutes...while I was there...talking about the deep underlying philosophical meaningfulness of having a symbol for *nothing* and one for *infinity* and how something could be bounded *and* infinite at the same time. Hallelujah! Next, algebra, which I'm doing a refresher course on because it's been a long time since undergrad. Their geometry is already pretty good, though."

Her specialty had been Classical technology, including the intellectual side like math, which meant keeping up her modern math too so that she could make comparisons.

"Well, *I* could have used the winter to keep fiddling with the McCormick reaper back at the villa," Jeremey said judiciously. "I know I can get the goddamned thing working for more than twelve feet at a time *eventually*."

And I'm not eager to meet the Marcomanni up close, nosiree Bob, as granddad's granddad would say. Or the Vandals or the Quadi. Nor the Langobards neither.

"But everyone on the villa was wowed with the cradle scythes this harvest, which beat sickles all to hell. Cut more than half off the time to get the grain in and that pushed yields up a bit because there's less lodging or shattering when you finish quicker. Saved a mint on harvest workers, too. Five, six thousand denarii easy, and everyone in the district is talking about it."

"Everyone's talking including big landowners who have friends and relatives all over," Paula said thoughtfully. "And write to their friends and relatives, all over. And the friends and relatives do likewise."

Jeremey nodded. That would spread things around faster. Paying harvest gangs was an inescapable heavy cost for big operators that suddenly *wasn't* anymore, or at least only one-tenth as inescapable. Which would have unpredictable follow-on consequences.

Cutting the market price of wheat, just for starters, especially when you add in the riding plows and seed drills and threshing machines. And reducing incomes in the places the harvest gangs come from. But everyone who buys their bread will have more money to spend on other stuff, like meat now and then...

"Threshing got done in jig time too. And the corn and potatoes and sunflowers and soybeans and tomatoes and whatnot did fine, next year there'll be plenty to *use*, not just keep for seed. The hops are doing well too."

He smacked his lips.

Mark muttered. "Real beer! Thank *God*!"

Jeremey went on: "We planted six acres of corn last year, this spring we planted three hundred and sixty. It looks like we'll get four times the yield per acre or more since we got it in timely and the spring rains were good, call it eighteen to twenty-four thousand bushels once it's off the cob, plus we've got people lined up to buy it so *they* can grow it. The locals turn out to actually *like* polenta and cornbread. And it's pretty much the same ratio with the rest too, tons of spuds and stuff. God but I love having French fries and more-or-less Heinz ketchup again whenever I want 'em."

Paula chuckled evilly. "I don't think the locals realize quite what the spinning wheels and treadle looms with flying shuttles *mean*, besides ten times the output for the same work," she said. "I do just purely *love* disrupting things here. Rome may be all the civilization going here and now, but this *civilization* needs a kick in the ass *so* bad. Multiple kicks. Kicked over and over until it squeals and blubbers."

Filipa made an enquiring sound and the black woman went on:

"Before, with hand spinning and all, it took one hundred and fifty labor hours... all by women, of course..."

"...of course," Filipa said.

"Why not?" Jeremey said innocently.

Then he whipped his legs up under the table as they both tried to kick him, grinning.

Paula glared and continued: "—to produce one middling quality plain wool tunic. That's just the spinning and weaving. With the new stuff, it takes *ten* hours, one long day's work instead of more than two weeks. Same-same on the fulling, bleaching and dyeing. Going to be a *lot* of women saying goodbye to perpetual distaff and spindle in every spare moment. Giving them time to *think*, hopefully."

Jeremey laughed. "You know Quintus, that furniture-maker apprentice guy we took along to the villa our first summer, to help out with the woodworking side? I looked in on him in Vindobona to chew the fat... he's not a bad sort. That carpenter's shop he started? He's got eight men and a smith working for him now full-time and he's turning out four or five spinning wheels a *day*, he took my hints about division of labor to heart, real little Fordist assembly line there. And three or four of the new looms every week too. And he's got a team of girls going around demonstrating how to *use* them, in the city and the countryside both, run by his elder sister. They get a commission on sales."

"You suggested that?" Filipa said.

"No, Quintus came up with *that* on his own. Smart cookie! He's making money hand over fist, paid off that loan he got from Josephus early and he's buying a house 'cause he's about to marry upward. But others are starting up, in Sirmium and here in Carnuntum, and probably further away soon. The army buildup helps. They're buying all the cloth they can get and paying top dol... well, top denarius. That keeps the established players from grumbling too loud. And it means they can afford the new stuff."

"Type A invention, like the Prof says," Mark said. "Nothing

the locals can't make with the tools and materials they've got. They just needed a demonstration of the *idea*, and why it's worth the trouble."

Fairly soon everyone was wiping out their bowls with the last heels of the—tasty, if gritty—brown bread and draining the last of the second cup of Falernian, which was quite good if you didn't mind your wine sweetish.

Though today it would be even better warmed and spiced the way Austrians did it for cold days when I visited here back uptime.

One thing riding all day in the chilly wet was guaranteed to do was work up an appetite.

Wine hits you differently too, when you don't spend the day sitting in front of a screen.

Filipa gave a signal to Sarukê, who got the guards moving. With a word, and also by grabbing the one who was chatting with the big-busted barmaid by the collar of his mail shirt and hauling him off with an admonition that the five-finger discount was cheaper.

Jeremey saw the *caupona*, who he'd picked up was called *Mistress Umma*, had the change ready on the bar: two sestertii, one dupondius and three copper as. More than half the cost had been ordering the Falernian, which came all the way from south-central Italy, rather than the local stuff.

"Oh, keep it," he said, with a waving gesture. "Excellent bean soup, mistress Umma. I liked the bits of ham."

Ham here in Pannonia was more like the Spanish *jamón serrano* he'd tasted a few times in Europe than the blander American product, or something halfway between that and the *Wien* style; about like Smithfield from Virginia, but he thought it tasted even better. The Americans and their guards spent a moment getting their now merely damp hooded poncho cloaks back on, and adjusting their hats—it was still raining out there, and had gotten darker and colder.

"You know," Paula said as they left, "that Falernian isn't bad at all."

Then shifting to English for a moment: "But God, what I'd give for a diet Dr. Pepper or a Coke Zero!"

Mark looked around at the gray, wet late afternoon with a shudder. "On a day like this, cocoa with rum, or a cappuccino, definitely," he replied in the same language.

"Oh, we'll all have hot cider with cinnamon and nutmeg, to go with our cheeseburgers with the Prof," Filipa said. "Or maybe Nene Chicken with *kongnamul bap!*"

"Coconut cream pie for dessert!" Paula said, and they drew up their hoods.

"We'll have sugar next year from the sugar beets and we've got cream—I'm working on a separator and pasteurization. Coconuts...those will take a while!" Jeremey said.

He swung into the saddle, prompting another sigh from the horse, and looked back over his shoulder at a choked-off sound. Mistress Umma was standing in the doorway, staring after them with a hand to her heart as if she was having a sudden attack of angina, her mouth open and eyes bulging.

Well, yeah, it was *a really big tip, but* that *reaction's a bit much,* he thought as the plock-plock-plock of hooves in mud sounded again.

Then he put it out of his mind. Pretty soon they'd learn what the Prof had in *his,* for better or worse.

Wonder what he *was doing today?*

❧ CHAPTER TWENTY-ONE ❧

Municipium Aelium Carnuntum,
Capital of Pannonia Superior
November 5th, 166 CE

That morning, Artorius had looked up at the stern of the river
galley with satisfaction.

The little ship was pulled up right now, which was done
when it was under repair or when the Danube froze, which it did
some years in January or February. Or just when the ship wasn't
needed, to keep the hull from getting heavy and waterlogged.

Not much like the reconstructions, he thought. *Well, we were
working from limited evidence. Wood rots, most of the time. The
exceptions we dug up don't have to be* typical *and it turns out
they weren't.*

The Fleet Prefect—a modest equestrian rank, this post just
wasn't considered important enough for someone of senatorial
lineage—in charge of the Pannonian stretch of the Danube flotilla
was near him, with his cloak wrapped around his body. It was
a cool overcast morning, promising drizzling rain later moving
in from the northwest up toward Vindobona, and the man...

Nonus Helvidius Drusus, he reminded himself. *From Apulia,*
originally.

... was nodding slowly. He was about Artorius' age, thin
and dark and missing the little finger and part of the next on
his left hand.

"This turns the ship better than steering oars, esteemed Tribune?" he asked.

"Yes, honored Prefect, it does. Faster, and with less effort. And it's more sheltered from enemy action."

"I see that. Much harder to get at when it's in the water."

The prefect's main subordinates were present too: a pair of *navarchii*, squadron commanders, and each ship had a *triarius* as captain. The terms were Greek originally, because that was where the Roman land animal had first picked up its nautical skills.

Romans are like jackdaws that way, Artorius thought. *The gladius is Spanish, chain mail is Celtic... If they see it works, they'll pick it up and run with it. For which, thank all the deities operational in this era. The Romans borrow, steal and appropriate Gods wholesale, too.*

A legionary centurion was there too, a lateral transfer who commanded the marines, who were technically auxiliaries. Everyone on a Roman naval ship was a free man and part of the military and would fight at need—Ben-Hur had gotten that drastically wrong.

Pity. Both movies were great otherwise, though the 2016 one was better... Row well and live! Mind, we historians are biased about historical flicks.

But the marines were specialists in boarding and landing actions. One thing that caught his eye was that the sea soldiers all had their tunics dyed a dull blue-green that wouldn't show much against the water, and the ship and its sail were the same color.

The legions didn't have a standard color for their clothing, unless it was the drab gray-brown of undyed wool, or bleach-white for special occasions like getting a decoration. Scarlet was for officers. The belt and sword and hobnailed boots were what marked you as a soldier.

The slipway the ship rested in was one of twenty along a stretch of the south bank of the Danube; the river ran nearly west to east here, after a northwest-southeast stretch a bit upstream, where Vindobona lay. Each was a shallow U-shape of stone, with wooden rollers set into it and flanked on both sides by chest-high masonry walls, which in turn supported heavy timbers that upheld the tile-clad roof above. One thing this part of the world was *not* short of was really, really big trees. A windlass stood at the inland end, ready to haul the ship up; gravity, poles and pig grease took care of getting it back in the water.

That made it convenient as a place for major repairs and reconstructions too. He'd kept those to a minimum, because he had a nasty feeling that time was a factor. The stern of the vessel curled up in an extension of the keel, which made a convenient place to put the rudder, needing only reinforcement and bracing inside.

"This round pole has inset iron rods, and it's bound by iron hoops shrunk on. It runs up through the keel timber to the deck, where a staff through it is used to turn the *rudder*. Three and a half parts in ten of the rudder are forward of the turning post."

That made it a *balanced* rudder, a Victorian innovation; the force of the water moving past it aided in swinging it.

"It's thickest on the forward edge, with a curved surface at the front tapering to the rear."

The rudder itself was made of adzed oak planks pegged together. Somewhat to his surprise, the river galleys themselves turned out to be built with oak framing and edge-to-edge softwood planks nailed on; caravel construction, technically speaking. There was an outrigger for the rowers, fifteen to a side, and the deck was fully planked under their backsides.

A scaled-down Liburnian, basically, he thought.

"It's as deep as the keel, but no more so," he added. "And if you release this pin, you can pull the whole thing up."

That was important because these were shallow-water craft, and needed to be able to beach themselves; they didn't draw over three feet even fully laden, so the marines could jump overboard into water no more than thigh deep.

"Now, let's go to the deck."

They climbed up what was essentially a big stepladder; the little ship...or large boat...didn't have a high freeboard either. The officers gathered around as he demonstrated how the tiller turned the rudder, with a T-handle at the front for two men. They all took turns pushing it themselves and looking over the side at the stern to watch it pivoting below.

"Ah, it can take a *steeper angle* to the water than a steering oar," one of them said. "Clever!"

"And it's bigger," another said. "So it *displaces* more water too, and all from exactly at the rear. More than two steering oars, if you have them. More...more *push*."

Bless you, my children, Artorius thought to himself, and went on aloud:

"The next change is to the sail."

That was a secondary device for these oar-powered craft, but they did use it when they could to keep the rowers fresh. Sail and mast could be taken down and lashed at head height to a fore-and-aft rack. This one was up, and he'd substituted a simple gaff sail for the square one... though a gaff sail actually was four cornered. At his nod the crew hoisted the spar up, and then demonstrated lowering it and reefing the sail to the *lower* spar.

"Why is this better?" one of the captains said. "Though I can see it does make it easier to reef," he added. "Faster to take the whole thing down when you need to, too, with that hinge-and-collar setup."

"You can point much higher into the wind with this rig," Artorius said. "You can do that a little now, by warping the spar of the square sail around. This does that much better and more easily."

He pointed out the pulley arrangements.

"All you have to do is put the helm over and the sail will swing of itself until the rope on the end of the lower spar stops it; you set the angle with the rope. That way you can't be caught with the wind plastering the sail against the mast when you try to tack."

The technical sailing term was *taken aback*, which didn't quite have a Latin equivalent.

As far as I know, that is.

"And it's easier to raise and reef the sail. A square sail is better if the wind is from there"—he pointed back, pivoting from left to right in a cone sternward, showing the wind coming from abaft either beam or right behind them—"to there. This fore-and-aft rig is better at all other times, and it always takes fewer hands to work. In a tight spot, the wind's *never* where you want it."

That had *all* the sailors nodding.

He'd enjoyed handling a little sailboat himself while living on the East Coast, taking the family out for a day on the water now and then. Despite he and Mary both having been born *high and dry*, as they put it in the Panhandle. That had been one of the few compensations—besides the libraries, bookstores, concerts, and restaurants—for living in Boston. Put all of it together and it *almost* made up for the sense of being insanely overcrowded twenty-four seven.

Most of what he was saying now was simplified versions of things he'd gotten in history courses at West Point, though.

"Now I've shown you how this ship can maneuver better, let's see how she *fights*."

He signaled to the capstan at the head of the slipway, and the crew hit the chocks and took up the slack on the cable at the rear. The ship slid down with a rumble and squeal, and bobbed into the water after throwing up a moderate wave to either side of the prow. The spectators all put an experienced hand to something secure while they were in motion, then walked further forward as the ship settled and the thirty rowers sitting on their benches ran out the oars.

In the bows, above and a bit back from the mostly symbolic ram and unhindered by the now cut-down bow, crouched a ballista. These river patrol boats all carried one, but they were a light type of bolt caster. This was based on his *carroballistae* for the land forces.

"Now, you've all seen the new field ballistae for the Legions, that are cocked by the same teams that draw them into the field. I'm afraid we can't do that here—six horses would crowd the deck, though you might not get some people to realize it."

That got a few chuckles; it helped that he wasn't an obvious landlubber. The Roman navy was very much an afterthought to the army and they resented it, in a muted nothing-to-be-done way.

"Instead what we've got here is a toothed-bar lever system."

That was as close as he could get to saying *rack-and-pinion jack* in Latin.

The catapult was mounted on a turntable. Two slanting bronze shields flanked the throwing trough, with the upright bronze tubes that held the ox sinews that worked the throwing arms piercing them. At the rear of the turntable, and linked to the catapult with a cable nearly as thick as a man's wrist, was what looked to him like an old-style lever-operated car jack.

But set on its side and doubled so that it worked from *both* sides. There were two six-foot poles working on pivots at their inner ends, and rower's benches with foot braces.

Artorius nodded, and two crewmen stepped up, sat and grasped the handles.

"Each time the men on the levers pull like the oar stroke, the swinging iron tooth on the end of the shaft engages one of these slanted notches. When they pull the oar, they pull the bar back a set distance every time. Then this spring-loaded pin here engages to hold the bar against the pull of the cable, which attaches to this hard wooden block, which has the cords on the side to the throwing arms. Then they stroke again, the pin slides out because that side is sloping, they bring the bar back another notch, the pin pushes up because of this spring, and engages to hold it, and so on until the weapon is cocked. Then the cable is disconnected from the block and the catapult is ready to fire."

"Ah, just levers!" one of the nautarchs said, a man with a reddish beard and a Greek accent in his Latin. "Like oars, but pushing against the tension in the ox sinews, rather than against the water."

It was as simple a machine as you could imagine; a lever on a pivot with another on the business end, a catch mechanism, and sloping notches. All the parts were big, too, no little gears that had to mesh perfectly.

Getting it so something wouldn't snap under the strain, and everything engaged smoothly...Dr. Fuchs's measuring gauges in combination with hand files had worked, more or less, with lots of time and a couple of nasty accidents that had left one man dead and several crippled. He'd assuaged his conscience by getting pensions for them, and the widow and orphans. Going to the funeral and visiting the wounded had been a bit lacerating, but everyone involved seemed to appreciate it.

And each set they produced was unique, only roughly similar, which put someone raised with interchangeable parts on edge.

No snapping a spare in if something breaks, the whole thing *has to go back to the shops. And it took us weeks to figure out how to make the parts* not *break all the time. Improvements needed! For the* next *iteration...*

"The mechanism multiplies the force, at the expense of speed. Go," he added to the crewmen.

Heave-grunt-*clack*, as the rowers—they had been rowers, until recently—threw themselves backward, feet braced against the timber, thick muscles rippling in their arms and shoulders. It was about the same effort as their usual jobs at full stroke, and they worked with the smooth united ease of long practice.

Heave-grunt-*clack*.
Heave-grunt-*clack*.
Heave-grunt-*clack*.
Heave-grunt-*clack*.

Heave-grunt-*clack*.
Heave-grunt-*clack*.
Heave-grunt-*clack*.
Heave-grunt-*clack*.

God, I wish I could just make cannon, he thought. *Working on that but it's damned hard. We needed something right* now.

The cable from the jack had a hook on its end, and that ran through an eyelet sunk into the back of a hardwood block at the rear of the throwing trough, which also had the cords from the throwing arms attached. There was a squeal from the twisted ox sinews in their bronze tubes, and the arms moved backward. It went on until they were very nearly parallel to the throwing trough, and there was a solid *click* as the trigger mechanism engaged.

"Load solid shot," Artorius said; that was granite chipped into a fairly smooth ball.

The crew chief spun the—also laboriously hand-cut—elevating screw, peered through the simple ring-and-post sights...

"Stand back," Artorius said, as the crew flipped the hook from the big jack out of the block's eye, someone pressed on the retaining pin and another shoved the grooved iron rattling forward again to be ready for cocking the catapult for the next shot.

He was gratified when everyone *did* stand back—respect for his *devices* was now universal. You could lift a car weighing several tons with a simple one-handed jack, and this was the same thing but considerably more powerful. It wasn't as fast as six horses and pulleys and a long rope, but it *worked* and it was a lot more compact.

"Shoot," he added, and the crew chief pulled a lanyard.

Tunnggg-WHACK.

And less than two seconds later, a sharp multiple crackling.

"Di Immortales!"

The *Praefectus classis Pannonicae* swore softly as the twenty-five-pound stone ball blurred away and struck a substantial rowboat anchored halfway across the Danube, about a hundred and fifty yards to the north and amid a collection of derelict barges and boats bought cheap and placed there for this demonstration. Broken planks leapt skyward along with a gout of water, and wreckage drifted away.

"Of course, this engine can also throw the thunderballs, which you have seen."

They had, and the news that they too could wield the thunder perked them all up. He judged they'd been glumly resigned to the Army getting a monopoly on that.

"Either the type stuffed with lead bullets set around the thunderpowder"—the phrase he used, *plumbum offa*, literally meant *chunks* of lead, but it was also the one generally used for shaped lead shot from slings—"or one with only the thunderpowder. That one is more deadly close-to, and better at shattering structures such as a ship, but less so at a distance from the *crepitus*."

Which meant roughly *crash, rattle, clack*, and had been taken up to mean *explosion*.

"Or it can shoot this."

While he spoke the big jack had done its work again; Artorius checked covertly that none of the teeth on either side showed any signs of strain or yielding, and that the retaining pin on its brass lever spring was still moving correctly. Anything this large made of iron had to be hammer-welded from smaller pieces and it was hard to tell when the heavy stress was suddenly going to find a weak spot in the join.

He nodded to the crew, who lifted a round ball of rough-fired pottery into the trough, then lit its fuse with one of the new flint-and-steel lighters with reservoir and wick. Which items were wildly popular because they were so much easier to use than an ordinary flint-and-steel, and were fetching so much on the black market that heavy punishments had been necessary to check them "vanishing."

Which lighter I have succeeded in christening the Ronson. Or at least the Ronsonius, *pronounced* Ronsonio'. *Hello, granddad!*

Josephus was financing an expansion of the workshop in Vindobona that made them, and sending samples to other members of his family, who'd pay him a royalty for those they sold over half the Empire, all in partnership with the Americans. The Romans didn't have a patent system...

Not yet.

...but that would place his relatives in a position to make major moolah for a while.

Romans understood the concept of mass production and division of labor, along the lines of Adam Smith's famous description of a pin works, more or less—they did it for some things like *terra sigillata* pottery. Which were made in standard forms, fired in giant kilns thirty or forty thousand at a time and shipped out to mass markets often hundreds of miles away. Impoverished huts in the wilds of northern Britannia had held fragments of them for archaeologists to discover in the twentieth century.

That just wasn't practical for most trades, where things were done by individual bespoke orders.

It would be practical for the *Ronsonius*...and eventually, for a lot of other things.

Two more men pushed at poles set in the turntable at the crew chief's hand signals for the traverse. The fuse was made up of soaked cloth wrapped around the pottery shape. It flared up with a chemical stink, and:

"Shoot!"

This time the projectile struck a much-repaired old barge that had spent its working life carrying things like bricks, logs, building stones, cattle, grain and pigs or their carcasses up and down or across the Danube.

The Romans had all seen incendiaries used...but not, he thought, like this one.

WHOOOF!

There had been endless disputes among historians and archaeologists about the secrets of Greek fire, the weapon the Byzantines had used to incinerate a number of Arab fleets heading for Constantinople...which was still simply the medium-sized Greek city of Byzantium here, and hopefully always would be. He'd had Mark Findlemann and Paula comb through the references Fuchs had on the external drives, and combined it with some hints he remembered from his Academy days—

Naptha and quicklime and pine resins, oh my! And speaking of Paula and Mark, does he realize she's making a play for him? Not yet, I think. There's a reason the others call him Mr. Oblivious. That would be a good match, all things considered. I don't think he'd be happy with a local, and that goes double *for her.*

The ceramic shell hit the edge of the barge, and the liquid within sprayed out in a fan from the point of impact. It caught immediately, and flared up with a savage actinic light. Red answered, as the timbers caught, and smoke billowed upward. Within seconds the whole central section of the wooden barge was in flames as spatters flew about the interior.

"Notice that it burns floating on the water," Artorius pointed out helpfully. "It can't be put out by splashing with water, only by being completely submerged or covered in sand or earth... *much* sand or earth. And it clings like glue. If it strikes a man, it burns inextinguishably down to the bone."

There was a long moment of shocked silence.

"I call it *ignis Romanus*."

Which meant *Roman Fire*.

"*Euge!*" the naval prefect said after a moment, and then they were all cheering and waving their fists in the air.

One of the *nautarchs*, the one with the red beard, asked: "What is the range on this catapult of yours, most excellent Tribune Artorius?"

"Two hundred to two hundred and fifty paces, depending on the wind and what you're shooting," he answered.

As one, every head swiveled north. That was Roman double paces, a yard and three-quarters by American reckoning; it was still considerably more than the width of the Danube here, or nearly everywhere from here east to the gorge of the Iron Gates. Which was about four hundred miles distance as the crow flew, more by water or road.

"*Euge!*" the prefect said again.

"We must reequip all our ships with this!" one of the squadron commanders said.

"Mine first!" the other replied, in tones much like a three-year-old seeing a chance of a sibling getting a candy before he did.

Artorius lifted a hand. "Next, we will demonstrate what this ship can do now sailing *and* fighting."

He reached into a sturdy wickerwork basket lashed to the rail, lifting a waterproof lid of hard waxed leather, and produced two balls. Each just the size to be gripped in an average man's fist, one of bronze and the other of pottery, and each with a crimped fuse dangling from the top.

"Out there, we can also demonstrate what can be done with these *malogranatum*. One with notched iron wire inside, one with only the thunderpowder."

Someone chuckled. "They *do* look a little like pomegranates!" he said.

Artorius nodded; that was the original word from which *grenade* derived.

"And thrown into a ship before you board, or when they lay

alongside and try to board you, they are very *malo* indeed," he said.

That got a general guffaw; *malo* meant bad or evil.

I've gotten to the point where I can make puns in Latin about blowing people up or burning them alive with napalm, he thought wryly. *Hurrah for me, Linguist of Death.*

One of the captains exclaimed: "We've got to send word of all this to Misenium!"

Which was the HQ of the Roman navy as a whole, and of the Mediterranean fleets, located not far from what he thought of as Naples and which was right now still a mostly Greek city called Neapolis.

"Oh, no we don't," another snorted. "Those idle Egyptian *vigiles*—"

He'd called them *police* (or night watchmen, or firemen, which were all the same word) with malice aforethought. In this era the main Roman fleets in the Middle Sea had nothing much to do but antipirate patrols, and piracy was rare...as long as the patrols were vigilant. And a lot of them *were* recruited in Egypt. It was the fleets of the Rhine and Danube and English Channel—aka the *Oceanus Britannicus*—that did most of the actual fighting on the water these days, against barbarian pirates and raiders. Some of *them* came from as far away as Norway and Sweden, though the Romans called them all "Saxons."

By which they meant basically *German bandit in a boat.*

"—wouldn't believe it if we just *wrote* them. *Deodamnatus*, would *you* believe it if someone wrote you a letter? We've got to send for some of them so they can come and see it with their own eyes!"

"We can convert one ship per day, now that the *Dacicus* is done," Artorius began, slapping a hand against the flagship's mast. "We're already working on the *Victoria*, and the *Fides* will be next—"

"You're probably all wondering why I've called you here today," Artorius said, later that evening.

Josephus looked puzzled as the Americans snickered. Sarukê sighed, bent and whispered something in Filipa's ear that made her giggle, and then looked a question at Artorius. He nodded and she sauntered out; probably to do something involving horses or weapons or get in a little hunting, which she adored and to hell with cold and wet.

Or at this time of day, to recite Sarmatian epic poetry to herself, something else she liked. She knew thousands of lines of it and there wasn't anyone else in town who could understand a word. For that matter, not a word of that ancient North Iranian tradition had survived the next few centuries, as far as he knew; not the poetry, not the legends, not the songs or jokes... nothing. Probably there were bits of it that went back to a time before the *Rig Veda*, when Sarukê's ancestors were inventing the war chariot east of the Urals in what a different age would have called Chelyabinsk Oblast.

All that would be lost when the Huns came west, the end of a tradition already more than two thousand years old.

Which is sad, in a way, he thought. *Maybe in the history we're trying to make, someone will write it all down. Maybe Filipa will! And maybe the Huns will stay where they started and if there's an Attila he'll spend his life tending sheep.*

"Sorry, a jest from our land," he said to Josephus. "Seriously, I've got a problem... and I've got no time for it, which is why you four had to ride all day in the rain, and our friend Josephus has kindly agreed to take some time off from his own business."

"That is not a problem, my friend," Josephus said. "Keeping the barbarians out of the Empire... and particularly my home province here... *is* my business too, after all. My wife and children live here, and some of my other kin. And I've got a lot more property to protect than I did last year, thanks to you five!"

Dang, but we were lucky to meet him! Artorius thought, something he did quite often. *None of that* what have you done for me just lately *with Josephus.*

He went on aloud:

"The Emperor is arriving here in three days, to consult with the provincial governor—and me—about the plans for next year; he's staying over the winter here, which is a big deal."

"Plans?" Filipa asked.

"Plans for the campaigning season next spring. I've been getting ready for that, not least by refitting the Danube fleet... that should be well underway by the time he gets here... and this."

He waved a hand around. The room was a fairly big one, in the second story of the praetorium of the fleet, the headquarters building that was about fifty years old. It had a fireplace; every permanent building of its type in Pannonia probably now had at least one, as the military units competed with each other to have the very latest thing.

That was easier for the military; in the Roman Empire, if you had a big building project, you went first to the soldiers. Both for the planning and the execution by skilled workmen, anything from a road or aqueduct to a giant domed temple.

It flickered pleasantly on a dark rainy night, and the scent of burning pine overrode most of the less pleasant odors of a river port and made it comfortable ... at least by second-century standards, which meant you didn't have to blow on your fingers or hold a fire-warmed brick wrapped in cloth. The walls were simply plastered, and he'd had them crisscrossed with soft wooden battens that could support pinned-on maps, carefully done up from the ones in the library Fuchs had sent along. Naptha lamps hanging from the ceiling with tulip-shaped blown-glass chimneys like an old-style kerosene lamp and burnished metal reflectors cast more light than anything the locals had used.

"Good work on the maps, by the way, Mark," he said.

The ex-graduate student grinned sheepishly. "I just sort of found the guys who could do it, mostly they're artists," he said. "And checked that the proportions are right. They weren't the first time, but we kept working on it and I managed to convince them that *accurate* meant more than *pretty*. Eventually. Long live dividers and protractors!"

"It's important," Artorius said. "Very."

It was. Romans had the *concept* of maps, and made some. The great marble-mosaic sixty-by-thirty map of the world in the Portus Vipsania in Rome, the Map of Agrippa, purported to show the whole world. But despite being able, practical land surveyors, whose grid layouts were occasionally still visible on landscapes in the twenty-first century, they had no idea of how to accurately transpose it visually to paper ... or papyrus or parchment, or for that matter marble slabs.

Instead for practical work they used an *itinerarium*, rather like a strip map along the route of a journey, studded with marked distances and descriptions. That worked ... after a fashion ... but not when dealing with moving overland into unfamiliar territory. There they went by trial and error and rumor and verbal descriptions and Eyeball Mark I.

"I was talking to the Emperor last month, and he mentioned the Baltic in a strategic way...and it turned out he thought it was about a hundred and fifty miles north of here. They call it the *Sinus Codanus*, by the way. And they think Sweden is just an island in it."

Josephus nodded. "I *thought* it might be more distant than that," he said. "Just from talking to amber traders. Though none of them go directly all the way to the northern sea, the amber is passed from hand to hand four times or more, which helps to account for the ridiculous price. It just didn't seem very important before this. It will if the Imperial border moves north, though."

In reality, it was about *six* hundred miles as the crow flew from Carnuntum to the Baltic, more if you were traveling by land and river, which was about twice the overland distance from here to the Adriatic. Thirty days' march on a good road, and there wasn't anything better than deer trails up there. Marcus Aurelius had been shocked, but willing to listen, especially after Artorius had called in Josephus and others with local knowledge.

"All right, I have to deal with his visit which will involve a lot of conferences, and what I'm trying to do with the fleet here, and a bunch of other stuff."

"All those bronze founders and ingots?" Paula asked.

"Right, cannon...for next year, if we're really lucky. And not many of them even if we are, so at least ammo per tube won't be a problem. What I want *you* four to do is help Josephus collate all the information we're getting on the Marcomanni and Quadi."

He jerked a thumb toward the river, and the night-dark forests on the other side.

"As I like to tell the Emperor's inner circle...repeatedly... they're barbarians but that doesn't mean they're all *stupid*."

"Even we blondies can have brains. Sometimes," Jeremey said dryly.

Artorius nodded. *Dumb blond* wasn't just a joke here, it was a genuine stereotype and not one only aimed at women, either. Not surprisingly, an empire founded by people from central Italy thought people who looked like Italians were the bee's knees all around—brave as northerners, smart as southerners, not too hot, not too cold. Fortunately *Marcus Aurelius* didn't think that way. *Much*.

"Everything we've done publicly, their chiefs and kings know about by now. They're starting to feel pressure from other tribes further north—the Goths are moving down from what was our Poland, for starters, from the Vistula delta—and they'd very much like to go somewhere else. The Emperor has made clear that he intends to cross the Danube and make sure they don't try to force the borderline again."

"The Marcomanni got beat pretty bad in the spring," Jeremey pointed out. "If they were crowded before, they've got more room now."

Artorius nodded. "Heavy losses. That doesn't mean they're going to sit still and wait for us to wallop them, while we get stronger and they get weaker and the reinforcements pour in like a slow avalanche."

"Will they have heard about the new legions?" Filipa asked.

"You betcha," Artorius said. "The recruits are pounding double-weight wooden practice swords on wooden posts and doing route marches now, but they'll be ready in the spring, another twenty thousand men with the auxiliaries being raised, and we'll be getting *Legio XI Claudia* too. When the Romans wind up to hit someone"—he made a short punching gesture—"they *hit* them, by God. But the new legions and auxiliary cohorts and cavalry *ala* are training and some still have to *walk* here from Italy. Or the newest legion will walk to the lower Danube while the veteran legion from *there* walks *here*. The guys on the north bank are here *now*."

Jeremey frowned. "What do you want us to look for?"

"If I knew specifically, I wouldn't have had to drag you into this! What you need to look for is *patterns*. Josephus has the local contacts; he'll get you the raw data and pursue any line of inquiry you find. You collate and analyze. You're students of history, right? So look at this as a research project... one that needs to be done as fast as possible. I have a bad feeling about this, but I just can't spare the time to look into it. I don't have anybody but you four who have the right... habits of mind."

"Who you gonna call?" Mark said, grinning. "*Us*, that's who!"

"And Mark, you're in charge of the analysis—you divvy up the data, and say who's going to look at what, and collate their findings."

Mark Findlemann scratched his head; the other Americans all checked reflexively to make sure that if it was head lice *they* hadn't gotten any.

"Why me?" he asked bluntly.

"Because of all of us, you're the best at seeing patterns in large heaps of information. I don't know why; maybe it's because you're not neurotypical, but you do. They leap out at you, I've seen it before. And remember, we're pressed for time. Something is coming to bite us on the ass. I can smell it. Work this hard."

Mark sighed, yawned and shook himself. "All right. Let's get to work. Paula—"

Two of the bodyguards Artorius had sent to collect the others fell in with him as he was walking back toward his quarters, their oval shields in their left hands, their right on their belts near their sword hilts.

They'd take turns being outside his door all night. Artorius sighed at the thought, but Sarukê said it was essential that he had an armed guard as close to twenty-four seven as was possible because assassins struck when the target *wasn't* guarded if they could. He had to admit it was logical, and she did have years of experience in the specialist field of bodyguarding.

Her obligation was to guard his life, not cater to his wishes or whims, and she took it seriously.

One of those things that's a pain in the ass until you need it, and then you need it very, very badly. But it's one reason among many I never wanted to be president . . . and you couldn't pay me enough to be emperor here. Presidents *had Secret Service types handing them their toilet paper and it's worse for Marcus Aurelius. The last four Emperors died natural deaths . . . probably . . . but a lot of their predecessors didn't and lot of Marcus' successors wouldn't in the original history either, starting with his son Commodus. No wonder the Roman sense of privacy is distinctly odd!*

He'd mentioned that he *did* have his own ex-gladiator guards to Marcus Aurelius, simply to avoid having half a century of Praetorians assigned and following him around like disconsolate scorpion-blazoned hound pups.

It's a good thing I'm a Roman officer now and expected to lead from the front.

You more or less couldn't be one and prioritize personal safety. Even the legionary tribunate did the *follow me!* thing; and centurions had a higher casualty rate than rankers. A commanding legate rarely survived a real disaster.

And now I'm a military tribune. Otherwise I'd be immured in a tower somewhere with a legion camped around me glaring outward. They'd pat down my own image in a mirror to make sure it wasn't going to knife me.

A Roman *castra* at night was fairly easy to navigate, and not just because there were covered torches burning at most of the intersections. It was because they all had roughly the same layout, anywhere from Scotland to the Euphrates, with only occasional deviations to allow for local terrain. The Pannonian fleet's was a bit smaller than most, which meant he didn't have far to go from the *principium* to the small suite he'd been assigned, probably a senior centurion's originally.

Like most people of this era, Roman soldiers hit their bunks at sundown, unless they were on night watch or out carousing on leave. The base differed from the town in that respect only in that it was much neater, and smelled a bit better; most of the scents were of the trade of war, metal and leather and—here—cut wood in the shipyards, plus tallow and oil, and the woodsmoke that was everywhere. There weren't many lights apart from the torches, nor much sound except sentries pacing on the stone fighting platforms of the wall and the low U-shaped towers that projected out from it.

That probably saved his life; he heard the *rutch* of a shoe on damp pavement just as someone lunged at him.

Reaction was instant. Pivot outside the lunge of a blade—steel blackened with soot so it wouldn't gleam—on the end of an arm, mostly by slacking the knee of his right leg and letting his weight push him. Grab the wrist, twist to lock it, spring off his braced right foot while wrenching the wrist back and smashing with his forearm at the place the also-locked elbow would be.

Thud.

And beneath that a crackle of snapping tendons and joints—elbows had no give in them in that direction. The man gave a breathless squeal that ended as Artorius whipped the bladed palm of his right hand from a position by his left shoulder across and into the man's throat. The edge of his hand brushed something—a beard—and then thumped into the target with a force that he knew of old.

The sensation was like crushing a fibrous cardboard tube wrapped in veal, more or less. It meant the man was dead, even if he wouldn't know it for a few seconds.

"*Sir, watch out!*" Dablosa shouted.

Amid the clash of steel on wood and leather and sometimes on steel; he and the other bodyguard were fighting dark-clad figures too, sword and shield. Artorius had already started to pivot, but the Dacian's cry speeded it up.

He brought the whatever-he-was who'd just tried to kill him with the turn, and threw him at the new attacker. There was a meaty chugging sound in the dimness, and a sword appeared out of the man's side.

That turned a triumphant scream of:

"*Dawi, wikkô!*"

Oh, I am getting so *sick of hearing that Proto-Germanic phrase directed at me!*

—into a strangled wordless scream of *frustration*. Whoever it was wasted a second withdrawing his sword—if you jammed a yard-long piece of iron through a human body, you were quite likely to find it harder to pull out. Artorius used the instant to jump backward while he drew his own sword and poised.

Both the bodyguards had their men down, and even in that moment Artorius made a mental note to thank Sarukê; without the pair, he'd have been as dead as fusion-bombed Vienna was in the time he'd left. The remaining Marcomanni very sensibly spun around and ran.

Dablosa cursed in Dacian. His comrade was originally Germanii himself, of a far northwestern tribe in what Artorius had called the Netherlands. They were known to their Imperial neighbors as the Chamavi; he was a medium-tall man with a collection of facial scars.

Some remote academic part of Artorius remembered that that tribe later on had been one of the confederation known as the Franks, who'd given their name to France. The man had a pointed reddish-brown beard, and would have regardless of fashion because shaving was out of the question for his mutilated face. He also carried a light throwing axe in a loop on his belt at the small of his back. In the original history that tomahawk-like weapon had been known as the *francesca*, and was a national marker for the Franks for centuries.

Right now, Balþawiniz dropped his sword, whipped out the tomahawk and threw in the same motion. The man with the dripping sword was ten feet away and gaining speed, a dimly seen shadow. The axe spun through the air, and then the curved edge struck between his shoulder blades with a hard thump-crack sound.

"Bold friend indeed," Artorius said—that was what the ex-gladiator's name meant.

A quick glance showed he and the Dacian both had rather minor wounds; somehow Artorius had gotten a nicked earlobe, which he hadn't noticed at the time and stung badly now. Balþawiniz and Dablosa both chuckled at the wordplay, and Artorius walked over to the man lying on his face with the short haft of the throwing axe standing up between his shoulder blades. He didn't approach immediately—that would have been reckless. Dablosa trotted off and came back quickly with a lit torch from the bundle kept under the ones at the cross streets.

"He's dead," Artorius said as Dablosa raised it and poised his sword.

Both the ex-gladiators nodded; the body had twitched half a dozen times just now and they could smell the stink of bowels released in death, which happened fairly often though not every time. The Dacian went to one knee and flipped him over, holding the torch high in his left hand.

"Suebi, like the others," Balþawiniz said, picking up his sword and using it to touch the hair knot over the man's right ear before he sheathed it.

That prompted a thought, and Artorius leaned closer, sheathing his own—still-clean—blade.

"I know him," he said.

The family resemblance was striking, especially with the distinctive hairstyle, though this man was in his midtwenties, rather than a teenager like the killer at the Villa Lunae or in his late thirties like his uncle Prince Ballomar.

Firelight helps, Artorius thought; that first one had been at night too.

"He and his brother tried to kill me last year, at the Villa Lunae. His brother died, he ran."

"He ran this time too," Balþawiniz said. A grin, and: "Not fast enough to outrun my axe, though."

Gladiators evidently had an even grimmer sense of humor than combat soldiers. Artorius nodded.

"If anyone asks, this was personal vengeance," he said. "Family feud."

"Well, if you killed his brother, sir, it probably *was*," the proto-Frank said cheerfully.

"Among other things," Artorius said.

The ex-gladiator put a foot under the dead man's shoulder and lifted so he could wrench the tomahawk free; then he wiped it on the corpse's jacket.

Dablosa cleared his throat.

"Yes?" Artorius asked.

"Sir, it's a nice change to bodyguard for someone who knows what they're doing in a fight," he said. "The *wirapta* was right about you."

Which is a compliment, Artorius thought.

"You two also do," he pointed out, nodding toward their fallen opponents.

"Yes, but we're not rich men," Dablosa said.

He and the German expertly frisked the bodies, coming up with pouches and a few personal ornaments as well as bundling the weapons—those would fetch a few score denarii. All of that was part of the perks of their job. Hobnails sounded on pavement, moving quickly—that would be the base night watch heading for the sound of a fight, who wouldn't enjoy having to dispose of the bodies. A tip ought to settle that.

Artorius sighed and put a wadded handkerchief to his ear.

I wonder if any letters from Julia have come, he thought. *It would be nice to have a* good *surprise, for once.*

≽ CHAPTER TWENTY-TWO ≼

Municipium Aelium Karnuntum,
Capital of Pannonia Superior
November 8th, 166 CE

Dearest Husband, he read, three days later.

For a moment he closed his eyes and smiled. If there *was* a somewhere...afterward, outside of time...he thought Mary was smiling too, and from the best neighborhood, she and their children. Mary and Julia would have liked each other and little Claudia would have gotten on with the kids like a house on fire.

I told Mary not to mourn me too long if I died in the field, and she said the same thing back at me—said a car or a stroke could do the same thing as an IED. Fortune loans things to us, it doesn't give them.

Next to having Julia here—and that wasn't going to happen until he was convinced it was safe...

Which recent events have shown this is not, yet, he thought, touching the scab on his ear.

—reading Julia's letter was as close to complete happiness as he was likely to get. Especially since he was sitting next to a fireplace, with a good lamp, a mug of watered wine and a bowl of dried figs. The cut earlobe had been disinfected and now was only an itch. He read on:

The vilicus *is at last convinced that you indeed meant to convey your* auctoritas *here to me and accordingly the timber*

329

for the new construction at the vicus *you wish to establish
on the estate is being cut and stacked to season.*

That meant by this time next year the married couples in
the *familia rustica* would all have their own three-room cottages,
starting with ones a bit bigger for the *pars rustica's* managerial
staff. Each cottage would have a fireplace-cum-brick-stove in the
kitchen and all would stand around a village . . . *vicus*, in local
terminology . . . square. One with a school and a clinic.

That would free up the *pars rustica* for business, not least
enlarged spinning and weaving rooms where the womenfolk could
earn some cash, which was a valuable idea of Paula's.

Not much cash, but any wage was a start.

*Then we'll gradually extend the principle and eventually end
up with a free labor force . . . one quite a bit smaller than it is
now. It's not as if they don't have the* concept *of regular wage
labor here, though it's low status from an aristo's viewpoint.
And I'll see that the ones we won't need on the villa get a
good start, land north of the river or enough to set up in a
trade, they deserve it.*

The school was possible right away because there *wasn't* any
law here against teaching slaves to read, the way there had been
in the South before the Civil War. Quite the contrary, slaves were
often trained in things like accounting, or apprenticed to trades,
or were schoolteachers or doctors or whatnot themselves; their
masters regarded it as a profitable investment and the slaves got
a better chance of eventual manumission.

Rural slaves working in the fields usually didn't get any education except from their elders, learning by doing . . . but then,
neither did free peasants, mostly. The plan for gradual emancipation on the estate would follow.

Even *bankers* here tended to be either slaves or more often
freedmen or their sons; it could be a lucrative occupation, but
was rather low status.

Artorius grinned: he'd started on the free-labor project with
the *vilicus* himself. The man had been planning on self-purchase
from his *peculium* anyway, and had leapt at the chance of a

contract, with him as a cost-free freedman paid a share of the profits...and with double-entry bookkeeping to keep him honest.

The tricks to get around that hadn't been invented yet, though he supposed they would be as soon as the new system spread very far. There was always some wise boy or clever girl who went *aha!* and reached for the shears when an opportunity wandered by bleating and blinking.

He read through the rest of the letter, chuckling occasionally at little Claudia's innocently acute questions, or Julia's observations like:

> ...*it is amazing how many more social calls we receive from the ladies and daughters of the gentry hereabouts, now that I am no longer the scandalous widow of a bankrupt spend-thrift gambler living in semi-exile on her brother's charity, but instead the wife of a wealthy Imperial* comites *who owns this estate...and now that the Emperor himself attended our wedding ceremony. Which I hardly noticed...*

"Dry, that's my Julia," he said to himself. "But she'll be impeccably polite...and even enjoy their company."

> ...*my mother the lady Claudia is reconciled to a journey to Carnuntum when you say danger is past, especially in the new coach with brass springs, which she has enjoyed using on visits in the neighborhood, not least for the envy and emulation it arouses. The prospect of dining often with the Emperor has proven an even* more *amazing tonic to her health. The house you suggest sounds very comfortable; especially the fireplaces. For which I thank you, dearest one who warms my heart... and the rest of me too.*

"You're welcome," he said, grinning again at the triple play of metaphor. "You are one clever lady. Smarter than I am. And it was your idea to buy the house and then make her a present of it instead of renting. Which will make your brother happy too, since it's even further from Sirmium than the villa is."

> *And last but not least, you may expect your child, hopefully a son, soon after the ides of July of next year.*

He read that twice before it sank home. He gathered his breath for a whoop, but a knocking at the door interrupted it.

An armored marine guard opened the portal, and Artorius had made clear that he wasn't to be disturbed except for something important—or for the Emperor, who'd arrived a couple of hours ago and after a brief greeting had retired for a snack and a good night's sleep. One thing you could count on with Marcus Aurelius was that he wasn't going to spend the day on a couch having grapes dropped in his mouth, or all night partying. Or even having a philosophical *symposion*, which was his version of a wild night out.

"Your client Marcus Triarius is here, sir," he said. "Will you—"

Mark burst through, waving a sheet of paper. "Got it! Got it, Prof!" he caroled. "We got it, we got it, *sooooogottit!*"

Gritting his teeth, Artorius made himself set the letter aside. Duty called...

In a shrill, unpleasant voice, as the man said. I'd forgotten the many reasons... besides getting blown up myself after Jake getting blown to bits all over me... I decided to get out of the Army.

"Chisels and saws and axes and adzes... is that a word?... and nails," Mark burbled as he sank into a chair—or onto a stool, more accurately. "Oh, my."

"Who?"

"The Quadi, half a dozen of their chiefs, acting through agents. Multiple purchases of woodworking tools, and starting months ago. It's not as if they can't make this stuff themselves, so you can assume their own smiths are working overtime too. People have been selling all they can make or get. Here, and in Vindobona and some other places too. Prices up too. That was what first put us on to it, before we got to the who. There have been complaints from camp prefects, boatbuilders..."

"Boats," Artorius said. "Someone's building boats over on the Quadi side... up the north-bank tributaries. Moving them at night, hiding them in marshes..."

"*Lots* of boats, evidently," Mark said. "Got the basic data from Josephus—he activated his contacts around here and told them to get him info on any unusual purchasing. He says the... tensions was the word he used... are probably the reason why nobody else noticed this yet."

There hadn't been a formal declaration of war on the Quadi; then again, they weren't really at peace with Rome right now either. They didn't really have governments yet in the sense he—or the Romans—used the word, though they were on that road. There just *weren't* any authorities that could stop raiding by subchiefs or ambitious would-be chiefs on other tribes or the Romans anyway.

Only fear, the dread of retaliation, kept would-be raiders in line.

All that meant trade continued, but with everyone doing it as fast as they could, in out-of-the-way spots, and keeping quiet about it. And nobody venturing far into the other side's territory. Which would reduce the quantity and quality of gossip, for a while.

"What are they building boats *for*?" Artorius asked the air.

"Ah...to cross the river?" Mark said.

"OK, but why?" Artorius said, as much to himself as to the other man. "All right, they know we're going to attack them, so they're planning on doing unto others, meaning us, before we get a chance to do unto them. But where, and why?"

He popped a dried fig into his mouth and offered the bowl to Mark, who took one absently and poured himself a cup of watered wine.

"Well, it would let them cross the river *faster*," the younger man said, in intervals between chewing. "More of them doing it all at once."

"Bingo. But *why*? The *Pannoniorum classis* isn't...couldn't be...big enough to patrol the whole river at once, so they just have to go where the Roman ships *aren't* and cross there. It's only three hundred yards, not the English goddamned Channel!"

"Ummm...another fig? Thanks, I skipped dinner without noticing, doing the final collation and cross-checking. So maybe they want to cross all at once because they're planning on attacking somewhere the Romans...we Romans, I suppose...*are*, instead of somewhere we're *not*? Then they'd need to get their men across all at once, wouldn't they? So the first bunch wouldn't all get chopped up before the second lot arrived?"

Mark Findlemann had little interest in things military, and not much knowledge of them—his chosen specialty area had been the spread of libraries in the Roman Empire and the Roman publishing industry, of all obscure and arcane things. But there was absolutely nothing wrong with his ability to worry compulsively at any problem with the fangs of logic.

"Attacking into the teeth of a waiting Roman army would be suicide, especially given our new weapons, unless—" Artorius began.

His eyes grew wide. He looked out the window—this room had one, four-by-six-sized piece of glass in a wooden framework.

Looking out at a dark rainy autumn night, twenty hundred hours, nearly everyone's asleep, including the Emperor and most of his Praetorian guardsmen. The perfect time and place to force a close fight, at knife distance, where artillery is irrelevant, it's all chaos and unit discipline doesn't matter nearly as much because it's just a gigantic brawl...

Artorius sprang to his feet, and snatched up his new *spatha* where it lay across a table with the belt wrapped around the scabbard. Four steps took him to the door and he ripped it open. The two marine sentries stiffened.

"An attack! Attack from the north bank! Sound the alarm, sound the alarm! Notify the fleet prefect, the Praetorian Prefect"—who would take care of informing the Emperor—"the legate of the Fourteenth and the town garrison! Turn everyone out! *Now, now!*"

He'd look like a wimpy idiot if he was wrong. If he was right...

Ah, now I could purr, speaking of leopardesses, Filipa thought.

She was lying in a happy, drowsy tangle with Sarukê, who'd said between endearments and gasps that making love on sheepskins in front of a fire was very homelike, reminding her of a wheeled hut on the Pontic steppe in wintertime, only with more room and privacy.

Their bedroom here in the *castra navalis* had a fireplace, one so new you could still smell the mortar setting. It was perfectly useable, though. In fact, the bricklayers had diffidently advised her to keep at least a low fire burning as much as she could when she arrived four days ago, because mortar set slowly in wet chilly weather.

That I have no objection to, she thought.

Stone buildings were perishing *cold* here this time of year. With only heating systems designed for the Mediterranean, the lower-status wooden structures, or the small houses of the poor, were often more comfortable than anything more upscale that didn't have the expensive luxury of a hypocaust.

This room was usually occupied by some sort of midlevel officer, probably. There was a fair-sized bed with the usual Roman stuffed mattress—stuffed with chicken feathers, in this case—on leather lacing across the frame. She'd had new bedding set up as soon as it arrived from Vindobona with the wagon carrying their personal gear, including the American novelty of linen sheets; there were a couple of chests, and a cupboard with drawers below. They didn't waste glass windows at this level, but the shutter was good and tight.

And Sarukê was starting to nibble at her neck again. Filipa sighed happily—

Trumpets blared, *cornua* and *tubae* and then someone began banging thunderously on a naval drum. Neither was very far away, nor were the growing chorus of shouts and yells.

Sarukê shouted in her own language as she rocketed erect, and Filipa squawked as she was dumped aside. Normally she only felt the other woman's sheer strength as an added, exciting bonus; it could be disconcerting when it showed this way, despite the muscle she'd put on herself with all the riding and arms practice and the sheer effort of living without machines.

The Sarmatian dropped back into Latin:

"Attack alarm is! Get ready, quick! Quick!"

They scrambled into their clothes, then the quilted *subarmalis* pullover jacks you wore under armor, then helped each other into their mail hauberks and fastened their sword belts. Sarukê slung her round shield over her back, her bowcase-quiver to her belt, and snatched up her helmet.

She didn't put it on yet—it restricted your vision, and more so at night, and the Roman model she used had a convenient handle on the neck guard for carrying it around. Filipa did likewise, suddenly conscious of how dry her mouth was.

"Get you shield," Sarukê said, all carnivore focus.

She'll run toward the fight, Filip thought numbly.

As she picked up her shield—which she'd painted with 한국, for "Korea," as a mordant joke. As far as she remembered the Three Kingdoms were just getting started back there, and Buddhism hadn't even arrived among her remote ancestors yet.

It's Sarukê's instinctual response, and she really, really meant that stuff she said to the Prof, and she just assumes I'll do the same. And I am, aren't I?

"Stay behind me little bit in fight. Right side," the Sarmatian said. "You guard, I lead, sword-sister."

The door banged open and they trotted out and toward the second story of this barracks block, where the Prof had his quarters.

I'm running toward *a knife fight in the dark with frothing barbarian savages,* Filipa thought, a little dazed. *This* must *be love!*

"This is going to sound really strange," Paula said. "But would you mind giving me a hug?"

"Not at all," Mark said. "*I* could use a hug."

They were alone in the map room, standing by the window. It was warmer than their private quarters—by mutual unspoken consent they'd all let Filipa and Sarukê have the one with the fireplace. Mark had found Paula still there when he returned, and they'd been chatting nervously. Now they simply stood with their arms around each other, looking out into the foggy dark-ness. Mark was uneasily aware that he was sweating, and that it wasn't because they'd stoked up the fire, but he could tell she was too. Lights were going on outside, but he couldn't see any details through the thick streaked glass.

"You don't think I should..." he said.

Paula snorted into his chest. "Don't think you should grab a snickersnee and make an idiot of yourself and get in everyone's way and get pointlessly killed?" she said. "No, I don't. Any more than *I* will. We have bodyguards with us to handle anything personal."

They were outside the door right now. A tribune—the Prof's current official rank—couldn't have private guards in a strictly military context.

"Fil will," he said, and then, to keep his teeth from chatter-ing: "I'm a poet and I don't know it."

"Fil's being an idiot because she's in love with Sandahl Bar-barian Bergman redux," Paula said. "Also she has *some* idea of what she's doing, she and Sarukê work out at it every day, for better than eight months now. Jeremey's being an idiot out of machismo, I think. The Prof is doing what needs to be done and he *does* know what he's doing."

"But I—" Mark began.

"You are the reason we're not getting attacked *in our sleep*," Paula said sharply. "So the Prof and the others get a chance to do something but wake up and say *huh? whuzzat? ouchie!* while someone spears them."

"Well..." Mark said; the thought did perk him up. "Yeah, I sort of am, aren't I?"

Mind you, this is a military base, she thought. *They've got sentries and walls and barred gates. They wouldn't have been totally taken flat-footed. But the Prof did seem to think every second counted.*

"Well, you guys all helped," he said.

"We did, and so did Josephus...but you're the one who picked out the pattern. The Prof is right, you're the best at that. We might have gotten it in a day or two...but he was right about being in a hurry, too."

"Hurrah," he said, giving her final grateful squeeze. "You know, looking out the window isn't going to do jack, so why don't we have a drink by the fire and talk about...oh, our long-term goals?"

"Anything but tonight? Or you could tell me about growing up in Midwood. I'll swap you stories about my 'hood." She hesitated for a moment. "Or we could go to bed."

He frowned. "I don't think I could sleep..."

"I meant *together*, Mark."

"Oh!" he said. Then: "*Oh!*"

"I've been dropping hints."

He winced. "I'm really not good at the nonverbal stuff, you know."

"Duh, Mark. That's why I just asked you straight out. Unless there's someone..."

"Uh, no. Certainly not! Ummm...yeah? Let's. By all means! But why me, if you don't mind me asking? I mean, you're really gorgeous, and..."

"And I really like you. You're always smart. Funny a lot of the time. You're kind even if you forget people *exist* a lot of the time. You're not bad looking. I feel less lonely with you around."

And you're not a Roman man, she thought. *Which makes you a real catch.*

She could see he was warming to the idea.

And I can't think of a better distraction from that battle out there, too.

⇒ CHAPTER TWENTY-THREE ⇐

Municipium Aelium Carnuntum,
Capital of Pannonia Superior
November 8th–9th, 166 CE

"Loose the cable!" Artorius shouted from the rear of the galley.

The *triarch* of the *Dacicus* didn't even look up from where he and his under-officers were shoving the still-sleepy rowers to the benches.

A voice rose in a shriek-scream, punctuated by the thud of blows with a stick on a back:

"No, you Gods-detested wide-arsed imbecile of an irrumātor, you don't run out the oar until you hear the command! It'll break off against the slipway! And kill you, you son of a clapped-out whore! I hope!"

The slipway team hesitated, then one of them took a wooden mallet and knocked out the pin that held the cable to the stern-post of the ship.

Out of the corner of his eye he saw Sarukê scramble on board, using ruthless elbows and the boss of her shield; Filipa followed in her wake, and behind her Jeremy, clutching at the new cross-bow he'd brought along—one of the first out of the workshops.

Down in the slipway proper, three teams of two swung their own mallets against timbers braced against the hull on either side of the ship and scrambled back to the pavement up the inset ladders behind them. For a long moment nothing happened, save that the scramble of the last of the crew to get onboard made the now-free hull rock back and forth. That was the marines, still hopping and struggling with items of gear and screaming insults when someone juggled a spearpoint too near their faces or posteriors.

That rocking broke the hold of friction and cold lard on the rollers. The ship started to move, only an inch or so, then a jerk, then faster as the last marine made a dive from the stepladder onto the deck.

Going a lot faster than last time.

The galley was tiny compared to the oceangoing varieties; that didn't mean it didn't weigh multiple tons. Once it was moving, it surged down the slip with ponderous, gathering speed. The rollers gave a squealing shriek that built rapidly along with a frying sound and a smell like the world's dirtiest bacon grease burning from whiffs of smoke, cutting through the white-noise burr of voices and thousands of pounding feet and braying trumpets and pounding drums.

Artorius ran forward, past the ship's captain looking around and shouting volleys of orders full of Graeco-Latin technicalities, past the catapult, where the two ex-rowers were stolidly pumping away to cock it as the weapon's crew settled in.

Then the ship's ram plowed into the water of the river in two broad gull wings of spray; he managed to catch a stay and hold himself upright, while dozens fell and rolled over the deck about him and the heavy feel of inertia levered at him. One luckless marine went overside with a scream, but it was probably shallow enough here for him to wade back to shore.

Of course, that means he'll be there when the Quadi arrive.

A shout and a flourish of trumpets, near enough to be metallic-scream loud, the trierarch's own signalers. "Out oars" was nearly inaudible under that, but thirty of them *did* shoot out, in near unison. Then the *hortator's* drum and voice began to sound: stroke... stroke...

There was a jerk as the long ash shafts bit into the river, and steerageway came on the galley. Water began to curl back from the bows. There he found the man who'd been stationed at the forepeak, and he was ready. The first of the four-foot paper cylinders had been jammed into the iron holder, but the crewman was still standing waiting to be told what to do. The American flicked his own *Ronsonius* and touched it to the twist of paper at the top. It caught with a hiss of burning saltpeter and a chemical smell.

"When it's done, start another right away!" he shouted in the man's ear. "As long as you've got more or until someone tells you to stop."

He'd thought about rockets. They wouldn't be all *that* difficult. When he had *time*.

Roman candles... which he'd christened *candelabrum Romanum*... were even simpler. You put successive charges of gunpowder in a thick paper tube, separated by clay wads and each topped with some very basic pyrotechnics for the stars, with a fuse running down the center from top to bottom.

Whump! sounded with a flash and burnt-sulfur stink, and then less than a full second later: *pop!*

There were already more and more lights coming on; lamps like tiny yellow stars, the more violent flare of crescents, and from the tops of the low towers that studded the walls of the *castrum* the whooshing, spark-spewing rush of heaped pinewood in iron baskets, kept tinder dry with greased leather covers over wicker for just such an occasion as this.

The greenish light of the new star overhead was brighter. It lit up quite a stretch of the gray-blue Danube, in fact, beneath the low overcast and through the chilly fog that wasn't *quite* rain now.

"*Je—*" he began to shout.

He caught himself in midyell and modified it to: "*Jeboza!*"

Someone might remember him calling on Jesus.

Not a smart thing to do. Though Marcus Aurelius does say he's seriously considering making changes there.

He still felt like swearing at what he saw, and since blaspheming Roman deities just wasn't very satisfying yet he settled for:

"*Pedicabo me!*"

There were *thousands* of Quadi warriors on the water, in everything from coracles to dugout canoes through rowboats to big barges holding a hundred or more men; he even saw some sitting on logs turned into crude outriggers by lashing on branches, and paddling with their hands. The dribs and drabs and masses stretched out of sight in either direction, where the light of the Roman candle didn't reach. The Quadi had shown far more discipline than he'd thought them capable of by staying quiet enough to be inaudible under the Roman shouts and screams and martial music growing steadily less ragged.

Whump!—pop!

Another green light overhead.

Whump!—pop!

Now the enemy roared, and water leaped higher as they rowed and paddled with all their strength in a heart-bursting spasm of energy.

And more water burst twenty feet into the air as the rest of the *Pannoniorum classis* came down the slipways, throwing plumes on either side of their bow rams.

Then there were more of the high bright green lights, from the other ships that had been refitted. He went back toward the stern, where the galley's commander stood, pausing just long enough to shout:

"Load Roman Fire!" to the catapult's crew chief before he ran back between the rowers' benches.

At the tiller he called to the captain, who was looking around as if he didn't quite believe in either what he was seeing, or the light he was using to see it with.

"There!" Artorius said.

Pointing eastward toward the largest concentration of barges— they were just big rectangular boxes of planks, hurriedly thrown together and probably leaking like sieves. But then, they only had to float for a few hundred yards, and only once; then their passengers would be either victorious or too dead to care.

"Attack that clump, Captain!"

Those barges also bristled with banners, horns and skulls and crude daubed cloth on poles. There seemed to be a lot of helmets and mail hauberks there too, which indicated commanders, chiefs and their full-time warriors. With any luck it might even include Ariogaesus, which was the way the Romans rendered the name of the leader of the anti-Imperial faction of the tribe and its would-be king.

There were six other Roman galleys in the water now, that he could see, and they swung into a ragged line; even then he felt pride as he saw that the other three which had been modified did it faster than the trio still relying on steering oars.

And whatever the Roman military's other faults, you *couldn't* fault the way their training produced a reflexive ferocious aggressiveness, a desire to get stuck in and start spilling blood.

Whump!—pop!

Another star shot skyward from the bows of the *Dacicus*.

As if that had prompted them, which it probably had, the other refitted ships began to fire theirs again.

And I nearly decided to put that off until spring! he thought, and broke into a cold sweat as he imagined trying to do this strictly by firelight.

Whump!—pop! over and over, and the light grew brighter as they drifted slowly downward.

A bit to his surprise the big barges didn't alter course, but kept driving straight for the southern bank of the Danube. They did sound lowing, dunting ox horns and tall upright trumpets with the heads of snarling beasts. Even more to his surprise, a small or not-so-small fleet of canoes and rowboats of various sizes and types turned toward the Roman ships, including a long raft towed by a dozen other craft and with scores of warriors on its sides beating the water to a froth as they tried to paddle with everything from oars through spears to shields and their hands. A few were slipping into the icy water, holding on with both hands and thrashing with their feet.

The *triarius* spoke in a worried tone. "Tribune, if any substantial number of those smaller boats get alongside, we'll be swamped. We have fifteen marines on board. Even Hercules can't fight two."

Artorius nodded; the rowers could fight at a pinch, and had weapons under their benches...but it wasn't their specialty and it would immobilize the craft.

"Let's do what men can do," he said.

He raised his voice: "Men! We fight under the Emperor's eyes! He will be watching from a tower in the *castrum!*"

That *did* seem to stiffen a few backs.

Tunnngg-WHACK!

The catapult cut loose, surprising him. He followed the burning fuse with his eyes—

"Short!" Then: "No, it isn't, not quite!"

They'd shot at the biggest target in reach, the raft. The wobbling ceramic container shed a thick coil of sparks as it flew, the passage whipping the fuse brighter and brighter. Then it struck, just a few feet from the foremost edge. The warriors there jerked up their shields in instinctive reflex.

That was the worst possible thing they could have done; if it had plowed into someone's stomach, it might not have shattered.

Though...let's see, twenty-five pounds, travelling at about three hundred feet per second...yeah, it would have killed the man it hit, certain-sure.

Instead it ran into a wall of wood and metal and hard leather, disintegrated...and rained gobbets of clinging white-hot fire in a flying fan for yards back of the point of impact. Even over the growing white-noise burr of combat, the shrieks of agony were loud. Men on fire were jumping into the water, and either landing in patches of floating flame or coming back up in them and having their coating of Roman Fire blaze up again.

He felt a grudging respect when the Quadi kept right on coming.

The ones on the raft did surge back a bit, reforming their shield wall, and many of them behind the front line raising their oval or hexagonal shields overhead in a crude imitation of a Roman *testudo*, a tortoise formation.

Tunnngg-WHACK!

That was good time, only about twenty seconds from the first...but then, the crew had a very strong incentive to hurry.

This time it was one of the bronze balls. It slashed out, invisible in the murk and dark save for the fuse leaving a thin trail of sparks. They'd left that a bit too long, and the bronze sphere struck the raft and bounced back to head height, pinwheeling and wobbling because of the way it had bent out of shape.

CRACK!

This time the wrong setting on the fuse had worked to their advantage; the ball exploded at about six feet over the Quadi shield wall. The red flash of the explosion flicked through the dark, but the smoke was invisible against the patch of fog drifting past. That mercifully hid the details of what happened between the raft's surface and the center point of the shower of high-velocity lead. Another twelve feet of the close-packed Germanii simply vanished or went up into the night in pieces. Another ten feet to the rear of that collapsed backward, blasted off their feet or killed by bullets that made nothing of shields or helms or chain mail.

Half a dozen of the boats that were pulling the raft cast off their towlines and swung into the sides of the raft; warriors scrambled to board...and then the boats headed for the oncoming Roman vessels.

God damn the poor brave bastards, he thought.

Then he yelled at the marines hefting their pila javelins:

"Don't forget the pomegranates!"

Because with grenades, Hercules can fight two.

He pushed forward himself and snatched one out of the wicker baskets tied to the rails, snapped his *Ronsonius* to light the fuse and threw, blessing days spent in the Little League.

Crack! and it burst in a rowboat. Water and bits of board . . . and probably of the occupants . . . rose into the night.

Half the marines grabbed grenades of their own, their *Ronsonii* making a flicker through the darkness. Just then the *Dacicus* lurched; the ram had slammed into a dugout canoe. It didn't slow the galley down, and there was another chorus of screams as the hollowed-out log and its occupants went under, thumping down the keel and the hull planking. A lit grenade went skittering across the deck, dropped when the boat heaved, and Artorius made a headlong dive after it. He snatched it up, threw—

Crack!

Something struck his helmet and his head whipped around; fortunately only a painful wrench as something went *spang* against the iron above his left ear. Low-velocity shards like that were why metal helmets had come back into use in his great-great-grandfather's day, back around 1915.

He came back to his feet, shaking his head; just then there were slamming, grating noises from both sides of the ship forward. Artorius swept out his sword and dagger and started forward; some distant part of him admired how the rowers ignored *everything*.

Tunnngg-WHACK!

The shell arched off eastward; it wasn't going to help against whoever had grappled the *Dacicus*, but it did burst—with malignant precision, this time—right over a clump of boats and canoes heading their way. Froth leaped upward, and then fell back, and what remained floating drifted away. Then he had something more immediate to worry about, as a helmeted head came over the starboard side, a gilded wolf crest on top and the metal below that framing a snarling bearded face. Hands clamped on the rail and the boarder heaved himself up. Spearpoints gleamed behind him.

Artorius charged flat out, and swung his foot at the man's face at the last moment, catching him just before he could draw his blade. The boot heel landed precisely as the man was swinging a leg over the rail, and there was a crackling *crunch* sound and a shock that jarred up his leg. Hot droplets spattered into his face as he recovered with desperate speed.

As his right foot thumped down on the deck, he translated that into a downward slash with his *spatha*. The next boarder had managed to get his arms across the rail; the blade took his left off just below the elbow, and the jet of blood took Artorius right across his midsection, soaking through the padding under the mail. A familiar hot-rank metallic scent washed across him, like rust and seawater and sweat all at the same time.

The injured man toppled straight back with a shriek. There was a deep *twang* sound from just behind him and the one who'd been about to hit him with a one-handed war axe suddenly stopped as Jeremey's crossbow bolt took him in the face.

"Thanks!" Artorius grunt-snarled as he wrenched his sword out of the oak and the man fell back.

Two of the *Dacicus'* marines dashed up. They dropped lit grenades over the side and then crouched with their shields upraised. Artorius did likewise, putting his back to the rail. Jeremey was lying on his back, with a foot in the stirrup of the crossbow, drawing the string back with both hands.

Crack! Crack! from behind him, and more screams.

That position let him see what was happening on the other side of the bow. A warrior vaulted the rail and lunged a spearpoint at Sarukê's face. She went forward under it with a fast, graceful dipping motion that left her on one knee; as it touched the deck she slammed her shield downward, the ironshod rim cracking into the top of the Quadi's foot in its soft moccasin-like shoe.

It was too noisy to hear the crunch, but there were a lot of small bones in a foot. The warrior jackknifed forward, his own motion adding to the impetus as she sprang upward and punched the upper rim of the gryphon-painted shield beneath his chin. His jaw shattered and he fell backward. Just then another rammed his spear at her, but Filipa was in striking distance, and she did strike—a straight thrust to the throat.

The steel slid home in a gout of red. The Korean-American woman froze for an instant: you could virtually see—

I just stabbed *someone in the* throat!

—running through her mind.

In a remote sort of way he sympathized with that flash of buck fever, but another warrior had his spear back. Sarukê pivoted with a dancer's grace and her backhand stroke flashed across his arm just up from the wrist. The hand flew free, the spear pinwheeled away, and his recoil put him in the path of the man following; the Sarmatian tucked her shoulder into her shield, took two quick steps and ran into them in a body check that bowled them over the rail and bounced her back into fighting stance.

This is like fighting in your bedroom! Or a broom closet!

Then more marines ran up on that side too, tossing grenades or throwing their pila directly downward. The heavy lead-weighted seven-foot javelins probably went through the bottoms of the boats as well as anyone who got in the way, and half a dozen grenades crackled there.

And the galley's oars kept moving, a steady stroke...stroke... stroke...probably crunching on swimming men as well like giant bone-breaking clubs.

Jeremey was getting to his feet; Artorius put a hand down on his shoulder and used it as a lever to come erect, panting like a wheezing bellows inside the constriction of armor and padding. There was a cut on his left forearm that he hadn't noticed until now; it stung like white-hot fire all of a sudden, and he worked his fingers to make sure nothing vital had been cut before he let a crewman wrap a bandage over it.

He poured double-distilled superwine over it too, and Artorius swore imaginatively—in English. Then it died away to a painful throbbing, which practice let him ignore for now.

There was more light; the Roman candles had stopped, but the burning raft and half a dozen other craft more than made up for it. Ahead of them the *Victoria* plowed into the first of the big barges, just as it touched bottom in the shallow water of the shore. The oars backed almost instantly, but the downward surge of the barge trapped the galley's ram for a moment. Scores of Quadi launched themselves over the rail from the barge—

CRUMP!

Artorius fell on his back again as a surge of water made the *Dacicus* buck like a restive horse. When he managed to get his head up once more he saw that the whole bow of the other galley had disappeared, its boards and timber vanishing upward and outward; so had the barge that held it. Spurts and gobbets of liquid flame traced lines through the air as well, falling among the packed Quadi vessels crowded with men.

Someone touched off the magazine and all the ammo went up, Artorius thought, half dazed; probably three hundred men had died in an instant, and twice that been badly wounded. *Possibly accidental, but I'd bet any amount someone over there did it deliberately when he saw they were going to be overrun.*

There were times when these Romans reminded him a fair bit of studies he'd read on World War Two Japanese in some basic attitudes. At least the ones you met under arms here on the frontier did.

"Duty, heavier than mountains; death, lighter than a feather," he murmured to himself.

Jeremey was doggedly trying to reload his crossbow. Behind Artorius the catapult cut loose again:

Tunnngg-WHACK!

A fire shell arched out and landed in another of the barges; it had just grounded, and the flames seemed to chase the Quadi ashore, but in moments the fire was leaping up across the crude heap of wood.

The *CRACK! CRACK!* of more shells sounded. The gates of the naval fortress opened; units of marines poured out, and he thought he saw a cohort of Praetorians coming too, their distinctive scorpion-blazoned shields up. Signal fires flared up from the *castrum* of the legion, and columns would be double-timing out of it. The four unmodified galleys were ramming the rear of the grounded barges, but doing it more cautiously—starting to back water before they hit, so they could retreat before the Quadi swarmed onto them.

The barges settled, and he noticed smaller craft turning about smartly and making for the northern shore again. He turned to the catapult crew and pointed his sword to the clots and straggling groups of Quadi wading ashore at the foot of the slope up from the water. Some of them were carrying long wooden scaling ladders, showing what they'd had in mind for the fort originally. They threw them down now, and massed for a charge.

"That's your target," he snapped.

Tunnngg-WHACK!

CRACK!

The bronze shot arched out and exploded almost exactly where the Danube's water met the mud of the foreshore. Black gobbets and chunks of warrior flew. The other two surviving retrofitted galleys fell in line with the flagship; their captains were conforming automatically, and the massed warriors were an obvious target. Their charge toward the Roman troops forming up in front of the wall collapsed as volleys of bombs shredded it. Bolts and rocks rained down from the older engines on the fort's walls.

Artorius caught his breath; someone passed him a canteen of water mixed with near-vinegar wine; he gulped down half of it, and passed it to Jeremey. A little way away Filipa was sitting on the deck with her head between her knees; Sarukê was squatting beside her, honing a nick out of her sword and leaning over to say something to her.

"You did good," he told the younger man, and thumped him on the shoulder. "Very good for your first action. Kept your head, shot that, ah, *nasty person* trying for me."

Jeremey coughed and drank again. "Well, seemed the thing to do, Prof," he said. "Frankly, I'd rather be farming...and I don't like farming much."

There was a crashing bark of: "*Roma!*"

Artorius looked up. The Roman formation under the naval fort's walls trotted forward; there were trumpet and *tubae* calls, and the first rank stamped down their left foot, twisted their bodies and threw their *pila*. The weighted javelins disappeared in the darkness in shallow arcs, invisible save for the odd glitter of a pyramidal point catching firelight.

Then they sleeted down into the Quadi faces and shields and chests, a thousand or more of them.

Firelight glittered again as the Roman short swords snapped free of their sheaths and the pace of their formation went up to a quick trot, the sound of the hobnails pounding in unison carrying through the damp air.

He snorted and turned to the captain. "We should check up and down the river for a mile or so. There must be little parties of the enemy coming ashore. We'll wreck their boats so the shore parties can handle them."

The captain nodded respectfully.

"Yes, *sir!*" he said.

Optio Aulus Petillius Brucius, First Century, Second Praetorian cohort, was not in a good mood.

First time I was going to get laid since Savaria, he thought.

And now I'm tramping up and down the freezing muddy godsfor-saken Danube, my balls cold and looking for trouble.

Trouble appeared despite the wisps of fog that restricted vis-ibility; a wrecked biggish boat, and thirty or so Quadi wading up onto the shore just ahead, dripping and in some cases crawl-ing and coughing and puking; the boat must have been sinking, probably a brush with one of the patrol galleys. They all looked as drenched and chilly as he felt, but he could have sworn that even twenty paces away he could wind their stink over the sweat and iron of his own men.

Thirty was about as many men as he had with him; half the *Prima Centuria* left on their feet, after that cluster buggery at the naval base all night.

Ave! to Artorius, though. If he hadn't called the warning... *What a man! With him and a fine Emperor like the one we've got, what can't we do?*

Half of them had minor wounds; he was limping slightly from a bone bruise on his shin that sent a stab every time he came down on it. Still, it wouldn't do to let the remnant sweepings of the bar-barian host go wandering off to rape the provincials' sheep and shear their daughters for wool. He couldn't really complain about the senior centurion of the Guard's orders to patrol aggressively.

Besides, after losing my chance with that fluffy little blonde piece, I am not feeling well disposed to these scum. To Hades with taking prisoners for the mines. They'd suffer more there, but I want to kill them myself, sink my blade in their guts and watch them die.

"Deploy!" he rasped, his voice hoarse from shouting orders over the roar of battle through the night. "Double line, open order intervals!"

The men shook themselves out in two staggered lines with drilled-in ease, two *contubernia* in each, the eight-man squads who shared a tent or a room in barracks. Minus the night's dead and badly wounded, of course. Three feet on either side of every man—to give full room for sword-and-shield work—and the second line covering the intervals in the first.

"Advance at the double-quick!" he called, trotting forward himself at the right of the front rank.

That was usually the centurion's position, but he was in charge here. Hobnails grated in unison on dirt and rock, and the hoops and bands of their armor rattled and clashed. It was about dawn. Or what passed for it in this miserable, rainy fog-begotten wilderness—he'd been born in decently warm and sunny Campania, southeast of Rome—but there was enough dim pale light for work. At least trotting in armor warmed you up a bit, though he'd be glad to get his weight off the damned leg for a while.

Preferably somewhere with a fire, wine, good bread and oil, hot soup and a pretty barmaid rolling her rump like Venus Callipyge.

The enemy were shouting, in that grunting, squealing language of theirs that always reminded him of—

"It's a boar hunt for some Quadi hogs!" he snarled.

Then, when they were close enough to see mouths gaping in horror or bellowing some uncouth challenge:

"Front rank, pilum ready..."

The shields came up as the long javelins cocked back.

"...*iacite pila!*"

A chorus of grunts as the left feet came down harder, the shield was brought down too, and the heavy throwing spears flew. Each one had a head like a long narrow metalworker's punch on a two-foot iron shank, with a tang slotted into the wooden part and secured by a pyramidal block and rivets and iron cullet. Behind each of *those* was a three-pound lead ball to add punch when they hit. They weren't long-range weapons, but they didn't have to be. Screams of fear and then of pain sounded almost but not quite human among the animal snuffling and grunting of what passed for a language among these savages.

Some of the enemy had their shields up, but the simple plank types they used here hardly even slowed a *pilum* down. The *tock-tock-tock* sound of impact was accompanied by more screams as they smashed through into arms and chests and faces.

"Second rank, pila ready—*iacite pila!*"

Once the spears were all in the air, twenty-nine callused hands slapped down in the reversed grip on the grooved hilts of the *gladii* slung high on their right hips and snapped them out in a long ripple. The broad blades glinted as the weak sunlight caught on their honed edges and sharp points.

He pointed his own sword forward, lips peeling back from teeth behind the scorpion-stamped cheek pieces of his helmet:

"Time to make some bacon, boys! *Charge!*"

✧   ✧   ✧

Abgar bar Mirhbandaq looked closely and anxiously at his bow. The damp climate of Pannonia was not kind to the glue that held laminations of horn and sinew on either side of the wooden core. Nothing seemed wrong right now, and the surface of melted antler he'd brushed on to preserve it was only lightly beaded with moisture.

"Praise and honor to *Tar'atā*, the Great Goddess; I pledge her a dove in sacrifice," he said in pious thankfulness, using the hem of his tunic to wipe it down.

"Silence in the ranks," the decurion snapped, the nasal Palmyran accent strong in his Aramaic.

The men poling at the rear shoved the barge further along; the water was shallow here, and the mud stank of rot and ancient sewage as it was stirred up. The wastes from the naval base had been accumulating for a long time.

Not as shallow as it is over there, the Syrian archer thought cheerfully.

In the dark this particular band of Quadi had grounded their barge hard on the mudbank, probably because they couldn't see it, black mud in the black night with a thin film of water over it anyway. Then the Roman galleys had struck it with a pair of granite balls to smash the flimsy improvised thing to fragments and a firebomb to set the splinters alight. It had burned right down to the bottom planks, leaving nothing for the survivors to stand on.

They'd leapt out into the mud rather than be set alight, and were now standing thigh deep in it, looking like a field of a hundred statues coated in glistening black muck. Roman soldiers were all taught to swim; evidently the local barbarians weren't, and the ones who could or who could find a chunk of intact wood had all struck out for the north bank hours ago. With Romans on the water, not many of them had made it.

Since the rest weren't going anywhere, they'd been left for the after-battle cleanup. He could smell the ones who'd burned, even hours later, a singed-pork stink under the smoke of wood and the odd smell of the new Roman Fire that was like scorched metal. Over on the south bank of the Danube fifty yards away half a cohort of ordinary auxiliary infantry were leaning on their spears. Or hooting invitations to the Quadi to wade on over, and making mocking beckoning gestures, blowing kisses, occasionally hiking up their tunics and mail shirts to wave their privates or slap their buttocks.

Or yelling jocular greetings along the lines of:

"Got any messages for your wives and daughters? We'll be seeing them before you do!"

The barge stopped, and the decurion called: "Front rank to the side, and nock shafts! Ranks will rotate every ten arrows!"

Abgar stepped forward, drew a shaft from the quiver at his belt, put it to the string and locked his thumb under it. The string rested on the metal ring that protected his drawing thumb, and two fingers clamped firmly over the top of the digit. The side of the barge rose to a handspan below his breastbone, which shouldn't be a problem, but he scuffed his feet to make sure there weren't any more loose kernels of barley under the soles of his boots. That had been the barge's last cargo, evidently, and he didn't want anything he could skid on under his sandals.

Some of the Quadi tried to run. Abgar frowned as many of his comrades laughed at the heaving, floundering mess that created. Killing was serious business. The auxiliary infantry spearmen on the shore were falling about in helpless, hooting, staggering mirth, but he felt the ancient, much-honored *Cohors Prima Syriaca Sagittaria* should show more dignity.

"Draw!"

Thirty bows creaked, and Abgar's heavy arm muscle knotted as the string came back to the angle of his jaw, tickling a little as it brushed the thick black curls of his full beard. The short sleeve of his mail tunic fell back with a chinking rustle as he raised the bow carefully, estimating the range with experienced eyes.

A chorus of despairing shrieks and pleas came from the mudbank, and some of the Quadi covered their eyes. Others waved their weapons and tried to wade toward the barge with the archers, wrenching a leg free with each slow bogged-down stride and gasping out war cries.

"*Shoot!*"

"You have been wounded and shed your blood in Rome's service, Tribune," Marcus Aurelius said.

There was a somber approval in his voice. One of the *seriously* wounded from the ship groaned as he was helped down the gangplank behind Artorius, red glistening on the bandages that encased his left leg.

"Sir!" Artorius said.

He was startled; he hadn't expected the Emperor to be down at the dock when the *Dacicus* tied up a little after noon. He looked down at the sword in his hand, then wiped it and sheathed it before he saluted. The seawater-and-rot smell of blood was heavy in the air by the docks, only slightly muffled by the chill, and a shriek rose from where the *medicii* had set up a forward dressing station—at a guess someone had slathered on the new disinfectant.

Better some pain now than gangrene later, of course.

I'd forgotten that stupid-tired sensation after a hot action. How not *nostalgic feeling it again is! I'm not twenty-two and hot to trot anymore either. Old enough to know down in my gut how quickly and easily a man can die. Julia and I've got a child coming now, for God's sake!*

His left forearm twinged, but the last thought warmed him and he said dismissively:

"It's only a scratch, sir."

The Praetorian Prefect snorted derisively; by his scarred face he had a right to comment:

"The difference between *a scratch* and *death* is about two digits, Tribune," he said, holding up two fingers pressed together.

There was an underlying stench of burnt flesh lingering in the damp cold air too, and of burning in general, and the harsh scent of Roman Fire. Working parties along the shore of the Danube were throwing corpses into two-wheel oxcarts. Occasionally they made sure that the bodies *were* corpses. Even after a half day's labor the numbers were impressive, drifts and lines and piles up from the shore halfway to the fortress walls, blind eyes staring up into the slate-gray overcast that dripped like tears.

Marcus Aurelius stepped forward. "Go now, eat and bathe and rest, soldier of Rome," he said, gripping his shoulder briefly. "Have your wound seen to—by Galenos himself. Tomorrow we will meet to discuss all this, and the campaign to come."

Artorius saluted again; that sounded like a good idea.

And I could really, really use a drink. The peach schnapps tastes *like cough syrup, but damn that, it's the* effect *I want.*

⇒ CHAPTER TWENTY-FOUR ⇐

Municipium Aelium Carnuntum,
Capital of Pannonia Superior
November 9th, 166 CE

Marcus Aurelius looked at the men in the map room the Americans had made in the Praetorium; his *comites* were there, and the provincial governor and higher local commanders, all seated at the table. Logs crackled in the fireplace behind him, and even then some of them who hadn't seen the innovation yet gave it an appreciative glance for the way it took the wet-chill curse off the air. Those same eyes went up to the new-style suspended lanterns with glass chimneys that gave a fair degree of brightness to an overcast November morning on the middle Danube. The sun wasn't going to do that, during the short period it deigned to lift over the southern horizon at all.

He doesn't miss much, does he? Artorius thought, reading the monarch's glance.

"It seems I owe you yet another debt," Rome's Emperor said to Artorius. "And, possibly, my life."

The American shook his head. "You were secure in the fortress, and well guarded by good troops, Caesar Augustus. The Quadi were desperate and made a reckless throw of the dice that had little chance of success. I do hope my warning made our victory swifter, less costly."

"Very much so," Marcus Aurelius said.

There were nods from the others, some friendly and done

with a smile, some grudging of this alien newcomer's swift rise among men of *good family*.

None of the men in military garb were ready to deny the warning had helped. Surprise multiplied force, they all knew it and knew the others did too. It was impossible to say how much more damage the Quadi might have done with that on their side and their scaling ladders on the fortress wall before the garrison turned out.

"And since you deny that you read the stars or do auguries, Tribune, *how* did you realize that the Quadi would attack that very night?"

"I...and more immediately, my clients...simply examined all the intelligence available, sir," he said, and outlined what he'd set Mark and the others to doing, and what they'd found:

"So I was then certain that the Quadi expected to attack, and attack a place where Roman forces were strong. Given that advantage of ours, added to by the new weapons, a night attack was only logical, because it minimized our strengths. I was *not* certain that that would be the day...the night...the Quadi attacked, or that the *castra* of the fleet in Carnuntum would be the target. But it seemed very likely, and better safe than sorry, as the saying goes, sir. Better I look a fool shying at shadows than Roman soldiers die because I *feared* looking a fool. But I was lucky."

"Luck is what happens when preparation meets opportunity," the Emperor said.

Then he sighed and shook his head. "I would not have thought barbarians such as the Quadi would have the intellect...and the patience and discipline...to carry out such a plot."

Artorius shook his head ruefully too:

"Where I come from we have another saying, sir. If you play at *latrones* long enough with good players, you will become a good player yourself. Rome has halted on this frontier and the Rhine for over a hundred years; and the Quadi and others have learned from the Empire, in more ways than one. Their forefathers in the days of the first Augustus could not have done this, but they most manifestly can. It is not safe to leave a *good player* on the frontier."

Latrones—the Game of Soldiers—was a Roman board game basically similar to chess. Marcus Aurelius took the meaning immediately; he could see the others getting it in a ripple of amusement, discomfort, or dawning thoughtfulness. The head of the Praetorians looked as if he'd bitten into something very sour.

"What do you recommend, then, Tribune?" the Emperor said, an edge of amusement in his voice. "It is your place to advise me, after all."

"Exactly what you had planned, sir. Cross the river as soon as the weather is good and our forces gathered, then *vincere superbos* until there's nobody left up there but obedient Roman subjects."

He thought for a moment and went on: "What the Empire needs and needs badly, sir, is...how shall I put it...a *finalem solutionem Germanis problemata.*"

Which meant: a final solution to the German problem. Mark made a choking sound behind him. One of the officials from the office of the *Praepositus a rationibus*—basically the treasury—was also almost whimpering, though for a very different reason:

"Great Caesar Augustus, the *cost*! The garrisons necessary—"

"The equivalent of four legions and an equal number of auxiliaries," Marcus Aurelius said thoughtfully. "Suitably distributed. And a network of roads and fortresses. That to begin with. Eventually, cities and towns and harbors and much else."

The Praetorian Prefect nodded; he was as close as the Romans had to Chief of the General Staff. That prediction meant about forty to fifty thousand men, which would be something around fifteen percent of the Empire's current armed forces.

Oh, please, *Parthian Kingdom,* stay *beaten for a while!* Artorius thought, as close to a real mental prayer as he'd come in a while.

We'll probably have to conquer Parthia—before the Sassanids take over and make it a real menace.

In the history he'd studied, that was due in 224 CE, just short of sixty years from now. But the changes already in place made the date utterly unpredictable either way.

The Parthian state was a ramshackle affair; it had a succession crisis every time one of its shahs died, and the Roman wars against it were manageable. The Sassanids were a different kettle of fish entirely; for starters they were convinced that Ahura Mazda had commissioned them to re-create the ancient Persian Empire.

At times they'd overrun everything from Anatolia to Egypt. Eventually they and the Byzantine successor to the Roman Empire had crippled each other with one massive war after another and so enabled the early Arab conquests.

Not that anything's going to be remotely the same in a couple of centuries from now . . . but not another Parthian war just yet, pretty please! *Let's settle the Germanii first.*

The Emperor went on to the man of the *fiscus*: "But within ten years, if we do not make large mistakes in the manner of Varus, and fortune favors us, it would be possible to move the Danube garrison units north instead to the *new* frontier. And of course, new territories mean new, additional revenues."

"Oh, Caesar Augustus, they wouldn't come near—taxes on barbarian lands with little trade and only weedy little patches of farmland . . . then the roads and fortifications necessary—"

Artorius cleared his throat. "May I speak, Caesar?"

"By all means, Tribune. You are frequently . . . instructive."

He rose and went over to the room's southern wall and pulled the cord that scrolled up the linen curtain that covered it. There was a murmur of astonishment from the spectators—to begin with, the Romans hadn't come up with that arrangement for moving curtains yet. What was behind it was a huge map, twelve feet from top to bottom and twenty-four long. It covered the Mediterranean, North Africa, Europe all the way north and the Middle East as far as the Zagros and the Gulf. There was a rustling and the sound of stools scraping as men shifted to look comfortably.

"My former people had considerable skill in making very accurate maps," he said. "Which I and my clients have shown to the local artificers."

This would look different from any map they'd ever seen before, but thunderpowder and the other innovations and just lately warning of the Quadi attack had given him a lot of credibility when he made a claim. The borders of the Roman Empire were shown, its neighbors across them and its provinces within, and the major cities; so were the rivers and the larger mountain ranges, and in the *Barbaricum* the tribal territories and the names of the major peoples beyond the frontier, all neatly handprinted in the same block letters used for inscriptions.

"Like a view from the halls of the Gods!" someone murmured.

Artorius picked up a pointer and tapped it on Carnuntum.

"We are here."

Then he moved it north and a bit west, to what would have been Prague, the capital of the Czech Republic in his time.

Or a mass of radioactive ruins and scorched bones very shortly after *my time,* he thought grimly. *A pity, very pretty town. Mary loved it when we had that holiday there.*

It was less than two hundred miles, but until recently most literate Romans had thought that took you all the way to the Baltic shores. He went on aloud:

"This is the former land of the Boii, a Gallic tribe, overcome by the Marcomanni over a hundred years ago, and it is now the core of their realm. With regard to the fiscal issues just raised, there is a very large silver deposit... here."

He tapped the site of what another history would have known as Kutná Hora—Cowl Mountain—in central Bohemia. It was marked by a small cross.

"Large, excellent Tribune?" the fiscal official said, looking less silly and more intent. "How large?"

Large enough to supply a fair proportion of all the silver used in Europe for three centuries, he thought, and went on:

"Comparable to the largest of the silver mines in Hispania."

Especially with better ore-refining techniques like pan amalgamation, which we will helpfully supply. That'll up the output in the mines they've already got, too.

Spain was where much of the Empire's silver coinage came from. The news went through the watching men like a jolt of electricity; and by now they took what he said very seriously indeed. Even Marcus Aurelius' eyebrows shot up, and others were grinning like so many hungry carnivores contemplating a bound, gagged and nicely plump victim. The rabbity little man from the *fiscus* blinked and began to smile himself.

He's seeing himself freed from sitting in a bathtub with three drains and only one plug. Where likely as not he'd be blamed when it ran dry, not the Equestrian Order guy who's head of the fiscus.

"There are other large... though mostly not *so* large... deposits—"

Tap... tap... tap... tap... tap...

His pointer flicked to locations on what some twenty-first-century tourist guides had called the Silver Route, all the way up into Saxony, all helpfully picked out on the map with the same little crosses. That silver had financed a *lot* of impressive medieval and Renaissance architecture, which people had still come to gawk at in his time. Fuchs's ever-helpful baggage had included specific locations, complete with detailed topographical maps, cross sections of the ore deposits, plus total reserves and grades.

"Ending with another *very* large deposit here—"

His pointer went to what would have been Rammelsberg, in central Germany, on the northern edge of the Harz mountain range where it sank toward the great flatland that ran from the Atlantic to the Urals.

"Silver here on a very large scale, also copper, lead, sulfur and zinc."

"Ah, sulfur," one of the military men murmured, as if reminding himself; now very necessary for thunderpowder.

One of the watching Imperial legates actually ran a hand across his mouth and wiped it off on the skirt of his tunic. That was even fairly appropriate if you knew what a tasty morsel it was.

Metaphorically speaking.

Mining in Rammelsberg had started not long after Charlemagne and lasted a continuous thousand years, only ending in the 1980s.

The officer of the *fiscus* muttered under his breath, his fingers moving in patterns on the table, as if he was flicking the markers on a counting board: "Call that sixty-five hundred talents of silver annually, thirty-nine milliards of denarii, minus costs of..."

The Emperor brought them down to earth:

"Let's not try to shear the sheep before we have it in the pen, gentlemen," he said evenly. "But this is important news. Money is the fuel of war, and war is, alas, necessary to safeguard and extend the *imperium* of the Senate and People of Rome. Silver on that scale turns this from a sorrowful...and expensive... necessity to an opportunity to secure both our frontiers *and* our treasury, without a lasting increase in taxation."

He wasn't having the visceral reaction most of the others were, but there was an ironic acknowledgment in the glance he gave the American, a sort of tip of the hat thank you.

Artorius had just solved two difficulties for him at the same time; the long-term financial problem of paying for incorporating the *Barbaricum* or big chunks thereof into the Empire, and the political one of getting his inner circle—and eventually at least most of the senatorial class—on board with his new policy despite its up-front costs in men and money. No individual senator or even clan could oppose the Imperial will...but Emperors who alienated too *many* important, wealthy, powerful families usually didn't have long lifespans.

Precious metals were technically an Imperial monopoly, but visions of leases to exploit them under contract were certainly already running through any number of heads. The necessary *societās* and *collegia*—the closest things Romans had to joint-stock companies—would be handled by businessmen of equestrian rank as far as the management went, but a lot of the money would come from the upper aristocracy and even more would...

Flow right back into their hot little hands. Making the rich richer is always popular. With the rich.

Plenty would spill over along the way to encourage swift Romanization of the new territories, not least by luring settlers from the older provinces. And rich mines made farming anywhere within reach profitable as well to feed their labor force; plus they bred cities, whose own demands bred villas and villages around them.

And within reach is the operative word, but in a year or two...or five...we'll introduce long-distance canals with miter locks, starting small; hard graft, but a lot more doable right away than railroads. The Chinese have already built big chunks of their Grand Canal; ultimately there's no reason we can't join the Mediterranean and the Atlantic...the Bourbons did that in France in the seventeenth century...and the North European Plain all the way from there to the Baltic and Black Seas...eventually, to the Volga and the Caspian. And link the Danube and the Rhine as well. That'll cut transport costs to a fraction of the overland haulage prices and feed plenty into the Mediterranean too.

He'd also just given the wealthy men *here* a leg up on the process of exploiting the new mines, which would make them happy, and he'd given the Emperor vast new patronage to hand out. Bassus, governor of Pannonia Superior, had a calculating look in his eye; at a guess he was wondering who'd get the governorship of the *new* provinces.

The high-ranking freedman from the *fiscus* was virtually squirming in delight. Better than three-quarters of the Empire's revenues went to the military and there was never, ever enough. The Spanish mines of the High Imperial period were so massive that they had left traces across the globe. Scientists in his own time had detected their airborne pollution as far away as deep-drilled ice cores from Greenland.

The prospect of duplicating that revenue flow had the treasury man nearly in ecstasy. Everyone else was fairly happy too, enough that there was only a little well-disguised grumbling when the Emperor told them that Marcus Claudius Fronto would be the second-in-command when he arrived in the spring with the Eleventh Claudian Legion from Durostorum on the lower Danube.

As the room emptied, Marcus Aurelius signaled Artorius to remain. He stood silent as the Emperor of the known world went from one end of the map to the other, close enough that his short-sighted eyes could see it all clearly.

Glasses, he thought. *We should be able to make a pair of glasses that'll help him. That's a medieval invention, thirteenth century, and we can skip the development phase.*

When he reached the Danube, he reached out a hand and Artorius put the pointer in it. It was marked off in Roman inches, and a scale at the bottom of the map showed the conversion into Roman miles, all units much easier for an American to think in than it would have been for a metric-raised European. The local foot was 11.65 American inches, and the inch *they* used was 0.97 percent of the one he'd grown up with. Roman miles were five thousand feet, very slightly more than nine-tenths of his.

The Emperor measured the distance from Carnuntum to the Baltic Sea, and his lips moved as he used the new *Pannonius arithmetica* to calculate.

"Just as you said, about six hundred and forty miles...is there *any* truth in the story you have told of your origins, Tribune?" Marcus Aurelius said.

He'd dropped into Greek, which was what Roman aristocrats often did when they wanted to keep a conversation between themselves private from the help. This wasn't a culture where anyone important could expect to be truly alone very often. The Praetorians at parade rest just inside the door with their scorpion-blazoned shields presumably spoke only Latin, or at least he thought they did—and Artorius was willing to bet on his knowledge. The Guard regiments got nearly all their recruits in rural and small-town central and northern Italy in this period, anyway, where there weren't many Greek speakers.

I expected this but not so soon, as the man wrote on his tombstone, Artorius thought.

He fought down an impulse to bare his teeth, and his stomach clenched.

That's the downside of having a brilliant thinker and trained logician as boss. They notice things. And they draw conclusions wherever the logic leads them.

He licked his lips, and they were dry; this could get sticky. Everything was in the balance at this instant. He knew Marcus Aurelius by now . . . a little. But at seventh and last, he was a man of this century. How might he lash out?

"Just about all of what I said about where I . . . we . . . came from is *true*, sir . . . but I will admit it is not *complete* in some crucial respects. If you don't mind me asking, what made you think so?"

"I was not certain until today. Your new engines, the thunderpowder, the mathematics, all these might well simply come from a people with more knowledge of natural philosophy and the mechanic arts than ours. So could your knowledge of mapmaking. But why would a distant people . . . across the very ocean itself . . . know so much of the *Barbaricum* just north and east of the Empire? If your knowledge came from books—from Tacitus and his *Germania*, shall we say—then it would be limited by *ours*. I put that together with the puzzle of your appearance here on the middle Danube when you say you came from across the western ocean, and certain other facts, and eventually my doubts became certainties."

Artorius glanced involuntarily at the door the others had left through. Marcus Aurelius followed the thought without effort, and chuckled dryly:

"No, I have confided these doubts in nobody but Galen, and he shares my analysis . . . and is also a man who knows how and when to keep his mouth shut. The others"—he shrugged—"are now convinced of your worth as an oracle, and do not doubt your story of vast riches, nor will they likely bother to puzzle at how *you* know when once they accept that you *do*. And now that prospect of a war winning great wealth preoccupies their minds; some from greed, others seeing in it the good of the State. Many both, like Marcus Iallius Bassus. There is no harm in ambition securely yoked to duty. So if—"

The Emperor raised an eyebrow, and Artorius nodded confirmation that the deposits were really there.

"I do not doubt your claim is true, to the inch. You have yet to make one that was not borne out, some much more extraordinary than the location of a mine. What I would like to know, Tribune...what I *must* know, and must insist you tell me...is *how* you know what you know."

Artorius told him, down to the way they'd left Fuchs's laboratory and awakened here.

The Emperor's face remained impassive, as usual, except for the rise of his eyebrows; this was a man singularly difficult to startle. Artorius was close enough to see his pupils expand, though, and several times his breath caught.

Artorius concluded:

"It is...as if *you* were suddenly conveyed to the Troad in the days of Agamemnon and Achilles and Odysseus, sir. Or to the time of Romulus and Remus on the banks of the Tiber, when Rome was a new-founded village of thatched huts. But longer, for me and my companions. We came from the year...two thousand seven hundred and eighty-five *anno urbis conditae*."

Which was the equivalent of 2032, if you were counting from the legendary foundation of Rome in 753 BCE, a little under a thousand years before this night. He wasn't going to go into the putative future history of Christianity and its dating system just yet. It wouldn't necessarily happen that way now in any case.

He glanced over his shoulder to make sure the angles were right to conceal it from the guardsmen, and pulled out his phone.

"Mary and me, sequence one," he murmured in English. Then aloud: "If you would examine this, sir?"

Her picture appeared, holding little Maddy, and Vincent standing beside his father, then segued into another view.

Marcus Aurelius nodded, and came to look at the picture. He reached out a wondering finger and touched the surface of the phone, blinking until the alien medium suddenly became real to him, and then murmuring astonishment at the lifelike rendering and the way pictures appeared and disappeared.

"Almost like sorcery in truth...but perhaps merely art, refined by many centuries. Your first wife, your children?" he said, when the sequence froze at the first shot again.

"Yes, sir. Severed from me forever, and probably...almost certainly...dead," Artorius said as he tapped the phone closed and put it back in his tunic's pocket.

"Ah, that is a great grief, and I can see that you feel it keenly. Yet you bear it manfully, and do not let pain crush your spirit, recognizing that love is a loan from fortune, not a gift that we may securely possess. I am sorry for your loss, Tribune, much though it has rebounded to my advantage, and that of Rome. That was this war you said sent you into exile? That you now say destroyed the mechanism that delivered you to the neighborhood of Vindobona, across the gulf of years?"

"Yes. Compared to the weapons used, the thunderpowder you have seen is as a little child's toy wooden sword. Or as a figure scrawled on a wall by an idler with a stick of charcoal is to *this*," he added, tapping the phone.

Then the Emperor fell silent for long minutes, walking to the window and gazing out through the thick, wavy, rain-streaked glass before he turned back. Artorius' tension grew.

"One thousand, eight hundred and sixty-six years," he said quietly at last. "I believe you; the alternative is that the Gods are making sport of us...and I do not think They do so, whatever Homer and the other poets wrote. And hence your knowledge of arts arcane to us, as Agamemnon or Aeneas would know nothing of the forging of iron or the building of aqueducts in the Age of Bronze. And once all men wandered, living by the hunt, and dressed only in skins, long before Troy...What would *they* make of Rome, or Alexandria or Athens, with their myriads of folk and great buildings?"

"Yes, sir," Artorius said. "Knowledge accumulates over the years. And past a certain point, if certain discoveries are made, knowledge breeds knowledge faster and faster. But knowledge is not the same as wisdom...witness the way only unimaginable flight saved us from a war fought with the weapons of Gods, but wielded by ordinary men consumed with fear and hate. Men willing to see a whole world go down to destruction, if only they could take their enemies with them."

The Emperor stroked his beard. "You bring us knowledge as Prometheus brought men the gift of fire, something that may warm in winter or cook a meal...or burn them to death in the ashy ruins of their homes. Yet something of us remains in your time, apparently."

"Yes sir, though our knowledge is incomplete," Artorius said.

Marcus Aurelius suddenly laughed, his grave face growing lively for a moment.

"Thus your tears of joy at reading all of Euripides, as your lady wife Julia told me! And she mentioned your Jewish client's *dance* of joy when he saw Claudius' histories! You knew only a few of the great playwright's works in your time? The histories of my predecessor were lost?"

"Precisely, sir. Though your book of philosophy—it is called *The Meditations of Marcus Aurelius*—that *did* survive. I kept it with me when I served my own Republic in war, to ponder in my moments of rest. I'm afraid I've quoted it to you, passing off your wisdom as mine, but it sustained me in a dark and bloody time."

The Emperor laughed again; twice in one day was unusual for him.

"Is it passing off another's work as your own, if you quote something not yet written? Most of it will probably be nothing but my poor renderings of Zeno, Diogenes and Attalus."

He sobered. "And is it possible, then, to frustrate the Fates and turn the river of time from its course?"

"I do not know with certainty," Artorius said honestly. "But I am convinced that it is. The man who invented the device for traveling upstream against the current of time thought so. And much of what we have already introduced here, things that now spread widely and cannot be expunged, would not have been thought of for centuries, some not for many centuries. The footrest saddle, Marcus' paper and printing, distilling, thunderpowder. Filipa's mathematics, Paula's preventative for childbed fever, Jeremey's new crops, and the rest. And these will change the course of events in ways no mortal man can foretell."

"This war with the Germanii we are fighting? It happened in your . . . your history? So odd, to think of there being more than one! Yet has not every man said to himself, *if only* I had done this otherwise or decided that differently, how changed my life would be? And as for men, so with cities and with empires."

"Yes it did, and you won it, though at great cost and with much loss," Artorius said. "But it took you fourteen years, and exhausted you and the Empire, and ultimately your successors—"

Let's not mention that that means your son Commodus the tyrant and prancing Neronian-style lunatic. Not just yet.

"—abandoned what you had taken. Ill came of that."

"Ah," the Emperor said; his face became intensely thoughtful. "And that you are from the years yet to come puts some of your advice in a different light . . . yes, indeed. For instance, at your wedding you told me that suppression of the Christian cult would not work well...that too was foreknowledge?"

"Yes, sir. The Christians of my time were descendants of those of this age, and they had a saying: *the blood of the martyrs is the seed of the Church.*"

The Emperor's brows went up. "Were you a Christian yourself?"

"Not as a man of full years, sir, no. My study of philosophy...and the experiences of my life...convinced me that the world was not such as a single all-knowing and all-benevolent deity would fashion."

"Indeed, that seems reasonable. Though not certain; would merely human thought be able to fully fathom the plan of such a God?"

Artorius chuckled. "That argument was made to me, sir! But many of my family remained steadfast in that faith; my wife, for one."

Marcus Aurelius nodded again, his brows knotting in thought.

"And tell me then, does Rome fall in the end, as Troy did and Athens after, and Alexander's empire later still? Despite our pretensions to empire without limits or end?"

"Yes, sir. Though not in your time; three and a half centuries from now. Then there is...will be...was...a long age of darkness and ignorance and petty wars before civilization advanced again. But memories of Rome remained, of her greatness, even the ruins of which spread awe. And memories of the Roman peace that stretched so far, for so long. Hence my own country of America was ruled by a Senate from a domed building with Corinthian columns and marble floors, and statues in niches! I...and my companions...hope to aid you, so that there will be no fall, and no end to that wonderful peace either in time or space. No terrible war such as destroyed our world. Instead *one* world, *one* law and *one* strong hand enforcing universal peace. Truly an *imperium sine fine.*"

Marcus Aurelius nodded soberly. "That too explains a great deal. Why you spoke of Rome as...something seen from a distance. Now I know it was a distance of years more than miles. But this must remain between us! You did right to keep the secret, for it would sow fear and unpredictable chaos if revealed. Does any other know?"

"Only Josephus the merchant, sir. He is a man of very keen

wit, and he saw us just after we...arrived, and deduced that we arrived by no normal means. He even noticed that the coins we brought all looked new minted! But he has proven...very reliable, and a true friend. To the best of my knowledge, he and you are the only human beings of this time who know the truth, and he is fully with me in the plan to strengthen Rome."

"Let us keep it so, then. Or nearly so; Galen will have to know, and he can bear the knowing. I trust his discretion implicitly, and it would be very useful for him to know the *source* of the medical knowledge he finds so confounding."

He looked at the map again, shaking his head. "Let us hope that together we can—"

He moved his hand from left to right in a sweeping gesture, indicating the stretch of miles.

And of years, Artorius thought.

"—draw an even better map than this, eh, Tribune?"

By God, this is a man I can follow!

❧ CHAPTER TWENTY-FIVE ❦

Exploratores camp, north of the Danube,
Kingdom of the Marcomanni,
Barbaricum of Germania Libra
April 4th, 167 CE

Back in the Rangers, by God, Artorius thought, in the chilly light of first dawn, with a mixture of anger and resignation.

The Emperor would, as Mark puts it, plotz *if he knew I were here. But* we need *this intelligence data and need it badly. Otherwise it's going to be hard to get enough force assigned for long enough. Everyone screams when their particular part of the frontier is stripped, understandably so, but . . .*

Trees stood all round them, old-growth hardwood, oak and beech, lime and ash and hornbeam, most with straight trunks and crowns of tender-green new leaves high above, filling the air with an intense green smell mixed with pungencies and odd drifts of sweetness. It was open at ground level, save here and there where a fallen tree let in sunlight through the canopy and produced a riot of saplings and brush.

This was the sort of mission the Rangers pulled, or the Special Forces of various breeds. For the Romans, that meant what they called *exploratores*—scouts.

There were eight of them here, plus himself and Sarukê and Filipa; he judged the latter wasn't enough of a handicap to outweigh having the former, and they *did* need someone good at it to wrangle the horses, since they were all mounted but the mission would mean a lot of time on foot. The rest of the ex-gladiators were back guarding the other three Americans, thank God.

The eight Roman scouts were wildly varied, from someone who was what he'd have called an Arab and who considered himself a Nabatean by the name of 'Abdu l-'Uzzá, the noncom in charge of the squad, to a lavishly tattooed redhead from somewhere near Hadrian's Wall. They all spoke reasonable Latin and all had a certain cat-quiet feeling, as if they would always land in a crouch if suddenly picked up and thrown in the air.

They'd all taken up his suggestion of hooded tunics and leggings tie-dyed in what he thought of as camo patterns with loops for bits of vegetation, and they were all lightly equipped with sword, knife and bow—except that Artorius and Filipa were carrying crossbows instead, and he took the lariat of braided rawhide from his saddle and looped it bandolier fashion from left shoulder to right hip.

Crossbows because you don't have to start in your cradle to get good with them, he thought ironically. *Not all that different from a rifle, learning-wise. The lariat because roping a man and a calf are basically similar.*

They all saddled their horses—with the new style of gear—and strapped their bedrolls behind the cantles. Filipa went from one beast to the next, pouring out some cracked grain fodder on the ground for each; after the scouts left on foot she'd bring them buckets of water from a pond nearby. Well-fed and well-watered horses were ready for sudden effort; they were also much quieter and less given to trying to stray.

Plus she's just good at getting horses to do what she wants; good when we arrived, even better since. And the horses think it's their idea.

They hadn't made a fire when they camped here, just gnawed hardtack and cheese and pieces of salted ham last night, with hardtack and dried apricots for a change this morning. A little more of the fruit had gone into their pouches. Artorius approved of that last; the sugar would give the immediate energy boost you needed. And they'd all crushed handfuls of leaves and rubbed the juices on their bodies strategically to hide the distinctive human smell.

This bunch are probably absolute hell on deer in their spare time, he thought. *Not to mention boar, bears, wolves and aurochs.*

Filipa looked up from soothing the mounts to keep them quiet and checking that their reins were properly over the picket line in a double loop, ready to be flipped free but immune to a straight pull.

"Like a national park," she said softly and wistfully, in English, looking up at the great trees through the umbrous green haze and obviously remembering camping trips and long hikes. "Even a bit like Muir Woods."

"More like a DMZ," Artorius said, also softly, and bent to span his crossbow and slip a quarrel into the groove.

She did likewise, but he went on when she looked puzzled at the term, showing that she hadn't actually been *born* in Korea. Or possibly she'd only discussed it with Korean speakers, who'd say *bimujangjidae* instead.

"Demilitarized zone. Buffer territory. The German tribes keep an unpopulated area around their core lands, nice and natural for hunting ... and hunting each other, and hiding raiding parties to keep life on the farm from getting dull. But it is pretty, yes."

The more so as the sun climbed minute by minute, birds flitted between the boughs, and red squirrels chittered; there weren't enough humans, or enough noise, to scare them off. Somewhere close a heavy weight crashed through some brush; everyone glanced that way, but only for an instant—it was wild boar, a distinctive sound, followed by snorting flatulent grunts. Boar could move quietly when they wanted to but generally didn't bother, assuming that anything that knew what they were would avoid *them*.

Sarukê touched Filipa on the shoulder with a smile, and then slipped away. The Arab went with her, and the others after him. Artorius touched a finger to his brow to Filipa and brought up the rear.

She's not safe *here and she knows it,* he thought, remembering the taut alertness of her face. *I'd rather be where I am than all alone with eleven horses in the middle of the woods. But she's more worried about Sarukê than herself, and bearing up very well. Not a combat virgin anymore, really. Though not a combat slut like me.*

They were heading north and slightly east, advancing from one terrain feature to another according to memorized mental maps. This was far from the first time that *exploratores* from the Danubian legions and auxiliaries had crossed the river, and fortunately only a few of them had gone east with the *vexilliationes* sent against the Parthians. You relied on men with local experience for scouting work, when you could.

Artorius felt a little quiet pride that none of them found him a burden in the sneaking-through-the-woods department; they'd trained together enough on the Roman side of the river to establish that, and for Sarukê too.

He'd been a bit surprised that someone raised on the steppe was so good in thick forest. *She'd* been surprised when he asked. It turned out that besides her experience living around Sirmium and traveling throughout most of the middle Danube country with Josephus for the last few years, her particular tribe's home territory was in what he thought of as *western* Ukraine, south of the site of Kiev-that-wasn't-yet and westward from the right bank of the Dnipro. Most of that was open grassland, but also a fair bit of forest; along the rivers, fringing it to the north, and islands of woodland in the steppe gradually thinning out toward the Black Sea.

They traded and hunted in those woods, too, and also feuded with and raided the farmers who lived northward. From her rather contemptuous descriptions those were probably some sort of pre-proto-Slavs or possibly early Balts. Sarukê's account of them made the Germanii of the *Barbaricum* look like miracles of techno-cool urban sophistication by comparison.

Some time later:

"*Goo-ko. Goo-ko. Goo-ko.*"

The Sarmatian's voice sounded, in an excellent imitation of the call of a cuckoo—even in a descending minor third, which was the type of call it gave specifically this time of year.

"*Goo-ko. Goo-ko. Gooo-koo.*"

That was the agreed signal for *found the trail, trail empty now*; three times, a pause, then three again. The actual bird sometimes went on for twenty calls or more, but not consistently, so the pattern was recognizable if you were expecting it but just forest noise if you weren't. Cuckoos weren't common in dense forest, but finding them along a deer path was quite likely.

More light came from ahead, and there was brush, unlike the cathedral openness of most of the woods they'd traversed in the last couple of hours. And a yeasty-musky smell like turned earth and barnyard. Artorius slowed, came up beside her where she knelt beside a scrubby hazel, drifting like a ghost or whisp of smoke.

"Not only deer," she said very softly, without turning her head.

He looked both ways along the curving track. It had undoubtedly started as a game trail, following the contours of the land, often ones so slight a human couldn't detect them. There were fresh scars on nearby trees, at head height from beasts rubbing itching antlers in the spring, or lower down and made by boar, and swatches of cinnamon-brown hair where bears had used bark to deal with an itch; he could faintly smell the scat of them. But there were also human footprints, and the prints of horse hooves, unshod variety, horse dung and the occasional marks riders would make. An inconvenient low branch lopped off by a blade, for example, or a gnawed pig bone with cut marks on it tossed aside.

Artorius turned, smooth and quick. The Nabatean grinned at him, snaggle teeth in the green dimness; he'd been *very* quiet, but knew he'd been sensed.

"Block force back around bend, *there*. Me, three men," he said, in fluent but guttural Latin; it reminded him of the Praetorian Prefect's accent, but much stronger. "I lead that? Hidden until you shout, that for signal?"

Artorius nodded, and the dark man ghosted away; you couldn't do final arrangements until you'd eyeballed the terrain.

Though I sorely miss tac-net mikes and earbuds, he thought. *Wouldn't mind a nice silent flight of AI drones, either.*

The scout from north Britannia grinned at him too through a wild red beard with tattoos swirling beneath it, and drifted over to an oak tree ten yards east and across the trail, accompanied by another scout who was slight and dark and also came from Britannia—but from what had become Wales later.

The last two were from Pannonia—they could talk to the Brits in their respective Celtic dialects with a bit of trouble, though the two groups apparently found each other's accents hilariously thick and strange—and settled down directly across from him. Between them stretched a braided leather rope they rubbed into the soft dirt with artful handfuls of mud and leaves to cover it. They took half hitches around convenient trees at both ends, and then became very difficult to see.

The mechanics of an ambush are different here, Artorius thought. *You don't need to worry about sprays of automatic fire hitting your own men.*

Then they all squatted or knelt in their selected cover and

waited. There was a quarter moon and they'd wait until it set, early next morning. If nothing came along the trail by then, they'd go home. Which would be very bad because that would raise the possibility that they'd been lured into a trap by a double agent.

Artorius noted with amusement that Sarukê used the same technique for keeping limber while not moving that he did; you clenched and relaxed each muscle group in turn at long intervals, shifting very slightly. Probably hunters had worked that one out as far back as there were human beings, or possibly some *Homo heidelbergensis* genius had skull sweated it behind their thick shelf of brow ridge several ice ages ago. He'd learned it from his father on hunting trips, and refined it in the Rangers.

A final glance made sure that nobody was visible from the trail; and if you stayed very quiet, you didn't frighten bird and beast into silence either. That could be a dead giveaway, if the other side included anyone woods-wise, which the attendants of a German war chief most certainly would.

They waited while the sun crept higher. He let his mind sink into the moment, strings of thought drifting in meaningless slowness through his consciousness, until sensations—even a mosquito bite—were just there, without stopping in your forebrain to *mean* anything or invite thought. He knew from experience that you were extraordinarily hard to see when you were in that state, for some reason. Even if you were in plain sight, which he wasn't.

A rufous fox came trotting by unconcerned within arm's length of him, then took his scent when the light breeze shifted and did a comical double take. Followed by a horrified sideways leap, and a leaf-spewing scurry into the trailside brush. Even his smile at the sight was distant and fleeting.

Later ... hours later when he checked by turning his eyes upward to catch the position of the sun through the leaves ... Sarukê's head moved very slightly westward. Artorius cocked his head, breathing out softly and letting the sounds sink in, and setting a hand palm down on a patch of bare dirt. Definitely the soft thudding of multiple unshod hooves on moist ground.

"*Goo-ko. Goo-ko. Gooo-koo.*"

The second use of that meant: *enemy in sight*. The Nabatean's call was a bit less convincing than Sarukê's, but then he hadn't grown up with cuckoos. It would do, to anyone who wasn't in this state of trance-like immediacy.

The hoofbeats came closer and closer. Then the first two horsemen came around the gradual bend about a hundred yards eastward at a fast walk. They were Marcomanni, young men... too young to raise much of a beard... with hair knotted on the right side of their heads, yellow-brown and dark-brown respectively, carrying spears and bright-painted hexagonal wooden shields, their clothing and cloaks drab. Both had cuts on their left cheeks, scabbed over—a mark of mourning and a pledge of vengeance, probably for fathers or elder brothers killed in the multiple disasters their people had suffered since last year.

Behind them came another clump of men, half a dozen strong. Their clothing was the same Germanic pattern of long-sleeved tunic jacket and cloak and narrow-tailored cloth pants with soft leather shoes or low boots, but colorfully patterned in ways not common here among the Suebic tribes north of the Danube. And they and the older man just behind them had different haircuts—cut closer at the sides, long on top, brushed back and braided into a queue at the rear.

Several of them also wore mail shirts and had helmets slung at their saddlebows, and they all had swords as well as spears, ranging from Roman-style *spathae* to long single-edged choppers.

The older man was a graying blond in his forties, with striped clothes under his mail shirt and one of the long cutting weapons at his waist; his shield was round and slung over his back, painted with a stylized raven. There was a man of his own age beside him, a Marcomanni richly dressed but in the checked style that group preferred, with long dark hair in the Suebic side knot and a golden torc around his neck. *His* remaining followers were apparently bringing up the rear, another half-dozen men.

Just what we wanted and what the spy said would be coming this way, Artorius thought. *The ones with the different haircuts are from well west of here, west and north. Everyone traveling fast and light, an envoy from the Marcomanni coming back with a panjandrum to talk business with his peers, and only a couple of pack horses for baggage.*

Then he stepped into the trail, and the first two Germanii pulled up in confusion. That they'd probably never seen anyone dressed as he was or carrying a crossbow probably added to their startlement.

"*Uzlaubīth!*" he shouted, which in the local tongue meant...

"*Surrender!*"

"*Surrender in the name of Rome!*"

He didn't expect them to *do* that, but it was as good a signal to the Nabatean and his men as any.

"*Rūmōnīz!*" one of the young Marcomanni pair in the lead shouted, in horror and rage. "*Romans!*"

Well, yeah, using the word Romans *loosely,* drifted through his mind. *Come on, let's see some hormonally driven youthful aggression, boys.*

The two youngsters kicked their horses into motion, spears held level and point forward above their heads. Even then he noted that they were using old-style Roman four-horn saddles... but that their chief further back had one of the new type with stirrups. Things did spread...

He brought the crossbow up. It had a simple ring as the rear sight, and a post on a bridge over the forward stock. Then he waited until the man was only about ten yards away, breathed out, stroked the trigger—

Tung.

Recoil thumped the stock back into his shoulder.

Almost immediately followed by a heavy meaty *thwack* sound. The leading Marcomanni went over his horse's crupper with the short, thick bolt buried to the feathers in his chest just to the right of the breastbone, and a spray of bright blood bursting out of his mouth as he fell, bounced, twitched once, and slumped.

This is where that M7 would have come in really *handy, and Fuchs was a fool,* some distant part of his mind thought, as he let the forward end of the crossbow drop, put his left foot in the stirrup and hauled back with both hands.

There was a sharp click as the string engaged the trigger mechanism; the pull was two hundred fifty pounds, not hard with both arms and when you were able to put your torso and leg into the draw.

Then he slung it and *unslung* the lariat.

I could have finished off all the ones we don't want to take alive nice and quick and safe with one magazine of six-point-eight. Safe is good. Christ but I hate this part of the job. Though not as much as what's coming. So much for the quiet life of a professor at Harvard... though if I'd stayed there I'd be finely divided particulate matter now... for a truly weird value of "now."

When he straightened and began to whirl the lasso, the second Marcommanic youth was falling too. Sarukê had shot him through the throat with a slashing broadhead, and he landed sprattling and coughing and flailing for a moment before he went limp as the blood pressure to his brain dropped. Artorius pivoted aside from the bolting mount of the man he'd killed with a swaying motion, annoyed at the interruption.

"Damn!" he said.

The horse went by close enough to stagger him a little; Sarukê dodged nimbly and whipped her bow across the backside of the second as it followed the first. In the depths of their dim little alarm-prone herbivore minds horses associated their stable or turnout pasture with home and safety, so that would likely be where they were heading. When a lathered horse in eye-rolling panic with an empty saddle splashed with blood came galloping in, people took notice.

"We're on the clock now," he said, realized he'd spoken in English, and dropped back into Latin:

"*Nunc cito!* Quickly now!"

The western chief's sworn guardsmen reacted with commendable speed, kicking their horses forward and screaming war cries. The twenty-yard gap between them and the Marcomannic vanguard—

Or between the visitors and their locally sourced Polish mine detectors, Artorius thought. *Well, brave lads, you Marcomanni say a ghost walks unless avenged. Sleep well, a bunch of assholes who used you as a live-but-soon-to-be-dead tripwire are about to join you.*

—was just enough for them to get their speed a bit up above a canter; the trail only had room for two abreast, and the others were eager behind them. They were building to a gallop with their spears held back for the first lunge at the pair of helpless unmanly archers when the four hidden *exploratores* heaved back in unison on their rope from both sides of the trail.

It snapped up under their horses' fetlocks, equivalent to a human's ankle and with similar results, except that tripping and falling at speed was even more serious for something weighing eight hundred pounds and carrying a man in armor than it would be for the man alone.

The first two horses were taken completely by surprise, and went down forward as if their legs had been sliced off with a supernally sharp ax. They screamed high and shrill and ear-shatteringly loud as they slammed down headfirst, throwing their riders in front of them. The screams of one ended abruptly as its neck snapped, and the whole weight of the beast toppled over and came down with a thud Artorius felt through his boot soles as much as he heard it.

Its rider had only time enough for a very *brief* scream of his own, before he disappeared under the beast and lay equally limp and thoroughly...

Squished, Artorius thought.

The other horse kept screaming, because it was still alive as it lay threshing and bugling with bulging eyes, with broken bones poking shards through the skin of its forelegs illustrating exactly *why* horses were righteously nervous about falls. Its rider flew free and even then tried to do a tuck and roll in midair.

Unfortunately for him that was extremely difficult when fully armed and in forty pounds of mail shirt with only a second or two to do it; his shield went one way, his spear another and he landed on his right shoulder, which was better than on the face and neck but still very not good. There was an audible *snap*, and he reared up to his knees clutching at his right shoulder with his left hand. His face contorted for a shriek of agony, but he didn't have time.

That rearing motion put him in position to take Sarukê's next arrow just above the bridge of his nose, the bodkin point designed to pierce armor snapping through the bone on both sides and the brain between. He collapsed, bent in a bow, with his knees still in the dirt and his suddenly limp body falling backward until his helmeted head hit the trail. The gray feathers of the arrow pointed directly backward between his sightless eyes.

The four *exploratores* on either side of the trail had dropped their rope as soon as the hideous perfection of the surprise hit the two horses' legs, snatching up their bows—the dark Silure and his redheaded Briganti friend both used yew longbows, the Pannonians the composite recurves that were the Roman Army's archers' standard weapon.

One of the riders managed to slug his mount back onto its haunches before it ran into the tangle of dead and dying human and horse flesh before it. The other three were crow-hopping and sidling and frantically wheeling, as their riders instinctively struggled to regain control and the horses even more instinctually and desperately dodged running into an obstacle.

Two arrows hit the superb rider as his mount reared, and the horse stood shivering and stared in bewilderment at the bleeding corpse at its feet. A sleet of shafts emptied the other three saddles in the next four seconds or so. Sarukê took an instant to send one into the injured horse, probably an act of mercy.

She *liked* horses.

The two chieftains had just time enough to grasp what was going on before the forward part of their party ceased to be. Both reacted instantly; the Marcomanni shouted:

"*Fleuhadiz!*"

Which was an emphatic way to say *flee!* or *run awaaaaay*! and he suited deed to word, hauling on the reins to turn his horse.

Unfortunately for him the western chief he was riding beside tried to do exactly the same thing and draw his long sword at the same time, and they lost a little time as their mounts jostled in the tight space, already upset by the sound of horse pain and the scent of blood. The Marcomanni rearguard were already under way by then, and charged around the curve in the trail to lead and clear the way for their chieftain, with getting out of bowshot of five good archers an added bonus.

That put them out of sight but in easy earshot. The chorus of human and equine screams as they met the Nabatean and his half squad at fatally close range halted the flight of the two chiefs in its tracks, amplified by the quartet of riderless horses that came back around the bend.

Everyone here understood the principle of following up surprise and not letting an enemy get his mental feet back underneath him; that fear-struck bewilderment was a big part of what magnified your force when you took someone unawares.

Artorius already had his lariat whirling as he dashed forward. Skills he'd practiced in endless hours as a teenager had come back quickly, and now the weighted loop flew out and opened wide as the western chief turned his horse to confront the *exploratores* dashing in. It must have been about then that he realized they were throwing down their bows because they wanted to take him alive.

He obviously also knew that for him being taken alive was quite literally a fate *worse* than death, and started to spur toward the Pannonians on the south side of the trail, to break through or at least force them to kill him. He'd probably also never seen a lariat and possibly never even heard of one; their use in this era started quite a ways east of here. It settled neatly around the man's shoulders from behind, and Artorius set his feet and hauled with a half hitch around his left forearm. That wrenched savagely as the line came taut; he'd used a bronze hondo ring rather than an open knot, and the noose whipped tight automatically.

The blond chieftain flew over the rump of his horse and thumped down on his back, knocking the wind out of him with an explosive grunt. The *exploratores* pounced in a flurry of kicks; one connected with an elbow and set the slashing sword spinning away. He tried to rise, but another kick went home in a belly, accompanied by one to the small of the back that brought a breathy grunt of pain. A Pannonian took the opportunity to shove a ball of knotted cloth into the man's gaping mouth and tie the rag tails together behind his head; they all had a couple of those tucked through their belts.

Heaving and muffled shouting followed as hands and ankles were trussed; the black-haired Silure caught the horse he'd just come off and the others slung him over the saddle and lashed him in place.

The Marcomannic chief was a quick thinker; he decided that the two Romans he'd seen step out into the way at its eastern end must be all of the blocking force there, took a chance and headed straight for them with his sword raised to break through and get home. His horse took the piled bodies in a soaring leap and landed neatly, its rider taking full advantage of the new stirrups to cushion his landing and leave him poised to strike.

Artorius and Sarukê skipped to opposite sides of the trail. The American drew his sword, which caught the man's eye; he probably discounted the Sarmatian's bow because he knew the enemy didn't *want* to kill him. In a sense making them do that would be a victory.

The American darted in, and beat the lunging leftward stab of the Marcomannic chief's spatha aside with his own, a hard ringing *clang* as metal met metal. That would have let the man ride on homeward at a pace nobody on foot could match...except that from point-blank range on the other side of the trail Sarukê shot him in the knee with neat precision.

Illustrating that saying they have here, even Hercules can't fight two. *Except with grenades, now...*

The chieftain screamed in surprise; so did the horse, as the shaft from the powerful steppe bow slammed through flesh and bone and the flap of the saddle beneath, to prick the beast painfully. It spun in a circle; Artorius darted in, grabbed the left stirrup and heaved before the spinning horse buffeted him back, only a thump into a tree keeping him on his feet.

The scream became a squawk as the chieftain catapulted sideways. The arrow tore free of the saddle, and the beast stopped circling and simply ran eastward flat out, away from whatever had bitten it.

That let him see the Sarmatian economically clubbing the German across the back of the head with a two-handed swing of her bowstave, just hard enough to stun without endangering the knowledge inside the Marcomannic head. They cooperated in trussing the mumbling man, Sarukê shoving another of the pre-knotted cloth gags into his mouth. Artorius let a long breath out as he looked up and saw the Nabatean and his squad trotting around the curve of the trail, waving that all was well and leading a dead Germanii's horse.

"Ambush so pretty-pretty. When it work," Sarukê said.

She visibly decided with a glance not to bother yanking the arrow out of the Marcomannic chief's knee; it would do to plug the wound right now, and *taken alive* did not mean *uninjured.* The prisoners were going to be wrung dry, and then probably end up as heads on spears and headless corpses slung into pits anyway.

Geneva was the Roman town of Genava right now and nobody had heard of the Convention.

"And a *failed* ambush is a nightmare," Artorius observed.

She nodded with a grimace. "How I be gladiatrix," she said.

The Sarmatian slid her recurve into the combined bowcase-quiver at her belt and took the reins of the horse carrying the Marcomannic captive, holding them gently but firmly not far under the jaw, and trotted off. The redheaded Britannian had the other horse, and the two of them took the lead; Artorius followed, and the rest deployed in a semicircle after them.

They'd be going back faster than they'd come—jog a hundred paces, a slow run for another hundred, jog a hundred. Usually you stopped for a brief rest every hour when you used that pace, but they only needed three hours to make the rendezvous... which would be a little before sundown. That pace could run horses to death, though fortunately they didn't have that far to go.

Very fortunately, because sure as fate they're going to chase us, Artorius thought grimly.

Well, it could be worse, he reminded himself, catching the murderous glare of the blond chief from the west as he bounced in his position belly down over the horse's back.

If you were the one shot in the knee and tied over a horse for transport to the interrogatores, *for instance.*

⤜ CHAPTER TWENTY-SIX ⤛

North of the Danube,
Kingdom of the Marcomanni,
Barbaricum of Germania Libra
April 4th, 167 CE

"They come," the Nabatean said two hours later, rising from where he'd been pressing his ear to the forest floor. "Many horses."

This would be a perfect time for extraction by chopper, Artorius thought. *Or maybe a tiltrotor. Fly away and leave the locals biting their thumbs and stamping their feet and pouting.*

Instead they simply pressed the pace. He looked up and took the time. A little less than two hours to sunset, which would make it just before the eleventh hour in local reckoning; he still had trouble adjusting to the way the twelve hours of the sunrise-to-sunset Roman day shrank and expanded drastically depending on the season. Which this far north meant that summer hours were *much* longer.

And the ones chasing us are mounted, he thought, looking over his shoulder. *Not as much of an advantage as it would be in open country, but this is climax forest, mostly fairly open. And it's not far enough for humans to outrun horses.*

You *could* do that.

Which was why armies in the old days...or these days... left a trail of foundered horses; fit humans just had more long-range endurance. The only way cavalry could stay ahead of good infantry over a week or more was to have a bunch of remounts and change off frequently. The way Mongols would have done it in a thousand years from now ... or the way Sarukê's relatives did when foot soldiers tried to invade their steppe.

But over this distance, four hooves beat two feet, he thought unhappily; it took days to outmarch a horse. *They'll be traveling twice, three times as fast as us.*

Then he recognized the scar on a tree, and whistled sharply. The same sound came back at him—which meant Filipa was still alive, free and just ahead of them.

They all put on a burst of speed. Sarukê tore ahead, urging the horse she was leading into a trot and hanging on the saddle herself—and ignoring the man bound across it as he flopped and banged and whimpered.

Then they were in sight of the horses, where Filipa was stripping the reins from the picket line with swift skill. The Sarmatian tossed her the led horse's reins, ran right on past her, and vaulted into the saddle of her horse. It pivoted in place and she was galloping back northward past them with her knotted reins dropped on the saddlebow and an arrow on the string, teeth bared.

"I slow!" she shouted as she passed Artorius.

He took that as *I'll slow them down,* and didn't waste time on answering as he ran for his mount. His leap wasn't as spectacular as the Sarmatian's, but it got him into the saddle quickly.

"Move! Now!" he shouted at Filipa, who was hesitating.

She turned her horse. The two Britannians were already nearly out of sight heading for the Danube, and one of them had the leading reins of the captive's horse in his hands as they galloped.

Now it's our advantage; these horses are fresh except for the ones carrying the prisoners, and it doesn't matter if they founder as long as they hold out for the next little while. Whoever's chasing us has been going as fast as they could for a couple of hours now. Close bet. Either they'll catch up in time to kill us ... or they won't. Ain't war exciting?

The others followed, and then Filipa, with Artorius and the Nabatean bringing up the rear.

The swarthy man was grinning tautly and had an arrow on his string as he made the same calculations; he was the only other horse archer in the group.

"This Sarmatian, she one fine killing bitch!" he said.

There was a sound behind them of blurred shouting and

then a massive thudding sound, unmistakably a horse *hitting* something at speed.

Horses didn't like doing that.

"I doubt her. I wrong!" he added.

Artorius concentrated; riding at speed through a forest, even a hardwood climax forest with not much undergrowth in most places, wasn't easy. Sound was tricky in the woods, but...

Another shout, a choked off scream, and the massed thudding of hooves drew back a little, fading. Two horses came into sight, both galloping flat out. One was Sarukê's; but she was bent over the neck of her mount, and an arrow stood out of her back below the left shoulder. The other was a Marcomanni, one with a forked beard and a helmet with a bear crest, his torso covered in a tunic of metal scales on leather; he was gaining and drawing back his spear for a thrust.

The Nabatean fell off a little. He stood in the stirrups at the gallop and drew his bow in the thumb-ring eastern fashion, holding the draw for a long moment as trees flashed between him and his target. Then he loosed, the bowstring slapping his bracer.

"Too low!" Artorius cursed.

Then, in savagely enjoyable self-criticism: "No!"

'Abdu l-'Uzzá was either a very good shot—probably, given the way he'd quickly grasped the benefits of stirrups for mounted archery—or very lucky or both.

Both, Artorius decided.

The arrow flashed down the fifty yards of distance, barely missed the trunk of a hornbeam...and plunged into the left fetlock of the German's horse. Right at the joint; that *had* to be luck, you couldn't do that deliberately even with a sniper rifle and mildot sight at this range, not on a moving target you couldn't. Good luck, just as Sarukê running into a competent German archer was the opposite.

Plenty of the Germanic tribesmen *hunted* with bows, but only those who couldn't afford anything better took them to war.

Maybe they were having a deer hunt as part of this conference at the Barbarian United Nations & Let's Kill Romans Alliance. Not at all unlikely.

The wounded horse bugled shock and went over, its own speed and momentum ensuring disaster as the leg buckled; there was *another* massive thud as it pivoted and plowed left-shoulder-first and downward into the roots of an oak. That gave its rider only time for one startled yip before he smashed into the tree at thirty miles an hour himself... and the mass of his horse smashed into *him* at the same speed.

The tree remained stationary.

"I good killing bastard too!" the Nabatean shouted gleefully as he bent and clapped his heels to his mount's ribs.

Saruké's horse was slowing because she wasn't signaling it with heels and balance any more. Only the new saddle and a training that had begun as a toddler kept her from toppling off.

"I'm coming, Saruké!" Filipa shouted, and angled back.

"Oh, *hell*," Artorius said, and joined her.

What was it Plato had said about an army of lovers?

Right: "Or who would desert his beloved or fail him in the hour of danger?"

Seems he had a point. Filipa shouldn't be here! But then, arguably neither should I. Right now I feel the force of that argument more and more. Approaching spearpoints will do that.

Filipa came in on the Sarmatian's right side. She leaned far over, grabbed the other's right arm, and slid it over her own shoulder; her own left gripped the mane of the Sarmatian's horse and kept them close, galloping like a chariot team. Saruké's horse matched the speed of Filipa's automatically, from herd instinct. Artorius came in on the other side and snatched up the reins loose across the front of the saddle.

"Keep up!" he snarled, as he spurred forward and all three horses went to flat out.

He glanced over his shoulder, one of the benefits of equine autopilot driving. The beast did the detail work, which was great as long as you remembered horses weren't cars and didn't necessarily *want* to do what you wanted them to do.

Pursuers from *Marcomanni & Friends* were in sight, their spearpoints and the polished, gilded or silvered crests on many helmets catching the declining light from the west, along with the cold gray glitter of mail.

Lots of decorated helmets and lots of armor and lots of good well-mounted horsemen.

All three were serious status markers among the Germanic tribes.

Either there's a really exclusive Marcomannic polo club right

*around here, or we really did interrupt a high-level diplomatic
conference of bigshots. The ones with poor impulse control came
after us. Because they don't know what they're chasing us into,
and if they don't catch us before that...but they probably just
automatically thought they could cram us up against the Danube
and that would be that.*

They were in the floodplain of the great river now, a district
his century had called the Lobau; they were also following a
marked path that they'd checked out coming in yesterday. That
was another reason going out had been much slower than coming back.

The river was getting higher as the snows melted further
up. The trees got bigger around them with fertile soil and lots
of water, and then he blinked and squinted against the sudden
late-afternoon brightness as they came out into wet meadow
where the water table was too high for tree roots. Spurts of black
muck went flying from the pounding hooves of the horses, and
he could feel his mount starting to labor hard, panting like a
bellows between his knees. Patches of shallow pond glimmered,
with white water lilies just opening, buzzing with insects and
busy with the birds that fed on them.

Mud slowed them, and the shouts of the pursuers grew even
louder and even more savage as they saw bloody revenge laid out
before them like a varied, tasty buffet dinner.

Artorius looked over his shoulder again. The pursuers had
gained on them, and were closing rapidly. No more than a hundred yards, and he could hear their wolfish howling. Big shaggy
hounds ran with the horses. This might very well have *been* a
planned hunt in exactly the wrong place at the wrong time. That
was just the sort of thing the chieftains would do at a gathering,
along with drinking and boasting and sacrifices to the Gods and
occasional duels.

Bad luck for us, or bad luck for them, but I think for them,
went through him tautly. *Far too close, though.* Ask me for anything but time, *as the man said!*

They quartered left, and the pursuers gained again; some of
them tried to cut the cord of the movement, and he heard their
screamed curses as their horses bogged. Ahead of him 'Abdu
l-'Uzzá slowed for a second and shot behind him, the arrow zipping
uncomfortably close to Artorius' face. One of the bogged-down

men toppled off his horse and landed facedown and thrashing in the calf-deep water and mud, and two more jumped down to try and help him.

Artorius followed the Nabatean around the bend. Ahead the marsh grass was chest high on the horses, save where a sandspit reached through, dry and showing bare spots. The barge waited at the end of it, covered in another innovation—camouflage netting this time, studded with tufts of grass that hadn't had time to go limp. Crewmen with oars threw it off as the riders thundered into view.

A ramp led up to the tubby vessel, and the two Britannians took it scarcely slowing, with the crew ready to help secure the captives. Filipa was next, calling out to the men to handle Sarukê carefully and fetch the *medicus.*

Beyond the sandspit was fifty yards of open water, then a long, low island overgrown with willows and other water-loving trees. Artorius reined aside and turned his horse.

"Ready!" he called.

Worth it, he thought to himself.

A risk, but only a slight one.

Do some wholesale decapitation on the other side. And I do not like these proud and noble-savage sons of untamed nature and various bitches. No, I do not like them. At all. Not in the abstract, and not in the personal sense of being married to Julia now, and we have little Claudia and another child coming and a home to defend. Debellare superbos!

Half a century of Syrian archers rose out of the tall grass; he suspected that some of their guttural Aramaic war cries were curses on his name, for having them wait this long squatting ankle deep among the mosquitoes and leeches, with the added strain of keeping their beloved bows from damage by the damp and the skirts of their long tunics sopping up swamp water.

"Take it out on them, boys!" he called, pointing behind him.

"*Draw—*" the decurion in charge of the archers called. "*Shoot! Rapid!*"

The Germanic diplomats didn't see the men for a moment, with the blowing grass breaking their outlines. By the time they did they were well within range of the powerful laminated recurve bows, no more than fifty yards, and their hurtling pursuit turned to chaos as they tried to pull up. There was marsh on either side, deep and sticky. The gap of firm ground behind them had been easily wide enough for the *exploratores*, but it was badly crowded with forty or fifty riders.

The first flight of arrows slashed down just as the headlong rush slowed, and it continued to sleet long shafts until the decurion called out:

"Cease shooting! By *contubernium*, board the boat! Fast! *Fast!*"

They were trotting aboard when the two galleys came around the islet just offshore. One was busy for the next few minutes hooking and hauling up the buoy with the towing cable for the barge, and making it fast to the stanchions by the stempost. The barge lurched just as Artorius led his horse into its crowded hold, the last aboard; the beast snorted with laid-back ears, rolled its eyes and tried to rear, but he kept a firm grip on the bridle and calmed it.

"Soooo, boy, soooo," he said. "We're safe now. For now."

Tunnngg-*WHACK!*

A shell full of Roman Fire went by overhead. Artorius frowned; not the load he would have chosen...

He glanced around and grinned like a shark himself. The catapult crew *were* using their heads. It was good to have men fast on the uptake backing you.

They'd aimed high, and the twenty-five-pound load of ur-napalm landed *behind* the clot of chieftains and their retainers. The tall grass there was damp, but the firebomb had it burning briskly almost at once, with copious sparks and lots of thick black smoke.

Some of the men were shaking their fists at the galley, and doubtless cursing the unmanly distance weapons in end-stage Proto-Germanic. The smarter ones, mainly Marcomanni and Quadi who'd had some experience with the new Roman gear, were trying to flog their horses through the barrier of burning grass, or get around it without bogging their mounts.

Or just running through it afoot with their arms in front of their faces; those were the ones most likely to live to see next morning.

Just why that was a good idea arrived with another tunnngg-*WHACK!* as the catapult's throwing arms hit the stops. The fuse was different this time, the slight spitting trace of saltpeter-soaked cord rather than flaming cloth. They'd lit the fuse at just the right length, and...

CRACK!

The red spark and puff of smoke was right in the middle of the surviving riders. Hundreds of lead bullets flayed them. It wasn't quite like having a Victorian steam gunboat shooting up some luckless natives, but...

"Close enough for government work," he muttered to himself.
CRACK!

❧ CHAPTER TWENTY-SEVEN ❧

Municipium Aelium Carnuntum,
Capital of Pannonia Superior
April 5th, 167 CE

The evening of the following day Galen washed his hands in the bowl of alcohol-infused water on the table by the door, and stepped aside as he dried them.

"This takes me back to my earliest days as a physician," he said quietly.

Artorius nodded. He knew that the court doctor had started out treating gladiators in Pergamum, in what was here and now the Greek-speaking half of Asia Minor, west of the Proto-Kurds and Armenians and that odd easternmost clump of Celts known as Galatians.

The junior-officer bedchamber Filipa and the Sarmatian shared was now reorganized as a sickroom; the bed for Sarukê, a cot for the American, and a table for medications and fresh bandages in covered pots. There was a fire burning in the grate, with a clay pot of water bubbling quietly to supply sterile washings, and several lamps gave the little chamber a soft glow, with a faint scent of peaches as well as the sickroom smells.

Filipa was sitting by her partner's side now, holding her hand; Sarukê was dozing facedown, heavily dosed with a new tincture made of dried opium sap dissolved in alcohol. It was probably fairly close to classic Victorian-era laudanum.

Galen bent his head as he paused before leaving, so that they could speak privately.

"If only I had known then what I do now! The legionary doctor cleaned the Sarmatian woman's wound thoroughly, and he used the doubled superwine disinfectant liberally on his arrow spoon and the injury itself," he murmured. "I could not have done much better myself. But though this decreases infections drastically, it is not infallible, as you yourself pointed out to me."

Artorius nodded. "Especially if foreign matter remains in the wound," he said.

"Or if the arrow is dipped in dung," the Greek said, his narrow clever face somber. "Which I am told is often done by the barbarians here. I *am* sure there is no extensive nerve damage—there is feeling and movement in the arm and finger muscles. Full function may well return, if this infection subsides, but it is worrying."

He began packing his bag, and his hand lingered over a recent addition to it, besides the brass-and-leather stethoscope; a translation of *Gray's Anatomy*, with woodblock illustrations painstakingly copied from the original...which had been a paper version of the 2015 edition.

"I was so *close* to being right about so *much*!" he said, with soft bitterness, letting the well-thumbed pages fall closed.

"You were right about many things, more so than anyone else of this time," Artorius said sincerely. "And would have been even more so, if—"

"If the rules of superstitious dolts and cretins...and I must admit, my own squeamishness...had not kept me from doing human dissections!" he said. "What more might have Herophilus' students have done in Alexandria, three hundred years ago, if they had been allowed to continue his work! Those laws have crippled medicine ever since."

"But now you have the results of innumerable dissections," the American pointed out, nodding toward the thick tome.

"Yes, and your *stethoscope*, and even more the *microscope*, revealing a new world to me," the Greek replied. "I will achieve undying fame...mostly by taking the credit for the work of others, in these books of divine insight you brought from your own time."

"You already *had* undying fame," Artorius said, slapping him on the shoulder. "For uncounted generations you were *the* physician; I studied your life in school, nearly two thousand years from this night!"

That was obviously some consolation. He went on:

"If others saw further, later, they did it standing on your shoulders. Now that fame will be still greater...but you still deserve it. And think of the suffering the new books under your name will prevent, the lives saved and prolonged, the illness and crippling injury reduced!"

"Under my name," the Greek said wryly.

"And given power by your name and reputation. It is your position in the present that makes it likely they will be widely heard and believed. Nobody knows me from a hole in the ground"—there was a brief startled chuckle at the unfamiliar turn of speech—"save as rumors. *You* are physician to the Imperial family and court."

The Greek brightened. "Yes...yes, it is so, my friend."

"And think of the *Galenus de institutis medicis*," the American said.

That meant *Galen Medical Institute*; it would be a medical school and hospital outside Rome, and lavishly endowed from the Imperial *res privata*, with rents assigned to support it. There, dissection of human cadavers *would* be allowed, to teach surgical skills. In the original history, Galen had lived into his eighties—until 217 CE, in fact. If he equaled that here, he would have a full half century to revolutionize the Roman Empire's medical practice. With official backing too...

"I do, I do! Already I have scores of pages of notes...your client Marcus has been invaluable as we worked together to translate the works you brought; if only I can persuade him to be one of the teaching staff! And to run our *printing* enterprise. From there, knowledge and skill will spread over the whole Empire."

He used *libri terunt* for printing; literally, book stamping, which seemed to be the term that would stick. The Emperor had already sent a sample press and men to run it back to Rome, with Greek and Latin type, with Arabic—here and now entitled *Pannonian*—numerals as well. Josephus had helpfully arranged papermakers too, an enterprise to be run by his young nephew with financial backing from Josephus himself and others of their family.

Marcus Aurelius had been musing about an authoritative compilation of Roman law and the opinions of the *iūris consultus*, the legal experts who later ages would call jurisconsults. Hundreds or thousands of copies could be distributed, so that every magistracy in the Empire would have the up-to-date references on hand for lawyers and judges to check.

And we can sneak some of our *ideas into that, yessiree. Paula already* has *some ideas about how to do that inconspicuously but with steady long-term effect. Like ending legal guardianship for women at twenty-one or marriage, whichever comes first, the same way Augustus did for women who'd had three children. Interesting that women here don't* need *a Victorian-style Married Women's Property Act, though—Roman law's already advanced that way. And it pays to know the boss!* What the Emperor desires has the force of law, *you betcha.*

"Mark...Marcus...has my leave to assist you, once matters are settled here on the Danube," Artorius said, smiling. "I think he would enjoy seeing Rome."

When the Greek had left, he pulled up another stool and sat beside Filipa. He touched his fingers to either side of Sarukê's face below the angle of the jaw.

"Definitely feverish," he said.

"Hundred and two. And the wound's draining, and it looks inflamed," Filipa said.

There was a wondering tenderness as she looked down at the Sarmatian.

"She's been dreaming...calling my name sometimes, and the name of her lover Tirgataô, who was killed when she was captured. Dreaming of both of us, I suppose."

Artorius reached into the pocket of his tunic and pulled out a cloth; it was wrapped around a square of aluminum-and-plastic foil containing tablets.

"Three a day until the infection's cleared up and the wound's healing solidly," he said. "Shouldn't take long. The bugs here are defenseless."

"I hope Jeremey didn't object that they were *irreplaceable*, the way he did with Josephus' kid," she said.

Artorius smiled and shook his head. "He didn't *object* even then, exactly. Just wanted the reasons for the decision made explicit."

They were all uneasily aware that even the crates full they had wouldn't last forever, and that they'd all used some of them already, mostly for stomach problems. Not until they were showing symptoms and getting worse, though, which meant their immune systems were getting *some* education for the new environment.

He went on: "And now both his girlfriends are pregnant, which makes it more...immediate for him, too."

"Has he—"

"Bought and emancipated, so the kids will be full Roman citizens, and he's going to formally adopt them."

Which would legitimize them too. They'd be citizens, and affluent ones. Besides the Emperor's generosity, Jeremey already had a couple of profitable sidelines going, and was drawing up plans for a sugar refinery next year on the estate he'd been granted from the *res privata*, complete with a rum distillery.

"Children change people. Not to mention that he knows we've been dosing the Emperor since not long after he arrived in Vindobona, and he hasn't said a word about *that*."

She looked up, eyes widening in alarm. "Marcus Aurelius is sick?"

"*Was* sick. From what Galen says about his symptoms, and from what the textbooks say about those, he has ulcers, bad ones—though he's so damned Stoic about it you'd hardly know. Must have been excruciating. That's probably what killed him eventually, fifteen years from now; at least that was the academic consensus in the twenty-first and it seems to be right. *Mostly* ulcers are caused by bacteria, though stress can make it worse."

"Galen lived into his eighties the first time 'round," she said.

Artorius nodded. "There's no reason the Emperor shouldn't too, and it looks like his insides are clearing up steadily. Augustus made it to his midseventies, and *he* was sick off and on incessantly and at death's door three or four times. Forty years of Marcus Aurelius would do the Roman Empire a world of good. And..."

And Commodus might well be out of the way by then, he always burned the candle at both ends, to put it mildly. For that matter, his other son Verus might well live now, he died of an infection after they took a growth out of his ear. We'll see...and if we have to, we'll see to it.

Filipa nodded and took out the first of the tablets. Artorius helped her hold the other woman, and she gently administered the medicine and a sip of watered wine. Sarukê's eyes fluttered open, and she smiled and murmured Filipa's name and something in her own rising-falling language before closing them again.

"Get some sleep yourself," he said gently.

She nodded absently as he rose and left, closing the door gently behind him.

Julia will be waiting.

⇒ CHAPTER TWENTY-EIGHT ⇐

Danube bridge, south bank,
Entering former Kingdom of the Marcomanni,
Barbaricum of Germania Antehac Libra
May 5th, 167 CE

Aha, me proud beauties! Artorius thought.

As the cannon rumbled onto the planks of the pontoon bridge that spanned the Danube just upstream of Vindobona, Artorius automatically gentled his horse as it shied a little at the thunderous drumbeat sound. Then the iron tires of their wooden wheels crunched off onto the pounded crushed rock of the macadamized road now making its way north toward the Marcomanni heartland, and the noon sun glittered almost painfully on the surface of the Danube.

Odd how war smells *different here,* he thought. *No burnt hydrocarbons or nitro powder or electronics. Lots of horse byproducts, though, lots of leather and dirty wool cloth. The shit and sweat and dirty feet and old blood... those stay the same.*

"You're looking good, sir," Artorius observed to Marcus Aurelius.

The Emperor was, with better color than he'd shown when he arrived most of a year ago, and holding himself easily, without the hint of painful stiffness the American had noticed earlier. He also had speckles of blood on the hem of his tunic—one surprise had been just how much time an Emperor's religious duties took, sacrifices and whatnot at every significant event and throughout the calendar.

"I *am* well, Tribune. My stomach is at peace night and day for the first time in many years; for which, my thanks to you and to Galenos. What is the advantage of these over the *carroballistae* throwing thunder-powder bombs?" Marcus Aurelius asked.

Likes to be indifferent to things like physical discomfort . . . and he really is. There are worse affectations!

"Because the fiscal officials complain to me daily of their greater cost!" he went on with a slight smile.

The little joke showed that he *was* feeling better. And that he hadn't asked until now reflected his management style; he trusted Artorius, so when told they were necessary had simply agreed.

"They throw projectiles about six times as far and the shells travel about eight times as fast, sir," he replied. "Solid shot from them hits much harder—hard enough to knock down thick stone walls, with repeated hits—and at close range, a hundred paces or less, it can be loaded with hundreds of lead bullets traveling about as quickly."

After checking that nobody was in hearing distance besides the brace of his own bodyguards, he spoke more quietly:

"My great-great-great-great-grandfather used very similar weapons in a terrible civil war fought in America."

That generation of Vandenbergs fought on both sides, come to think of it. Let the dead past bury its dead . . . And that's now about as dead as a past can *be, since "now" it never existed at all except in my head and in Fil's and Jem's and Paula's and Mark's. Or possibly but untestably in another timeline, as Mark would say.*

He'd made the guns as close a duplicate as he could of the twelve-pounder Napoleon gun-howitzer of the Civil War era, as giving the best combination of mobility and firepower. Basically just a tapering bronze tube with a barrel of 4.62 inches caliber and a little under six feet long, weighing in at a bit over half a ton.

A good crew, and they all were now after months of hard practice drill, could get off two or three rounds a minute. Every elderly dung heap in three provinces had been torn down for the saltpeter, and orders and plans for leaching grounds had gone out Empire-wide. Getting powder production going had been a struggle, but as with most of the innovations once you reached a certain point, things started to pyramid.

And having the Emperor on your side certainly helps. Thank God and Professor Fuchs for those measuring gauges, too, he added to himself. *We'd never have gotten the insides of the bores acceptable without them to measure the cutting bars, even if we have to keep rechecking and adjusting every dozen turns. And we've tested these guns enough that I don't think any of them are going to blow up unexpectedly. Granted, about half of them* did *blow up during the testing, at least to start with . . .*

The *testing* had been done by loading a double charge of powder down the barrel, lighting a slow match set in the touch-hole and then sprinting and diving into a slit trench. Followed by examining them *very carefully* for stress cracks or distortions.

Oddly enough, it was Mark who had saved them a lot of time and possibly lives when he remembered that it was better to cast the guns muzzle up and then saw off the two feet or so of spongy bronze at the top weakened by air bubbles rising through the molten metal.

That was another gift of Martin Padway. Though for some reason *he* hadn't known the actual formula for gunpowder, odd in an archaeologist, even a fictional one.

Or maybe not, that book was written a century ago . . . well, nearly, 1938. Damn, but the English language is not intended for time travel, and Latin's even worse.

Training the crews hadn't been too hard, except for the ones who couldn't take the noise. He'd used *carroballistae* men as cadre, and they were all proud as peacocks now, and would have tattooed thunderbolts on their foreheads if he'd let them. Three batteries of six guns each, nine men to a gun and a few more for the ammunition wagons, and a flexible-minded young centurion for each battery; one slightly more experienced from *Valentia Edetanorum*—what he thought of as the Spanish city of Valencia—in overall command.

Now if only the Marcomanni are obliging enough to charge into the muzzles . . . probably not that stupid, though . . . but sometimes you can force an enemy to do something they know *is stupid because all the alternatives you present are worse.*

The legate who'd sent the two new *Italica* legions to the Danube and brought the *Legio Claudia* from its lower-Danube home guided his horse closer, his entourage falling back behind him; he was from Asia Minor himself and named Marcus Claudius Fronto, a bearded olive-skinned hawk-faced man of forty, tanned dark by ferocious eastern suns.

The *Legio IV Italica* he'd left at Durostorum wasn't really ready for this campaign, and the Emperor had sent it to the lower Danube to complete its training and get some practical experience, in exchange for the veteran unit whose home was there.

Fronto had also been a legion commander on the lower Danube for a while, then on the Rhine, and effectively in overall command of the Parthian war for several years, given that the co-emperor Varus was something of a nonentity, though fortunately an unambitious one.

Romans wore their decorations in the field; Artorius had a small replica of the *corona graminea* on his chest. It was all alone, but it was also the equivalent of the Medal of Honor squared.

The ones across Fronto's muscled cast-bronze legate's breastplate were impressive in their own right. The *corona muralis* had pride of place, which meant he'd been the first man to scale an enemy-held city wall. Seeing that award was rare, because men who survived doing that were even rarer. And the *corona vallaris*, the *corona aurea* and four *hastae pura*, which were miniature gold spears. His formal rank was *Legatus Augusti pro praetore*, which meant he was qualified to govern a province or lead a force of more than one legion.

Oddly enough, I've campaigned in territory quite close to what's now western Parthia. Not in this century, though! I wonder if it looks much different... or smells better. Heat's probably just as bad, and the sandstorms would be all too familiar.

"I have seen these new *tormentii* at practice, sir," Fronto said to the Emperor, with an affable nod to Artorius. He was second-in-command of the field force, which meant effectively its general under the Emperor's...

General supervision, Artorius thought.

The word *tormentii* meant literally something like *torturer* in Latin and was the term for "throwing engines" in general, but they'd picked it up as a specific term for cannon.

"They'll be useful anywhere there's a fight bigger than a large skirmish," the general said. "But they'd have been even *more* useful against the Parthians, sir. We must have *plenty* of them the next time we have to fight them—which we will, of course."

Marcus Aurelius made an enquiring sound, and the man went on:

"They rely on their horse archers in the big open spaces

there; that's what destroyed Crassus' army, back in the divine Julius' time."

The Emperor nodded; he'd read about that . . . read nearly everything historical the Romans had, in conscientious self-training. Roman soldiers still winced at the memory.

"We've learned countertactics since then of course, but they're still a hard problem, *very* hard to bring to battle if they don't feel like it. You have to head for something immovable they value highly; but they harass and do hit-and-run on a large scale all the time. With their armored cataphracts hovering about with their barge poles ready to run up your arse, so you have to be cautious and stay in close formations. With enough of these new *tormentii*, though, they wouldn't dare come to within bow range in any numbers. Not in daylight!"

"And cavalry are very difficult to coordinate in darkness," Artorius observed, and Fronto beamed at him. "In any substantial numbers, that is."

"Just so, Tribune! They couldn't peck at us and run and peck again, they'd have to either get out of the way or try to charge home and come to close quarters. And then at close range, just about long bowshot . . . odd to say close about *that* . . . then the new *carroballistae* with thunderballs would slaughter most of them before what was left impaled themselves on our iron."

"Where I was born we had a saying: *Caught between the demons and the deep blue sea*, Legate."

Fronto laughed; he seemed a cheerful sort, and it was always better for morale to be attacking.

"These *tormentii* would be even more useful against the Iazyges and Roxolani on the steppes north of the Danube east of here for the same reason," he added. "And they're nomads with no cities to defend, so they're even harder to bring to battle than Parthians. You can set grass fires to destroy their pasture for a while, but that's awkward."

The Iazyges and Roxolani were the Sarmatian tribes who'd moved down from the Pontic area and occupied what Artorius knew as eastern Hungary and eastern Romania. They flanked the Transdanubian Roman province of Dacia on either side, which was a monumental pain and which the Romans appreciated better now that they had accurate maps of the region . . . and were reminded of that strategic awkwardness every time they *looked* at the new maps. Which augured ill for those troublesome nomads, once the Marcomanni and Quadi were dealt with.

Wait a minute, that reminds me, I do remember Fronto's name. The Iazyges killed him about ... three or four years from now, while he was commanding in Dacia. Those tribes pitched in on the Marcomanni side, in the original history.

Artorius shivered a little inwardly. That was about the sum total of what the books said about Fronto, who was known only from two inscriptions and a few passing mentions ... and here was the living, breathing man, with a black curly beard and hair thinning at the front, sitting a little uneasily in the new-style saddle and visibly reminding himself to press down on the stirrups now and then.

As far as looks went, he reminded Artorius of a Turk who'd run a shawarma stand near a base he'd been stationed at in Germany right after he was commissioned. The part of wasn't-going-to-be-Turkey his family came from was Greek speaking now, but apparently physical appearances hadn't changed as much as language and religion.

He's already doing things he wouldn't have done ... the first time through. Maybe he'll live a lot longer.

Or maybe he'd slip getting out of bed tomorrow and break his neck, or take an arrow in the eye from a German guerilla north of the river. There was no way to tell, now. Just because he knew *a* future didn't mean he knew *the* future, the one that was coming at him one inescapable second at a time. That future was like all the others; it didn't exist until you got there.

The only certain *thing is that we're* all *going to die someday, somehow.*

"Unfortunately, night attacks are more practical here," Artorius observed, putting aside the oddly disturbing feeling of talking to a man he knew would ... would *have* ... died soon.

Time travel does odd things to your mind, too. Thank God it only happened to me once! If it was routine I'd go bughouse.

"Yes, I heard the reports of the night attack on Carnuntum," Fronto said.

An American would have said read *the reports.*

"Good work there, Tribune."

"Thank you, Legate," Artorius said. "I was at the right place at the right time."

"And *did* the right thing, in the right place at the right time," the Emperor remarked.

A cohort of infantry from the new *Legio II Italica* came next, tramping in unison. They were in marching order—each man's name, legion, cohort, century and his commanding centurion was written neatly on the leather cover that protected the shields slung over their backs, in formal *capitalis monumentalis*. Their helmets hung on their chests with the cheek pieces splayed open or folded in, and their pila and *furcae* were over their shoulders; each carried an oak stake pointed at both ends, a *pilum muralis*, for topping the wall of a marching camp as well.

A furca was a long pole with a crossbar fastened a foot from the top by notches and rawhide thongs. It was named after an instrument of judicial torture, though.

Soldier humor, you betcha.

You tied your *dolabra* or spade or turf cutter to the upper side of the furca, put the shaft of your pilum next to it on your shoulder, and from the crossbar of the carrying pole hung the rest of your gear. Everything from a mess kit and rolled cloak, spare socks and a folded blanket to a loaf of bread and hunk of cheese and little jar of olives and oil, in a leather satchel and in bags and nets hanging down your back. He supposed it was more awkward than a rucksack, but you could shed it instantly at need, or lean on the pole with the weight off during a rest stop.

There was something, something besides their being at full strength, all four hundred and eighty of them...

Ah, they're younger *on average*, Artorius thought. *Newly raised unit, two years ago. Only the officers and noncoms are long-service veterans, and it shows.*

He'd been surprised at how mature most legionaries were; nearly thirty on average, about the same as the US Army in his own day, but it *wasn't* surprising when you remembered that they all enlisted for twenty-five years rather than the average of eight to twelve in his time. The longer hitch balanced out the higher everyday mortality.

These looked as if they were mostly in their early twenties, with far less in the way of scars and weathering, though they were also visibly mostly outdoor workers from childhood.

And their equipment was a bit more varied than usual, probably because it had been pulled out of long-term storage to

meet the sudden demand. Older and more complicated styles of
the hoop-and-band *lorica segmentata* were nearly as numerous
as the newer model. Here and there a man wore a sleeveless
thigh-length mail shirt with doubling flaps over the shoulders,
outfits which had probably been gathering dust in an armory
for generations with periodic maintenance. It was still perfectly
functional, though a bit heavier than the plate lorica and more
typical of auxiliaries, though occasionally they wore the *lorica
segmentata* too.

For the rest, the soldiers of the Second Italica looked just as
you'd expect from a bunch of Italian farm boys and laborers'
sons and blacksmiths' apprentices. Though taller than average
because the Roman army's minimum was about five foot five,
and no gimps or squints or hernias or mouths empty of teeth
because of the medical exam.

Add in plenty of good plain food every day for going on two
years of very hard training and long, long marches in full kit,
and they were visibly tough and bullock strong; arms and legs,
shoulders and necks corded with hard muscle. They marched in
step with a springy endurance, and sang out something rhythmic
in a harsh male chorus that seemed to go:

> "*Exurge Mars!*
> *Mars Ultor!*
> *Roma et Imperator!*
> *Sumus filli lupae Capitolinae—*"

His mind translated it. More accurately than he would have
two years ago, before he'd come to speak this century's Latin as
a living tongue, even though the Italian accent was fairly distinct
from the slight Pannonian one he'd picked up. About as different
as General Californian was from what they drawled in a small
rural town in Alabama:

> "*Awake the War God!*
> *Vengeance God!*
> *For Rome and the Emperor!*
> *Sons of the Capitoline she-wolf,*
> *We suckled on blood from her bitch teats:*
> *Out of our way or we'll drink yours too!*"

> *We follow our Eagle wherever it leads*
> *To barbarian forests or burning sands—"*

"They're shaping well, sir," Fronto said to the Emperor. "Now they just need to be blooded a little and they'll be...almost... the equals of veterans like the Claudia."

Artorius smiled. "I think the Marcomanni will see to that," he said. "And hopefully supply most of the blood."

Fronto chuckled, though Marcus Aurelius stayed grave; he was in a blackened bronze muscled cuirass with golden decorations and purple sash and cloak, and wore it with the ease of long practice, but you could see he wasn't really a soldier himself.

None the worse for that, Artorius thought. *He's the big-picture man. He's got us for the hands-on side.*

"Not only the Marcomanni," the Emperor said gravely. "We have had good intelligence"—his eyes flicked to Artorius for an instant, holding both reproof for taking the risk and acknowledgment of the results—"that there is indeed a great barbarian conspiracy against Rome. War bands and chiefs or the sons of chiefs from all over the *Barbaricum* have flocked to join the Marcomanni and Quadi against us."

"Which is both good and bad, sir," Artorius said.

Fronto raised his brows and spoke:

"The bad being their numbers, and that those numbers won't be farmers with a spear they keep over the doorway of their huts, they'll mostly be nobles and their retainers. Better equipped and real fighters. There is a good side to that, Tribune?"

"Yes, Legate," the American said. "Feeding them will run the local tribes' supplies out earlier. It's the hungry time of their year, just before harvest, and we want them desperate enough to fight us head on as soon as possible."

"True," Fronto said. "You have to remember that the other side has supply problems too!"

"And really *coordinating* a huge mob like that will be impossible, not to mention that half of them have blood feuds against their neighbors...and unlike the local Germanii, they'll not have any real experience with our new weapons. They will likely discount them out of blind bravado—and be all the more inclined to panic when they find out the rumors are true."

The Emperor nodded gravely. "We have five legions, and as

many auxiliaries. Even with line of communication and fortress garrisons, we should have thirty-five-thousand troops or more in one mass if we can bring the barbarians to a decisive battle. And when we beat them, survivors will carry a tale of defeat from here to the northern sea."

"From your mouth to the ears of the Gods, sir," Artorius said, which made Fronto chuckle again.

I'm getting a rep as a real wit, too.

They all turned their horses and trotted across the bridge themselves, ironshod hooves loud on the thick planks covering the barges. Fronto's tribunes and clerks and their Imperial equivalent followed behind, while a *turma* of the Emperor's horse guards went before, behind and to either side.

They passed the cannon and the *Italica* cohort, and then a train of big wagons pulled by long hitches of paired oxen pulling on a common chain, each twenty-eight beasts strong—the Americans had had them done up by local wainwrights, but based on Artorius' memories of what he'd read about the freight wagons used in South Africa during the Boer War period, or in Australia around the same time.

"Large!" Fronto said, interested.

If you'd survived multiple campaigns, not to mention won them, you took logistics seriously. Roman wagons were fairly good—iron tires, iron bushings for the axles and wheel hubs, and they did have pivoted front wheels for some of the bigger ones—but not quite on this scale. The broad rear wheels of these were neck high on the men walking beside them, and the top of the loads more than twice that height.

Interesting, Artorius thought. *The way the best designs for us are often from just before mechanization finally won. The same way sailing ships peaked a few years before steamers completely supplanted them. Competition from something new forcing people to wring everything possible out of an old design that loafed along being "good enough" until then. So we can skip right to best possible, sometimes.*

"Six-ton loads," Artorius said, and the general's eyebrows went up; that was well over twice what the largest Roman vehicles hauled.

"Grain and beans, hardtack and cheese, salted meat and dried fruit," Fronto said approvingly. "And spare sandals, extra pila and arrows and bandages...and now, thunderpowder and spare shoes for the horses, as well!"

He waved toward the northern horizon. "I doubt we're going to be living much off the land here."

Artorius hadn't been looking in that direction. He did now. Pillars of smoke marked the horizon there, from the edge of sight on the west to where the sun had risen bloody tinged that morning. Burning homesteads and villages; burning grainfields, where they were dry enough. Forest fires as well, spread by the sparks. Where the grain wouldn't burn, teams of Roman cavalry were dragging heavy brush or logs across it to spoil the harvest. And they were having a grand old time stealing everything that wasn't nailed down.

Flocks and herds had come back over the Danube, or been eaten by the Roman advance parties. Trains of brutalized captives in chains and under guard had stumbled by too. What couldn't be securely used by Rome was destroyed. Or was carried north by hordes of terrified refugees, who the Marcomanni would have to feed somehow, now in the season before late summer's harvest. And in lands where, unlike the Empire, grain hardly ever moved more than two days travel from where it was cut.

In addition to all the allies the Great Barbarian Conspiracy had brought them, who'd have arrived hungry and expecting a splendid feast from their grateful hosts. Great chiefs and kings in the *Barbaricum* moved around with their retainers to eat the surplus from each district, rather than having it shipped to them. The tens of thousands of newcome allies would be inclined to simply steal supplies not freely given.

Vastatio indeed, he thought, and then:

Exactly as I predicted, they're falling back and doing all the ambushes and tricks they can. And the Praetorian Prefect from Not-Yet-Tunisia was right too.

How did you fight a successful guerilla campaign against someone ready, willing and able to simply kill *everyone* and leave an empty, foodless, shelterless wasteland?

The answer was simple: you couldn't.

Guerillas have to depend on the people, ultimately. And these people are farmers, not nomads: you can't drive off a crop that's already planted in the dirt and grain is heavy. So eventually they'll have to stand and fight to control the ground that feeds them, or be driven out and mostly simply starve to death. They're just trying to delay the battle as long as they can stand it, to stretch our supply lines and pull us deep into their territory.

"We'll see," he said, half to himself.

Fronto chuckled again. "That's why we have wars, Tribune. To see."

"Yes," Marcus Aurelius said—with a sigh, rather than a smile, but with flat sincerity.

➤ CHAPTER TWENTY-NINE ➤

Barbaricum of Germania Antehac Libra
June 25th, 167 CE

"Two years exactly since we arrived," Artorius said through the window of the traveling coach.

It looked a lot like a Western stagecoach, though the Roman artisans had painted it in gaudy designs of red and orange and vibrant green, including *putti* and mythological scenes on the doors. Whoever had first associated Classical times with white marble had been using his imagination, or just forgetting what two thousand years of weathering did to stone.

Or just had a fetish about "purity," he thought. *Romans slather bright primary colors on anything they can reach. This coach makes an old-style Costa Rican oxcart look restrained.*

"Hurrah," Mark said from inside.

He and Filipa had been avoiding looking out at the swath of carnage the Roman army was cutting through a bright June day as they came north. Sarukê was riding on the other side of the carriage and looking absolutely unconcerned, as were her arena-recruited Brute Squad of bodyguards.

The four of *them* just looked as if they wished they were participating in the killing, rapine and pillage.

Those are some very hard men ... of course, they'd be dead if they weren't.

Artorius suspected Jeremey was only *pretending* to be grossed out. The young man had a very hard edge himself. Some people just did, wherever or whenever they were brought up and regardless of what was typical or average for the time and place.

Paula was back in *Vindobonum* with the fifth guard following her like her shadow, discussing medical education for young women with Galen, who was proving surprisingly receptive to the idea. Apparently there had been occasional women doctors in Athens and some other parts of Greece for a long time. It was a product of the near-purdah Athenian women had traditionally suffered, which made their menfolk reluctant to let a male physician into the women's quarters, but often wanting someone with more formal training than the midwife.

Paula has more than occasional in mind, and cunning plans to encourage it.

As Paula had said, she'd sold her soul to the devil, or the Roman Empire, but that didn't mean she had nothing better to do with her time than take a guided tour of the slums of Hell.

The smell of smoke and decay was heavy in the air.

Clink-clink-clink...

The sound of hammers on rock echoed from the forests to either side, where broad bands of stumps showed where the woods had been roughly cleared back and circular scorch marks marked the points where piled brushwood and trees had been burnt to get them out of the way. More was stacked, neatly split, by the roadside for the troops to use as needed. A fair mob of prisoners—containing no males over about twelve—was sitting by the side of the road, using smallish hammers to turn moderate-sized rocks from local deposits into smaller ones that would fit through a screen of two-inch iron rings.

The screen hung from a tripod of tall poles by ropes. Once the stony road metal had been shaken through that screen—and the ones left too big had been returned to the workers by the simple expedient of soldiers throwing them *hard* at the captives, whose bruises and bleeding showed the result—they were shoveled into wheelbarrows and taken to the cambered dirt of the roadbed. That and the roadside drainage ditches had been shaped by Fresno scrapers, a horse-drawn device of cunning simplicity from the late nineteenth century.

The crushed rock was spread across the dirt in a mass a little higher at the center than the edges. Then it was raked to a careful shape under the watchful eye of military engineers.

And then pounded by more captives, this time with hardwood blocks on poles lifting them and ramming them down. These gangs *did* include a fair number of adult men, all in ankle fetters and watched carefully by the auxiliary infantry guards. Unlike the traditional Roman way of building a paved road—something rather like a fortress wall laid on its side—this didn't require much skilled labor, just careful supervision, and it was much, much faster. As an added bonus it was also vastly easier on hooves than blocks of stone.

One of the auxiliaries cheerfully kicked a laggard, hard enough to knock him down.

The threat of another kick got the man back on his feet.

"That's right, Hermann," the auxiliary said, or jeered.

In what Artorius now knew was Latin with an accent from southwestern Gaul, near what he thought of as Bordeaux and was now Burdigala. The dwindling local language there was some sort of collateral predecessor of Basque, not Celtic.

"Welcome to the first day of the rest of your short, sad and sorry life. Now *work*! Or you get more of the same!"

Artorius grimaced slightly.

War's a brutal business, he thought.

Then, dryly:

What an original observation!

That was one reason apart from nearly getting ripped to pieces he'd changed professions. When you came right down to it, war amounted to beating on people until they did what you wanted. Or beating on them because *you* didn't want to do what they were trying to beat you into doing.

And then...

Hi-di-ho, we all change partners and the dance continues. The Germanii aren't any nicer; more savage, if anything. The Romans are just more ... systematic. And in the Empire, war's usually limited to the borderlands. Inside it, cities often don't even have walls anymore and a man with a sword is a rare sight on a busy street. Among the barbarians, it's all border, all the time. Men take a spear along to go water the bushes every day of their lives because raiders might come screaming out of the bushes when the first drop hits.

He'd still be glad when this was over.

✧　　✧　　✧

Artorius looked down at the map across his saddlebow on the morning of the first day past the Ides of Augustus—or the 14th of August, to use the calendar he'd been brought up on.

Calendar reform, he thought; one of the innumerable mental notes he made every day. *Gregorian calendar, suitably altered to use local names.*

The sun was bright, or would have been except for the thin haze of smoke, and a smell like the ashes of the world's biggest campfire.

"Well, sir," he said to the Emperor, tapping a spot. "It looks like they want to try and fight us around *here,* from what the *exploratores* say."

The upcoming battlefield was about halfway between Brno-that-wasn't and Prague-that-wasn't-either, in what was the heartland of the Czechs in his native century. Here and now the pre-proto-Slavs were wading around spearing fish and boiling porridge and dodging marauding Gutthiuda—Goths—in the Pripet Marshes a long way northeast of here. Right now this was where most of the Marcomanni had lived since they beat and then gradually assimilated the Celtic Boii. Acquiring things like Prince Ballomar's Gallic name along the way.

I wonder what Chopped-Off Head *would be in Boiian Celtic?*

The Roman force had been marching roughly northwest for some time now. Their course was quite near to the alignment of Euro Route E65 according to Fuchs's maps, since the topography hadn't changed much and that was the best Vienna-Brno-Prague passageway. And they'd moved through weather as warm and dry as this part of Central Europe ever got, even in the Roman Warm Period, which meant it only rained about one day a week and not too long even then, you sweated freely in the daytime, and you didn't need a down sleeping bag at night.

About half the land was in forest, particularly the hillier bits, and half in plowland and pasture, the cleared proportion getting bigger as they approached the central part of the Marcomanni territory; a lot of the forest looked second growth, fields abandoned when they stopped yielding well. The thatched hamlets of rectangular houses half buried in the earth had been mostly abandoned and the livestock driven off by the time the Romans arrived and put them to the torch. By now they weren't bothering with burning the equally abandoned, half-harvested grainfields that had been frantically worked up until the last minute, and they carefully preserved any heaps of sheaves found.

We'll find them very useful ourselves, and if absolutely put to it the soldiers could harvest the rest.

That was one reason every *contubernium* carried a sickle.

I don't mind the smoke being thinner, either. It's eerie, though— we might as well be marching through a world where humanity just vanished yesterday morning.

The occasional hilltop palisades of the Marcomanni elite's fortified halls were all empty and stripped now too, when the first fringe of Roman cavalry arrived to check for valuables and then set them on fire. A few demonstrations of what the new thunderballs and *ignis Romanus* could do to a not-very-large wood-and-earth fortification had sufficed to drive that lesson home, though the Romans could have taken them with their traditional gear too, if less briskly. The new weapons made it easier and faster, and the fear they spread even more so.

Legate Fronto was on the Emperor's other side, also on horseback. He blinked for a second as he craned to look, being a bit less used to the new maps, and then nodded as it clicked into his mental picture of the terrain. He had a very good eye for ground, which wasn't surprising.

"They've realized they can't delay us much more, Tribune," he said. "Not without being pushed so far back that half or more of them would starve anyway, and this is harvest season here. They didn't expect us to move this fast."

"Nor did I," Marcus Aurelius said thoughtfully.

"It is largely the new things, so we could not be sure in advance," Fronto said, inclining his head to Artorius. "Not any single one of them, but the effect of them all together, each magnifying the other. That new method of paving a road is quicker, *that* lets us use the new heavy freight wagons and bring up supplies more quickly, the thunderballs and Roman Fire reduce forts more quickly... particularly these rickety German ones. Quickly enough that after the first week they didn't even *try* to hold them against us. Add it together with other things, and they haven't really been able to slow us down at all. It's like a training march combined with a roadbuilding project. Just enough skirmishes and ambushes to give the men practice and keep them alert."

"An interesting thought!" Marcus Aurelius said. "The sum is greater than the total of the parts, then!"

"We Americans had a word...first made from a combination of Greek terms...*synergy*," Artorius said.

Romans certainly *used* synergy, but Artorius didn't think they had the abstract concept yet, or a single term to express it... except that he'd just given it to them. Romans as smart as the Emperor—and Fronto paled only in comparison—would take it and run with it, and often do things with it he hadn't thought of himself.

"Ah, from *together* and *work*," the Emperor said.

Romans with an upper-class education would also discuss matters of language at the drop of a hat, or less, and often stop anything else they were doing for the pleasure of hashing a term out.

Artorius hid a grin; he'd really put the cat among the pigeons a little while ago, having dinner with the Emperor and Galen and a few others, by pointing out that Greek and Latin—and Gallic and Germanic and Persian and Armenian and Sarmatian—were all descended from a common ancestor language. Then he'd listed the word correspondences and similarities of grammar which showed it. *That* conversation had lasted late into the night, and the Emperor intended to write a book on the idea when and if he had time.

"Yes. As trained and disciplined men working together are more effective than if they were merely individuals added one to the other," Artorius said aloud.

"*Synergy*," the Emperor murmured to himself several times, a trick he'd noticed people in this century used to commit a new term to memory. "I like the word. It is...*compact*. Heavily freighted with meaning."

"I wonder why they have picked this precise place," Fronto said, getting out his own map.

"The lie of the land, with enough open space to deploy most of their host, sir," Artorius said. "At a guess, they plan to entrench and force us to come to them. Or at least the Marcomanni and Quadi leaders do."

Fronto's brows went up; this wasn't his first encounter with the European *Barbaricum*. Germanics of this era prided themselves on aggression, at throwing themselves on an enemy and overwhelming him by their ferocity and contempt for death.

Then he smiled like a shark with an exceptionally low sympathy quotient...even for sharks.

"Ah. The Marcomanni have told their so-called *allies* enough to make them realize what running the gauntlet of the new *carroballistae* throwing thunderballs...and now your even newer *tormentii*...can do to an enemy charging through the beaten ground before them."

Artorius frowned. "But I doubt they have really taken the realization to heart, Legate," he said thoughtfully. "And they have no idea of the increased range of the *tormentii*. Something might be done with that."

⪼ CHAPTER THIRTY ⪻

Barbaricum of Germania Antehac Libra
August 15th, 167 CE

"Well, there they are and here we are," Mark said, standing in his stirrups and using a pair of binoculars from Fuchs's hoard.

The sun was up enough that he could do that though the people he was looking at were to the east. He went on:

"Someone's going to lose their temper if we're not lucky."

He said it in Latin, and Sarukê laughed aloud where she lounged in her saddle. Filipa was riding beside her, and her face had been a little strained; now she relaxed and chuckled. Jeremey was looking that way too and the other guards were stolidly watching with the interest of spectators.

"Har. Har-di-ha-har," Jeremey said sourly, drawing out each syllable. "Chr... by Mars, but there's a lot of them."

Mark had made up a bunch of notepads with paper between thin board covers held by spirals of copper wire at the top. He'd also come up with something that worked about as well as a pencil, involving graphite from deposits not far from the Villa Lunae packed into a wooden tube, though it was soft and crumbly.

Now he wrote on the pad he had braced across the pommel of his saddle; his riding had continued to improve, in the manner of a skill for which you had no talent or liking, but were forced to practice constantly anyway.

"Approximately... sixty thousand," he said as he wrote. "Possibly... more... behind... northeastern... ridge."

Then he signed it and tore off the page and handed it to a messenger who galloped off.

"How do you *do* that?" Jeremey asked. "Get an exact figure?"

"Ummm...it's not exact. Not to within a couple of thousands. You just take an area, count the men in it, then multiply it by the number of times the area is—"

"Oh, forget I asked, that's why the Prof has you here," the young man from Wisconsin grumbled, and looked over his shoulder, and visibly found it reassuring. "Our army's pretty big too. Not *as* big, but quality has a quantity all its own."

"That's not what Stalin said—"

"I *know*, Mark. That was *irony*."

The field of battle both sides had chosen by unspoken mutual consent was an undulating slope a little over a mile long, gentle overall and facing southwest. It had been in fields of wheat and rye, laid out in long rectangular strips and nearly all stubble when the Romans arrived. And pasture, plus supposedly bare but actually weedy fallow. An occasional tree or small grove dotted it; most of those were still there, though the buildings near them were smoldering cinders. Forest crowned the ridge behind the Americans, and patches of woodland more or less defined the sides; the ground declined from the Marcomanni position to a fordable stream, then rose to a wooded ridge.

The Marcomanni and their allies were a swarming dun mass made individually tiny by distance, studded with standards of cloth and wood and bone, each amid a glitter of polished helmets and the often-gilded sparks from crests of animals real or mythical, or the actual gold of torcs and armbands. You could smell them too; that was as many people as a small city like Vindobona, and composed of men with little sense of personal hygiene.

They normally lived fairly thinly scattered, where sewage wasn't much of a problem and bushes did duty for latrines.

"If they don't get to move, they'll all die of dysentery in a couple of days," Jeremey said, wrinkling his nose as they got a wind carrying a whiff.

Behind them and much closer, the Roman army was an ordered array of iron and bronze, the standards of legion, cohort, century and ala instantly recognizable.

"Like the pieces at a wargaming convention," Jeremey said, glancing their way. "I went to those when I was a teenager."

Five legions were drawn up by cohorts, a bit under twenty thousand men. The two new legions, *Italica II* and *III*, were close to their theoretical strength. The two legions of the Twins from Vindobona and Carnuntum were at a bit over half, and the Claudia from Durostorum was around three-quarters because it had gotten the survivors of its *vexilliationes* back and they hadn't yet. The auxiliaries were as many again, including about five thousand horsemen.

Before the legions were their new *carroballistae*, 126 now; then blocks of archers and then a thinner line of auxiliary infantry, and the cavalry on the wings in a forest of lance points and pennants.

Some of the horsemen were out skirmishing with their Germanii counterparts, and getting very much the better of it to judge by who ended each clash running as fast as they could, and who came back leading captured horses and triumphantly waving the odd gold or silver torque or bracelet.

Sarukê watched that with interest; she was still a little thinner from her illness, but the wound had healed solidly and her color was good. The First Victorious Thracians trotted by, victorious once more, as another ala cantered out to take their place and let them rest their horses. Several of the First recognized the Sarmatian, and shook their new lances in the air.

"Like fighting men with one hand tied behind their backs, *wirapta*!" one of the troopers shouted to her with a gap-toothed smile as they passed. "We knocked 'em heels over ass with every passage, the way you did me! Only they're dead!"

"You stay *right here*, sword-sister," Filipa said to her a second later. "No rushing off for heroics!"

The ex-nomad blinked pale eyes at her. "Why, of course!" she said. "What you say, I do!"

And added, with an obviously counterfeit simper:

"*Mâtar.*"

Which meant "mother" in her language. She grinned and dodged a punch on the shoulder from Filipa that was only half playful. The guards all laughed too.

"Here they come," Jeremey said.

They all looked around. The *tormentii* were coming out, trotting with the left-hand mounts in each six-horse team bearing a man each, guns and limbers bouncing along behind over the rutted, uneven surface that had been plowland, and the rest of the crews following on their own riding cobs. They went past the Americans on their slight rise, then swung right and deployed before them.

That started with the first gun when it reached its firing position; the rider on the lead horse swung the team around and halted. That left the muzzle pointing toward the enemy. Men sprang down from the saddle, including two whose rotated duty was to hold the individual mounts.

The *optio* who led each gun crew whipped the circular wooden tompion blocking the muzzle free by its rope handle. Others were lifting the trail that connected the gun carriage to the two-wheeled limber free of its joint and letting it drop to the ground. More hands unhitched the limber from its connection to the horse team, and threw open the wooden doors, exposing the tubes that held thirty-two rounds.

Artorius spurred his horse from the battery and toward them.

"Here comes the Prof," Jeremey said. "Prepare to be convinced. The man missed his vocation, he should have been an Evangelical minister."

Artorius drew rein. "All right," he said—in English. "Gather 'round."

They did, as much as you could on horseback. "First," he went on in the same language. "You've all seen some really bad shit since we crossed the Danube."

Mark looked queasy, and Filipa gave a curt nod. Jeremey looked...blandly attentive.

I'm not really a fan of vastatio *either,* Artorius thought grimly. *Though it* works, *no dispute.*

"Bear in mind a few things. First, the Marcomanni started the war. Second, in our history this war went on for *fourteen years*, with the *same* bad shit on both sides of the river and as far south as Italy. For every single one of those fourteen *years*, and it didn't settle squat. So it got refought over and over for the next century and a half. And then Attila the Hun arrived, and then...eventually...human beings blew up the planet fast, because it wasn't satisfying enough to fry it slowly. If we pull this off, we settle *this* war in two years instead of seven times that long, and it's a step toward people possibly *not* blowing up the world. That's worth some spectators' PTSD. Am I right?"

He caught each of their eyes. Mark and Filipa nodded... reluctantly. Jeremey gave a broad smile and an *enthusiastic* nod.

Which is not all that convincing, Artorius thought. *I think it's more like watching old episodes of* House of the Dragon *to him.*

He dropped back into Latin:

"Sarukê, you listen too."

She obviously did.

That lady has an admirable ability to exclude the irrelevant and focus on the necessary, he thought, and continued:

"OK, those guns"—he pointed to the eighteen cannon just finishing their deployment, neat as a parade exercise—"are not going to destroy *that.*"

His finger swung northeast to the barbarian host.

"What we want to do is break their *patience,* and make them attack, because that makes it much more likely we can win this without screwing our own army up beyond repair. We want this to be a *decisive* battle, the *last* big battle in this war, so the Marcomanni and Quadi surrender and the *vastatio* ends. Mark, you're here because you're good at visual assessments. Filipa, you're here because you're the best we've got at estimating ranges on the fly."

And because you won't let Sarukê go into danger alone and she won't let me *do that, but leave that aside for now.*

"Jeremey, you're here because you thought with your balls, not your brains. And you're quite competent at this stuff, our second best at visuals and ranges, so I'm glad you volunteered."

"Thanks, Prof...I think," the younger man said.

Filipa and Mark looked startled as they realized why it was a good idea to have a spare to fall back on.

Welcome to the Army, infants, Artorius thought sardonically, and continued aloud:

"So if the enemy charge and keep coming long enough for the guns to shift to canister, get out. Ride over to where the Emperor is. I'll give you a heads-up, but even if I don't, get going then."

He pointed southwest, where the Imperial standards and a cohort of Praetorians were grouped under the great black-red-and-gold banner.

"Believe me, I'll be right on your heels. Julia and I have a baby coming any day now and I want to see him or her grow up. And we're planning on more."

He or she could already have been born. Probably has. Messages take a while to get here.

Artorius thrust the thought of Julia dying in childbirth out of his mind. Little Claudia had come with no problems at all, he'd heard, and Galen and Paula and the midwives they'd put through the new training would be there. Plus Paula had their store of uptime medical supplies on hand, apart from a few packages in his baggage.

"So Sarukê, when I give you the high sign, you and your squad get everyone out of here, understand?"

She nodded cheerfully. "I do, lord. Fake retreat—draw them in."

Her horse-nomad people used that tactic all the time; unlike the Germanii they had a whatever-works attitude to war almost Roman in its pragmatism, though less sophisticated. *Barbarian cultures differed from each other as much as civilized ones did.*

"Right, let's get started."

They rode with him over to the artillery battalion's—*cohors tormentorum*, in Latin—HQ, standing neatly not far behind the gun line, with the supply wagons and a horse-drawn ambulance not too far off.

Just like the Civil War, only everyone's in a Mother Hubbard sack dress as Jeremey so accurately puts it, helmet, lorica segmentata *and hobnailed sandals,* he thought. *God, I wonder what Netflix would have made of this, back in the day?*

He raised his binoculars again. One of the things he'd done in the last couple of months was to collect—and send couriers to collect—descriptions of banners from all over the *Barbaricum.* He scanned carefully along the front of the enemy host.

"Marcomanni and Quadi in the center," he murmured. "They put this alliance together, they get the post of honor."

Plus they've dug a ditch and heaped up a berm . . . sort of a berm, it doesn't look too solid, their warriors don't like digging . . . in front of their position, too, he thought.

They hadn't exactly learned quickly, but they *had* learned something. That was the problem with fighting the same people for too long; they picked things up, they came up with counters to your specialties . . .

Their *problem is none of their* allies *have yet. Let's not give them a chance to wise up and shed their illusions. We want to boil this Froggie as fast as we can, not give him ideas about jumping to a better lily pad.*

He handed the glasses over to Filipa.

How the skills do come and go. I'm used to getting ranges

with equipment that just tells me to a fraction of an inch, or aims itself. Usually anything that shot could take ranges and adjust its own sights automatically. Now it's a crucial eyeball skill again and I turn out to just not be very good at it beyond a couple of hundred yards.

"See that banner, on the left? Looks like a mummified horse head on top, and a white figure with a sword on the green cloth hanging from the crossbar?"

Filipa hunted for a moment, locked on and thought for a moment.

"Yes, got it, Prof. Eighteen hundred yards give or take ten."

He turned to the cohort commander. Who looked the way Antonio Banderas had in his first big roles back in Artorius' father's youth and was called Gaius Baebius Miccius.

"Centurion, cohort will load solid shot, all tubes," he said.

The orders were relayed. The two-hundred-odd men poised waiting broke into action as stylized as a dance routine in a Bollywood film. The man at each limber pulled out a round—a cylindrical linen bag of powder, topped by a round wooden disc tied on, and the cast-bronze ball strapped to the disc by thin copper bands looped over the top of the shot in a cross and nailed to the sabot's sides. Bronze turned out to be a bit heavier than cast iron, so the ball had been made with a slight hollow in the center.

And the quartermaster begged us with tears in his eyes to retrieve the balls for recasting; bronze isn't cheap and stone's too brittle. We must get around to cast iron, in our copious spare time...

The first man walked briskly back and handed the round to a second, who turned and slid it into the waiting muzzle. Since this was the first round, the man with the rammer could push it down without swabbing out first; he did it with a couple of smart two-handed lunging motions. A third stepped up to the breech as soon as the round was solidly planted and plunged the sharp end of a thin bronze spike through the touchhole to pierce the powder bag; it had a ring on the other end, and was attached to his wrist by that via a leather strap. A fourth inserted the primer, which was a quarter-inch copper tube, filled with fine powder, sealed on the bottom with wax and topped by a short length of quick match. He stood by with his *Ronsonius*, lid pushed up and ready to flick.

All eighteen guns were ready within fifteen seconds of the

order. The centurion nodded somber approval—doing something in a drill was one thing, but doing it equally well in action was *real* discipline.

"Targets, Tribune?" he asked Artorius.

"Take a look at the banner at the end of their right flank, Centurion," he said.

The man raised a brass-and-leather tube to his eye and adjusted it. The first telescope had gone to the Emperor, the second to Legate Fronto, and all eight of the rest were in this cohort, for now. They weren't perfect—no more than x3 magnification, blurry and weirdly color streaked. But they worked.

Sort of. Better than Eyeball Mark One, at least.

"I have it, sir."

"It's eighteen hundred yards—extreme range. All tubes on it, and on my word. Two volleys, then switch to the next, work your way right, until you reach the Marcomanni banners. Ignore them, traverse across to the other side of them and the Quadi, and start with that one—the antlers on a bear's skull, see it?"

"Got it, sir."

The centurion passed on the orders. Each battery centurion trotted between his six guns, pointing out the target. The *tesserarius*—crew chief—clipped the removable ladder-and-ring sight into the slot at the rear of the guns, adjusted it to the maximum eighteen-hundred-yards setting and straddled the trails to peer through it. He made hand signals, and the men who'd run a metal-shod pole through the horizontal ring at the end of the trail heaved on it. The muzzle moved in increments, left and right, while the gunner worked the screw-mounted handwheel that elevated the muzzle as high as it would go...

"Tube ready!" each gun chief shouted, as he stood aside and raised a hand.

"Battery ready!" came from the three junior centurions.

Artorius pulled felt-and-leather earplugs joined by a thong out of a pouch and distributed one to each of the party, including Sarukê and the bodyguards. The gun crews were pushing theirs in.

"Do you know how you can tell a retired gunner?" he said—in English, as they draped them around their necks.

"No, Prof, how can you?" Filipa said.

Artorius put his cupped hand to his ear. "Eh? What's that you said? Speak up, don't mutter!"

It took a moment to sink in, and then the three younger Americans all chuckled.

"That one's ancient," he added, noting that Filipa and Mark at least looked a little more relaxed.

He took a deep breath, and switched to Latin: "Centurion... on my signal...*unleash hell*."

The man looked slightly baffled, the more so as the Americans all chuckled again, but it was a good idea to look relaxed and confident in a setting like this. Some of the men had glanced over their shoulders at the command group, and they'd probably be saying something to their mates as they turned back at crisp barked commands.

Then there was a sound, a sort of massed growling booming mutter coming from the Germanii, loud even at a mile's distance as tens of thousands of them took it up.

Ah, the barratus, he thought. *Unpleasant, when you realize how many people are right there and really, really have a yearning, burning desire to kill you.*

They were bellowing into the hollows of their shields. In *his* history the Roman Army had taken it up about a century later, a mark of their becoming more and more like their principal enemies and recruiting heavily from them in the desperate traumas of the third century as the Empire came within a hair of collapsing. Right now the ordered ranks were resting behind them in their traditional disciplined silence...

He raised his hand and chopped it downward, with his field glasses trained on the Anglian standard.

Strange to be blowing up his own linguistic ancestors...probably a few physical ones too, though the first of the Vandenburg family to settle in America had been Dutch originally, back in the early eighteenth century. Or Germans from Lower Saxony, which had been a distinction without much difference back then.

Only vague family legends remained; Border South dirt farmers mostly didn't bother keeping detailed records. The same legends said that the ones who'd moved to Texas in the 1830s had had urgent, practical reasons to leave West Tennessee. Involving either bad debts they didn't intend to repay, or accusations of horse theft, or the un-mysteriously pregnant daughter of a very irate neighbor known for his marksmanship.

And we became purebred American mongrels anyway, fast

enough, once we got off the boat in Philadelphia ... English, Scots-Irish, touch of Cherokee, probably the odd octoroon who managed to skip out, move two hundred miles over and pass ... then a couple of Tejano girls grafted themselves onto the Vandenberg family tree once we got to Texas ... and then there's Dad's grandfather's mom, who arrived as a pregnant war bride from Seoul in 1953. And my descendants here are going to be Romans. Who are just as ... eclectic.

The centurion barked an order. Eighteen *Ronsonii* flicked—none more than twice—eighteen quick matches sputtered, and eighteen men skipped briskly to the side because...

BOOOOOOM!

Each bronze tube shot a long plume of dirty-white smoke that reeked of rotten eggs ... or of hell, if you thought about it. The recoil also shot the whole one-and-three-quarter-ton weight of gun and mount back about six feet, with the crews standing well clear. Plenty of practice with live ammunition drove *that* point home well and truly, or left crippled or dead examples of *why* you should take it to heart.

As soon as the recoil stopped men flung themselves on the wheels and ran them back up.

The moment the piece was back where it started the rammer was back at work—this time running the big wet sponge on the other end of his rammer down the barrel with a long *hsssssh* sound of steam, dipping it in a bucket and doing it again.

That was to get any embers or bag fragments well and truly put out. Practice also drove that lesson home. What happened if you tried to ram a bag of gunpowder down on top of hot embers had to be seen to be believed, and Artorius wished he hadn't had to see it. The rest of the routine was the same as the first time; sponging out added about ten seconds to the process.

Artorius had his field glasses up and was looking at the end product when it hit around two and a bit seconds later. Eighteen twelve-pound shot struck the densely packed shield wall around the Anglian banner, with only about thirty yards between the leftmost and rightmost hit, good practice at nearly a mile with round shot from smoothbore tubes. Most of the balls were still in the air when they struck. The impact was shattering—literally so, because a man struck by twelve pounds of metal still travel-ing at nearly a thousand feet per second disintegrated instantly.

He *spattered*, and the ball plowed on through to do the same to the man behind...and the one behind him...and the one behind him...and the same for several more repetitions.

Some of the balls hit short and bounced, with very much the same effect. The ones which hit shorter still and rolled still tore legs off right at the hip if they struck anywhere on the limb from the foot up. It was all doll tiny with distance even with the binoculars, but he still winced a little at the sight.

Not too much, he'd seen things just as bad, up close and personal. The *scale* here was a bit daunting, though.

BOOOOOM!

The sound was spread out a little more, the guns firing as fast as their crew chiefs considered them ready.

"Cease fire! Shift to second target! Load and stand ready!" the cohort commander called.

Filipa and Mark were carefully not looking at the fall of shot; they were both naturally shortsighted, but they'd also had the surgical correction routine in their generation. Jeremey was looking, and he had better than 20/20 natural vision, even if he didn't have a telescope or field glasses.

"Why don't they drop flat? Take cover?" he asked, frowning and shaking his head. "That would cut their losses. A lot."

"Because that would mean showing fear in front of their lords and oath comrades and kin," Artorius said quietly.

"You think they'll break and run away eventually?"

Artorius shook his head. "No, we can't kill nearly enough of them with the cannon to do that. If we had a hundred guns, then maybe. Or two or three hundred. Like one of Napoleon's *grand batteries*, but sure as hell not with only eighteen. Not against a host that large."

"Then what's the point?"

No flies on Jeremey, not at all, Artorius thought, and went on with the lesson:

"The ones from outside the Marcomanni and Quadi territories are mostly what passes for professionals in those tribes, not called-up farmers who fight once or twice a year or steal the odd cow or pig. They left the ordinary peasants home when the Marcomanni envoys convinced their kings and chiefs that the Romans need slapping back before they got big eyes about the whole *Barbaricum*, and dangled visions of loot in front of *their* eyes. They're mostly brave as hell, and they take that feasting-with-the-Gods thing seriously."

He smiled thinly; he knew from the way it felt it was an expression he'd seen in a picture someone had taken of him, back in his Ranger days. Memories of it had been one more reason he'd switched trades. It wasn't a smile you wanted to see in the mirror very often, or at least he hadn't.

"But they're used to being brave at sword's length or spear distance from the ones trying to kill them, or after charging a hundred yards with a few arrows and javelins and slingstones falling. That's a different thing entirely from standing still and taking it from people a mile away you can't hurt. And as I like to say, they're not necessarily stupid."

Jeremey made an enquiring sound, and he continued:

"After a while, it's going to occur to them ... the young hot-heads, the berserkers, *and* the chiefs who have to stay standing around those banners too if they want to keep the young warriors' respect ... that we can keep this up all day, and that they have a choice of running away, being smashed to bits as helpless as sheep until sundown, or running *toward* us and seeing how that turns out. Pulling back would be the smart thing to do. We don't want them smart, we want them *angry*."

Jeremey nodded. Filipa grimaced, and Mark blinked.

"Ah," Jeremey said, smiling at seeing a point. "That's why you're *not* having them shell the Marcomanni and Quadi? It'll make them angry at the people who got them into this, too?"

"Right. Among other things."

Mark spoke, frowning: "That's logical." The gangly student of ancient publishing history added, "But ... you know, usually I approve of logical thinking. That ... I don't know ... seems sort of ... weird."

"No, it's not weird, Mark. It's just *nasty* logic; we've put them in a position where all their choices are bad. But this is a nasty business we're in right now and they were doing their best to do unto us, first. Hopefully, we're not going to be doing this much longer. I'd rather be reducing maternal and infant mortality and increasing food security, you betcha."

BOOOOOM! BOOOOOM!

More hell-stinking smoke drifted back around them as the sound thudded through the air and into chest and gut with palpable impacts, and Filipa grew white around the lips as she kept calling the ranges, as regular as a machine.

BOOOOOM! BOOOOOM!

Is this what Kitchener felt like at Omdurman? he thought, his own lips drawn thin in resigned distaste.

That had been where the British brought the Sudanese Mahdists to battle and broke them in 1898 in one overwhelming blow. The losses had been about 15,000 deaths to 48 in that one—a classic Maxim-machine-guns-versus-spears colonial massacre, complete with things like bayoneting the wounded. To a degree that had shocked even the Victorians, a little, though what the Dervishes did to enemy wounded when they got the chance made that look like a love pat.

No, from what he said, Kitchener was mostly concerned about the expense of wasted ammunition. And anyway, I don't have Maxim guns here, or Lee-Metford rifles, or even Martini-Henrys. This battle is going to be decided the old-fashioned way, with swords and what the participants can arm power in the other direction. The cannon are just...what were those guys in a bullring called? The ones who get the bull worked up for the matador by jabbing those barbed darts into it? Right, picadors. This is picador work.

BOOOOM! BOOOOM!

⇒ CHAPTER THIRTY-ONE ⇐

Barbaricum of Germania Antehac Libra
August 15th, 167 CE

BOOOOOM! BOOOOM!

Artorius looked up; it was nearly noon, and the rate of cannon fire had dropped off, because the barrels were burning hot and needed a lot more sponging. And to be picked free of red-hot debris with a corkscrew-like arrangement on the end of a pole. The breeze had kept the smoke from getting too bad—the fog of war needed still air to form—but the stink of burnt sulfur was very strong.

"How time flies when you're having fun," he muttered. "Didn't think they could hold themselves back this long."

Then louder: "Here they come!"

Messengers from the Marcomanni leaders had been coming out more and more frequently and running around to their allies, and there had been stirrings and heaving more and more frequently in the flanking forces. Now a substantial chunk, looking like better than a thousand men, were trotting forward toward the Romans. That was from the left, the Germanii's right flank, which had just started getting its third drubbing from long-range cannonballs.

"Just about time for the allies to start screaming at their hosts: *You're not the ones getting shot to shit,*" he said to himself, with a baring of teeth.

He rode over a dozen paces to the cohort commander, who was sweating freely, pacing back and forth and calling the commands in a hoarse voice, along with arm signals.

*And doing his job well, which is why I haven't been bother-
ing him for the last hour. Never interrupt someone doing it right.
Someone on your side, that is.*

"Centurion!" he called.

The man faced around with a jerk. Artorius raised a hand.

"They're coming now, Centurion. Remember your instructions."

The man looked half mutinous, under a disciplined veneer.
"Sir, I hate the thought of abandoning—"

"The enemy probably won't have time or tools to do much
damage to the guns," he said. "And if they do, we know how to
make them now. Replacing trained men who can train others
would be more difficult. How are we for ammunition?"

He knew the answer, but he saw the man blink again and
come down from that exalted focus of absolute concentration on
one limited task.

"Ah, we've replaced the round shot four times, sir. Still have
the cannister, of course."

"But we're not going to have enough time to fire sixteen rounds
of that per gun," Artorius said grimly. "Not after they get—"

He pointed out into the open space. Three hundred and fifty
yards out, a line of white stakes had been driven into the ground.
That gave everyone an instant reference point; it was also the
limit of cannister range from these guns. There was another line
of stakes fifty yards out.

The gun crews would have been working stripped to the
waist if this were the American Civil War; it was a hottish day,
and they'd been doing shatteringly intense physical work. They
staggered as the cohort commander went down along the line,
giving the battery centurions his heads-up.

Artorius had business to do as well. He rode his horse back
to the clump of Americans and their local guardian angels.

"Get going!" he said, after another glance. "All of you!"

More chunks of the barbarian host were milling about or running forward in scattered masses. As he watched, the Marcomanni
and Quadi came over their berm too; their leaders had decided
that if there was going to be a charge, they might as well join in.

*They can hope the charge will work, and they know their alliance
would really be screwed, and for good, if they bugged out and let
the others fail for want of numbers. Rock and a hard place, dudes.
You really shouldn't have let Prince Ballomar have his head last*

year. He lost his head, his nephew lost his head, then his other nephew did, and now you're going to. Ain't karma a cruel bitch?

Sarukê hesitated for a single instant, since he was obviously not coming along right away.

"Now!" Artorius barked. "See you later," he said to the three Americans.

With their bodyguards behind them they cantered away toward the Imperial banner.

The cohort commander was barking: "Targets of opportunity, adjust range!"

BOOOOM! BOOOOM!

They had time for another six rounds of solid shot as the Germanii host streamed down the slope toward them, concentrating on the Marcomanni now...which slowed them a little, and prevented the enemy from massing into a single fist. They were aiming short, deliberately, and the bounding bronze shot plowed swaths though the dense formations. The enemy were operating on reflex—you had to, which was why having the *right* reflexes drilled in was so very important.

Up until now, dense formations had meant survival. Reality had changed, but reflexes took longer.

Artorius felt his gut tighten. This was going to be close...

"Now!" he called to the Antonio Banderas look-alike.

This close, I can judge ranges pretty well...with the ranging stakes to help. Also start seeing those spearpoints distinctly. Julia, I'm not going to leave you alone if I can help it!

"Switch to cannister!" the centurion called.

The loaders worked their ballet, only a little ragged. Then as the foremost of the charging enemy came to the outer line of stakes:

"*Shoot!*"

BOOOOM! BOOOOOM!

The sound was a little different. It looked different, too. The cannister shot was pitched low like the solid shot; he'd remembered how the Civil War accounts said that made them bounce gut high...or crotch high...when they hit the target. Spreading cones of dust smoked up as the hundred lead balls from every muzzle hit and fanned out across the dirt and nine-tenths of them rose and bounced on, and then swaths of the charging warriors dropped in the same neat conical formations.

Absolutely nothing neat *about the results* inside *the cones, though.*

By the second volley even the charging barbarians were slowing a little; eighteen tubes pumped out nearly two thousand of the bullets into a target where few of them could miss. Half a thousand men or more were dying or going down in screaming agony at every volley, every thirty seconds, swept away in an instant each time a gun fired. Even in that stunning-large host, it hit home.

Again, again—

"*Now!*" Artorius shouted.

The screaming of the advancing ranks was loud, but the gun crews had drilled in this a dozen times, and they'd been waiting for the word, for the hand signals too. Only a few had to be grabbed and butt-booted into attention. Every man threw down what he was holding, turned, and ran for his horse. In moments they were all mounted, except for one who'd tripped and struggled to get into his spooked horse's saddle. They'd have to take their chances.

The charging barbarians saw their tormentors running, and came on faster still, but horses kept ahead of them...except for one who went down somehow. They galloped on, through the narrow gaps between the auxiliary infantry cohorts, grim-set faces under the helmet brims, then past the archers setting cord to string.

Past the long line of *carroballistae* batteries, then between the legionary cohorts, through the little stream, then up to the higher ground where the Imperial command group waited.

He panted as he drew rein beside Marcus Aurelius and Fronto and turned his horse, saluting and taking out his field glasses.

➤ CHAPTER THIRTY-TWO ➤

Barbaricum of Germania Antehac Libra
August 15th, 167 CE

Just as he reined around, the TUNNGGG-*WHACK!* of a hundred and twenty of the catapults shooting within a second of each other sounded. They were firing over the heads of the auxiliaries, into the still-huge mass of the enemy.

CRACKCRACKCRACKCRACK—

Even at eight hundred yards' distance, a hundred and twenty-six of the exploding projectiles made a sound that was stunning; that was more than half a ton of gunpowder going off in the space of a few seconds. The enemy host staggered; probably more men died in that instant than had all the long hours from the beginning of the cannonade.

Instants later the survivors rammed screaming into the front line of the auxiliaries' shields. More of the bombs arched over their heads, and arrows from five thousand bows in singing clouds. The Roman infantry rocked back a step, and another; every twenty seconds a new flight of bombs went by, and the arrows fell without cease. The explosives were landing well back in the huge mass of Germanii behind the front lines; it stretched more than far enough. And in this battle, unlike any they'd experienced before, being well back put you in *more* danger not less . . . and you couldn't strike back.

Ah. There some of them go, Artorius thought grimly; a fringe from the rear of the enemy formation were simply running away. *Sensible, though it's probably panic and not Deep Thought. The very first might get away. Might.*

Fronto nodded and pursed his lips, like a farmer looking out over a field of wheat ready for the blades. Marcus Aurelius had lowered his telescope, and was simply waiting impassively, eyes turned upward toward the blue of the sky. His breathing was very controlled, long and slow—a Stoic method of meditation.

"Now they're dung for our pitchforks," the general from Asia Minor said, hearty satisfaction in his voice. "Good work, Tribune, very good! It would have been ugly if we'd had to open the dance with a mass attack. Even if it worked as well as could be expected, we'd have lost...ten times the number of dead and wounded we'll suffer today. That or more. *And* every one the new weapons killed is one less at sword's point with our men."

Artorius nodded wordlessly. *Well, that's some comfort,* he thought.

The auxiliaries rocked back, and again, retreating to orders while the bombs flew and sleets of arrows dropped. The enemy hesitated, visibly wavering, even the front rank starting to look over their shoulders, and Fronto nodded and made a sign.

Horns and trumpets sounded. The archers trotted off in files between the legionary ranks. The *carroballistae* crews ceased fire, and clamped the trails of their weapons together while the limbers were harnessed. They went off behind the bowmen at a slow canter; then the auxiliary infantry followed. First the ones who were limping, or helping wounded along, or carrying the seriously injured on stretchers of cloaks and spear shafts, then the rest.

Their dead would be collected later for burial and ceremony; the enemy fallen would be left for the crows and foxes, and their wounded finished off if they looked too badly injured to be worth keeping to sell.

Many of the auxiliaries were grinning—their losses had been light for a pitched battle of this size, and they'd taken the edge off the enemy charge and halted them under a rain of death for long crucial minutes.

The enemy hesitated, panting, looking across a gap of thirty or forty yards at the fresh, untouched ranks of the legions and the flashing polished gold of the Eagles.

"Sound *legions will advance in wedge by cohort!*" Fronto called.

The signalers sounded it, and *cornua* and *tubae* sounded from legion, cohort, century.

Should have heard a shink-shank *sound like a rifle bolt being cocked. It's like machinery moving,* Artorius thought, watching.

Even after seeing Roman troops in operation before, it was impressive. All along the long legionary front, the line turned into a set of blunt cohort-sized wedges in less than fifteen seconds, with the banner of the *pilus prior*—the senior centurion of each cohort and its de facto tactical commander—at the fore.

A human saw blade, he thought, caught between admiration and horror. *And now it cuts. Or it's the teeth of a very large carnivore, and now it bites, I suppose.*

A single long shout roared out, after the long silence in the ranks:

"*IUPPITER OMNIPOTENS! ROMA! ROMA!*"

The line of wedges moved forward at the double-quick, armored men with their big, curved shields up and covering them from nose to shin, *pila* ready.

The barbarians tried to resume their charge, or a lot of them did; some others were standing their ground, and some were edging back. All of them had just run a mile under fire with a desperate fight at the end, and they were wrung out and panting with fear and anger and uttermost stress. Another set of calls from the trumpets, a growling brass scream.

The pila flew, each cohort's first line in unison, all of them within a half minute. Even watching from nearly three hundred yards distant from the front line, the massed whistling was distinct; almost immediately followed by a long rippling, thudding clatter as the long lead-weighted javelins slammed home. Thousands of them, some in earth, some with their narrow punch-shaped pyramid heads punching through plank shields and mail armor. Far more into half-naked human bodies. The whole front of the barbarian host rippled and wavered and fell.

More weighted seven-foot javelins arched out, and more and more. The wedges moved ahead at a pounding trot with the fanwise crests of the centurions and the banners at the front. At the double-pace, shields up with each man the regulation three feet from his neighbor, the sharp points of the *gladii* flickering by each man's side. You expected a thud when the masses struck, but instead there was a long scream from tens of thousands of throats, like some great beast calling—half rage, half pain and panic at naked death approaching.

Then the legionnaires were fighting as they endlessly drilled, at quarters too close for the long thrusting spears or chopping swords of the enemy to be used at their best. Smash with the scutum shield, often punching for the face with the metal boss, or slamming the iron-sheathed edge of the twenty-pound weight down on a foot or up under a chin, or a lunging at a knee. Or a sideways sweep to hook the smaller, lighter barbarian shields aside, or a shoulder-in buffeting to knock the other man back on his heels.

Then the *gladii* flickered out, economical upward stabs for the gut or crotch, less often a stooping, hocking strike at knee or ankle with the shield held up, now and then a thrust to the throat or face. This wasn't like the one-on-one melees that Hollywood had loved to show; the Roman wedges put two on one as often as not, and the Roman soldiers acted in a unison that was like a monster with ten thousand barbed tentacles.

Ten minutes, and a rippling all along the long front of death as the first rank rotated backward and the fresh men of the second rank stepped forward while the men who'd fought first recovered their breath eight files back. A trickle of wounded going to the rear, but surprisingly few.

Smash-stab-chop, smash-stab-chop . . .

And I'm watching why Rome ruled a third of the human race for centuries. They're impressive at any aspect of campaigning, but this is what it's all for.

"Dung to our pitchforks," Fronto repeated. "They'll break now, but not before every second or third of them die. Then the cavalry goes in and they can pursue for days."

In the next twenty minutes, a third of the barbarian host, a third of the ones who'd made it over the killing ground so far, died or went down bleeding and screaming. The metallic copper-iron-seawater stink of blood was stunning, and the ground would be muddy with it at the line of contact.

The toothed line of the legions moved forward, the rear ranks finishing off the writhing enemy wounded as they passed if they looked at all dangerous, often with a casual stamp of a hobnailed sandal boot or downward stroke with a shield. More and more of the enemy were melting away, running or limping back the way they came, an increasing thick scatter of Germanii backs presented to their view. The rest were backing up faster and faster, and looking over their shoulders more and more.

The problem with not being able to face death any more is that running away leaves you with your back *to it.*

Which meant a case of damned if you do...

Fronto shifted his telescope to his left hand and waved.

The brass scream sounded again: *Cavalry, general pursuit!*

...and damned if you don't.

A rumble in the earth as thousands upon thousands of iron-shod hooves pounded down, and the *alae*—regiments—swept forward in two horns to encircle and hold, their silk dragon banners hissing with the gathering speed until the horns met a half mile behind the line of contact.

The points of the lances dipped as they went, taking running men in the back...and behind them the saw of wedges advanced, smash-stab-chop-smash...

Fronto looked over at the Emperor.

"Sir, this will be as great a victory as Roman arms have ever won in a single day! They'll surrender within a month, as soon as we can find someone who *can* surrender the women, children and the ones who ran first. The Marcomanni and Quadi won't have anyone left to fight *with*. And there were just enough fugitives that this tale will be carried and sow terror and beshat barbarian trousers all the way from here to the German Sea."

Marcus Aurelius closed his eyes and sighed again, looking older than Artorius remembered him.

"Peace," he said after a moment. "Won by bloody work, but *peace.*"

⇒ EPILOGUE ⇐

L ate the next day, in the marching camp behind the battlefield—
that was already a mass of corruption you could smell from
here, five miles away, and the flocks of carrion birds were like
drifting wisps of smoke overhead as they flocked toward it—
Artorius spoke quietly to Sarukê.

"I'm glad Filipa has you," he said. "She needs...a true comrade like you badly now."

The Sarmatian nodded, smiling with fond pride.

"She brave, lord," she said, and thought before she went on:
"But...sweet. Tenderhearted. I go back to her now. See if I can
get her eat some. Maybe drink a lot. Hold her."

*Tenderhearted? I wouldn't have said so, not unusually...Well,
not by our standards, but it's all what you're used to,* he thought.
*There were more dead in that battle than the total population of
some of the smaller state capitals like Juneau or Helena back...
back in the twenty-first. Not back home, this* is *home now.*

She strode away with the basket of rations on one arm, an
amphora of wine sticking out of one corner and the edge of a
round loaf opposite it.

Then his head came up. A courier with sweat-stained clothes,
smelling strongly of horse, pushed up to the Praetorians standing
in the gateway of the Imperial tent compound. He waved, and
Artorius went over to him.

The Praetorians had been in the battle, too; some of the
ones here had bandaged minor wounds to show it. There was
deep respect in the looks they cast him, behind the stiff drilled
discipline.

He took the message cylinder with a nod of thanks and the

courier staggered, as if his strings had been cut. They had, the strings of willpower that had kept him focused until now. His horse was lathered and dull eyed too where it stood behind him.

"Serious news, Tribune," the courier said.

The message he unrolled within was from Paula Atkins, and it was short and in English, hence absolutely secure:

Other bigwig arrived.

That was Imperator Caesar Lucius Aurelius Verus Augustus, the co-emperor, returned from finishing up his campaign against the Parthians.

He and many of entourage ill. Administering antivirals to himself, prognosis good. Others in quarantine. Definitely smallpox.

Then, less formally:

This is a fight I can really get behind, Prof. We're ready and so are the calves with the shaved tummies. All and sundry being vaccinated.

"Good," Artorius said grimly.

Smallpox they could do something about, and they'd been making preparations. If it had been measles...

The courier looked at him, gaping.

"Good news indeed."

➤ AFTERWORD ⬅

FOR NERDS LIKE ME:
CONCERNING TECHNOLOGICAL
INNOVATIONS AND TIME TRAVEL

Travelers from the future bringing inventions to the past are a staple trope of science fiction. *To Turn the Tide* continues that grand old tradition. Bear in mind that this is a well-read amateur writing, *not* a professional historian... and they disagree on things (or more commonly, the implications and interpretation of things) too.

Sometimes it's shown as impossible for the time refugee in question; Poul Anderson's classic story, *The Man Who Came Early*, is an example, and Harry Turtledove and Judith Tarr's *Household Gods* is another; both very good, by the way.

There the time travelers are single individuals, and don't know much about either the period they're in, or the things they vaguely think they should be able to introduce.

At the opposite end of the spectrum, sometimes there's a riot of modernization. Look no further than Mark Twain's seminal *A Connecticut Yankee in King Arthur's Court* for a good example, where the Yankee in question is the up-from-the-ranks manager of a Victorian-era engineering firm. Twain also has a hilarious game of baseball played in full plate armor, introduced to give the Knights of Camelot something to do once they're obsolete, with modifications to the rules dealing with things like fastballs bouncing off breastplates and helmets.

Perhaps one of the best and most realistic (given what was known in the 1930s), not to mention funniest, is Sprague de Camp's

Lest Darkness Fall, which displaces an American archaeologist named Martin Padway to post-Roman Italy in the Ostrogothic Kingdom of the sixth century. Padway—rechristened Martinus Paduei, "of Padua," by the locals, or "Mysterious Martinus"—has both successes and failures. He knows the period in detail, and has a good practical grasp of a number of other things...like how to make a still.

Incidentally, there's an unspoken convention in a lot of science fiction that the characters in the stories don't *read* or *watch* science fiction themselves. I've always considered this rather odd! Particularly considering how dominant the genre has become in our popular culture.

Hence my protagonists in *To Turn the Tide*, Gen-Z American Ivy League academics specializing in Classical history in a slightly alternate early 2030s, *have* all read the de Camp novel, though several only read it once and long before. This is by no means unrealistic; my friend Harry Turtledove has said that reading it was precisely what made him decide to study Byzantine history!

They've all streamed *Gladiator*, at one point or another, too.

History has been my hobby for a disturbingly long time; I originally considered a career in some university history department, but on investigating how that worked I went to law school, and after *that* decided to pick a more secure, practical, down-to-earth way of making a living...writing science fiction and fantasy. With a specialty in time travel and alternate history!

My research—and research is one of the pleasures of the job for me, though you have to keep it under control—has led me to the conclusion that for a time traveler to introduce innovations would be very hard, or *relatively* easy, depending on whether the innovation was, as my protagonist puts it, a Type A or a Type B. Type A means it can be done by the people of the time with the tools and materials they have available once they have the idea; Type B means that it's necessary to make the tools to make the tools to build it.

And of course ease of innovation depends on whether or not the time traveler is locked up as mad, sold as a slave, or burned as a witch or not. And whether or not they just starve to death in the gutter or get a raging bowel infection and die in a pool of their own wastes. There's a reason crossing to a new watershed with a new set of bacteria used to be *very* risky.

Even with the pandemic, since the 1950s we've lost a sense of the continual menace of infectious disease. My mother grew up in Peru before the Second World War, where one of her close friends died of rabies (caught from a bat) and another person she knew of bubonic plague—the actual Black Death.

My American viewpoint characters in *To Turn the Tide* are professional historians, or aspire to be. When they're unexpectedly dumped back into the early summer of 165 CE in Pannonia Superior (eastern Austria south of the Danube, roughly) they're ready and eager to change history...not least because the modern world destroyed itself with thermonuclear war just as they involuntarily departed, mere instants after being informed (and not believing) that they were in the presence of a time machine.

Everyone and everything they knew and loved has gone into the stratosphere as radioactive ash. They can't control every consequence of changing the course of events, but what could be worse than *that*?

They don't know if their changes will create a new parallel timeline, or simply change the history that led to them. There's no way for them to know or check on that. Either way, they aim to create a better course of events. And a big part of that will be introducing "discoveries" long before they were made the "first time around."

They do have the advantage that they know *something* about the period. Though their knowledge turns out to be incomplete and not necessarily accurate. Little details like whether the Marcomannic Wars start that year or the next or the one after that aren't definitely known. A difference of three years may not seem overly important from eighteen hundred years later, but when you're the one on the ground waiting for Suebic types with homicide and arson on their minds to arrive, spears in one hand and torches in the other...

And they don't know for sure what disease caused the Plague of Galen, which killed somewhere between a tenth and a third of the Roman Empire's population in the next decade, until they see it. The ancient descriptions could be any one of a number of infections, from smallpox to measles. They could *possibly* do something about smallpox; there are reasons vaccination started with that disease, and in the eighteenth century. If it's measles, everyone's screwed, blued and tattooed.

They all know Latin, and some of them Greek...though it also turns out the locals can't understand them through their thick, weird accents at first and they have to learn how to *speak* the local Common Latin dialect. Even then, their book-learned Classical Latin leaves them sounding like a scholar down from Oxford and stranded in Cross Plains, Texas, in 1930. Only they're from Mars as well, in other respects.

And since the wicked Austrian physicist who sends them back by deception (and unintentionally dies in the process) was planning on landing there himself, and used pilfered R&D money on strategic purchases, they have a ton of baggage.

Quite literally: one metric ton, twenty-two hundred and six pounds and a bit.

This includes a lot of money in the form of replica Roman coin of the period, and synthetic gemstones the Romans can't tell from the real thing. Also crates of antibiotics, and lots of books and working scale models of various simple machines. Along with potentially very important seeds of maize, potatoes and other New World crops, improved true-breeding varieties, at that. They manage to avoid having their throats immediately slit for their goods and make a friend in the Jewish merchant who discovers them right after arrival. For further details, I recommend the book!

They've landed in the Roman Empire at its absolute peak. At that point, Rome had one thing in common with China: it encompassed a large proportion of the human race under one government and one law, dominated by one culture.

There were probably about 200 million people or a little more alive on Earth in the year 165 CE; the Roman Empire had somewhere around 55 to 75 million of them, perhaps a third of the total, on just under two million square miles. From what's now Scotland to what's now Iraq, there was one ultimate source of authority—and you could travel that distance on Roman roads, and talk to anyone of note in Latin or Greek, the two dominant languages, and spend the same money and plead the same laws in the same courts.

Those people of note would read the same books, watch the same entertainments, worship different flavors of the same melange of deities, build similar mansions and temples and share the same basic view of the world. That would be more and more so as time went by, because there were powerful forces pushing toward uniformity—witness the fact that Latin replaced most local languages north and west of the Greek-speaking zone by the time of the Empire's fall.

Which is why Romanians between Transylvania and the Black Sea today say *veni* for "come" and *bună* for "good" and *unu, doi, trei* for "one, two, three." Latin equivalents, *venire, bonum*, and *unus, duo, tres*. There's a reason they're called "Romance" languages, and it's not because they're good for courtship. And "Romanian" means...ah..."Roman."

Things peaked in the 100 to 200 CE period, and then everything...to sum up briefly and oversimplify just a little...went to hell. To give one example, Roman Britannia in the late Roman period had around twice the population that England would have on roughly the same territory in 1086 CE, when Domesday Book was compiled; it got back up to that level in 1300...and then the Black Death arrived and hi-ho, a century later they were back to Domesday levels. England didn't *consistently* exceed the *provincia Britannia*'s population until the later 1600s.

So, my time travelers are well placed. What can and cannot be done? What's easy to do, what's hard when it comes to technology? For the politics and personal stuff, once more...see the book!

My protagonist uses Type B for innovations that *do* require a chain of other developments in materials and manufacturing. The example of Type B he uses is Watt's steam engine.

James Watt had the idea for his improved machine in 1763–5, while he was working as an instrument maker at the University of Glasgow. It took him a full decade of trial and error and the financial backing of the businessman Boulton's substantial supply of money to produce the first practical engines for sale in 1775–76. This was when steam engines stopped being a proof-of-concept thing useful only for pumping out coal mines where fuel was a free good and became a source of general energy for industrial purposes.

Getting the required precision for the cylinders, the valving...it was an R&D nightmare even for a brilliant engineer in the center of the most advanced manufacturing technology available on the planet at that time. It was probably the earliest time someone *could* have made a practical steam engine using available technology. Though it required generations of theoretical work—investigations of atmospheric pressure and the power of the vacuum—before the *idea* became available in the first place.

In Roman times it would be even more difficult; the boring machines that Watt used for his cylinders were adapted from those used to ream out cast-iron cannon, for just one example. The Romans didn't even *have* cast iron, though the Chinese at this time did, produced in the world's first blast furnaces.

At the other end of the spectrum is the first "invention" my characters introduce, the wheelbarrow, the Platonic Ideal of a Type A. Which was invented by the Chinese as well, by the way, and not long after the time the story is set.

A wooden wheelbarrow with a few very simple metal parts was easily within the skill set of a Roman carpenter and blacksmith. And it's surprisingly important; the alternative for short-distance transport of heavy materials like grain, bricks, sand, manure and so forth was dragging them or lifting and carrying in a basket or sack, or loading up an oxcart, which isn't practical for really short distances or smaller loads.

For those tasks, this simple little machine gave a massive increase in labor productivity, reducing the number of workers for a given task by half or more.

Another example my characters introduce, and an even more significant one, is the cradle scythe, an American invention of the eighteenth century. It's basically the classic hay-cutting scythe with light wooden fingers fixed above the blade and parallel to it, which allows you to cut a swath of wheat, barley, oats or other small grains and then tip them off the "fingers" in a neat row rather than scattering them.

The Romans already had scythes, since they're a Celtic-Gaulish invention and were widely used before the Roman Empire incorporated the continental Celtic-speaking areas.

Which incidentally stretched at their peak from what's now Ireland to what's now central Turkey and included most of southern Germany and the Czech Republic and chunks of the Balkans. They got around!

Why is a simple little thing like a cradle scythe important?

Well, with a sickle, an average worker can harvest about one-quarter to one-third of an acre of wheat or barley a day. It's the original "stoop labor," too, requiring a bent-over posture even if you don't cut close to the ground. In some places it's even done squatting. That all means that if the harvest window is about fourteen days, one average worker can cut about three and a half to at most five acres in the whole harvest period, with weeks of sweating-hard labor.

With a cradle scythe, you can take between one and a half and three acres a *day*. It's a productivity improvement of eight times or more.

And getting in the grain *fast* is extremely important, even leaving aside the possibility of bad weather—which farmers don't. The grain has to be reasonably ripe to cut, but if you take too long after that, the grain "lodges," falling over and becoming difficult or impossible to harvest. A related problem of ripe grain is "shattering," when the heads break apart and the kernels drop out on the ground. You can stretch the harvesting period a little by staggering planting times but not by much. Essentially you have no more than four weeks and often only two or less to get the grain safely cut or the whole year's work is lost.

This narrow "harvest window" was the main labor bottleneck of food-grain farming in the ancient world. Even with primitive tillage gear, one worker could plant five times the area of wheat or barley (or oats or rye) per day that the same worker could harvest.

So every area producing the basic breadstuffs had to carry enough harvest labor within walking distance of the fields. Or in the case of big landowners, the magnate had to import migrant gangs from somewhere else at high wages plus their keep. And wherever it lived, that labor had to eat every single day of the year, whether or not it was underemployed in the forty-eight to fifty weeks that *weren't* spent harvesting the grain.

That had all sorts of knock-on effects, and was one of the basic reasons why the level of urbanization was limited—in the whole Roman Empire at its Antonine peak most likely a bit more than twelve percent. In Italy it was an astonishing (for a preindustrial economy) twenty-five to thirty percent, but the huge megacity of Rome depended on wheat, wine, wool and olive oil brought and bought (and taxed) from all over the Mediterranean basin.

So there's nothing complex about *making* a cradle scythe. Any competent carpenter could do it in about two hours with the materials to hand, starting with a scythe. But it changes the whole economic structure of agriculture, which was *the* major occupation until quite recently. Suddenly you don't need to carry eighty or ninety percent of that extra harvest labor year-round, or pay premium wages for temporary hires; it's not *necessarily* there on the farm or some nearby village or town or remote hill-country district eating some of the *last* harvest every day of the year.

You can sell that food instead. Other people can buy it and do other things.

Horse-drawn reapers like Hussey's or McCormick's are even better, but that would be much more difficult—there are Type B elements.

Another example of a simple concept with serious knock-on consequences is the wood-framed saddle with stirrups; possibly another Chinese invention, or taken up by them from the Asian horse nomads to their north. The Huns didn't have stirrups when they fought the Romans in Gaul in 451 CE, but the Avars did, when they arrived in Europe from the Asian steppes about a century later.

You can have workable cavalry, horse archers or even heavy cavalry in complete armor, without stirrups—but they don't work nearly as well as they do *with* stirrups, and the necessary skills are harder to learn and maintain. Without stirrups, a cavalry-man's weapons have to be used with the strength of the upper body alone, because his legs are holding onto the horse. This is, incidentally, probably why cavalry in the ancient world used an arm-powered stabbing motion with their spears.

With stirrups, you can brace your feet and use a bow or a sword almost as if you're standing on the ground, adding the muscle power of your core and legs. With stirrups and a raised cantle at the rear of the saddle you can also use a "couched" lance held underarm, with most of the weapon ahead of you and the momentum of the horse providing the punch behind the point. This was a very important tactical innovation that didn't happen until nearly a thousand years after Marcus Aurelius. If you take a look at the Bayeux Tapestry scenes of the Battle of Hastings in 1066, the Norman knights are still mostly shown using an overarm stabbing motion. Stirrups also make it much easier to guide the horse with your legs and knees alone, which made mounted archery at speed very much more efficient.

Try riding bareback at a trot and you'll see what I mean. It's possible but not easy, because you're using an inward clench of your thighs rather than your legs and knees to cushion the up-and-down motion. Try pulling someone out of the saddle if you're bareback and they've got their feet in stirrups. You're using your arms against their *legs*. Because *your* legs are otherwise occupied.

There's absolutely nothing in the saddles of the nineteenth century that couldn't be made in the Rome of the Principate. For that matter, with a few minor substitutions of wood and leather for iron parts, they could have been made by the Yamnaya, the Proto-Indo-Europeans who (probably) domesticated the horse, back in the fifth millennium BCE.

They just didn't have the *idea*. Nobody did, not for four thousand years and more of riding.

It turns out that there are a whole raft of innovations like this. The foot-treadle-powered spinning wheel, also handmade by individual craftsfolk, increases productivity by ten times over the handheld distaff-and-drop-spindle used in antiquity. A treadle loom with a flying shuttle, the final handworked version replaced by power looms during the 1820s and '30s, has an even greater advantage over the looms used then. For that matter, the Romans didn't have the hand crank—that thing you see in old pictures of people winding up a bucket from a well. They used spokes sticking out of an axle to turn it, and a rather clumsy camming system to turn rotary motion into linear from a watermill. They did have watermills, but hadn't thought of windmills...

And then there's gunpowder. The Romans had saltpeter, charcoal and sulfur, the first and last as medicines, fumigants and bleaching agents. They just didn't know what happens if you grind them up, mix them together wet in a ratio of 75-15-10, dry and grind and sieve the resulting cake...very, *very* carefully... and apply a light. It was, once again, the Chinese who worked that out.

This raises the question of the consequences of the innovations the time travelers introduce. Those don't follow in a one-to-one or obvious way, nor are they going to be necessarily the same as they were in the history where they were discovered.

Note that the Chinese were *extremely* inventive throughout their history. Up until the early modern period it was the Chinese who made most of the advances, or at least did them first—the ones mentioned, plus rockets, crossbows, paper, printing, sternpost rudders, long-distance canals...the list goes on and on.

Yet it wasn't the Chinese who had the first Industrial Revolution. It wasn't Chinese steam gunboats that sailed up the Thames and the Seine to thrash the natives, peddle cheap dope at gunpoint and burn down Westminster or Versailles to make a point and get souvenirs for the folks at home.

Like Queen Victoria's Pekingese pup, brought back from the sack of the Summer Palace outside Beijing in 1860. Which she named "Lootie," in a charming display of Victorian candor.

Why not? Why did Europeans end up kicking China around the block for generations, rather than vice versa?

This is the subject of a *lot* of historical controversy, to put it mildly. There are all sorts of political, cultural and religious factors involved.

One important reason among the others is that the Chinese innovations were introduced *gradually*. China had coal-fired blast furnaces on a large scale in the eleventh century, seven centuries before the same invention was (independently) made at Coalbrookdale in England and while those Norman knights I mentioned were stabbing overhand. They very nearly invented the "cotton jenny" in the fourteenth century. By that time they were drilling wells for brine thousands of feet deep and using natural gas to evaporate the water and produce salt. There were reasons they thought of themselves as the Middle Kingdom, the home of civilization, and everyone else as a deplorable fringe of barbarian savages...in addition to the standard human instinctual "my tribe good, your tribe stinks" reflex, that is.

Since China introduced these inventions gradually, the growth of population had time to absorb all the increase in productivity. Some historians have called it a "high-level equilibrium trap," and it's very Malthusian. You eventually get a bigger population, but one just as dirt poor on average.

In Europe, and specifically Britain, the inventions that led up to the Industrial Revolution proper were introduced in a long burst covering no more than a few centuries. They produced a huge surplus, which increased per-capita incomes (already higher than most of the world) to unprecedented levels, which provided a mass market for ordinary consumer goods, which in turn encouraged *more* inventions in a virtuous feedback cycle that enabled Western civilization to dominate the planet and escape the Malthusian trap. This is, to put it mildly, a gross oversimplification, but I think it's true as far as it goes.

When Western Civ wasn't expending its surpluses in ever-more destructive wars between its component parts, of course. The preparation for those wars also drove the process of innovation...

See Chapter 1 of *To Turn the Tide*!

The results when a suite of inventions are introduced from the *outside* can be more dramatic still; witness the astonishing rise of Meiji Japan. And they can be even more unpredictable than most of history, which is highly contingent anyway. It's my belief that if you could "rewind" history to any given point and then let it run forward again, even without time-traveler meddling, the results would be startlingly different most of the time. Next time Franz Ferdinand's driver won't take a wrong turn!

The Roman Empire spread a number of economic institutions and technologies. Together with the "Roman peace," which obviously did not end wars but did reduce them substantially, and the creation of a huge free-trade area with common currency and legal forms, this allowed an unprecedented degree of specialization and division of labor. This in turn resulted in a level of population, long-distance trade, monetization, literacy and urbanization that wasn't surpassed again after the fall of the Empire until the modern period.

For example, the Roman army's minimum height requirement was several inches taller than that of the army of Napoleon. The city of Rome had at least a million inhabitants in 150 CE, and that was the largest urban population in the world in one spot. No European city matched that again until London in the year 1800, though some Chinese ones did for a while, and Edo/Tokyo in the late eighteenth century.

That's the condensed version, by the way.

But the Empire is at its peak between 100 CE and 200 CE... and 165 CE is when my time travelers arrive, just when it's about to run into the wall and go splat.

Though not as quickly or decisively as you can manage with thermonuclear war. Isn't progress grand?

Effectively the time travelers dump, over the next forty years, 1,600 years of technical progress into the stew; first the highly significant Type A ones, and then more slowly and with difficulty some of the even more important Type Bs. Not to mention that they know the precise location of mineral deposits...including things like gold and silver.

Plus extra items of mental, *ideational* technology, like positional arithmetic, modern algebra, double-entry bookkeeping, joint-stock corporations, heliocentric astronomy, the germ theory of disease and antisepsis.

Many of those are Type A, too. Most of the drop in death rates in the First World between say 1853 and 1953 (the latter being my own incredibly ancient date of birth) wasn't due to antibiotics, which didn't come into play until the 1930s and weren't common until later. It was due to fairly basic sanitation measures informed by germ theory.

Though the time travelers get Galen, the famous court physician of Marcus Aurelius, to take credit for the medical stuff! If there was one thing Galen was good at, it was academic bunfighting, and that is not a modern invention.

And since the Empire is united and has good communications...and (slight spoiler) they get the Imperial government mostly on their side in the first few years...the innovations spread very, very rapidly. Helped along by things like paper and printing!

The consequences? Well, *I* think the way I worked them out is interesting. To find out, you need to read *To Turn the Tide* and its sequels!